LAURA TALBOT

(1908-1966) was born Lady Ursula Chetwynd-Talbot, eldest daughter of Viscount Ingestre, heir to the twenty first Earldom of Shrewsbury. Her father died on the eve of the First World War, before inheriting the title, and in 1917 her mother married an American diplomat. Thereafter the family was brought up largely abroad.

As a child, Laura Talbot was shy with an artistic sensibility and a sharp eye for the vicissitudes of class, which she was later to skillfully portray in her five novels: *Prairial* (1950), *The Gentlewomen* (1952), *Barcelona Road* (1953), *The Elopement* (1958) and *The Last of the Tenants* (1961). She also wrote a number of plays intended for broadcasting and a collection of short stories.

In 1930 Laura Talbot married Hector Stewart, who died of a rare paralysis five years later. Her second marriage, to his cousin, Lieutenant Commander Michael Stewart, ended in divorce in 1952, and in 1954 Laura Talbot married the writer Patrick Hamilton. This eight year period was her most creative; they settled in Norfolk where she concentrated on writing. After his death she married Dr William James in 1964. This happy marriage was brief in span — they died together in a plane crash on a private flight from Jersey, where they lived, to Alderney in 1966.

THE
GENTLEWOMEN

LAURA TALBOT

With a New Introduction by
POLLY DEVLIN

PENGUIN BOOKS – VIRAGO PRESS

PENGUIN BOOKS
Viking Penguin Inc., 40 West 23rd Street,
New York, New York 10010, U.S.A.
Penguin Books Ltd, Harmondsworth,
Middlesex, England
Penguin Books Australia Ltd, Ringwood,
Victoria, Australia
Penguin Books Canada Limited, 2801 John Street,
Markham, Ontario, Canada L3R 1B4
Penguin Books (N.Z.) Ltd, 182–190 Wairau Road,
Auckland 10, New Zealand

First published in Great Britain by Macmillan & Co. Ltd. 1952
This edition first published in Great Britain by
Virago Press Limited 1985
Published in Penguin Books 1986

ISBN 0 14 016.118 X

Printed in Finland by
Werner Soderström Oy, a member of Finnprint
Set in Baskerville

INTRODUCTION

Laura Talbot was the pseudonym for Lady Ursula Chetwynd-Talbot, eldest of the three daughters of Viscount Ingestre, heir to the twenty-first Earldom of Shrewsbury, Premier Earl in Peerages both of England and Ireland and Hereditary Great Seneschal or Lord High Steward of Ireland. In fact Viscount Ingestre died before his father, of pneumonia, just on the eve of the First World War and so never inherited the title — and his family believed that, had he survived the pneumonia, he would have died a few months later when his whole regiment was wiped out at the Marne offensive. Lady Ingestre, who had been Lady Winifred Paget before her marriage, was left a widow with three young daughters and an infant son, John, who became the twenty-first Lord Shrewsbury. When he attained his majority in 1935, he celebrated the event with a glittering party at Ingestre Hall, a Shrewsbury seat which had been closed for years: and it is Ingestre which is the model for the great house, Rushford, — almost a pantheon — in which the story of *The Gentlewomen* is set during the bleakest years of the Second World War.

Lady Ursula had a peripatetic childhood. Two years after her husband's death her mother married Richard Pennoyer, an American diplomat, and she and the children accompanied him on his postings all over Europe, except for Ursula's younger sister, Lady Audrey (Morris), who had delicate health and spent the greater part of her childhood at her uncle, Lord Pembroke's, house, Wilton, often lying, recuperating under the chestnuts in the sun. Wilton, too, plays a thinly disguised part in at least one of Laura Talbot's other novels.

Her mother was a great beauty, egocentric and dazzling, who, although she copied out great chunks of her favourite poetry into her commonplace book, and after her first husband died, sat desolate by candlelight writing poetry, seemed to have had not the slightest interest in her children's artistic aspirations. An old family friend recalls that like many of her contemporaries she was more preoccupied with their prospects in the marriage market than with them as people. One family legend remembered by all was of one of their aunts reading the engagement column of *The Times* and saying, mournfully, "There, *another* marquis gone." In such surroundings, such an ethos, this tall, shy young woman Ursula, or "La" as she was known to her friends, with a secret, inner life of her own and an acute eye for pretension did not feel a success. In fact she was shy to a degree of suffering and would turn back from parties, from balls, with a failure of nerve. Yet in other ways she was a remarkable woman and bore vicissitudes and tragedy with courage all through her life. Lacking in self-confidence she may have been, but her bearing, her manners, her sense of herself were impeccable and in every memoir her appearance is mentioned, as is her gift for making the many houses in which she lived uniquely beautiful, uniquely hers. She was blessed, or cursed as she would have it, with the Shrewsbury nose; and though photographs show a sleek and handsome young woman with wonderful legs (another characteristic of the family) and an elegance to match that of her stunning mother, she was, apparently, mortified almost to the point of obsession by her nose. In the 1930s she had it altered by plastic surgery, the operation was felt by her to be a great success, and she was always much happier with her appearance afterwards.

Though a shy and elusive woman who did not take the centre stage at any gathering, she was not merely an observer, though she certainly was that. "She simply didn't care about whether people saw her staring at them" Lady Audrey, her only surviving sister, recalls. "She would stare intently at whoever or whatever took her interest and make no bones about it. She'd take in every wrinkle and eyelash in a person and wouldn't look away until she'd finished. And you could almost hear her listening to people's dialogue." But she was also rather an instigator of scenes among her family and friends. She seemed to thrive, to be stimulated, by observing a drama develop from something she'd implanted into the conversation earlier, as though intent on having her art copy nature, by making a simulacrum of a scene for her artistic imagination, seeing how things would turn out in real life, watching how emotions work. It was the singular unhappiness of individuals within a family, or connected with a family, how the tangled connections between people gathered together under one roof could painfully pull at their roots, which interested her.

In her books she never tried to disentangle the roots, to run back along the tendrils and nerves, to get the hidden hurt — in short, she did not speculate or devise systems. She observed, absorbed and recorded, and her observations became perceptions as she wrote. "She was interested in detail" her sister remembers. "Everything was filed in its proper place, everything organised. Her will, for example; she loved making wills and she would make sure that every single thing was left to exactly the right person. She loved arranging things, was a marvellous decorator and did flowers like no-one else." (For some years, in fact, Laura Talbot wrote about flowers for *Country Life*.) And in *The Gentlewomen* there is a key passage, a set piece devised around an arrangement of flowers which is a brilliant metaphor for the characters concerned.

The woman behind the books, the ironic delineator of *The Gentlewomen*, seems from descriptions, to have been an enigmatic, contradictory character; timid, though daring in some ways, physically frail, yet spending years of her life looking after ailing husbands. Her sister recalls "She used to go to bed for months. I once asked a husband what was really wrong and he explained that she was so exacting that she exhausted herself. He said, for example, that if someone was coming to stay, well most people like to do flowers, to do three or four vases, she would do perhaps sixty or seventy vases." Perhaps the act of writing relieved the obsessive internalised passions and pressures of her nature. Certainly there is a strong undercurrent of passion and rage flowing in her books which rarely bursts through: just as open emotions are rarely displayed by her characters, who, although on the whole, members of a privileged class, suffer acute spiritual deprivation. There are blanks in their lives where there could be richness.

Laura Talbot came to writing late in life, just before her marriage to her third husband, the writer Patrick Hamilton. He was a well known, indeed celebrated, writer of the 30s and 40s, and was also an alcoholic. Her first husband, Hector Stewart, had died suddenly, tragically soon after their marriage. "I'm going to drop this cup" he said one day at teatime, and within three days he was dead of a rare paralysis. She married his cousin, Lieutenant Commander Michael in 1942, but they were divorced ten years later. Her marriage to Hamilton, in the 1950s when she was in her forties, though haunted by Hamilton's illness, was the most creative period of Laura Talbot's relatively short life. He had almost stopped writing, but she acquired from him, according to one contempory source, "the technical discipline of handling characters, situation and ideas in a moulded competition".

The Gentlewomen, her second novel published two years before she married Hamilton, echoes themes to be found in his work. In many of his books, most notably *Hangover Square* and *West Pier*, Hamilton concentrates with vicious intelligence on the mechanisms of snobbery, and his hatred of pretension, of flummery, was an animating force in his creative life. "The word 'class' is fraught with unpleasing associations" wrote R.H. Tawney, the British historian, in 1932. "So that to linger upon it is apt to be interpreted as the symptom of a perverted mind and a jaundiced spirit." Born as she was, in 1908, into the centre of the British aristocracy, Laura Talbot might well have taken the class system so much for granted that she might never have perceived the system's excesses. But she seems to have been disaffected from her very birth. Laura Talbot wrote five novels in all: *Prairial, Barcelona Sqaure, The Gentlewomen, The Elopement*, and *The Last of the Tenants*, some plays intended for broadcasting and a collection of short stories. Her books have slight plots which often turn into melodrama, wrenching the frail episodes to abrupt, alarming conclusions, which, though perhaps meant to be wholly tragic, are often tainted with the ludicrous. She never wrote with an animated or comic pen — she was very serious, though she had a light touch (in speaking of her, her friends always mention how amusing and witty she herself was). Occasionally the force and size of the things that happen to the people in her books outweigh the capacity of the writing and characters to accomodate them so that there is, occasionally, a bathetic quality to the writing; but there is a skill in devising circumstance and motive, a gift for storytelling and a flair for writing dialogue that contains all the significances of the plot, yet sounds plausible. Indeed it is in the dialogue, especially in the many question and answer sessions in the book, that the reverberations, the depths behind her skimming presentation are heard and shown. In a review of *The Gentlewomen* in the 50s a critic wrote that the book was "composed of emotional clichés, but the dialogue is written with skill". For all the low-key tone of the writing there are moments of verbal violence which are all the more shocking because they erupt so harshly into polite luncheon conversation. Miss Bolby's impassioned harangues in defence of her good name and family are, in their rhythm, bleakness and context, reminiscent of Ivy Compton-Burnett.

Laura Talbot's preferred way of writing was to make a pastiche — putting fragments of dialogue, glimpses of a setting, clues to the atmosphere, together to make a whole. The end result has an extraordinary feel, not just of the period about which she is writing, but also of the time in which she was writing. Even while pasting up the collage to show the period of her setting she does not conceal her contemporary way of feeling and seeing, and it makes for a curious and singular style. A correspondent in *The Times* wrote, "Her novels, though widely different in setting, showed her skill in conveying, through natural dialogue and unforced confrontations, the many-sided facets of a social attitude taken as a theme — as, for example, snobbery in *The Gentlewomen*."

The Gentlewomen is an extraordinary presentation of a social disease. Nearly everyone in the book is infected with it: except the children and the sweet-natured, dotty secretary, Miss Pickford, who is the scapegoat for the mendacity and uncaringness of most of the other adults in the book, especially Miss Bolby, the governess, who is obsessive about her place in society in general and at Rushford in particular. Miss Bolby has never known comfort, has never been at rest. All her life she has been harried and hag-ridden, in her early days by her mother's pretensions and unease, in her adult days by her own pretensions, her own desperate insistence on her gentility.

She is a governess, a member of a race that has vanished from the earth. They must often have led lives of quiet desperation, these women who had to be sexless, poised between being servants and family, neither one nor the other; yet they were gentlewomen, women of good families, who were often treated slightingly by their employers. The famous fictional example is, of course, Jane Eyre. But in the nineteenth century there was hardly any other occupation for a young woman who needs must earn a living.

Lady Audrey believes that Laura Talbot herself wanted to be a governess. "She adored children and would have made a marvellous teacher — all her nephews and nieces loved her. It was a great grief to her that she had no children." Ironically, in the times of which she writes, her own social position would have precluded her being a governess, yet two centuries earlier she could well have been one. Then, in her heyday, a governess was "a gentlewoman with a right to instruct princesses and duchesses" and was treated with respect, often continuing to be the friend and confidant of her erstwhile charges when they had entered public and powerful life. But by the time poor Miss Bolby steps onto the stage at Rushford Hall she is an anachronism and knows herself to be. Just another source of unease and discomfort for a woman whose only wish was to be secure, secure and accepted.

When the book opens she is in a genteel boarding house in fog-ridden Birmingham. Here life is a continual fight, both to preserve her position and her own precious ideas of herself. But even when she accepts a post at Rushford Hall, the seat of Lord Rushford, things there are not all she thinks they should be. Like any true snob, she finds those whom she envies lacking in exclusivity, falling down on those matters of form on which she must needs be an expert. One cannot like her. Her refusal to acknowledge the hunted creature who is within herself is alienating, though one can feel pity for the external person who has been so *depisté* by life and circumstances that she has to feel ashamed of herself. Not because she has behaved badly but because *she* her own person and soul, is *déclassée*, not good enough for Miss Bolby the governess. She, of course, takes her grievances out in a subtle way on the children, though she would never consider her behaviour as revenge. Her unkindness is pronounced; and she has a cruel heart: and yet, and yet, it is Laura Talbot's skill that one sees the might-have-been under the story. She would never have been a kind woman, she would always have been a snob, but she might have been a contented one. She lives in a state of arrogant and pitiful delusion, and the moment of revelation when delusion is, for a stark moment no longer possible, when she sees the worthlessness of her loyalty, the lack of regard in which she has been held by those she considered true gentle-persons, *worthy* of her benediction, is utterly without consolation. And it is part of Laura Talbot's understated, reticent style that she simply presents the moment, no embroidery, no speculation. There is layer upon layer of snobbery in the book, peeled delicately but pitilessly away by Laura Talbot, who seems not to have been overburdened with compassion. Only the children and the old, autocratic peer, Lord Curwen, are granted simplicity and the integrity of their own untrammelled reactions.

It is hard to comprehend now the extent of the rigidity of the class system which obtained even until the last war, nor how it bedevilled England. The diminution of class distinctions since the 1930s is very real, as is class consolidation, though the class structure has remained much the same. People still cling to their places on the social ladder, but then a step downwards was, for some people, a banishment and the term "a lady" had a far more specific meaning than it has now. For some ladies, including Miss Bolby, manners were more important than morals. *Debrett* was the bible to be consulted; for remote cousinships and aquaintances to be traced in order to show a connection with a grand family. But there was no connection in the Forsterian sense. The gaps were unbridgeable, cold chasms, that people tried to bridge with pathetic credentials.

Both Miss Bolby and Miss Pickford, when writing in confidence to Lady Rushford, state as part of their curriculum vitae and references that they are gentlewomen. It is important to Miss Bolby, whilst waiting for Miss Pickford to arrive, to find out if she has described herself so. Only then will she know how to treat her. One remembers Surtees' remark, "The only infallible rule we know is that the man who is always talking about being a gentleman never is one." The same, I wager, goes for the female of the species; and Miss Bolby is very female, with her shawls and Indian bracelets, not to speak of a natural allure which she suppresses with such repugnance and success that when she does try to lure a man, the effect is repellent.

Miss Bolby could not lay claim to any of the qualities of the original meaning of gentle: but (and to her this is far more important) she could lay claim to the breeding. "Even when Victorian society was at its most rigid, a duke and an Indian Army subaltern, both being gentlemen, were equal in class, however different they may have been in rank and wealth." This is at the nub of the book: for by becoming, or having to become, a governess, and thus having to be in the employ of those who are her peers, Miss Bolby fears that she has forfeited her status. And her status is her only defence against a cruel world. In fact Miss Bolby, so insistent on being treated as and called a gentlewoman, is not one in any sense. She is a lost, haunted woman, who is on occasions demented, who has turned her back on love and who cannot understand her failure. So circumscribed and entailed are her emotions by her rigid insistence on doing the right thing, preserving face, keeping up appearance, that her responses have atrophied. She is a bundle of horrid social reflexes, an empty woman.

In *The Gentlewomen* Laura Talbot did something remarkable. She presented the decaying life of a great house, the tocsins ringing, the wheels running down, the kind of harmonious whole that was a great house falling apart in a slow, ungraceful discordance. She shows the fraying of nerves and the fraying of a family and presents it against a backdrop of war. War is not described, yet the atmosphere of wartime Britain is adumbrated most effectively. The irritant, uneasy quality of life on the brink, the meannesses, the curtailments and deprivations, the sense of doom, the graininess of life, the grit in its everyday texture infects every page. She evokes the atmosphere of a lugubrious boarding house in Birminghan more successfully than she does that of Rushford. The house lies, like a kind of web, full of spaces at the very centre of the book, but only once or twice does it come alive for the reader, when Lord Rushford comes back from the war, sees the house from a certain point through the trees and feels his heart turn over; and in the heat of the summer, when the house is deserted, open, baking and the Italian prisoners of war are in the gardens, singing.

The Gentlewomen was, perhaps, Laura Talbot's most successful book. She continued to write until her death in 1966 in an aeroplane crash during a private flight from Jersey, where she lived with her last husband, Dr Bill James. She had been warned that the plane was probably unsafe, but she was never one to hold back from adventure. In her obituary in *The Times* the prescient writer concluded, "she was an author of quiet, unheralded distinction who in a future generation may well be resurrected to fuller recognition". It was as much a prophecy as an epitaph.

Polly Devlin, Somerset, 1985

Snob. '. . . Person with exaggerated respect for social position or wealth and a disposition to be ashamed of socially inferior connexions, behave with servility to social superiors, and judge of merit by externals . . . .'

The Concise Oxford Dictionary

THE BEGINNING

1

MISS BOLBY heaved her bag up from the floor on to a
chair in order to get a better purchase upon its zip-
fastener: it was so full that its mouth gaped and its
sides bulged; the fastener halted, stuck with firm obstinacy;
then, after she had despairingly tugged at it, it completed its
wavy course with unexpected ease and a light tearing sound.
Nothing now remained but to turn out the gas fire and this she
had left till last because the room was so cold. Damp, clinging
cold pressed against the windows in a white tide. Now and then
it receded, loosened its clutches a little so that the harsh light in
the room dimmed, but it rolled back again, pushing its way
relentlessly through ill-fitting windows and doors; it seemed to
thrust itself between traffic and the street—between the street
and sound, so that wheels seemed to run upon a layer of
nothingness. Its penetrating whiteness made the room more
drab than it already was, revealing stains upon sombre wall-
paper, smudges upon a pattern faint with age. By the stillness
it brought with it, the fog seemed to give the day intensity; it
made movement deliberate and concentrated, it shrouded the
city of Birmingham in a mantle of delay.

Miss Bolby took a newspaper wedge from its niche between
the mirror and its frame; she had put it there for her own comfort, folding it and coaxing it until moulded to her purpose;
why, therefore, leave it for the comfort of others? As she threw
it into the waste-paper basket the mirror fell forward. It was a
mean sort of mirror, singularly unflattering; spots, brown
constellations that transfixed themselves on to the face,
were splashed across its surface. Her bracelets made a shrill

tinkling as she moved. Sounds which were not muffled were magnified.

'What pretty bracelets you have, Miss Bolby. Indian, aren't they?'

'Yes, they were my mother's. I was born in India.'

How seldom was the comment omitted. It marked a phase in each new environment, because her answer, to the accompaniment of the bracelets' light jingling as they slid back and forth over her wrists, seemed to set her a little apart. Today, heightened by the muffled sounds outside, the sound brought memories of other sounds: hooves upon hard ground and jackals' cries which had caused terror in the night. Bare feet upon bare boards. Male voices from the verandah, and her father's voice, louder, and the clink of glass against glass. Rain upon wide leaves. . . . These were her memories of India: sounds, and the vividness of canna lilies. Dust, and the faintly dusty smell of mosquito netting, and in terrifying detail a beggar's sores. When she had been sent back to England she had been seven. She had been told so much since that memories which had been sharp had become blurred by that which she had been told. It was difficult now to sort her own from Sita's and Mavis's. India had not faded with the journey home; from then on it had grown, had become as much a part of her own life as of her mother's and Sita's and Mavis's, through her mother and Sita and Mavis. . . . The bracelets slid back from her wrist as she tipped the mirror from its prone position. The face behind the brown disfigurations was no longer young. . . . 'And what, my dear Lavinia, shall we call the little dusky one?' 'Roona,' Sita and Mavis had crooned, bending over the cot. She had seen herself, 'the little dusky one', in a frame of draped muslin as clearly as if she had been Sita or Mavis; had heard her father's voice as clearly as if she had heard it boom from the verandah: 'Roona, my dear Lavinia, will be the beauty.' . . . But time and trains waited for no man—he had boomed this too—and from India, through a long vista of schoolrooms to this—the

2

mirror pitched forward again drunkenly as she let it go—had been a long road. . . .

Miss Bolby took two half-crowns from her bag and put them on the dressing-table—she and Mrs. Hurst and Mrs. Billings had arrived at an eventual system of weekly tipping—then she put one of them back, one was enough for Elsie. It would be joy indeed, soon to be in a house which was not a Boarding House where servants were not sluts. She put out the gas fire: cold seemed to close in as the fire hissed towards its final pop of extinction. There were still five minutes to spare. She rang for Elsie—Elsie took so long to come, thundering when she did so, two steps at a time, up the stair.

"Take down my bags, Elsie, will you?"

"Taxi's not here yet, Miss." 'Tuxie' Elsie pronounced it.

"I ordered it in plenty of time."

"Not never enough time for fog, Miss." Elsie heaved at a suitcase; she made a noise as she breathed—not unlike the gas fire. There were damp patches at her armpits, dark in her dark frock, her stockings were wrinkled and her once-white apron was stained; yellow hair fuzzed out from underneath her cap, the fog's white glare was merciless.

Miss Bolby took a last look at the room: at the mat beside the bed, dark and greasy as a bedraggled poodle, at the commode with a cracked marble top which had served her as a writing table, at the mirror lying drunkenly suspended, at the dead, cold fire. It was good to have a room to which one could return, though, in these dark chaotic times. She followed Elsie through the doorway. As she came out into the passage Mr. Howland came out from the room opposite.

"Miss Bolby, I see, or rather, I hardly see, out here it is so dark. After India you must find these damp fogs trying, Miss Bolby. This peculiar white intensity is rather special to the Midlands, though during the Blitz it was singularly absent—you can hardly have experienced enough of it to have become

3

accustomed to it. But I see you are in a hurry, and so, as a matter of fact, am I, and as we have already gone through our farewells I shall bid you, once again, my dear Miss Bolby, au revoir, but not goodbye." He shot down the stairs, brushing past Elsie. He did not pause to offer her any help with the bags, he was in too much of a hurry; but it flashed through his mind that Miss Bolby might at least have carried one of her own bags. To have relieved Elsie of the suitcase and carried it as far as the hall would have delayed him unnecessarily. It did not strike him that his oration in the passage had already done so—words flowed from him easily. As he opened the front door and then hurriedly slammed it, a fine layer of fog drifted across the hall and up the stair.

As Miss Bolby caught up with Elsie, Mr. Billings opened the smoking-room door, bringing with him a current of warmer air which intensified the cold in the hall.

"Miss Bolby! An unexpected pleasure. But about to leave us for higher society, I see. Well, I can't say I altogether envy you, and without our Miss Bolby where shall we be?"

"I'm in rather a hurry, Mr. Billings, I'm afraid."

"So I see, so I see, but I shouldn't worry, Miss Bolby. 'Time and tide' may not wait, but in a fog such as this, one can hardly say the same of trains. Well I hope we meet again, Miss Bolby, 'bye, 'bye."

Milly Tollmarsh opened the Tollmarsh's sitting-room door.

"Just off, Miss Bolby? Mother asked me to say goodbye. She won't come out because of her cough. Not that it's goodbye, really, is it? You'll let Mother know in good time when you want your room again, Miss Bolby."

"In plenty of time, you may be sure, Milly, though I feel it will not be for a *long* time. Say goodbye to your mother for me. And you've got my address correctly, haven't you, Milly?"

"Rushforth, isn't it? Was it Hall or Park?"

"Rush*ford*, Milly, c/o Lord Rushford, *The* Lord Rushford."

The Beginning

"That's right, Mother's got it. I wrote it down. Well, I mustn't stand here with the door open because of Mother's cough. Good luck at Rushford, Miss Bolby. 'Bye, 'bye."

Elsie had opened the front door by now and the fog was coming in in waves; it was no longer white, it was already turning, as the afternoon light lessened, to a dirty grey. The taxi, padded with the layer of nothingness, made a soundless imprint, as the wheels of a ghost car might, upon the gravel outside. Elsie struggled with a suitcase and heaved it into the taxi. The driver, as if infected by the fog, was deep in sullen apathy. Miss Bolby got in, Elsie heaved in the zip-fastening bag, then she slammed the door.

Elsie did not run in out of the fog, she was too cold to run; instead she watched the taxi bump its way through the gateway into Hillthorne Road : fog rolled in where the taxi had been; it rolled up towards her and clung to her cap in pin-point beads. The laurels on either side of the gateway were shadowy islands, the hollies on either side of the laurels had become ghosts of trees; a bird moved in the hollies, sending a shower of dead leaves on to the laurels with a brittle rattling, lightened, as the commotion made by the bird was loudened, by the fog, then silence rolled in where there had been sounds. Elsie gathered herself together and went in.

She was thinking how nice it must be to come from India, where, she supposed, there were no cold dank fogs, and where leaves, if there were leaves, were broad and green, and soft and rubbery, like the tropical plants in Mr. Lind's botany book, instead of yellow and speckled, and dark and prickly, like the laurel and the holly—and how heavy Miss Bolby's silver-backed hair brushes had made the suitcase, and how Miss Bolby, with a part of her, seemed to want to be nice, and how India, some-how, came between her and the part of her that wanted to be. Elsie's thought was not as lucid as this, but in a muddled,

5

woolly way this was what she thought. She slammed the front door and the hall was dark.

Dark and full of fog. She began to cough—so much of it had got into her throat while she was standing outside. She lifted her stained skirt and fumbled inside the elastic bands of her knickers for a handkerchief; her hands were so cold they were feelingless lumps. She was still sniffing and coughing and fumbling when the door of Mrs. Tollmarsh's sitting-room opened and Milly Tollmarsh's broad figure blocked the greying, dirtying light as it fell from the room into the hall. Elsie could see the fog from Mrs. Tollmarsh's room drifting round Milly's head, working its way out to mingle with the fog in the hall. She could hear Mrs. Tollmarsh's deep cough barking and rumbling its way up from her chair by the fire and filling the room behind Milly.

"Whatever were you doing, Elsie, keeping the door open all that time and letting the fog in all over the place? It's getting worse, too, every minute."

"I hud to get Miss Bolby's luggage out, Miss Milly."

"And a mighty long time you were, too. Look sharp, Elsie, or you'll be late with the teas." Milly shut the door. Elsie heard her pulling out the piano stool and pulling a bundle of music from the stand—as plainly as if the door were open she saw the plush cloth slip and its fringe of little bobbles tremble as it did when she dusted—she stood waiting for Milly to strike the first bars of Beethoven's Minuet in G. . . . She did not know it was Beethoven's Minuet in G, she knew it only as 'what Miss Milly played'. Milly began it twenty times a day. No one ever heard her finish it, she broke off abruptly at the same passage, pausing before it—taking it at a run, then breaking off, the passage struck the two dumb notes in the piano. But the first notes, as Milly struck them now, released something in Elsie; the cold numbness in her eased and she ran down the dark passage to the kitchen. Presently, as she set out the tea things and waited for the kettle to boil, plaintive tremulous murmur-

ings struggled into being, stretched into full-blooded sounds:
they came from Mr. Lorelli's violin in the room on the top
floor next to Miss Bolby's—Mr. Lorelli had come home early.
It was as if she, Elsie, as she brought forth sound from the tea
things, and Milly and Mr. Lorelli were defying the fog outside.
By the time the bell above her head had jangled its first sum-
mons, feeling had almost come back into her hands. The bell
would ring intermittently now, boarders summoned their tea as
they wanted it; she carried it through to the drawing-room on
small round trays: a small square tea-pot and a small squat
jug, and, for those who preferred this means of disposing of
butter, bread and butter.

When she carried the first tray through, Mrs. Hurst and
Mrs. Billings, Mrs. Rowcroft and Miss Hines were sitting, skirts
raised to their knees, before the fire.

"Miss Bolby gone, Elsie?" Mrs. Hurst ran the point of a
needle down a row of stitches.

"Yes, Mudum."

"And a mighty long time you was with that door open—
place is full of fog."

"Getting worse, too, Mudum. Got down me throat something awful. Miss Bolby's luggage was so 'eavy, thut's what
made me so long, Mudum."

"You ought to *h*ave got Mr. Billings to *h*elp you, Elsie.
Toast, Mrs. *H*urst?" As though fearful of being infected with
Elsie's dearth of 'h's', Mrs. Billings accentuated hers by allowing
little pauses to rest before them.

"Fresh as a daisy, eh, Elsie?" Mrs. Hurst prodded a rock
bun. "Just the day for toast, and my turn to make it, Mrs.
Billings. 'Ow many pieces?"

"One will be sufficient, thanks, Mrs. Hurst," said Mrs.
Rowcroft and Miss Hines in unison.

"Mr. Billings were in too much of a 'urry, same as Mr.
'Owland," said Elsie, still thinking of her struggle with the
bags.

7

"Seen Mr. 'Urst, Elsie?" Mrs. Hurst's 'h's' were as uncertain as Elsie's, as if in her case Elsie's disregard for them were catching and she did not care, she seemed almost to take delight in mislaying them. "I don't envy Miss Bolby, travellin' in a fog. If there's one thing I 'ate it's travellin' in a fog."

"Same *h*ere, Mrs. *H*urst," said Mrs. Billings. "Going into a new post in a fog, and especially for a governess, must be *h*orrid."

Mrs. Hurst ran the needle over the sock again in order to give the pattern a final check, then she picked up the toasting-fork and drew her chair nearer to the fire.

2

In the meantime, Jessica Rushford, becoming a part of the mass upon one of the platforms at New Street Station as she was poured into it from the train, edged towards the bridge which she had somehow to cross in order to reach a telephone booth. She tugged at her suitcase, uncertain what to do with it; it had already caused trouble enough in a troublesome journey, though it *had* made an island upon which to sit in the corridor between two not very sober sailors. There had been halts and pauses in which all hopes of reaching a destination had subsided—rushed out into the fog with the hissing of steam, pauses in which the train itself had become silent and still and the sailors' villainous breath had floated about her head in a white cloud to meet the white cloud which someone had let in through a window further down the corridor. Journeys in comfort were to Jessica little more than a memory, dimmed by a number of comfortless ones : journeys in reserved carriages to the seaside with picnic baskets and bananas had become hazy—Ruth and Louisa did not remember the bananas. "At least I can remember a banana," she said aloud, heaving at the suitcase.

Fog clawed at her throat. As though not content with the delay it had already caused, it seemed to thrust itself between the passengers—there was nothing to keep it out—the station's glass roofing had long ago gone: it had showered on to the platforms during the nights and had been swept into mounds in the mornings during the winter of 1940.

"Pardon *me*. Allow *me, Ma'am* . . . "

Jessica looked up, searching for the voice; the face looking down into hers was black and not very far from hers, because the gigantic figure to whom it belonged was bending down to talk to her; a black hand disengaged itself from the fog close to hers and she relinquished her grasp upon the suitcase's handle. "Well, it's awfully kind of you, thanks awfully. . . ." She was conscious of a flush spreading upward from her neck, she could feel it rising from under her jersey. . . . The suitcase had been lifted as if it were a feather and with the suppleness of a cat the face's huge owner mounted the steps ahead of her —she had almost to run in order to keep level with it. At the top it paused. "You remainin' at de top of dese steps? No, *Ma'am.*" And the black giant was off again. 'Hi, not so fast! I'm only going to the telephone-box." "Right heah? Yes, *Ma'am.*" He put down the suitcase and as suddenly as he had appeared out of the fog was swallowed back by it. Jessica, because her legs trembled, walked, instead of into the box, into the Queen's Hotel which was virtually within the station. Its back windows looked on to the station; it was possible to walk directly from the station into it, and she was on friendly terms with the hall porters. The Queen's Hotel was a refuge upon shopping expeditions; parcels, and even Ruth and Louisa, had been left there. She wanted to try out her voice before telephoning because her encounter with the soft-voiced, black-faced giant had made her feel unsteady and there was something sternly steadying about the foyer of the Queen's Hotel.

"Box four," the telephone operator said and she walked into box four, which was very different from the telephone booth on the station; this would hardly have held the suitcase and herself, and she began to wonder how she would have inserted the pennies and watched the suitcase in the darkening fog outside at the same time so that another black hand should not grab it, when there was a click and the buzzing at the other end of the line ceased.

"Hullo?"

"Lisbeth, it's Jessy."

"Jessy, darling! Are you safe?"

"Absolutely. Why shouldn't I be?"

"Well, the fog's awful."

"It is here, too."

"Did you have an awful journey?"

"Pretty awful. My train was awfully late."

"But you've got time to catch the three-twenty, haven't you?"

"I think so, if I don't go on talking now. I couldn't remember whether you'd said you'd meet me at Colsall or Huggley."

"It will have to be Colsall because there is so little petrol, and I told Miss Bolby and Reenie to get out at Colsall. You'll look out for them, won't you, darling?"

"I don't know how I'm going to see them in a fog like this unless I'm in the same carriage. What does Miss Bolby look like, and who's Reenie?"

"The new kitchen-maid, she's a friend of Vi's. She's been invalided out of the ATS."

"Oh Lord!" said Jessy. "And what about Miss Bolby?"

"She's thinnish; rather good-looking as far as I remember."

"Old, young, or middling?"

"Decidedly middling."

"Oh Lord!" said Jessy. "How awful!"

"But you can't expect to get a young governess in war-time. Where are you?"

"In the Queen's Hotel. I think war's horrible."

"Why particularly at this moment?"

"A black man carried my suitcase."

10

"I wish you wouldn't talk to people, Jessy. He wasn't fresh with you?"

"No, not fresh, just black, and it must be horrid to be black in a fog like this. Lisbeth, I absolutely can't travel with a coroneted suitcase again."

"Why not, darling?"

"It makes me feel so silly."

"I don't see anything silly about it."

"You would if you'd had to sit between two drunk sailors. Have you done anything about the Gymkhana?"

"Not yet, it's much too soon, and goodness knows what will have happened by next summer."

"Barby says you have to send the entries in months before."

"There are months before we need think about it, and I shan't forget. Have you had a nice visit?"

"All right."

"Haven't you had fun?"

"If you call washing-up fun. You know we're awfully lucky to have servants."

"They're such a worry that I sometimes wonder . . ."

"You wouldn't if you'd been washing-up all the week."

"You'd better hurry up, Jess, or you'll miss your train. What time is it?"

"I don't know. All the clocks are broken."

"Well, look out for Miss Bolby and Reenie, won't you?"

"O.K."

"And don't say O.K., darling, it's awful."

"Everyone says it."

"I know, but try not to."

"Righto," said Jessy.

"And, Jessy——"

"I must go or I'll miss the train."

"I've given Miss Bolby your room."

"Oh, blow!" said Jessy. She took the suitcase from the hall porter and went out into the fog and the station's clamour and bumped the suitcase down the steps; this time no black hand helped her.

3

Miss Bolby took Elizabeth Rushford's letter from her bag. 'Rushford, Colsall' it was headed beneath a small blue coronet. 'Rushford' conveyed nothing. Rushford Hall, or Park, or Palace, or Castle, or Towers would have given a suggestion as to its architecture and size, but 'Rushford' was irritatingly enigmatic, a little flat, somehow. It had been difficult to say in the smoking-room at Hillstone House : 'I am taking up a new post, I am going to Rushford.' It had not made any particular impression, so that she had been forced to add, 'Lord Rushford's place', and it had been Mr. Lind who had made the impression : 'That is very interesting, Miss Bolby. My wife used to know some of the Rushfords.'

Miss Bolby put back the letter and took out her ticket. 'Colsall Halt' it said. A journey to Colsall Halt must surely be an irritating one : a series of halts. In a fog such as this it was not easy to see the names of stations, and by the time the train reached Colsall Halt darkness would have fallen. The clinging vapour outside had already turned to a deep gun-metal, and platforms at halts seldom extended to the full length of the train—there was nothing to prevent one from stepping into nothingness. But I must not lose my head, she thought : I must not panic just because I am going into a new post. At my age, after all I have been through, it would be absurd. I have never lost my head. . . . 'If you can keep your head when all about you are losing theirs . . .' It had not always been easy, though. It had not been easy when she had found her father unconscious upon the study floor at the White House at Worthing, for instance—for the second time today she thought of her father—the agitation, the upheaval of leaving Hillstone House and the uneasiness of going into a new post had brought back flashes from the past with uncanny

12

vividness today. No, it had not been easy when first Mavis and then Sita had married, though she, Roona, had been singled out by her father as the beauty—true, they had been older and Ralph Barnsley *had* proposed and it had seemed at first as if Sita's marriage would make things easier, but it had not done so and Sita had married in India and it had not led where it should have led. If Sita's marriage had taken place in England . . . Miss Bolby attempted to push the thought from her. Ever since she had begun to pack yesterday, with the folding of a sari, the polishing of her silver snake-backed hair brushes or the putting away of a photograph, some phase of the past had thrust itself before her to disturb and disconcert: the White House at Worthing with its green shutters, the smooth lawn with its Cedar and its Monkey-puzzle tree. . . The Cedar had given it an air of peace, grandeur almost: had enabled her to pretend she was no longer at Worthing, but in some great house where there were many servants. Servants who did not move with the silent soft-footed dignity which had made her wince at her loud-voiced father—servants who were servants and not sluts.

She had been sitting under the Cedar when the telegram came from Sita.

'A telegram, Mother. It must be from Sita!'

'Open it, my dear child. I could never face a telegram, and we mustn't disturb Father.'

'Mother, Sita is engaged. Engaged to be married! To Arthur. . . . Arthur Atherton-something—it looks like Atherton-Broadleigh.'

'Let me see the telegram, Roona, and get me my fan which is on the piano. Don't stand there staring so. Is it so extraordinary to become engaged?' The shawl had slipped from her mother's shoulders and her hand trembled, agitating her bracelets; she had been resting upon the sofa. The french windows were open and the room was filled with birdsong and

13

the swishing of the Cedar; sunlight, through its branches dappled the shawl.

'Go gently to your father's study, Roona, wake him and tell him to come here immediately.' And her father had come immediately, ruffled from his afternoon sleep, but as always when her mother called, immediately.

'I'll bet you he's a penniless subaltern, Lavinia, and, if so, I won't hear of it. Send her a telegram instantly to say I won't hear of it without further details.'

'But he is an Atherton-Broadleigh, Bertram. The Atherton-Broadleighs are a very old family, related to Lord something, I feel convinced of it. Get me the Peerage, Roona.'

'But, Mother, if you don't know the family to whom he is related, how can you look it up in the Peerage?'

'Give me the Book—there are ways, my dear Roona.'

Hastily, feverishly almost, her mother turned the pages so that she, Roona, watching shadows from the branches fall upon them, said to herself : I must not be hasty, it is undignified; that, at least, I learned in India.

'I can't seem to come upon it. How very vexing, when I know it is here.'

'You are imagining it, my dear Lavinia.'

'I never imagine anything, Bertram. We shall have to compose a telegram.'

'Then you do it, you are better at telegrams.'

'Get me a telegram form, Roona.'

> 'Your father cannot give his consent
> without full details whose son
> cable immediately love Mother.'

'If you hurry, Roona, the post office will still be open. I know it's there somewhere, but the name escapes me. How very vexing. Even if we don't encourage it, we must at all costs take no steps to *prevent* this marriage, Bertram.'

14

The Beginning

She, Roona, had hurried to the post office. Her heart had thumped uneasily, not solely because the evening was warm and she hurried : Sita's marriage opened up new possibilities; she might even go to stay with Sita in India and thus escape, as Sita was about to, from Worthing.

On the way back she met Ralph Barnsley, sauntering.

'I say, Roona, whither with such speed?'

'Sita is engaged!' She blurted out the news.

'Golly! Who to?'

'That's just it, we don't know. I've been to the post office to send a cable. His name is Atherton-Broadleigh.'

Ralph whistled. It had been in very bad taste on Ralph's part to whistle, though she had scarcely noticed it at the time. Funny the way little details such as this seemed to imprint themselves upon the memory as though with invisible ink in order to irritate later.

'Sounds all right to me. Anything wrong? Aren't your people pleased?'

'Oh yes, Mother is delighted. It's just . . . I suppose—well, rather unexpected and exciting.'

'I should say it is. Why not come round after dinner tonight and celebrate? Oh, and I say, Roona, I was coming along, as a matter of fact, to ask if I might have the loan of your mower. Ours has broken down. Shall I come along with you now?'

'Yes, rather. I shouldn't say anything to Mother about Sita's engagement, though; it's—well, you know, as I've just said, rather unexpected.'

After dinner, to escape her mother's feverishness and the uneasy atmosphere of the drawing-room, she went round to the Barnsleys. The Barnsleys lived at the end of the street, with a copper beech and a laburnum in place of the monkey puzzle and the cedar, which made the house, though it was as large as the White House and set well back from the road, seem more suburban.

15

'What is this I hear, Roona? Sita engaged? You'll be the next and before you can say Jack Robinson!' Colonel Barnsley had gone down to the cellar to get some champagne.

'Give us a song, Roona,' Ralph said later. Ralph's sister Bertha sat at the piano. 'You know your voice has got beyond Mr. Middlethorpe, Roona. I think you're wasting your time. You ought to go to someone really first class—in London or Birmingham.'

'But how can I get away, Bertha, particularly if Sita marries?'

'Surely it will be easier if Sita marries. There'll be more money.'

'Not enough to make any difference.' The easy way the Barnsleys talked of money made her flush.

'Well, I don't see how you're going to get on with a career unless you get away.'

'Mother's dead against a career.'

'I know, but she's wrong. In any case you've chosen a pretty harmless one. I can't see anything wrong with singing.'

Ralph said : 'I suppose it's different from singing in a drawing-room.'

'Well, anyway, sing you must because you've got a magnificent voice, and if you confine it to the drawing-room you'll be a fool, Roona.' Bertha struck a chord on the piano.

Ralph walked home with her. He slipped an arm through hers as they went through the gate and into the road.

'I say, Roona, come down to the sea with me. I want to talk to you and we can't talk between here and the White House. Come down to the shelter.'

'Not at this hour, Ralph.'

'I suppose not; it would be scandalous.' He said it bitterly and at that moment she hated Ralph. Then he wheeled round to face her and without warning said : 'Roona, I'm going to the Sudan in a fortnight; will you marry me?'

'How can I, Ralph, in a fortnight? And there is my career.'

'Oh, blow your career. Don't listen to Bertha. What do you want with a career when you'll marry sooner or later in any case. You couldn't look like that and not. Come with me to the Sudan and forget about a career.'

'Marriage is no longer a woman's sole object in life. I will give you my answer in the morning, Ralph,' she said chillily.

But it was, it was, and it was galling that it was, because she had had many offers and she had let them all go, because none had seemed good enough once Sita had married an Atherton-Broadleigh. . . . Miss Bolby rubbed savagely at the carriage window with a discarded newspaper. Why did the truth assert itself so painfully today? It was as if the fog, by its density, clarified it, played the same curious tricks it played with sound. She threw the blackened paper under the seat and back came the house at Worthing with the ease and inevitability of a returning nightmare. . . .

A sleepless, agitated night. First Sita's engagement, and then, as though precipitated by it, Ralph's proposal. It had not seemed, until that moment, as if he would speak because he was going so soon to the Sudan. In the morning her mother, who got up late and directed the day's arrangements from her bed, as though sensing what had happened, sent for her.

'Aren't you seeing a little too much of Ralph Barnsley, Roona?'

'Not really, Mother.'

'He was here a great deal yesterday.'

'We met in the street as I came back from the post office. He came to borrow the mower.'

'And you were there after dinner.'

'Yes, Bertha had promised to play for me. He is going to the Sudan quite soon, Mother.'

'Ah!' leaning back against the pillows, relieved. 'How soon?'

17

'In a fortnight.'

'I must admit I'm glad, though Ralph himself is a nice enough boy, but the Barnsleys are not quite . . . not quite . . . but I hardly need tell you that; you were always perceptive, Roona.'

'Not quite what, Mother?'

'Well, rather *deuxième*. Not quite out of the top drawer. I do hope Sita will answer the cable quickly and not consider expense.'

'Which is difficult, Mother, with very little money.'

'An occasion such as this is not the time to be parsimonious. I can hardly bear the suspense.'

Then she, Roona, had gone down to the sea instead of to the drawing-room for her morning practice, feeling curiously flat. She sat in the shelter. Never had the sea seemed so flat. At Brighton it ran up to meet the sky, but Worthing itself was flat. She looked about her at the other occupants of the shelter: they were crooked and old and carried sticks, and everything about *them* was flat—their feet and their eyes and their greyish-green faces. Funny everything should be so noticeably so, just when so much had happend. What would Ralph do? Would he come back today for her answer, or would he avoid her? And what was her answer? No. No. No. Yet here was a chance to leave Worthing. For what? For the Sudan. No, this was not the chance to take; it was foolish to take the first chance, and there would surely be others. Hadn't Ralph said: '. . . you'll marry sooner or later in any case—you couldn't look like that and not.' Rather sooner than later, but not yet. And as her mother had said, the Barnsleys were not, well, not . . . She was not snobbish like her mother though, and they had money, and with money she could go on with her singing, but not in the Sudan. No. The answer was no.

In the evening Ralph brought back the mower. She did not sit, as she usually sat when the weather was fine, beneath the cedar, because she was afraid Ralph would come. She went up to her bedroom. She heard the noise of the mower in the road; and then her father's voice as it dispersed across the lawn, reaching its far corners as Ralph reached the gate: 'Ralph, my boy! That's what I call promptitude. Looking for Roona, I expect, eh?' Then her mother's, from the drawing-room: 'If she isn't under the Cedar, she must be out, Ralph. Won't you come in, dear boy?' It was the sweetness in her mother's voice that had sent her down; she had not meant to see Ralph when she had first heard the trundling of the mower.

'What about a stroll, Roona? Now that the wind has dropped it's nice down on the front, and you ought to see the azaleas in old Mr. Middlethorpe's garden.'

'She sees them twice a week, Ralph.'

'They were hardly out two days ago, though, Mrs. Bolby. They've blazed out suddenly, they really are a sight. I bet you she trills away in that dark stuffy room of Mr. Middlethorpe's without ever looking at the azaleas.'

'I'll go and get my hat, Ralph.'

They walked to the end of the road in silence.

'Well, Roona, have you made up your mind, or are you still deliberating the higher aims of woman?'

'I have made up my mind, Ralph.'

'Let's have it, then.'

'I can't marry yet.'

'You can't marry yet, or you can't marry me?'

'Neither.'

'What exactly, then?'

'If Sita marries I can't leave Mother. Father's blood pressure is so high, the doctor says he might—well, anything might happen at any moment, and Mother is so delicate.'

'But you'll have to leave Mother sometime, and you don't know for certain yet about Sita, do you? It looks as if none of you could make up your minds about anything.'

'But I *have* made up my mind. Ralph, I can't marry you.'

'Apart from your aspirations as a singer, may I ask exactly why?'

'You see, I don't . . . love you.'

'Yes, I think I do see. If you did, you'd throw everything to the winds, but yours was never a spontaneous nature, Roona.'

They walked down to the sea in silence, and back, almost in silence. At the gate he said : 'Well, there isn't any more to say, Roona, is there?' Just as something in her mother's voice had made her come down to the drawing-room—had almost made her change her mind and say 'yes' to Ralph, something in Ralph's voice decided her against it.

She tried to go straight to her room when she got in, but her mother called her. 'You look as if Ralph has proposed to you, Roona—a little feverish. What have you said?'

'I said no, Mother.'

'Very wise, dear girl. How I wish we could hear from Sita.' Then she hated her mother and hated Ralph and hated Worthing.

When the telegram from Sita came its effect was electrical.

'Son of the Dean of Waterbury and Lady Alice
Atherton-Broadleigh Lady Alice writing Mother
love Sita.'

She almost forgot Ralph until she met Bertha in the street. Bertha greeted her with her usual affectionate friendliness.

'You look a bit more cheerful. Anything on, Roona?'

'We have heard from Sita.'

'I say! All on then, is it?'

'We're waiting to hear from his mother, Lady Alice Atherton-Broadleigh.'

Bertha whistled. She had always hated the way the Barnsleys whistled, it was the one thing she disliked about Bertha.

'Looks a bit better for you, Roona. You may get a chance after all, with your singing. Don't go dashing off to India, though, will you? I'm jolly glad you're looking more cheerful.' Bertha said this as if she had known about Ralph, though she did not allude to Ralph.

'Surely the post is extraordinarily late, isn't it? Have a look when you go down, Roona, will you?' 'What can have happened to the post?' 'Just get me the Peerage again, Roona; somehow I must find Lady Alice.'

Then the letter from Lady Alice :

'DEAR MRS. BOLBY,' it ran,

'My husband and I are delighted to hear of our son Arthur's engagement to your daughter Sita. We shall be so delighted if you will bring your younger girl to stay with us here for a night. We have a girl of the same age and it would be nice if our girls could meet—this would also give us an opportunity to discuss Arthur's engagement. He is very young and impressionable and I feel sure you will agree that we should try to dissuade from too *hasty* a marriage.

'The night of June 20th or 24th would suit us very well.

Yours sincerely,

'ALICE ATHERTON-BROADLEIGH.'

'DEAR LADY ALICE,

'I was delighted to get your letter.

'My husband and I are overjoyed at the news of our daughter Sita's engagement to your son, Arthur, and my daughter Roona and I have great pleasure in accepting your kind invitation to visit you on June 24th, which is the better of the two dates you have given us.

'I look forward to the opportunity of discussing the forthcoming marriage. While my husband and I are wholly in agreement with you as to the inadvisability of *hasty* marriages, we do not approve of long engagements for young

21

people. I feel certain, therefore, that we shall be able to come to some very satisfactory arrangement.

'Yours very sincerely,

'LAVINIA BOLBY.'

'Bertha, we've been asked to the Atherton-Broadleigh's!'
'Lordy! All of you?'
'Just Mother and I.'
'For long?'
'No, just for the night. So that they can discuss Sita's marriage, and there's a girl my age. I don't think I've got the right sort of clothes, though.'
'Surely, just for a night. When do you go?'
'On the twenty-fourth.'
'The day after Ralph goes. My goodness, I *shall* be low with *no one* to console me.'

The train had begun its series of halts and the light had gone out above Miss Bolby's head; it could not be very far now to Colsall Halt.

'I shouldn't wake Father till Enid brings in the tea, dear.'
'No, Mother.'
'And don't forget to pack some music. I should like you to sing to Lady Alice.' She knew that her mother had gone to tea with Mrs. Butler-Clitheroe in order to tell her of their approaching visit. Since Sita's engagement her mother had daily discarded her invalidism. Would Ralph come to say goodbye? And if he came . . . no, no. With Sita's engagement and the approaching visit which might lead to other visits . . .
'Tea's in, Miss. Shall I tell the Colonel?'
'No thanks, Enid. I will.'
'Father, *Father*! Enid! Enid! Enid, get Dr. Beardmore *at once*. At *once,* do you hear? The Colonel is ill—I think

22

he's dying. . . .' And within a few hours her father had died, and she had not seen Ralph again; he had sent her a note of condolence. Not that she held regrets for Ralph. She was reminded of him sometimes by Mr. Billings. Not that he and Mr. Billings were from the same social stratum, but there was some sort of a resemblance between them. No doubt it had been her encounter with Mr. Billings in the hall this afternoon which had led, indirectly, to this searching into the past. It would be nice to get to Rushford if only to get away from Mr. Billings. She had never been able to make up her mind which she disliked most : Mr. Billings's distasteful remarks and perpetual patience-playing, Mr. Howland's flowing phrases and comfortable complaceny, or the political opinions of Mr. Lorelli—last night she had hated Mr. Billings.

'Well, what will you be doing tomorrow night, I wonder, Miss Bolby? You'll be glad to get into a decent house with comforts, I should think. Not that Milly doesn't try to run the place decently, but it's hardly what you'd call *comfort*,' Mrs. Hurst had said.

'I wonder if you could *h*elp me? I'm afraid I have lost a stitch, Mrs. *H*urst.'

'My word! You *are* in trouble, Mrs. Billings.'

Mr. Lind cleared his throat : 'My wife's brother-in-law had a cousin who married a Rushford, Miss Bolby; one of the Irish branch, I think.'

'Indeed, Mr. Lind? I didn't know there was an Irish branch. I remember my mother saying one should never travel without a Peerage, but that was long ago, when things were very different; when we lived at Worthing.'

'Rather a heavy book to carry around, I should think, Miss Bolby. Let me see, let me *see*. . . . The ace of *spades* . . . the ace of spades. . . .' Mr. Billings slapped down a card.

'Have you any idea who *Lady* Rushford was, Mr. Lind?'

'I don't know at all, Miss Bolby. I dare say my wife would know, and I dare say at Rushford you'll find a Peerage. Or, if you like, I could look it up for you tomorrow in the public library.' One had only to mention a thing and Mr. Lind would dash off and look it up in the public library.

'There goes Mr. Lorelli again—there you are, Mrs. Billings, a stitch in time. . . . Soon we shall have Milly at her minuet in whatever it is. It'll be nice for you getting a little *quiet*, Miss Bolby. Nice to get out of that room of yours, too. Of all the rooms in the 'ouse, yours is about the most sordid.' Mrs. Hurst was nothing if not candid, but she was not ill-mannered like Mr. Billings.

Then the telephone rang. The telephone at Hillstone House was in the hall. When it rang conversation in the smoking-room ceased, an expectant hush fell, then Milly Tollmarsh came out from the Tollmarsh's sitting-room to answer it and Mr. Howland rustled his paper and Mr. Billings slapped down a card and Mrs. Hurst, with a scarcely perceptible movement, agitated her steel needles and Mr. Lind cleared his throat. None of these little sounds, however, covered Milly's mono-syllabic replies and the conversation in the smoking-room, which had been half-heartedly resumed, flagged : each waited with a sort of halting inside. Then Milly said : 'Hold on a minute, will you?' and crossed the hall and threw open the door—Milly did not open doors, she threw them open with the same vigour with which she attacked Beethoven's Minuet in G. She stood squarely, surveying the room's occupants with her right eye, while her left travelled a course of its own, blinking before swinging back into focus : 'Miss Bolby, for you. Sounds like your new post, Lady Rushforth or some-thing.' Then she waited, not as if to watch the impact of her words, Milly was as incurious as Elsie—within the walls of Hillstone House only Milly and Elsie were incurious—but in order to draw her left eye into control before recrossing the hall and slamming Mrs. Tollmarsh's door.

'It's Lady Rushford here, Miss Bolby. Can you get the three-twenty tomorrow? I've got to meet a kitchen-maid on

24

it, and my stepdaughter, Jessica, who has been away on a visit, and we've got very little petrol and the weather is too bad to use the ponies for the station, so will you get out at Colsall Halt? And perhaps you'd keep a look out for Reenie —that's the kitchen-maid.'

The voice had been hurried and rather peremptory—very different from the voice at the interview. Or had she imagined this because she knew that in the smoking-room, intent upon their knitting, Mrs. Hurst and Mrs. Billings listened—and Mr. Howland, seemingly deep in his evening paper, and Mr. Billings, tut-tutting between his teeth as he held high a card before slamming it down upon the table; and Elsie, lifting her face with its vacant stare towards the sound, somewhere in the dark beetle-ridden region of the kitchen?

'All well, Miss Bolby?'

'Yes thanks, Mrs. Hurst.'

Why should it be she who had to look out for the kitchen-maid? Surely the kitchen-maid should look out for her.

'I shall say good night, Mrs. Hurst. I'm tired and I have my packing to do.'

Good *night*, Miss Bolby, but not goodbye. I take it we see you on the morrow?' Mr. Howland swept his paper aside. Mr. Howland's paper, it seemed, was solely for the purpose of smoothing, rustling, flourishing, an aid or a barrier, a part of Mr. Howland. It was only Mr. Howland who had his own chair. 'No, no. Pray don't move, Miss Bolby. They are all Mrs. Tollmarsh's chairs, all yours.' Nevertheless he had waited for her to move when she had inadvertently sat upon it.

'Don't go sittin' up all night packin,' now, Miss Bolby. You want to be fresh when you go into a new post.' Mrs. Hurst stuck her needle into the ball of wool.

'Well, night-night, Miss Bolby. Sleep tight, as the saying is.' Mr. Billings did not look up from his cards.

It would be nice indeed not to have to sit in the same room as Mr. Billings night after night. Later, when she had gone upstairs, she had heard Mrs. Billings and Mrs. Hurst come up for coats, then she heard the front door slam; they had gone, with Mr. Billings and Mr. Lind, to the George.

The train was drawing to a halt and this time it was Colsall Halt. Miss Bolby began to gather her things.

4

Elizabeth Rushford tucked the rug in under her knees; she had already waited half an hour : she began to think of all the things she might have done in half an hour.

Sitting outside the station here, she felt like a cocoon, wrapped in the fog's shroud. So much of war was spent in waiting : waiting for news, waiting for trains, waiting for servants who missed them and took a dislike to the place when they came. She herself had been fortunate enough not to have had to wait in queues; it was possible to sail in ahead of them because the order had been given by telephone : 'Oh, and by the way, Mr. Simpkins, if you've *got* any biscuits. . . .' Yes, there *were* advantages after all, even in war, in being, well, who one was . . .

Elizabeth took a duster from the pigeon-hole in the dashboard and rubbed the windscreen. She let down one of the clouded windows and fog floated round her head and into the dark body of the station van. An express thundered through the station and the floorboards vibrated; she sensed a stir and heard the hurrying of feet before they halted while eyes strained towards the darkness, attempting to penetrate the opaque wall beyond the orbit of the dim light from the lamps. She did not feel wholly at ease about Miss Bolby, or about Reenie, the kitchen-maid. How could one assess a personality during a hurried interview and judge whether or not it was suited to the role of governess or kitchen-maid? Especially now, when only the over-age, the feeble and the mentally deficient were exempt from the call-up.

"Lisbeth!"

Jessy's train must have come in under cover of the express.

"Jessy darling! Where are Reenie and Miss Bolby?"

"Oh Lord! I'd forgotten them." Jessy dived back into the station.

When Miss Bolby descended from the train she saw no sign of a porter, so she stood beside her luggage; it was too heavy to carry, besides, she had never yet carried a suitcase. It was simply a matter of waiting; if you waited long enough some-one came, and surely at Rushford there would be a man, *some* sort of man, some old retainer whose duty it was to meet trains.

"Ah, Miss Bolby," said Elizabeth, "at last! What *have* you been doing, Jessy? This is Reenie, Miss Bolby, Reenie Miller. Get in in front with me, will you, Miss Bolby? And you, Reenie, get in the back with Miss Jessy."

"Thanks, Lady Rushford," said Reenie.

"And by the way, you should call me m'lady, not Lady Rushford. We had better begin as we mean to go on, Reenie."

"Rightho, m'lady," said Reenie. She threw away a cigarette as she got into the car. She had been holding it inwards, pointing inwards, towards her hand. Errand boys smoke in such a way, and Benn when I come into the pantry and he hasn't seen me, and the Italian prisoners. I shall have to tell her not to smoke when she talks to me, and Mrs. Williams will have to tell her not to smoke in the kitchen. How tedious, Elizabeth thought.

Jessy climbed in over Miss Bolby's luggage and Elizabeth started the car. "I'm afraid you'll have to put your head out of the window, Miss Bolby, to tell me how far I am from the kerb. Do you know this part of the country? In any case, you must be used to our Midland fogs if you've been in Birmingham." Elizabeth ground the gears—she was not a good driver.

"My room in Birmingham is just my pied-à-terre. I don't belong there; I was born in India, Lady Rushford."

Over her shoulder, into the body of the car, Elizabeth said : "Did you have a good journey, Reenie?"

"Fine, thanks, Lady Rushford," said Reenie.

"India, did you say, Miss Bolby? Just put your head out of the window again, will you? At least there is one good thing about the fog, it gives us a few days' peace, rest from the bombers about us—a few days' silence. Rushford is barely two miles from an aerodrome, Miss Bolby, and it lies in such a way that they fly directly over the house when they're coming in—rather low, of course; in fact it's a wonder they don't fly *into* the house."

"It must be very disturbing, Lady Rushford."

"At first it was, rather, but one gets use to it, and we must be thankful, I suppose, that we're not a hospital, and we've no evacuees. Just a few land girls."

"Reenie, give this case a shove, will you?" said Jessy. It's awfully heavy and it's on my toe."

"Rightho," said Reenie.

The fog was beginning to play strange tricks. It was no longer an opaque wall; there were patches of clarity and then pockets of fog in hollows, and then clear hollows and layers of fog upon high ground, but it was floating now, it was no longer solid.

"Just at the moment we are not very well off for servants," said Elizabeth, "so you won't mind doing your room, Miss Bolby? Just making the bed and dusting. We have Winnie from the village and one or two others, but they're not very reliable, and there is Mrs. Williams, who cooks, and Benn, a very old butler, and a boy, and now we shall have Reenie, so you won't mind, Miss Bolby?"

"Most certainly *not*, Lady Rushford. It's a case of all hands to the plough, is it not?"

Why the hell do I have to call her 'm'lady' when this old bag calls her 'Lady Rushford?' Reenie thought.

Why, when Elsie makes all the beds at Hillstone House, and at Rushford they have Winnie from the village and this common girl, Reenie, must I make my bed? wondered Miss Bolby.

"And when all else fails," continued Elizabeth, "there are Nino and Otello, the Italian prisoners. They work on the land, but they've cooked before now; they have even cut Ruth's and Louisa's hair."

"When they cut Louisa's, she looked like an umbrella, they made it all bristly underneath so that it stuck out all round," said Jessy.

"Christ!" said Reenie.

"Ruth and Louisa, I should explain, Miss Bolby," said Elizabeth, as if Reenie had not spoken, "are my stepdaughter and daughter. Barby and Louisa are mine, and Jessy and Ruth are Lord Rushford's. His first wife died when Ruth was born. And then there is Bella, who is ours."

Why does she explain us so? I shall never explain, thought Jessy.

"Does Lord Rushford think it wise to allow the prisoners in the house?" said Miss Bolby.

"Oh, I think so. They're really quite harmless and most obliging, and Lord Rushford is as fond of the Italians as I am. He is in Italy now. It's nice for the prisoners as well as for me; you see, I speak Italian. Do you speak Italian, Miss Bolby?"

"I used to, in the days when I sang, but I fear it is rather rusty, Lady Rushford."

"Anyway, they're not *our* prisoners. I mean they're not

slaves, they don't belong to *us*; and it must be jolly unpleasant whatever you do, being a prisoner, I should think," said Jessy.

"Same here," said Reenie.

After this no one spoke for a time.

"You have no idea how much there is to do with Lord Rushford away, endless Red Cross work and so much correspondence, and the servants come and go so. I haven't been able to find a satisfactory secretary. I don't suppose you type, by any chance, Miss Bolby?"

"I'm afraid *not*, Lady Rushford."

They had turned now through the gates at Brixhall Lodge into Rushford's main drive. Here the fog was dense again, and Elizabeth's full concentration was directed upon her driving. As the car clanked slowly over the first cattle-grid—grids took the place of gates at Rushford—Jessy felt a tightening inside, a twinge of constriction as it were, about her heart. Upon every return to Rushford for as long as she could remember she had felt this same twinge, just here as the car bumped over the grid, because it was here that one first caught sight of Rushford, and even though now it was dark and nothing at all could be seen through the wall of fog, this clanking over the grid meant that Rushford was there: dark and symmetrical and serene, and for the space that it covered, forcing the fog to disperse, the folds of vapour to part.

As the car curved slowly round an oval lawn, invisible now, before the house, the silence was broken by yapping, then a shrill staccato bark, then a deep sonorous one; then, as Barby opened the door, shapes rushed forth from it into a thin stream of light: Messalina the sheepdog, tumbling over her own paws, followed by Larry Rushford's labrador and the poodles, and Chang Kai-Shek, Elizabeth's pekinese. Barby, no more demonstrative than the cats, Eleanor and Doushka, stood silently, silhouetted against the light, framed by the doorway. Because of the black-out, only the inner door, a narrow door, cut in the door itself, had been opened, so that the light thrown from the hall was a feeble one extending little further than the porch.

"Down, Messalina, down!" said Elizabeth. "She's quite harmless, Miss Bolby, only a little rough. I do hope you are an animal lover. This is my daughter, Barby. Get *down*, Messalina! Is Benn coming for the luggage? Do call the dogs, Barby."

"How do you do?" said Barby. "Hello, Jess."

"Hullo," said Jessy. They did not kiss or show any sign of affection; they were between the ages of kissing.

"If you can take your zip-bag, Miss Bolby, Benn will come for the heavy luggage. Do get out of the way, Messalina! Where are Ruth and Louisa, Barby?"

"Becca wouldn't let them come down. She thinks they've got colds. Lady Meredith is here."

"Good heavens, where? And she's Lady *Archie,* darling. How many more times must I tell you to call her Lady Archie and not Lady Meredith."

"Sorry. Lady Archie, then, she got stuck in the fog and she's in the hall."

Over and above Reenie's aching desire for another cigarette and her uncertainty as to whether or not she could light one under such circumstances, came the thought that this mass of turbulently moving bodies in the porch was not unlike a football scrum; she wanted more than ever to 'get a line on the place' from Vi. She coughed—no one had addressed her since she had got out of the car.

"Ah, Reenie!" said Elizabeth. "I had forgotten Reenie, who is more important than all. How pleased Mrs. Williams will be to see you. Come in, Reenie. Mind your head, Miss Bolby; you'll have to make yourself small, I'm afraid, as you go through the door."

Once inside it, the hall at Rushford was large, so large that its size at first bewildered; a broad staircase rose from it, sheltered from the rest of it by a lacquer screen; in the distance, beyond the screen, Lady Archie Meredith rose from a sofa by the fire: "My dear Elizabeth, what a shock it must be for you to see me."

"My dear Lady Archie—this is Miss Bolby, who has come to give the children lessons—and this is Reenie, Reenie Miller, who has come to help us out in the kitchen. Barby, take Miss Bolby to her room, will you? And you, Jessy, take Reenie to the kitchen. You must be tired after your journey, Miss Bolby, and you'll want to unpack. I expect you'd like some tea upstairs. Barby, see that Miss Bolby has some tea, will you?"

Dismissed, as it were, without a chance to reply, Miss Bolby followed Barby upstairs.

5

"This is your room, Miss Bolby, or rather Jessy's."

"Well, now that it's mine, I suppose it is no longer Jessica's, Barbara."

"I'm not called Barbara."

"So I'm to call you Barby?"

"And Jessy is not called Jessica."

"I see."

"And the bathroom, Miss Bolby, is at the end of the passage. There are two: one is the nursery one, which we use, and the other is for Reenie and Vi. I don't know which you're to use. I don't suppose it matters much, but the nursery one, ours, is always full of Becca's washing."

"Becca?"

"Becca is our nurse, our nanny, she was Larry's. Miss Rebecca Stroud."

"And Larry?"

"Larry is my stepfather."

"Lord Rushford? And you call him Larry?"

"We call him Larry and we call my mother Lisbeth, it's easier; if we call them Mum and Dad no one knows whose is which."

"I see. Your mother very kindly said you would get me some tea, Barby."

"Oh Lord, yes! I forgot. I'll get it from the nursery."

"And what time do we dine, and where? And does your mother change?"

"Heavens, no! At least, only sometimes, into a dressing-gown or something. She changes when there's anyone here, but I expect you'll have yours on a tray. She said Jessy and I could have ours in the nursery because it's Jessy's first night back."

"My former pupils always had schoolroom supper with me on *my* first night. On a tray *where*, Barbara?"

"In the Red Room, I should think. They generally do."

"They?"

"The governesses and secretaries, when it's not in the schoolroom."

"You talk as though you had had many?"

"Oh, masses. Nobody stays, you see. I suppose it's the war. I'll go and get your tea, Miss Bolby."

Jessy's room was long and narrow; there was linoleum on the floor, white-painted furniture, chipped and a little shabby, some book-shelves, faded chintz curtains and two or three mats. The dressing-table mirror, when Miss Bolby attempted to adjust it, fell forward. Was she to be dogged by this sort of mirror, even in this sort of house? As far as comforts were concerned there seemed no great improvement here in Jessy's room upon those in her own in Hillstone House, though its walls were cleaner and the fire before the grate was an electric, not a gas one, so that here no fumbling first with cold fingers would be necessary for shillings in the slot. But why Jessica's room? Why had she been given Jessy's room instead of the

33

Green Dressing Room, where Barby said Jessy was? Miss Bolby began to unpack.

'I expect you'd like *some tea upstairs*.' She smoothed and folded the tissue paper, which since the war had become so precious.

'And you won't mind doing your own room, Miss Bolby? *Just making the bed and dusting*.' She took out her nightgown case, shook it and laid it upon the pillow—the shaking eased her slowly mounting anger; it was embroidered with mauve flowers.

"Did you have a good journey, Reenie?" Just as she, Roona, had said: 'I was born in India.' She shook out her mother's sari and spread it over the top of the chipped chest of drawers in order to make the room look less like Jessy's and more habitable.

'The other is for Reenie and Vi.' Who was Vi? She spread her silver-backed brushes embossed with twisted snakes upon the dressing-table, and, holding the mirror to keep it firmly wedged, hung up a hair-tidy. Why should such a fuss be made of a common girl like Reenie, who was not at all the type of girl one would expect to find in such a house? A very different type from Elsie, not the kitchen-maid type at all. That was the worst of war, one came across such dreadful types everywhere. She put the brass pin-tray which had been Sita's last Christmas present upon the mantelpiece, then she took an apple and the remains of her monthly ration of chocolate from a corner of her zip-bag and put them at the bottom of the cupboard. Finally she took her ration book from her handbag and then from its cover in order to see that she had had her full share of all that had not been inevitably Milly Tollmarsh's and need not inevitably be Lady Rushford's—war made one mean. The stench from its stained greasiness made her shudder: it reminded her of the scullery at Hillstone House into which she had once penetrated when filling a hot-water bottle, it stirred vague memories of native quarters

and of crowded trams. There was a knock at the door. It
was Barby: she carried a cup of tea which had the flat look
of tepidity; it slopped as she shut the door, into the
saucer.

"Becca thought you wouldn't want anything to eat because
it's so late, but I can get you a bit of cake if you like."

"No, I don't want anything to eat, thank you, Barbara."

"And Lisbeth, that is my mother, says that as Lady Meredith is staying the night and Reenie is new and Benn has
lumbago, she thinks you had better have dinner with her and
Lady Meredith."

"I see. Perhaps if Lady Meredith—I mean Lady Archie—
is here she will change."

"I shouldn't think so, because Lady Meredith hasn't got
anything to change into; she got stuck in the fog. Lord Corwen wouldn't let her go back in case anything happened to the
car."

"You mean Lady *Archie*, Barbara. Your mother said she
was Lady Archie, therefore she can't be Lady Meredith."

"Lady Meredith *and* Lady Archie. Some people call her
Lady Archie, but mostly she's called Lady Meredith."

"If she is Lady Archie she can't be Lady Meredith and you
ought to call her Lady Archie."

"People like my mother do, but mostly people call her Lady
Meredith."

"I can see that I shall have to look the matter up to get it
clear. And who is Lord Corwen?"

"Lord Meredith's brother, I mean Lord Archie's. He's deaf
and very old, and he keeps birds, and Lord Archie does everything; Lord Archie is only about seventy. They live with
him."

"Who, live with whom?"

"Lord and Lady Meredith."

"You mean Lord and Lady Archie, I think."

"Well, Lord and Lady Archie, then."

"Live with whom?"

"Lord Corwen. At Bowborough."

"And what *time* is dinner, Barbara?"

"Oh, about a quarter to eight, I should think. It's bound to be late because Benn has lumbago."

"And I'm not quite sure how I get downstairs."

"Well, you just go down the stairs."

"But to where?"

"Into the hall. I expect you'll find Lady Meredith there. Becca said I was to take your cup to the nursery when you'd finished with it." Barby ran a hand over the sari.

"It's Indian. Do you like it? It was my mother's sari."

"Was your mother Indian? It's lovely."

"The British in India do not marry Indians, my dear Barbara. My mother was a great lover of Indian things; you see, I was born in India."

"Oh, I see. Can I have the cup if you've finished with it, Miss Bolby?"

Miss Bolby brushed and repinned her hair. It was dark, only faintly streaked with grey. Then she took a light cashmere shawl from a drawer. Even at Hillstone House, always she, and sometimes Mrs. Billings and generally Mrs. Hurst had changed, not into full evening dress, but they had changed. She wrapped the shawl about her shoulders—these great houses were cold—then she turned out the light and switched off the fire.

Jessy leaned against the nursery fire-guard. Barby's long legs were swung across the arm of a chair. Ruth and Louisa sat upon the floor, heads together, studying the *Radio Times*. Becca sewed a button on to a petticoat of Bella's.

"Becca, why is Lady Meredith Lady Meredith *and* Lady Archie?"

"Gracious me, Barby, now you *are* asking. It's because

36

she's Lady Archie Meredith, isn't it? Mind out or you'll burn all the marrow out of your bones, Jessy. Get away from that fire."

"It's because of Lord Corwen," said Ruth, without looking up from the *Radio Times*.

"What is?" said Barby.

"That she's Lady Archie. Lord Corwen is a marquess. What's Miss Bolby like, Barby?"

"Awful," said Barby.

"Pretty awful," said Jessy.

"Oh, come now," said Becca.

"How awful?" said Louisa.

"Indian," said Jessy.

"No, she's not," said Barby.

"She was born in India," said Jessy.

"Is she dark?" said Louisa.

"People aren't dark because they're born in India."

"But she *is* dark," said Barby, "and she's got snakes on her brushes."

"Don't you wish she was the secretary and not the governess?" said Louisa.

"Ruth is becoming an awful snob," said Jessy.

"What's a snob?" said Louisa.

"Well, Ruth's one," said Jessy.

"No, I'm not," said Ruth.

"Yes, you are. You shouldn't talk about marquesses."

"I didn't," said Ruth; "Barby asked me."

"It doesn't matter being a marquess, though, does it?" said Barby.

"You shouldn't talk about it, though," said Jessy.

"But I didn't," said Ruth.

"She didn't mean no harm, Jessy," said Becca, "and as far as I can see he's not doing no harm being a marquess."

"Well, I still don't understand why Lady Meredith is Lady Archie," said Barby.

"Me neither. Beats me, but I'm new to the racket," said Reenie from the doorway. "Excuse me, Miss Stroud, but Vi said I was to ask you if I could have a bath in case Miss Bolby was using it."

"I didn't know she was listening, did you, Miss Stroud?" said Jessy when Reenie had gone.

"I'm surprised at a girl of *that* sort calling me 'Miss Stroud'. Thank goodness there's a little etiquette left in this house, even if there *is* a war on. It's time for Ruth and Louisa to go to bed. I don't know what you think you're doing in the Nursery, Ruth and Louisa, now that you're in the Schoolroom. The Schoolroom it is, from now on, and mind you remember you've got a new governess."

"Righti-ho, Miss Stroud," said Ruth.

"And *not* 'righti-ho' Ruth, if you please."

"Vi says it."

"Vi is a land girl," said Becca.

6

In Elizabeth's voice as she turned to Lady Archie after Miss Bolby had gone upstairs there had been a query. In all probability Lady Archie had forgotten by now where she was.

"That poor woman, Elizabeth, do you think she *wanted* tea upstairs?"

It seemed that Lady Archie had forgotten, not where she was, but her reason for being here.

"My experience of governesses is that they don't like it upstairs. She seems promising, though, unobtrusive and rather handsome, but not young enough for it to matter. Where does she come from?"

"Birmingham. I think she was born in India. Her sister married a General Sir Arthur something or other."

"Birmingham ... and India ... and a General ... an ominous combination. General Sir Arthur *what,* my dear Elizabeth?"

38

"That's just what I can't remember, Lady Archie."

"Dear me, how one's mind jumps to fanciful conclusions. I was beginning to imagine . . . but one can imagine anything in a fog. Fog, some scientist was saying last night on the radio, is increasing, due to the Gulf Stream shifting in its course. Soon we shall be back in the Ice Age; I wish they wouldn't forewarn us of such calamities. What were we talking about?"

"Fog, Lady Archie. Barby said you got stuck in it."

"Just outside the gates, so I didn't try to go on. One mustn't waste petrol, and Hughie is so terrified of anything happening to the car. I rang up Bowborough and he won't hear of me leaving till the fog lifts. Can you *spare* it, Elizabeth?" Lady Archie leaned forward and speared a pat of butter. As she did so the pansies on her hat trembled. Remembering them upon a summer straw during the last, and many other summers, Elizabeth wondered whether she and Lord Archie, living as they did with Lord Corwen at Bowborough, were as hard up as people said, and in which room she would put Lady Archie if she intended to stay the night.

"But it may not lift for days, Lady Archie."

"I know, but if you'll let me stay the night I'll be off soon as it's daylight. I daren't risk damaging the car. Sometimes it's hard for younger sons and very tiresome for the wives of younger sons, very irritating everything being Hughie's and nothing Archie's. Archie and I sometimes long for something of our own. Grandchildren, for instance, or a grate with a hob on it, or an aspidistra, and we can't even have the aspidistra, Hughie's taste is too austere. Don't waste sheets on me; let me sleep on the sofa, Elizabeth. Do you think Barby remembered to *give* that poor woman some tea?"

When Miss Bolby came down into the hall, Lady Archie, as Barby had predicted, was sitting there. She had sagged a little into the corner of the sofa, as though tired. She looked up at Miss Bolby's approach; she had heard the bracelet's jingle upon the stair.

"Ah, Miss Bolby. So you and I are the only punctual ones. How the punctual suffer. Unpunctuality was considerably worsened by the aeroplane; it came in with the car. Very trying for the horse-trained. Have you come from far?"

"From Birmingham, Lady Archie. I have a room there. Just a pied-à-terre, you know, in these uncertain times. It isn't always easy to find the right sort of post any more."

"I imagine not. So many children have gone to America."

"And so few people have servants, and houses are so full and one is expected to do a hundred other things besides the work for which one was engaged."

"Well you're lucky here, Miss Bolby; they seem to have plenty of servants and no evacuees and two delightful prisoners and some land girls, whereas we at Bowborough have no one at all. No one seems to want the place, which is just as well; both we and it are falling into sad decay. We've offered it and offered it in the hopes of getting it repaired. Hughie—Lord Corwen, that is my brother-in-law—won't spend a penny on anything but his birds—but nothing ever comes of it, so we sit there rotting on our hill all alone. What pretty bracelets you have, Miss Bolby. Indian, aren't they?"

"They were my mother's. My people were army people, and my mother spent a great many years in India; I was born in India, Lady Archie."

"India revives memories for me, Miss Bolby, too. *Sad* memories—not of India itself, but of events connected with India. You must find our smoky Midlands very cold."

"My own memories of India are slender, Lady Archie. I left when I was seven, but my sister Sita, married there. She went out again when a girl to stay with Lord Chipperfield; she was a friend of Lord Chipperfield's girl, Lady Pearl Thrufell—written, as I need hardly say, Throughfell—such a difficult name for foreigners, I always feel. She married an Atherton-Broadleigh, Arthur Atherton-Broadleigh. You know the Atherton-Broadleighs, I expect, Lady Archie?"

Lady Archie sat up, as if she had received a shock. "The name, somehow, Miss Bolby, seems to ring a bell."

"She married General *Sir Arthur* Atherton-Broadleigh, a son of the Dean of Waterbury. He was then only Lord Chipperfield's aide-de-camp."

"I remember the Dean, Miss Bolby. Yes, I remember the Dean well. A great man, the Dean : a great dancer and a great tennis player, a great preacher and a great upholder of women's suffrage. We used to flock to his sermons, and he made us sew for the poor. It was a wretched world in those days for the poor—now it's wretched for all of us and still wretched for the poor. Lady Alice, I remember, was delicate; she wore wisps of tulle and had a baby every year, she couldn't keep pace with him at all. There were some quite young ones still, when . . . Well, at about the time your sister must have married Arthur, I suppose. . . . You bring back memories, Miss Bolby. . . . The warmth of a conservatory and the scent of geranium, and the sound of wheels upon the road outside. We lived in St. John's Wood then, my son Harry and I. Harry had just left Harrow, and we had a butler called Barrington who used to leave notes for Harry about my movements and notes for me about Harry's, so that our life ran very smoothly. I can see Barrington's butlerian handwriting now. My son Harry was killed in the last war, which at least saved him from this one. How he would have hated this one, poor Harry."

Conversation subsided and with it Lady Archie, who seemed to sink further into her corner. There was no sound now but a gentle hissing of logs from the fire and the dripping of leaves in the deeper silence outside. When Miss Bolby broke it, her voice, though it was melodious, sounded harsh.

"How small the world is, Lady Archie! Such an extraordinary coincidence! One of those extraordinary doubles you might almost say. Only today I was thinking of my sister Sita's marriage and the Atherton-Broadleigh family."

Lady Archie made no answer; she stared, as if into a crystal, at the fire. Then, as though dragging herself unwillingly into the present, she said: "Would you say the picture above the fireplace was a Canaletto, Miss Bolby?"

"Jessy, run down into the hall and give Lady Archie and Miss Bolby some sherry," said Elizabeth, running a comb through her hair. "I'm sure Miss Bolby is punctual and that they're sitting there together, and Lady Archie lapses back into the past so."

"I shouldn't think she'll get much chance to, with Miss Bolby."

"Why not? You haven't taken a dislike to Miss Bolby already, have you?"

"She's all right, I suppose."

"What do you mean, all right?"

"A bit Indian. All bracelets and saris."

"But she is a gentlewoman, though."

"What exactly is a gentlewoman?"

"Surely you're old enough to know that, Jessy. Reenie, for instance, isn't one."

"Yes, I see that. She's nice, though, and Miss Bolby is going to spoil all the fun on the Nursery Landing. Why did you give her my room?"

"I told you. I thought it better to have you in Grandfather's Dressing-room until we see if Miss Bolby settles; she's bound to want to change her room—they always do."

"Well, I wish you'd change it now. You *will* put me back in my room?"

"Yes, of course darling. As soon as I see if she's going to stay. I must go, Jess. I'm keeping those wretched women waiting. It's an infernal bore, having Lady Archie for the night."

"Why? I like Lady Archie."

"So do I, but I don't want her for the night, it means another pair of sheets."

"War makes everyone horrible, horrible and mean."

"By everyone, I suppose you mean me?"

"Not particularly. It must be ghastly to be a governess, mustn't it?"

"I don't know. I haven't ever thought about it."

"Think how ghastly. You'd be neither one thing nor the other. I'd rather work in a factory. Can I read Larry's letter?"

"Yes, do. It's on the table by my bed. He's got dysentery again, and a heat rash and a boil. Poor Larry!"

"Poor Larry! I wish they'd send him home."

"I wish they would, but he doesn't say any more about it. Put out the light when you've read it, darling, and go to bed and don't sit up talking to Barby all night."

"If *not*, a very good copy, I should say, Lady Archie," said Miss Bolby, looking at the supposed Canaletto. She could hear her voice falling.

"In fact, decidedly *not* a Canaletto, you think? Same here, Miss Bolby," said Lady Archie. "All the best pictures here were burned in the fire."

"Was there a fire?" said Miss Bolby.

"A veritable conflagration. The house was burned to the ground in Old Lord Rushford's day."

"All of it?" said Miss Bolby, as if, somehow, she felt a little cheated.

"All but its dome and its balustrade, and its rather fine façade. Bowborough is of a much later date and rather ugly, but we *have* got some very fine pictures."

"I should like to see them, Lady Archie."

"You shall, Miss Bolby."

Silence came down again between them; it seemed as impenetrable this time as the fog outside. I have offended her in

some way, Miss Bolby thought. This great link between us
has led nowhere. It was again Miss Bolby who broke the
silence.

"I was for some years with Lord and Lady Rowfont, Lady
Archie. Lady Rowfont was a Blatchington, and I seem to
remember her mentioning Lord Corwen's name. Was she not
related to Lord Corwen in some way?"

"It's not much good asking me, Miss Bolby, I never remember
relationship, at least, not that sort of relationship, and Hughie
—Lord Corwen, buried the Peerage at Bowborough during
the Invasion scare, though why he thought it necessary to
save it I can't imagine—poor Hughie, he was so agitated
about his birds—but there's bound to be one here, so we'll
ask Elizabeth and look it up after dinner. What *has* happened to Elizabeth? If she doesn't hurry we shall miss the
nine o'clock news and I hate missing the news, don't you,
Miss Bolby?"

In Elizabeth's room Jessy read the small shiny airgraph under
the bedside lamp. Its smallness and shininess made it a mockery,
as if its meaning had diminished with its size : as if Larry, sitting, pen in hand, before the broad white form, had been able
to think only of those who would censor and photograph it.
She put it back and turned out the lamp, wishing she had not
read it. Through its stilted phrases she realised how much she
missed Larry. Though Elizabeth seemed to have filled a
number of spaces, there were blanks where Larry should have
been.

7

"Come in!" Miss Bolby sang, rather than said the
words.

"I hope you are comfortable, Miss Bolby. I'm afraid I have
neglected you. It was rather a shock to me to find Lady Archie

44

here. I hope Becca—I mean Nanny—explained to you about the bathroom and you don't mind sharing the nursery one, or the other with Reenie and Vi?"

"One makes the best of the worst, so to speak, in wartime, Lady Rushford. I am forced to share a bathroom at my pied-à-terre."

"Well, good night, Miss Bolby. Now that we're so short-handed there is no Schoolroom breakfast, we all have it together in the dining-room, except, of course, Bella, who has it in the nursery with Becca."

"It takes a day or two to get accustomed to the ways of a new house, and tomorrow we must map out our time-table. I hope you'll forgive me for asking, Lady Rushford, but who *was* Lady Archie?

"She was a Burraby. Lady Blanche Burraby, a sister of Lord Vallance. She married Tom Meredith, a cousin of Lord Corwen's and Lord Archie's, who was killed in a polo accident, and finally Lord Archie. She is older than Lord Archie —almost as old as Lord Corwen."

"I ask because, by a curious coincidence, she knows some connections of mine, the Atherton-Broadleighs. My sister Sita, married an Atherton-Broadleigh, General *Sir Arthur* Atherton-Broadleigh. Thank you for coming up, Lady Rushford."

Miss Bolby seemed to have started off on the right foot; she had not so far complained, and she did not seem to harbour any resentment against neglect shown earlier in the evening, Elizabeth thought as she reached her room. Lady Archie, one way and another, had made her feel a little guilty about Miss Bolby. Perhaps the Atherton-Broadleigh coincidence was a fortunate one. Why was it and how was it that she knew the name? And what would Larry do in this house full of women if he *did* come home?

8

Before getting into the bed in the State Room, Lady Archie put a hand inside it in order to feel the sheets; as she had expected, they were damp. Everything was damp. How could it be otherwise with fog seeping its way through every crevice? A fine film of fog hung in the light from the dressing-table lamp; there had been no response, when she had touched the switch, from the bedside lamp, so that she stood in a dark pool of chilliness which must be crossed before turning out the dressing-table lamp. In preparation for this bold move, she wrapped the dressing-gown she had borrowed from Elizabeth more firmly about her. She saw that there was a coronet embroidered upon its left cuff, then she looked up and saw that there was one above the bed—a bold gold coronet, a part of the bed, with curtains draped through it: pink, or were they grey? Impossible to tell in this dim light; they were misty, made so by the fog. Nothing in this Midland area held its true colour for long. Coal dust blew across a wide stretch of moorland into Rushford Park, coating its chestnuts and its beeches.

Had the Corwen coronet been Archie's instead of Hughie's, would *she* . . .

Lady Archie crossed the dark, cold space . . . .

People were unfair to Elizabeth about the coronet. Why *not* make use of a coronet, if you had a coronet? it was such a graceful thing. It was unfair that nothing, not even a coronet, was given to younger sons. Elizabeth hadn't been very nice to that poor Miss Bolby; rather inhospitable, packing her off like that for tea. . . . And who would have thought that Miss Bolby would turn out to be the sister-in-law of Arthur Atherton-Broadleigh. . . ?

Arthur ageing: Arthur pompous, perhaps; surrounded by Indian gewgaws, married to Sita. . . .

Arthur sitting at her, Blanche Meredith's, feet upon a chaise-longue in the house at St. John's Wood. Light falling upon the floor from the Conservatory and the scent of geranium. . . . And she had not said, as anyone in a novel of the period, or anyone else, with any sense for that matter, would have said : 'Go, you foolish boy !' Instead, she had opened, and then shut her fan in a way which she knew, because of her delicate wrists, would ensnare Arthur further : 'Arthur, we have forgotten Harry.' Then the sound of cab wheels and of a cab stopping at the door. Voices in the hall. Arthur going out and Phil Somers coming in : 'Seeing rather a lot of the Atherton-Broadleigh boy, aren't you, Blanche?'

'He is Harry's friend, Phil.'

'All the more reason for not seeing such a lot of him, I should have thought.'

'Don't be absurd, Phil; he is half my age.'

'Though you hardly look your age, Blanche, that's exactly what I mean.'

'Have you come here to lecture and torment me?'

'I came as usual to tell you I love you, and I find as usual that the Atherton-Broadleigh boy has been here before me.'

'We have a new footman, Cyril, and he lets in all and sundry. Barrington is having one of his all too frequent indispositions.'

'I wish, Blanche, that you'd sometimes be serious.'

'But I am serious.'

'With the Atherton-Broadleigh boy?'

'Go, Phil. I'm in no mood to quarrel. I've had a long stream of callers. It's impossible to rely upon Cyril, he shows Harry's friends up to see me and mine up to see Harry. He knows none of our arrangements. I'm lost without Barrington.'

When Phil Somers had gone she took a pen and a sheet of paper upon which she wrote, in Barrington's hand :

47

'To Col. Somers.

Sir,

I have been asked by Herladyship to inform you that Herladyship is resting an does not wish to be disturbed. Herladyship as a bad headache.

I beg to remain, Sir,

'Yours obediently,

'BARRINGTON.'

Then she rang the bell: 'When Colonel Somers calls tomorrow afternoon, Cyril, give him this note, will you? That is, if Barrington isn't back amongst us by tomorrow afternoon. And if Mr. Arthur calls and Mr. Harry isn't in, send him up to me.'

Harry came in so quietly that she did not hear him open the door.

'Mother! Has Arthur been here?'

'Yes. He wondered where you were.'

'But I told him I was going to Lord's.'

'Arthur seems to have no memory.'

'Are you all right, Mother? You look a bit queer.'

'Quite all right, thank you, Harry.'

'Where on earth is Barrington? I haven't seen him all day.'

'Drunk again.'

'For at least the third time this week. You really ought to sack him, Mother.

'I couldn't. I couldn't do without Barrington.'

'I met Phil Somers coming up the stairs. I wish you'd get rid of *that* man, Mother.'

'I've been trying to for years.'

'Not very hard, though. I believe you really rather like him.'

'He never does what he says he will, he only comes here when he wants something, and he always lets me down, so

that I know exactly where I am. Men only become incon-
sistent when they try to behave well. Never behave too well,
Harry.'

'I'd rather behave well than like Phil Somers. He can't still
be in love with you after all these years, can he, Mother?'

'One wouldn't think so, but he says so, and I like him for
saying so. Always say so, Harry.'

'Mother, I'm trying to talk to you seriously.'

'I know, Harry.'

'Mother . . .'

'Yes, Harry?'

'I think you ought to see less of Arthur.'

'Would you leave me to the mercy of Phil Somers?'

'I know it's foolish of me, Mother, it's foolish to suggest such
a thing when he's so much younger, but I've got a sort of idea
that Arthur might . . . well, fall in love with you. Mother,
Arthur isn't in love with you, is he?'

'It's no good asking me such a question, Harry, and there is
nothing wrong in love. You must ask Arthur.'

August. And the light in the Conservatory golden—less
harsh, less light, and the house empty but for herself and Cyril,
and Barrington drunkenly sleeping in the basement, and steps
hollow in the street because the street, too, was silent. All of
London seemed empty but for herself, and Arthur, who was
coming at any moment now to say goodbye. . . .

'Blanche . . .'

'But you'll enjoy India, Arthur. There'll be polo, and parties,
and the jungle, and elephants and parrots and goodness knows
what, and the Taj Mahal. Think how exciting.'

Instead of saying: 'Do be serious, Blanche,' he had said:
'Yes, India *will* be pretty exciting,' and she knew that he did
not wholly love her—not enough to rebel against going to
India, to defy the Dean. Had the idea of his going been
wholly the Dean's? Was his going to India with such docility

a relief, an escape, so that he would not have to say at some
future date that he no longer loved her?

'And you'll marry, Arthur. Some Colonel's daughter who
will love you and then bore you, but I doubt if she'll leave you.
My poor Arthur.'

'Never. I love you, Blanche.' But he was not thinking of
her, though he said it with conviction; he was thinking of India,
of polo, no doubt, and pig-sticking, and possibly the Taj Mahal:
his words had lost their meaning.

The room's emptiness when he had gone was an abyss; not
because he had gone and he no longer loved her, but because
the meaning had gone from the word 'love'.

Then, as she lay there watching the light pale in the Conservatory, Cyril, because Barrington was drunk, had shown
Lord Archie in.

'Lord Archie!'

'I was on my way home. It's great luck finding you in.'

'I'm always in in the afternoon.'

'I've called before, you know, and Barrington said you
weren't.

'How very foolish of Barrington. He gets drunk sometimes,
but I couldn't do without him.'

'You look distressed, Blanche—if I may call you Blanche.'

'I am. A man much younger than myself was foolish enough
to imagine himself in love with me, because of which his father
is sending him to India—an unnecessary precaution as he
seems not unwilling to go. . . .'

'My poor Blanche, still searching for happiness. You'll never
find it, you know, in love.'

But she had—as much happiness as there was to be found—
and quite unexpectedly, with Lord Archie. And that poor
Miss Bolby, in all probability, hadn't, and Sita . . .

On coming out of this reverie Lady Archie realised that she
was standing in the middle of one of the spare rooms at Rush-

ford and that her feet were cold. She put out the light and floundered through the dark and got into bed and shut out all further thought: she listened through a blank blackness with forced intensity, so as to dismiss thought, to the fog, dripping as it condensed, sliding from the shiny surface of magnolia leaves. . . .

9

Because she had been angered and disturbed and then soothed and then disturbed again, Miss Bolby, when she looked into Jessy's mirror, was not pleased with what she saw there. True, it was not a good mirror. Where at Hillstone House there had been blemishes, here there were smudges; she tried to efface them with a corner of *The Times*.

The Times at Hillstone, had set one a little apart.

'Mind if I look at your *Times*, Miss Bolby?'

'Not at all, Mr. Billings, if you'll let me have it back.'

'Have you got my *Times*, Mr. Billings?'

'Memory like a sieve. Thanks for the loan, Miss Bolby.'

'Only if you've *finished* with it, Mr. Billings.'

'*Absolutely,* thanks, Miss Bolby. If I want to refer to it I can borrow Mr. Lind's.

Only she and Mr. Howland and Mr. Lind and Mrs. Hurst had taken *The Times,* and Mrs. Hurst had kept hers in her bedroom. One could understand why Mr. Howland and Mr. Lind, and even Mrs. Hurst, had taken *The Times*, but not Mr. Billings's anxiety to read it, and tonight, she, Roona, had been reduced to the status of a Mr. Billings. 'Might I borrow your *Times*, Lady Rushford? I have asked my newsagent to post it, it would be fatal to relinquish it, but the fog has held it up, and I do like to see *The Times*. Its news may be late, but it is *accurate*. And I like to look at the births, deaths and marriages, so as not to lose track of my former pupils.' 'I never read the deaths,' Lady Archie had said. 'Death depresses me, there is

51

so much of it about. In fact I never read *The Times,*' so that
she had wondered all the evening about Lady Archie, and who
Lady Archie was and why she used such phrases as 'It seems
to ring a bell' and 'Same here', which one expected from a Mr.
Billings, but *not* from a woman such as Lady Archie. They
seemed incongruous with her elegant and dignified appearance,
and not quite . . . well, they made one wonder who Lady Archie
was—they were the sort of phrases Bertha Barnsley might have
used. And then, just when she and Lady Archie had found a
bond, come upon an extraordinarily exciting coincidence which
had brought light into a chill, unwelcoming evening, Lady
Archie had said, as though with deliberate intent to snub :
'Would you say the picture above the fireplace was a Canaletto,
Miss Bolby?' She had insinuated, too, that the pictures at Bowborough were better than the pictures at Rushford. The seeds
of a pride of Rushford were beginning to take root within Miss
Bolby, though she was not yet aware of it; she was conscious
only of her seething resentment at the way she had been treated
earlier in the evening. At the way she had been met and
greeted—Lady Rushford had shown more interest and enthusiasm for Reenie : at the way she had been dismissed for tea,
with as little ceremony as Reenie. No one had introduced her to
Nanny or the younger children, or had taken her to the nursery;
and then there had been Barbara's insolence, and she had been
put in Jessy's room when in a house the size of Rushford there
must be many better rooms. And then on top of all had come
Lady Archie's snub, just when they might have had a talk about
the Atherton-Broadleighs. Even Lady Rushford's visit to her
room had not assuaged it. Lady Archie should have known
better; she had snubbed her, not as a governess, but as a relative
of the Atherton-Broadleighs, and she, Roona, had not met in
any of her former posts, anyone who had been on such intimate
terms with the Atherton-Broadleighs, although Lord Rowfont
had vaguely remembered the Dean.

'The Dean, Miss Bolby?'

The Beginning

The conversation had taken place at luncheon, shortly after her arrival at Rowfont. In those days luncheon had been the only meal not eaten in the Schoolroom.

'The Dean of Waterbury, Lord Rowfont. My sister, Sita, married an Atherton-Broadleigh.'

'Ah, yes, I vaguely remember the Dean, Miss Bolby. He and Lady Alice came over here once when I was a young man. I think, as a matter of fact, they came to my coming of age. He was rather good-looking and did great work for the poor. I remember my mother saying all the women put on their best hats in order to listen to his sermons. He made money roll from them like water off a duck's back—the offertory plates were piled so high, in fact, that sovereigns were simply overflowing. And he made them all sew. Yes, he was a great man, the Dean, and a great *ladies'* man.'

'I hardly knew him in that light, Lord Rowfont.'

She had flushed as she had remembered her first, her only visit to the Deanery, delayed by her father's death, with all its attendant miseries and humiliations. She flushed as she thought of it now.

'I don't see how I can go without you, Mother.'

'But you must, Roona, and you must take Enid. I'll get Bertha Barnsley to spend the night here. I'm sure Lady Alice will expect you to take a maid. I can't possibly go on a visit while in deep mourning, and my health is too broken. You can surely see, dear girl, how your father's death has affected my health. I must reserve my strength for our move, and we mustn't delay Sita's marriage any longer. It isn't fair to Sita or to Arthur.'

'Wouldn't it be better to get the move over first, Mother?'

'No, dear. It wouldn't be fair to Sita.'

She had known that her mother would have preferred to write to Lady Alice from the White House, Worthing, rather than from the address in the Cromwell Road at which they had taken rooms; the White House was to be sold.

'Mother, I've wanted to say this ever since Father's death, but I've been afraid of disturbing you. Now that we're so . . . well, so badly off, isn't it important for me to take up singing as a career?'

'Singing is not a suitable career for anyone in our walk of life—not suitable for a gentlewoman, Roona. Singing as a career is very different from singing in a drawing-room, and I know your father didn't approve of it.'

'But, Mother, Father is dead.'

'Roona . . .'

'I mean, if he had known, had realised about the money, Mother . . .'

'And where is the money to come from for your training? There is little enough money. Your father never nuderstood money and he never discussed it with me, and in future I don't wish to talk about it, but we must face facts, Roona.'

'But, Mother, one must be practical.'

'It's so long since I have been about, *dans le monde*, I mean, that I hardly know . . .'

'There is Lady Alice, and perhaps the Dean would . . .' at which point both shied away from the subject. But on the night before she left she said: 'Mother, wouldn't it be better not to take Enid?'

'Why, dear? I think Lady Alice will expect you to take a maid.'

'But, Mother, doesn't it seem a little odd to take a maid and seek a post as governess at the same time?' It was the first time she had said the word 'governess' aloud—she had circumvented it in thought, even. As it fell into the cold room it was stern and forbidding, though she was glad that she had said it—it gave her a queer satisfaction to see her mother flinch. For nights she had not slept because of the problem of Enid. Should she, or should she not, take Enid?

'Perhaps, on the whole, you are right, Roona. I have been thinking it over myself, and Enid is unused to the company of other servants; besides, the girl is a chatterer. In fact not the right type of servant for that type of house.'

So she had gone alone.

'Arthur is very young, younger than your sister Sita, I understand, and rather irresponsible, I'm afraid. As a matter of fact, it was I who sent him to India, because he had got himself rather involved—I think it better to tell you this, Miss Bolby—mixed up with a woman much older than himself, the mother of his great friend—a very delightful woman, mind you, and she kept him out of harm's way—one must be broadminded about these things. But people were talking too much, and—well, Miss Bolby, Arthur is very easily influenced; I'm not sure that he knows his own mind . . .'

Surely the Dean should have called her 'Roona' when she was the sister of his daughter-in-law to be. It had not been easy to advance Sita's marriage alone.

When she had left the room something had made her pause outside the door before she had wholly shut it. 'Not at all what I expected, my dear, but she is beautiful. You must admit the girl is beautiful.' The Dean's voice was resonant, used to great spaces. 'But how are we to know if the sister is beautiful, too? And, in any case, it won't do, Arthur.'

'*It won't do, Arthur.*' She had gone to her room, flushed, trembling with mortification. Somehow she must win over the Dean. And she had, because in the morning the Atherton-Broadleigh girl, Muriel, had knocked on her door. 'Mother is very anxious for you to stay another night, Roona; please do.'

'*Mother* is very anxious . . .' So that they can have another look at me, she thought, looking at her face in the glass; if I can stay another night I can sing. It was a beautiful face: large dark eyes and a dark, smooth skin.

She looked at it now in the blemished mirror in Jessy's room : her rubbings with *The Times* had not altered the reflection she had already seen earlier : the furrows were furrows, not the mirror's fault—a disturbing reflection. The furrows had deepened with the war. War was a lonely battle for the lonely, for those not urgently connected with it, and in her case a lonely battle for what? That she might continue to be a governess— she had not ceased to shudder inwardly at the word—in houses such as Rushford, continually reminded she was the governess, and there were few houses such as Rushford left. She must at all costs stay at Rushford, whatever the disadvantages; it would be better than giving daily lessons from Hillstone House in the draughty dining-rooms of Birmingham's suburbia.

'Roona,' she said, looking sternly at the reflection, 'where is your patriotism?' As the stern look eased she picked up one of her silver-backed hair brushes. It was this dreadful all-enveloping fog which held all in abeyance, even patriotism; it weighed the spirit down.

As she wielded the brush she was conscious of an atmospheric change, of a lifting somehow of the silence. From somewhere in the distance came a hint, a suggestion of sound; uneven, wavy : increasing and then diminishing; increasing again; as it increased in violence growing steadier—its very unevenness grew steady. It was coming nearer, becoming angrier, lower; seeking the house as if it were some object for revenge, charging towards the roof so that its roar filled the chimney and then the room and a tremor ran through the hair brush and up Miss Bolby's arm and down her spine. Then the dark, evil object above seemed to steady itself, to hover, and the roar became a drone as it grew fainter until it was a hair-line upon a barometer of sound. As Miss Bolby put down the brush she saw that her hand trembled and that the face in the mirror had a frozen, waxen look which seemed for an instant to have smoothed out the furrows. 'Roona,' she said to it; 'remember you are a Bolby, and you come from a long line of soldiers.' The words seemed to boom out at her from the past as if it were her father booming them from the verandah.' Remember, Roona, you are a Bolby,' he had said, straightening his shoulders as she had shrunk away from the body of a dead snake; and then, more gently, as she had straightened hers and he put an arm about them : 'And you are a beauty, remember that, too, Roona.'

Terror, for an instant, had brought back beauty as it had brought back her father's words, but only for an instant; the face was an old face, angular, and pinched about the mouth, marred by a deep frown. 'Roona,' she said to the old face; 'even you are no longer beautiful, *stick it*, you are brave.'

10

The roar woke Lady Archie. She reached for the eiderdown which had half fallen to the floor.

She had slid, through a long tunnel of blackness, to the accompaniment of dripping leaves, into the warmth of a conservatory where she had been sitting with a shadowy creature who had been Arthur Atherton-Broadleigh and had turned from Arthur Atherton-Broadleigh into Phil Somers and from Phil Somers into Lord Archie, and in the doorway, accusingly, had stood Miss Bolby.

Why should this old history return with such vividness and be so disturbing just because she had met Miss Bolby? Because it was night, and a cold night, and she was marooned at Rushford, it seemed that some sinister trick of fate had thrown her in Miss Bolby's path. Then she remembered that the roar above meant that the fog had lifted and that she would be able to return to Bowborough after breakfast. Then she began to wonder whether she would get any breakfast, Elizabeth had said nothing about breakfast. In an endeavour to keep warm she rolled herself in the eiderdown.

11

Though less intense above Bowborough than above Rushford because Rushford was three miles nearer to the aerodrome, the roar had woken Lord Archie and Lord Corwen who had fallen asleep in the library at Bowborough. The land sloped from Bowborough towards Rushford, and beyond Rushford to the river, and beyond the river to the aerodrome, which lay upon a bleak and treeless plain, so that the wind tore at the hangars and sheds unimpeded—went where it willed, and whenever the wind dropped fog hung about it. In Rushford park fog lifted intermittently, revealing islands; wide islands that were chestnuts, tall islands that were elms. But when it settled over the plain it was static until the wind took it, and as soon as the wind died fragments of fog knitted together again. No site, except for the fact of its unrelieved flatness, was less suitable as a bomber training station: when they had dropped, dark monsters, above Bowborough, and skimmed the roof at Rushford, and turned in towards the aerodrome above the elms, they ran, more often than not, into deep, opaque fog.

Lord Corwen's head jerked forward and an open copy of *Country Life* slid from his knees. "Archie," he said, "listen." He hurried to the window, darted behind heavy velvet curtains. Draught lifted the blind. As he pulled it away he discerned the lawn's edge, and then the lilac bush, and then the buddleia tree, and he saw that its branches moved. "Archie," he shouted, "it's lifting!"

The roar which had woken him came nearer; it set up a singing in the window frame, it sent a whistle down the chimney. "Hooray, Archie!" shouted Lord Corwen. "They're at it again." He did not think of aircraft as evil instruments of death, but as dark, clumsy shapes huddled together in hangars as pheasants huddle in woods, dependent upon weather. He was temporarily freed from his deafness by the bombers' roar; spasmodic sentences would flash across a room to him, so loud that the voices hurt. If only people would not shout so during moments when he could hear, he thought; if only they would talk less when he could not.

He came out from behind the curtain and stood before the fire; the roar was fading, was no longer a roar.

"I must ring up Rushford now the fog has lifted," said Lord Archie.

"Ring up what? Speak up, can't you, Archie?"

"Rushford," shouted Lord Archie, "to see what has happened to Blanchie."

"Blanchie's all right. She'll be back in the morning. I shouldn't bother about Blanchie."

12

Though Jessy had not slept, the sound startled her. Because she had been away and had come back in a fog she had forgotten it, forgotten that this intermittent roar was now a part of life at Rushford. She had forgotten all about the war. She had rushed ahead into an idyllic and imaginary summer in which war did not figure, and she and Barby won first and second prizes in the 'Best Child's Pony Under Fifteen Class' in the Colsall Gymkhana, which she and Barby had made up their minds to do last summer. But it was dreadful to have forgotten the war, with Larry in Italy with a boil and dysentery, and so much happening that was awful. She began to think of war in all its awfulness; all she had heard and read that was awful began to flash before her in a sort of newsreel. Then, as the newsreel faded, she began to think about Miss Bolby, of how awful it must be to be a governess. Elizabeth had not welcomed Miss Bolby, had ignored her almost, and Barby had not been particularly polite; she began to feel sorry for Miss Bolby. She was so wide awake now that she got up. With a quick movement, so as not to show a light, she parted the curtains and darted behind them as Lord Corwen had at Bowborough. There

was something sinister, she thought, about this furtive movement of curtains and continual imprisoning of light; it made
the dark outside seem full of the dark evil of war.

The curtains in Grandfather's Green Dressing Room at
Rushford were of a faded rose-patterned chintz; they had
shrunk a little, so that they fell short of the floor. Jessy pulled
up the blind and rubbed a pane; then she opened the window.
Cold caught her breath, seemed to pierce her through, but she
did not immediately shut it; she stood there shivering, listening.
The earth's pores were opening; fog was making way for spring.
From the hollies came a sound so faint that it might have been
a first movement of wings. Then she heard a jerking and spurting sound; a series of sounds, then a rumble; lorries, starting up
upon the road, jerking and spurting back into motion
after a long repose. War was emerging from a fog-bound
interlude, going about its business again.

HILLSTONE HOUSE AND
BOWBOROUGH

1

QUIET had fallen over the smoking-room at Hillstone House. No sound disturbed it but the click-click of Mrs. Hurst's needles and the flap-flap of flames in a coal fire; no startling shots such as dart from a newly laid fire, but the comfortable flap of a steady-going fire—like the flapping of a tent on a summer's day, Mrs. Hurst thought, as the steel needles flashed and darted, and the wool, with the lift of a finger, sprang backward and forward.

Mrs. Billings's hands rested in her lap and she stared unseeingly before her; the top half of Mr. Howland was invisible, it was behind his evening paper. Mr. Lind sat upon a hard chair, his body drooped forward and he dejectedly held a book. Mr. Billings, directly beneath the ceiling light, played patience at a table in the room's centre.

"*You* don't look too good, Mr. Lind," said Mrs. Hurst.

"I don't feel it, to be quite frank with you, Mrs. Hurst. A bit close in here—hic-ahem, I beg your pardon—is it not? Does anyone mind if I open a window?"

"Not at all. Not-at-all-not-at-all, not *at* all. Pray do, Mr. Lind, open a-window."

"A bit of the hair of the dog, that's what you need, Mr. Lind," said Mrs. Hurst. "That's what I always say to Mr. 'Urst, and, generally speaking, quite right I am, too."

"Case of kill or cure," said Mr. Billings without looking up from the cards. "Shall it be kill, or shall it be cure? Ah, here she is, the elusive little woman. It shall be cure. So says the queen of hearts, and so, ladies and gentlemen, who's for the George?"

"Seems funny without Miss Bolby, don't it?" Mrs. Hurst stuck the needles into the ball of wool and folded it into the sock.

"Hillstone House without Miss Bolby," said Mr. Billings, gathering the cards, "is like Indiah without the Taj Mahal."

"If you and Mr. Lind'll wait for us, Mr. Billings, Mrs. Billings and me will go and get our coats on. You not coming, Mr. 'Owland?" Mrs. Hurst folded the sock into a silk scarf.

"He is asleep, Mrs. *H*urst," said Mrs. Billings.

"As yet, no, but I hope very soon to be, Mrs. Billings," said Mr. Howland from behind his barricade. "Tonight, I must admit, infinitely regrettable though it seems to lose the further pleasure of your company, I feel more—drawn—shall we say, yes, drawn, I think, towards the lulling arms of Morpheus than toward Bacchanalian pleasures, so I shall hie me to my bed. *À demain, mesdames.*"

"Isn't Mr. Billings a terror, Mrs. *H*urst?" said Mrs. Billings in the hall. "He really oughtn't to have said that about Miss Bolby; she has very good connections in India. I don't say Miss Bolby is perfect, mind you, but which of us is perfect, Mrs. *H*urst?"

"Which of us, indeed," said Mrs. Hurst. She was puffing a little now, with the effort of mounting the stairs. "All the same, it does seem funny without Miss Bolby, don't it?"

"Yes, don't it?—I mean, doesn't it?" said Mrs. Billings.

The bobbled fringe which edged the cover upon the piano-top in the Tollmarsh's sitting-room trembled.

"What was that, dear?" Mrs. Tollmarsh thrust her ear-trumpet in the direction of the sound as the front door slammed.

"Off to the George," said Milly, "Mrs. Hurst and Mr. Lind and Mr. and Mrs. Billings."

"Again?" said Mrs. Tollmarsh.

"To cure poor Mr. Lind. He doesn't half crumple up after a bit of a binge, poor chap! If you ask my opinion, which no one does in this house, last night was to celebrate Miss Bolby's going and tonight's to celebrate Miss Bolby gone."

"I should be sorry to lose Miss Bolby altogether, though."

"Why ever, Mother?"

"Miss Bolby has some very good connections."

Milly began to whistle. "I shouldn't be surprised if she's telling that to Lord and Lady Rushforth." Milly got up and turned down the wireless; they had been talking against the latter half of the nine-o'clock news. She did not turn it off, but she turned it so low as to be barely audible. "Listen, Mother, the fog must have lifted." From somewhere in the upper distance came the burr of approaching aircraft.

"The what, dear?"

"The fog, Mother, *lifted*."

"Don't shout so, Milly."

"My word! How everything breaks out when the fog lifts! There goes Mr. Lorelli again! Even he packed up after tea. There's one thing you *are* spared, Mother, and that's listening to Mr. Lorelli." Milly whistled her way to the piano. She banged back the lid and dragged out the stool, then she thumped out the first bars of Beethoven's Minuet in G.

Elsie did not move at first when the kettle began to bubble. She had fallen into a semi-doze while waiting for it to boil for the filling of the hot-water bottles; they lay in a heap upon the kitchen table. She sat awkwardly, slumped in a kitchen chair, her skirt above her fat, ugly knees, her legs thrust apart, her cap at the angle of a music-hall slut's cap. She had been woken less by the kettle's surging than by her own snores; they were short, uneven, more like a dog's whimpering than snores. As her body jerked forward her cap jerked into her lap, it was not over clean. All seemed to happen at once with the bumping and clattering of the kettle's lid: a moan came from Mr. Lorelli's room upstairs and a fall of notes from Milly and the piano in the Tollmarsh's sitting-room, and from somewhere below the lid of her consciousness, by a sort of delayed action, the burr from above and the slamming of the front door. Water spurted from the kettle's spout as she turned off the gas; it hissed upon the stone floor and rolled away in little beads. If anybody worked hard, Mr. Lorelli did; and if anybody talked about not working others hard, Mr. Lorelli did, Elsie thought, as she took the nearest bottle from the table—five six seven, eight nine ten. Had she got them all? All except Miss Bolby's. Seemed funny without Miss Bolby's voice rising and falling between Mr. Howland's and Mr. Lind's and Mrs. Hurst's tables in the dining-room as if she could send it where she willed, throw it down to Mrs. Hurst's and hold it above Mr. Lind's and bring it back to Mr. Howland's over Mr. and Mrs. Billings's heads, shutting it off from Mr. Lorelli's. Whatever would Mr. Lorelli carry on about now that he hadn't got Miss Bolby? Not that he was ever anything but mum as mum and polite as could be in the dining-room; it was in the drawing-room that they got at each other, which was why Miss Bolby sat in the smoking-room perhaps, more than that she felt the cold because she came from India. Like red rags to bulls, they were—'rugs' Elsie pronounced it.

'You'd be better off, Elsie, if you smartened yourself up a bit more and took the fizz out of your hair and went to a house like Rushford, which is where I'm going when I leave here. It belongs to Lord and Lady Rushford. The Rushfords are one of the oldest and most historic families in England,' Miss Bolby had said.

'Don't you believe it, Elsie,' Mr. Lorelli had thundered. 'Not that I can absolutely condemn the upper classes, not having the good fortune to be on the same familiar terms with them as Miss Bolby. Don't you believe a word Miss Bolby says, Elsie. It's the Miss Bolbys of life I object to. Nothing but jumped-up tradespeople putting on airs. The silly old bag.' Mr. Lorelli hadn't half carried on about it. It wasn't always easy, either, to understand all that Mr. Lorelli said; he got so excited and used such long words. Seemed funny Miss Bolby going to the house of a lord from a place like this, but she *had* changed for dinner every night and her silver hair brushes with the twisted snakes had been pretty posh, heavy enough, too—the suitcase had weighed half a ton.

Elsie squeezed out the air from the last hot-water bottle and secured its screw. As she did so her eyes were directed towards the floor; she saw that a long line of cockroaches advanced across it from the scullery. They had not come out from their hiding-places of late; they had remained, folded and drowsy, as if they, too, hated the fog, beneath the sink in some dark recess.

2

"Why don't you go to bed? You look dead beat, Blanchie," said Lord Archie.

"I am. Not only dead beat, but I feel as if I'd spent the night in a third-class railway carriage. It's always the light above one's head which doesn't work, and the bedside lamp at Rushford didn't. Archie, ask Hughie whether he thinks it all right to wear a coronet on a cuff, will you? After my night out I'm too tired to shout."

"Eh?" said Lord Corwen.

"*Shout,* Archie."

"No need to; I'm not deaf, Blanchie. Personally I wouldn't, but I can't see any reason why one shouldn't."

"Hughie is in fine fettle," said Lord Archie. "Once the fog lifted he quite forgot to fuss any more about the motor."

"*Car,* Archie. Do try to remember to say car. 'Motor' went out with the last world war. To return to the question of the coronet. The question of where, and where not to put a coronet is a very delicate one. I just wanted to know what Hughie thought, whether it was or whether it wasn't permissible to wear a coronet on a cuff. I've always believed in erring on the side of understatement, and goodness knows that's got

The Gentlewomen

me into trouble enough. Do you remember all the fuss after
Tom's death, when I went to the Polo in grey, Archie? If I'd
gone in black or white no one would have minded, but I went
in grey. It was fatal. The only one who stood up for me was
Phil Somers—Phil Somers was pursuing me then and he
thought grey very becoming. You remember Phil Somers,
Archie? He was rather a bounder. Throw another log on the
fire, my dear Archie, I feel cold. Cold and shivery, as if I had
received a great shock, which indeed I have."

"How, my dear Blanchie?"

"Miss Bolby knows Arthur Atherton-Broadleigh—Miss
Bolby is the new governess at Rushford—her sister Sita, in fact,
married Arthur Atherton-Broadleigh, and I don't want all
that fuss unearthed again. It seems a terrible fate to have overtaken Arthur when he survived the fuss so well, he has become
a general. Miss Bolby is enormously pleased with the coincidence of my knowing the Atherton-Broadleighs; she pounced
on it. It's what she calls one of her doubles."

"I shouldn't worry, my dear. It was all so long ago."

"I suppose we forget, on our isolated hill here, how old we
are. We live too much in a shadowy, bygone world. We must
try to be more up to date and live more in this horrible world
of the present. I feel extraordinarily depressed somehow, but it
may be because the sheets were damp and the breakfast cold
at Rushford. I shall forget all about Arthur instantly and get
down to a little dusting, and we ought to clean the silver. They
keep the silver at Rushford beautifully. It's extraordinarily
clever of Elizabeth, the way she manages."

"You'd far better go to bed, Blanchie; you seem rather
over-excited," said Lord Archie.

"Well, if you or Hughie feel like taking the silver on, I will.
When you haven't got to do it for a living it gives you a sort of
lift, like changing in the tropics."

"A sort of what, my dear?" said Lord Archie.

"Lift. Haven't you heard the word? It's very modern."

"Rather a good one. Where did you get it?"

"From those nice boys from the aerodrome who came to tea on Sunday. I think I *will* go to bed, Archie. I'm very tired."

"Do, my dear. Would you like *The Times*?"

"You know I never read *The Times*."

"Rest yourself well, then, my dear Blanchie. *Au revoir*."

"*À tout à l'heure, mon cher Archie*. '*Au revoir*', you know, is very outmoded. You should say 'bye-bye'."

A WEEK IN LATE SUMMER

1

ELIZABETH RUSHFORD sat in the Office. The Office at Rushford, where since the war she had spent so much of her time, was in the dark back regions of the house. Currents of air rushed through a long dark passage and gathered in a whirlpool outside its door, so that anyone sitting there heard a slamming of doors and clicking of heels upon the back stair. When a bomber roared over the roof the sound vibrated through glassed-in bookcases and heavy files. In summer the Office was stifling and in winter like a vault. Today it was stifling.

In Old Lord Rushford's day it had been the sanctuary of Old Mr. Stiles, a model of neatly docketed order. As she surveyed the muddle before her, Elizabeth thought a little wistfully of Old Mr. Stiles, a long since deceased and now legendary figure who had ridden, bowler-hatted in winter and straw-hatted in summer, to and fro upon a bicycle. Incoming letters overflowed from the outgoing basket; wherever she looked there was disorder. There were letters headed with a Red Cross : letters asking her to speak in neighbouring towns. Letters from agencies about servants; letters about the Gymkhana, airgraphs from Larry; and somewhere beneath this chaos, though she could not lay her hands upon it, Miss Pickford's letter and Miss Pickford's reference. Had Miss Pickford said she was a gentlewoman? Miss Bolby, in hers, had unmistakably said so —Miss Bolby's, too, was somewhere here. When they said they were gentlewomen it smoothed the path of approach. It meant that Becca must be referred to as 'Nanny', and not as 'Becca', or 'Miss Stroud', though the days of trays in the Red Room were over.

'Where shall she feed, Larry?'

'In Father's day Old Mr. Stiles always had lunch with us, and his successors, who stayed in the house, always had dinner on a tray in the Red Room, but I suppose now there's a war on she'll have to muck in with the Schoolroom.'

But that had been at the very beginning. Now, except for supper, there were no meals in the Schoolroom.

Elizabeth had barely mastered the Rushford etiquette before the war came, and such fragments as were left were not always workable; they had to be altered to circumstances. Reenie, for instance, had never before been a kitchen-maid.

Elizabeth felt uneasy because she had not warned Miss Bolby of Miss Pickford's coming, and it would not do to upset Miss Bolby, she had settled in surprisingly well, and for the last six months all had gone fairly smoothly. It had not seemed it would at first, she was too much of a stickler; then all had gone smoothly since she had been put in Old Lord Rushford's Room. 'Grandfather's Green Dressing Room', as the children called it. It had been a mistake, short-lived and easily rectified, to put her amongst the land girls and the nurseries, in Jessy's room. Jessy had been right, as she was so often right. Jessy, for her age, was extraordinarily shrewd. But she, Elizabeth, should have told Miss Bolby about Miss Pickford; Miss Bolby would certainly resent a newcomer who would infringe—in any case for supper—upon the Schoolroom. She, Elizabeth, had delayed it, forgotten and then delayed it again, because in some way she felt uneasy; as if by telling Miss Bolby about Miss Pickford she would disturb the house's harmony. Had this smooth-running something to do with the tension outside? These continual telephone calls from London asking for a few days' refuge at Rushford? The mounting anxiety every time one picked up a paper or turned on the wireless? It was as if all in the country beyond the evil weapon's approach, since the onslaught of the flying bomb, had scarcely dared to breath, had been fearful to disturb in case they should entice it further.

Elizabeth shifted the outgoing basket in a final effort to find Miss Pickford's reference. Something must be done immediately about telling Miss Bolby about Miss Pickford, because Miss Pickford was arriving this evening, and it looked as if she, Elizabeth, would have to meet her in the car, because the weather was hot and the flies were bad and both Finch and the mare had been twice to the station yesterday, and both were old, and it seemed almost sacrilegious to ask old Finch to take the mare to the station when his thoughts ran solely upon the Gymkhana. Some sort of madness had seemed to pervade the stables during the last few days. Finch and the children had gone mad about the Gymkhana.

"Lisbeth, can we have a laundry basket?" Ruth hung on to the door as she came in to try to prevent it from banging; although there was no suggestion of wind outside there was a minor hurricane in the passage.

"What on earth for, darling? *Do* try not to bang the door."

"I couldn't help it, it banged. To put the gramophone on. Barby says Crowhurst must get used to music and we've only got a week. Today's Monday and the Gymkhana is a week today, and the gramophone is on the ground and the tunes go into the grass."

"Well, not now, Ruth. You've been out all the afternoon, and you know Louisa can't stand in the sun, and as for you, you look like a beetroot. Tell Barby and Jessy to take the ponies back to the stables and come in at once and get cool before tea. Oh, and, Ruth, run up and ask Miss Bolby to come and see me, will you?"

"Must I?"

"It won't take a moment, darling."

"She's cross, though."

"Why?"

"With Barby and Jessy."

"I'm not surprised. The Gymkhana seems to have gone to

70

all your heads. Run along, darling. I *must* see Miss Bolby. I
haven't told her Miss Pickford is coming."

"Who is Miss Pickford?"

"The new secretary. I've found one at last."

"When is she coming?"

"This evening."

"Who is going to meet her? Mr. Finch says Bess can't go
out again, she went to the station twice yesterday."

"I know. I suppose I shall have to. I told her to come to
Huggley. There's something I want to do there. Run along
and get Miss Bolby, and tell Barby and Jessy to come in at
once."

As Ruth shut the Office door she heard the telephone ring.
She paused, not with the intention of eavesdropping, but
because it is almost impossible not to pause when a telephone
rings and to put more time between herself and Miss Bolby.
Since the scene in the Schoolroom in the morning she had not
liked Miss Bolby's mood.

"Hullo. Yes, Colsall 322," Ruth heard. "Lydia, darling!
A *what* queue? . . . Exhausted? . . . Yes, you must be. . . .
It must be. . . . Yes, appalling. . . . *How* many? . . . She heard
it where? . . . Oh, at the hospital. . . . Eight killed out of twelve?
How *awful*, darling. . . . Oh, a *sweet* queue, I see. *Darling*, how
simply awful. Why on earth did they send twelve children—
think of having *twelve* children—into a sweet queue. . . . Yes,
of course, get on to the first train you can."

Ruth was no longer listening but she could not move: it was
not until the abrupt ring which escaped from the telephone
as Elizabeth put down the receiver ceased to disturb the
silence that she ran up to Miss Bolby's room; she was thinking
about the children in the sweet queue and not about Miss
Bolby.

Miss Bolby sat before the window in Old Lord Rushford's
room; she was sewing a dress-preserver into the armhole of

71

a mauve lace frock. She could hear Barby and Jessy calling
to each other, then Ruth and Louisa, whose voices, because they
were younger, were thinner and higher, and the gramophone's
shrill bark, muffled by long grass.

She was away from the children here, though a watchful eye
could be kept upon them, merely by looking through the window. The truth of the matter was, she was too old for children.
It was some time now since she had had a resident post and a
resident post required more vigilance. Not, since the war,
having been able to find the right one, she had preferred giving daily lessons from Hillstone House, because, on returning
to Hillstone House, she had been *someone*, with a room of her
own and a life of her own and a background in India. There
had been compensations at Hillstone House, once used to its
inconveniences; in the kinds of posts she had been offered
after the outbreak of war there had been none. In Mrs. Kenneth Bonder's house, for instance, life could not have been
called civilized. Then, after nearly three years of Hillstone
House, through a Birmingham agency—Mrs. Barton's Agency
for Governesses and Domestic Servants—it had worried her at
first that Governesses were procured through the same agency
as domestic servants, never until the war had she had the need of
an agency—had come the heaven-sent letter from Rushford
and the interview with Lady Rushford; her hopes had been
raised again, and then had come the bad beginning : her cold
reception, and Reenie's commonness and Barby's rudeness, and
Lady Archie's insult—if it had been meant as an insult—mixed
with joy at the discovery of a link with the Atherton-Broadleighs
which should put her on a better footing. Then sleepless nights
in Jessy's room, disturbed by the bombers' roar, then the removal to the Green Dressing Room, Old Lord Rushford's room,
and a new-found calm which had come with the room. Not
that the noise was less here, but by degrees one got used to it,
and she was away from the children, the hurly-burly of the
nursery landing and Reenie's commonness, and from it she

could see the park, rolling gently into miniature hills beyond the balustrade. She could see, too, who came to the front door; she could hear delivery vans rattling up the back drive and the slamming of the back door; and on still days, between the bombers' intermittent roar, lorries rumbling in the main road; and, best of all, the Italian prisoners in the kitchen garden singing.... She could forget then that they were prisoners.

The Green Dressing Room was a long, cool room, in which one felt serene. Through its inset mirrors she saw a cool, green vista, which became in the mirrors a long cool verandah—cool because night had fallen—and she tiptoed out on to it to say goodnight to her father, fearing the sound of her own footfalls would break some spell, some indefinable blend of childhood's magic and a knowledge of evil, prowling beyond.... It was not unlike the young girl's bedroom in the ballet, *Spectre de la Rose* : these resemblances, in some way, assuaged past humiliations and inconveniences and irritations. With what pleasure she had written of the room to Mrs. Hurst. With what joy, too, she had seen the startled look on Mr. Howland's face on the night at Hillstone House when she had mentioned Nijinsky's leap and having *seen* the ballet.

'I *say*, Miss Bolby, that is something, to have seen Nijinsky! 1911, wasn't it?'

'I was very young, Mr. Howland. It wan't long after I had begun giving lessons.' At Hillstone House, more than anywhere else, she had avoided the use of the word 'governess'. It had been impossible, too, at Hillstone House, to say 'teaching'—it was a convention amongst the married women at Hillstone House not to mention their former occupations—but 'giving lessons' had somehow been permissible.

'Lord and Lady Rowfont were in London for the season, Mr. Howland; Lord Rowfont gave me tickets.'

'My word! You *are* lucky!' Mrs. Hurst had echoed from the sofa.... Fully for the next ten minutes she had held the room's attention.... When she went back—and at some time or other she would certainly go back, if only to collect her trunk from the attic—she would describe Rushford. 'Very different from Hillstone House, eh?' she could hear Mrs. Hurst chuckling. . . . She began to feel uneasy about her trunk and to wonder whether the attic was damp and if she could ask Lady Rushford whether she could store the trunk at Rushford. As Elsie had dragged it across the passage and had been about to heave it up the narrow stair to the attic, the whine from Mr. Lorelli's room had ceased abruptly and he had come out from his room hurriedly, implying she had had no right to get Elsie to heave the trunk, so that she could not now dissociate the trunk from Mr. Lorelli, and she had hated Mr. Lorelli; she had come up against him musically as well as politically, and he was an atrociously bad violinist.

'Let me give you a hand. Whatever have you got there, Elsie?'

'I am afraid the trunk is mine. Thank you very much *indeed*, Mr. Lorelli.'

Yes, she would go back, just for a night or two, in order to fetch the trunk, fortified by Rushford against Mr. Billings and Mr. Howland and Mr. Lorelli.

'We'll always let you have the room if we can, Miss Bolby, won't we, Mother?'

'Eh, Milly?' Mrs. Tollmarsh had thrust out her ear-trumpet.

'We shan't ever let Miss Bolby's room *permanently*, will we, Mother?'

Miss Bolby securely fastened the thread before cutting it off with the scissors, then she paused before rethreading the needle. There was a knock at her door. Before she could answer Ruth came in. The children had a tiresome way of knocking and entering simultaneously.

"Yes, Ruth?"

"Lisbeth wants you, Miss Bolby, in the office."

Miss Bolby held the needle towards the light. She hated sewing. In those far-off days before the war houses such as

Rushford had generally boasted a children's-maid, or a school-room-maid, or a ladies'-maid, or even a housemaid whose duty it was to sew, and who, for a small fee, was willing to do her sewing. Sewing seemed an insult to the intellect somehow. She did not hurry with the threading of the needle; she deliberately dallied, in fact, so as to hide her irritation.

"And may I ask why your step mother wants me, Ruth?" It was excessively irritating to be sent for, and through one of the children, in the afternoon.

Ruth hesitated. "I don't know. What is that thing in your dress, Miss Bolby?"

A slow flush mounted from Miss Bolby's neck; from where she sat she could see herself in one of the inset mirrors. She saw the flush mounting. How dare the child make her flush?

"I've told you before, Ruth, it is very impertinent to ask personal questions. From Jessy and Barby I expect it. Jessy never thinks before she speaks and Barby doesn't think at all. Even though you are younger, Ruth, I thought you had more sensitivity."

Although Ruth's eyes had not left the dress, a number of curious sensations were hurrying through her : bewilderment, anger at the injustice of Miss Bolby's rebuke, and then self-pity, with a danger of tears. She was astonished when she looked at Miss Bolby to see that she had flushed, her own cheeks were burning. She knew that this meant that Miss Bolby was more than usually angry. Miss Bolby did not lose her temper—the angrier she was the more patient and painstaking she became; her anger reached its peak in a flush.

"May I go, please, Miss Bolby?"

"When I have finished talking to you, Ruth."

"I've got to tell Jessy and Barby to take the ponies to the stables."

"And Louisa is without a hat, I see." Miss Bolby had got up and was looking out of the window. "You know Louisa can't

stand in the sun without a hat. Tell Louisa to come in instantly.
You may go now, Ruth."

Ruth decided to walk boldly across the room to its far door
which led out on to a stair which ran up to the nurseries and
down to the Red Room. She did not want to hear the telephone
ringing in the Office and to be reminded of the children in the
sweet queue.

"Ruth." She had almost shut the door.

"Yes, Miss Bolby?"

"I can't see my bracelets anywhere. A new eye is better than
an old. Just have a look round before you go, dear."

Ruth came back into the room, but she did not shut the door,
she felt she could escape more easily by leaving it open. It was
she who was supposed to see that Louisa did not stand in the
sun without a hat, and Louisa had been without a hat all the
afternoon, so she wanted to get to Louisa; she also wanted to
get out of the house before the telephone rang—you could hear
it ringing in the Office from Miss Bolby's room.

"How extraordinarily tiresome! I must have left them in the
nursery bathroom when I washed my hands there."

"Shall I run up and see for you when I come back, Miss
Bolby? I *must* go now because Louisa hasn't got a hat."
Ruth did not wait for Miss Bolby's answer, she ran down the
stair.

Before going down to the office Miss Bolby leaned through
the window to call the children in. She was excessively irritated with the children; with Jessica for the scene she had made
in the morning, with Barby for being so coolly insolent, and
with Jessy for violently taking Barby's part. It had all happened over nothing, as it were, because of Jessica's irritating
habit of tapping the floor with her foot.

'Now that the holidays have begun, Jessica, and you only
have an hour's work in the mornings, surely you can behave
rationally during that hour.'

76

'What is rationally, Miss Bolby?'

'Get the dictionary, Barbara. I'm not at all surprised at your not knowing the meaning of the word, though you are quite old enough to do so.'

'But it's not holidays if we have an hour's work; that doesn't seem to be rational.'

'Don't be impertinent, Jessy.'

'But we've never had lessons in the holidays before. It's not fair.'

'You're behaving very babyishly, Jessica, like Ruth or Louisa.'

'I don't see why we should have lessons in the holidays just because you've got nowhere to go.'

'How *dare* you speak to me like that, Barbara! Leave the room instantly.' Then Jessy had thrown the book.

She had sent them both to their rooms for an hour, threatening that unless Jessy apologised neither should ride in the Gymkhana. Barbara's words, though only partly true, had been wounding. She *had* nowhere to go. It would be truer to say, nowhere where she *wanted* to go. She had no desire to spend the holidays at Hillstone House. Holidays since the war had become a difficulty. There was no longer any pleasure to be had from going to the South Coast, and she no longer wished to visit Bertha Barnsley—Bertha Barnsley brought back too many memories best forgotten. She had no relatives whom she could visit, so that when Lady Rushford had said: 'What are your summer plans? I suppose I daren't ask you to stay for the holidays, Miss Bolby? The summer holidays are so long, and I'm so busy, and the children get so out of hand', she had gladly agreed. There were already moments when she wished she had not.

She had been irritated, too, by Ruth's indelicacy. The children had been allowed to run wild; they said whatever came into their heads. It surely was not good to grow up wholly uninhibited. As she leaned through the window she saw the swing-seat on the grass below move. Bella was there. Bella, too,

77

was in a sense neglected, though this was partly the fault of the other children, Ruth and Louisa were as caught up in preparations for the Gymkhana as Barbara and Jessica. Some kind of madness had seized them: they had gone mad about the Gymkhana.

'Jessi-cah! Lou-i-sah.' She was not displeased with the sound of her voice as she called; it seemed to hang above the lawn: something atmospheric, voices hung so in heat—cries in the East—it was not like Nijinsky's leap, a matter of prowess. . . . As she withdrew her head, and then her body—it was a low window and she had been half-way out of it—she heard the familiar drone; it came hard upon her voice or she would scarcely have noticed it, as though hurrying to disperse it. Although her voice had already vanished, the harsh drone following upon it spoiled its effect, it disrupted thought and overpowered all other sound; it sent a wave of anger through her. How could anyone remain good-tempered against this constant disturbance by noise? Although one got so used to it that some days one scarcely noticed it, on others it left the nerves frayed, and today had not been a good day. The final straw was being sent for in the afternoon.

Just as she was about to go down to the Office she remembered her bracelets. They were in the nursery bathroom, of course they were. She remembered taking them off in order to wash, but she also remembered the irritation of sliding them over a wrist that was damp when she thought it dry. Or had that been another time? She remembered that she had not had them on when she had begun to sew. She pulled out a drawer and lifted a handkerchief sachet; she felt beneath a row of carefully folded stockings; she took the whole contents of the drawer and put it on the dressing-table. Then she pulled out another drawer, felt through it hurriedly; then she pulled out the writing-table drawers. No she never *did* put them in a drawer. Of *course* they were in the nursery bathroom and she could not go to look now because Lady Rushford was waiting in the

78

Office. She lifted the mauve lace dress, lifted the sewing bag, looked in the sewing bag. . . . Anxiety had made her hot. She would wait a moment in order to go down cool. After all, she *might* have been resting. It *was* the middle of the afternoon.

Outside it was uncannily still now, silent but for the rooks above the elms, circling in noisy protestation at the recent disturbance. Certainly the place would not be good for anyone with a tendency to nerves. . . .

Bella sat in the swing-seat, below Miss Bolby's room; she sat back against the seat's back so that her body curved with it, her short legs straight before her. She sat as a doll in a shop window might sit, or a Saturday night's drunk, slumped down upon the pavement. Her feet hung over the seat's edge, toes turned inward; her fat insteps bulged above her shoes; buttons strained at leather; her white cotton socks had fallen into folds. She knew that she could not have new shoes because there was a war. There were shoes in plenty in the cupboard upstairs, Ruth's and Louisa's shoes, which were like boats upon her feet. It was because of the blisters these had given her that Becca had made her wear socks. 'Don't know what to do with you, Bella. If there's one thing that's bad for feet it's wearing the wrong shoes. Seems a shame to grow up with crooked feet, though, even if there *is* a war on.' 'Don't kick the gravel, Bella sweetheart, or you'll stub the toes, and there's a war on.' Such phrases reiterated in Bella's head with the monotony of a merry-go-round, though she did not think in words. Phrases were groups of islands in her thought flow, centring round the word 'war'. Outside the islands were no words, her thoughts flashed and flowed. Beyond, in the park, rooks circled above tall elms. War, they cried, war, war, war!

The seat rocked gently now. When she had climbed into it, it had plunged forward at her, and then away from her, so that climbing into it had been difficult. Now it had ceased to rock backwards and forwards, but when she leaned sideways it rocked sideways, bumping against its supporting poles, bumping itself to a standstill. She could only see the balustrade now; the balustrade divided the lawn from the park. When the seat had rocked and dipped there had been stretches of green and stretches of sky, and the elms had been short and then tall, and she had seen Jessy, cantering in a circle upon Crowhurst, and Ruth and Louisa, and Barby telling them what to do, and then they had disappeared behind the balustrade and there had been another stretch of green, on *this* side of it, and then a stretch of gravel, and then it had begun all over again in smaller stretches until the seat was still. Now she could see nothing beyond the balustrade but sky, and the elms, which were tall and sedate again, and the rooks above them crying: War, war, war.

Bella put out a fat hand towards Miss Bolby's bracelets which lay upon the seat beside her, sending off darts of light so that they seemed to be moving, dancing; sultry afternoon sun filled the gap between the roof and the wall of the seat, brightening as it caught the bracelets although it had not yet reached Bella. Bewildered by this new angle of vision the seat's motion had caused, Bella had forgotten them.

When Barby had said: 'Coming, Bella?' and Jessy had said: 'Oh *no*, Barby, she'll only be in the way', she had wandered down the nursery passage and into the bathroom in search of comfort from Becca, and there upon the glass shelf had shone Miss Bolby's bracelets. By standing on tiptoe she had been able to reach them; she had taken them down to the swing-seat. She picked them up now, and slid them over a fat wrist; she slid them up and down her arm as she had seen Miss Bolby do. They flashed and jingled.

Bella's laugh pierced the stillness shrilly, more shrill than the bracelets' jingling; it traversed the oval lawn and reached the park, so that Ruth and Louisa heard it; Barby and Jessy were too intent upon Crowhurst.

Bella saw a shadow fall upon the lawn and her laugh and the jingling were lost in a bomber's roar as it bore down over the house, made a half-turn above the elms and bore down over the kitchen garden; lower, and then lower as the ground dipped, until it skimmed the river and reached the aerodrome. It had swooped down suddenly upon the house, sending a tremor through the swing-seat's poles so that Bella flinched. She dropped the bracelets; they wobbled drunkenly away from her and down the crack between the cushioned seat and its frame. Bored now, she slid to the ground, and, unbalanced by the seat and the shortness of her legs and her fat round form, she rolled, rather than walked, towards the house.

"Where's the laundry basket?" said Jessy.

"She says we can't have it today and we've got to go in now."

"Oh, blow!" said Jessy. Her hair had escaped from its slide and her shirt had come out from her breeches; it hung out at the back in a tail.

"Crowhurst has had enough, anyway. He's sweating like anything," said Barby.

"There's a new secretary coming," said Ruth, anxious to divert the conversation from the laundry basket before Jessy could return to it; Jessy, like Miss Bolby, had been in an evil mood all day.

"When?" said Barby.

"This evening," said Ruth, elated by a warmth inside because she was the proud possessor of news which had temporarily eclipsed the other news which had given her a funny sensation in her knees so that she had to wait outside the Office door before going up to Miss Bolby.

"Who's going to meet her?" said Barby.

"Lisbeth, in the car."

"I thought there wasn't any petrol."

"There's always petrol for the station," said Jessy. She meant that there was *not* always petrol when she and Barby wanted to go to a Gymkhana.

"My head feels funny," said Louisa.

"How funny exactly?" said Jessy.

"Like cotton wool," said Louisa.

"She means like saucepan wire," said Ruth, all her elation gone.

"Jess-i-cah! Lou-i-sah!" Miss Bolby's voice floated out from the Green Dressing Room window. It seemed to rest above the lawn, somewhere in the region of the sundial, before it reached them in the park. It was a melodious voice and it melted Jessy's rage.

She felt it melt within her suddenly, leaving in its place uneasiness. She had raged all day, since the scene in the Schoolroom in the morning; first outwardly and then inwardly against Miss Bolby, and then outwardly against Barby, and then against everything generally, and she had wanted to rage against Ruth for not bringing the laundry basket, only Ruth had forestalled her with the news of the coming of the new secretary. This was fortunate, because, however tiresome Ruth was, she always felt sorry when she had raged against Ruth, and she and Ruth, with the exception of Bella, who was almost too young to count at all, were the only Rushfords at Rushford now Larry was at war, and Rushfords shouldn't rage at each other, and Ruth was at everyone else's beck and call, therefore it hadn't been right to send Ruth in for the laundry basket. She was beginning to admit to herself, too, that it had not been right to throw a book at Miss Bolby. She felt the impotence and misery which follows an act of violence; all the hatred had gone out of her: stirred by Barby's cold insolence, it had risen as she had thrown the book in an uncontrollable wave, and now Miss Bolby's voice through the window had made her feel like a cushion with the stuffing knocked out of it. It was such a silly voice, affected and yet pleasing. . . . If only

Miss Bolby would sing naturally, hum about the house as the Italians did about the garden, one would not hate her at all; instead, when she sang, in church on Sundays, even when she called through the window, she seemed to draw herself together as if she had stepped on to the platform at a concert hall. . . . It was a pity hatred had such sudden collapses. . . . Miss Bolby was just an old woman with a rather melodious voice, affectedly calling through a window. . . .

Although the front stairs were shallow, Bella took a long time to climb them; she dragged her left leg up after her right leg as the very old and the very young do, as if one were shorter than the other; then she halted before putting the right leg forward again. When she had nearly reached the top she paused to look down through the banister; she hung on with both hands, pressing her head into a gap between its rails. The screen was at a curious angle, so were the rugs upon the floor; the hall had become a room she had not seen before, more topsy-turvy than the lawn and the park outside. It was full of the clock's ticking, which seemed as she listened to grow louder. Jessy and Barby were no longer calling to each other. Droning its way up through the clock came the sound which had startled her on the swing-seat. Because she was standing motionless and tense, it seemed like a new sound, one that she had not heard until today. For the first time she became aware of the sound. She clung more firmly to the banister, concentrating upon the clock's protective ticking, but it, too, was drowned.

"I'm sorry if I have kept you waiting, Lady Rushford, but I have mislaid my Indian bracelets, which is rather worrying. I've been searching for them everywhere. You sent for me?"

"Oh, there you are, Miss Bolby." Elizabeth had begun to wonder whether Ruth had taken the message. "I wanted to tell you that at last I've found another secretary. More satisfactory this time, I hope."

There had been several since Miss Bolby's arrival, each of whose stay had been of short duration, so short that any resentment of Miss Bolby, and Miss Bolby's misgivings, had been lost in the general failure.

"Her name is Miss Pickford. She seemed nice, I thought. You won't mind her having supper in the Schoolroom, Miss Bolby?"

"Certainly not, Lady Rushford. When is Miss Pickford coming?"

"This evening. I shall have to go and meet her now, in a few minutes; that's why I sent for you, Miss Bolby."

"I see."

"With one thing and another, and the children's excitement over the Gymkhana, I'm afraid I forgot to tell you."

"It *is* a little sudden, Lady Rushford, I must admit, but I know how busy you are, and the Gymkhana seems to have disturbed everyone. The children are quite out of hand. I have had to tell Jessica and Barbara that unless Jessica apologises to me for their behaviour in the Schoolroom this morning I shall be forced to forbid them to ride in it. Ruth seems very over-excited too, and Louisa had been out without a hat all the afternoon."

"I thought we had arranged that Ruth was to see that Louisa wore a hat, but I wish *you'd* see to it, Miss Bolby."

"I think it's really Nanny's job to see that Louisa wears a hat."

"Nanny has so much to do already, Miss Bolby." How tiresome it was to have to refer to Becca as 'Nanny', Elizabeth thought. But the formality must be adhered to because Becca disliked being called Becca by anyone but the children. 'Can't expect to command any respect and keep me place in the house unless I'm addressed in the proper fashion.' Such little tendencies to touchiness did not go towards the smooth running

84

of a large house in war-time. Sometimes it seemed surprising that Miss Bolby had stayed so long. "And my sister-in-law, Lady Lydia, may be coming, Miss Bolby. She says she can't take it another minute, but you know what that means, they seem to get a second wind. She was dreadfully upset at having heard that eight children out of twelve, all of the same family had been killed in a sweet queue. She didn't *know* the children, it was in the East End somewhere, but she seemed quite unhinged. They *are* having a terrible time in London, poor things, but at the same time it's extremely irritating not knowing whether or not someone is coming. I don't think anyone has any idea how difficult it is to run a house of this size in war-time."

"No, indeed, Lady Rushford. How truly appalling about the children. I think it would be advisable not to let the children here know."

"I certainly shan't tell them, Miss Bolby."

"It is difficult to throw oneself into their excitement over anything so trivial as a Gymkhana when such dreadful things are happening all round. I suppose one must try to be lenient with the children."

"I suppose we all have to look forward to something, Miss Bolby, in order to keep sane. I must admit I'm looking forward to having a secretary to clear me out of all this muddle."

"Well, thank you very much for letting me know." At the door Miss Bolby paused: "Forgive me for asking such a question, Lady Rushford, but is Miss Pickford a gentlewoman?"

Elizabeth, too, paused. "I understand so, Miss Bolby. Her father was vicar of somewhere—Stonechurch."

"I always think it helpful to know from what *milieu* people come, especially in these days when one so frequently finds the unexpected."

As soon as she was in the house again Ruth remembered she had offered to look for Miss Bolby's bracelets. She caught sight of her face in the mirror as she ran through the hall. It was indeed, as Elizabeth had said, the colour of a beetroot. She seemed to have been running all the afternoon, first on one errand and then another. She had not said she *would* look for Miss Bolby's bracelets, she had only offered to do so, and it was a long pull upstairs, and there was no need to go upstairs. Now that Larry was at the war and there was no man in the house but Benn they used the downstairs cloakroom; Elizabeth did the flowers there; sunbonnets hung there, frivolously giving a dejected air to Larry's coats. Once inside the cloakroom Ruth wavered, conscientiousness overcame her and she turned back and plodded up the stair—the front stair this time. Until quite recently they, the children, had been forbidden to use the front stair, but as the war had progressed, rules had become lax, and this seemed to be one of which Miss Bolby did not know. Miss Bolby, if anything, seemed to encourage the use of the front stair.

'I don't know what you and Louisa do, Ruth, messing about with Benn in the pantry and gossiping with Reenie in the back regions. Servants like you to keep your place, you know.'

'Mr. Benn says he likes us in the pantry, Miss Bolby.'

'Benn is a very old man, rather past it now.'

'And Reenie says *she* likes it.'

'Reenie is hardly likely to know what is right and wrong in a gentleman's house. One has to make allowances for Reenie, and don't please answer me back, Ruth.'

Ruth came upon Bella sitting at the top of the stair.

"War, war, war!" said Bella.

"Caw, Bella, *Caw!* Not *War.* What are you doing here all by yourself?" But Bella would not move.

Becca was washing out a frock of Bella's in the nursery bathroom. "My! Ruth, you look hot. Better get ready for tea, hadn't you?"

"Miss Bolby thinks she left her bracelets here, Becca."

"Well, they're not here now."

"Where's Louisa?"

"Lying on the sofa. Dizzy again. It's all this standing in the sun without a hat. *I* shall be thankful when the Gymkhana's over."

"I suppose it's my fault," said Ruth.

"Louisa is quite old enough to remember her own hat. You mustn't always go thinking everything is your fault, Ruth."

"Becca, if a buzz bomb fell in the middle of twelve children, wouldn't they *all* be killed?"

"Let's hope not *all*. Whatever made you think about buzz bombs?"

"Eight were. Only eight, though."

"Eight *what*?"

"Children, in a sweet queue. Aunt Lydia rang up. I heard it on the telephone."

"Well, don't say anything to Bella and Louisa, and don't go mooning about thinking about it. People have to get killed if the Germans *will* send over buzz bombs."

"You don't think they'll come here?"

"No, I *don't*, Ruth. Go and get ready for tea."

"I'd rather like to *see* one, Becca."

"I wouldn't, thanks very much. Not on your life, its bad enough having bombers thundering over the roof morning, noon and night. I can do without the bombs, thank you."

"There's a new secretary coming." This time Ruth hoped that her news would have the desired effect; so far it had not seemed to make much impression.

"Heavens alive! However many more are we going to have in this house? All I can say is, I hope she's not balmy."

87

"Might she be?"

"Well, they all seem to complain of something, don't they? If it isn't the noise it's the stairs, if it isn't the stairs it's the land girls. Some people don't seem to know when they're lucky."

"Becca, would you say Miss Bolby was balmy?"

"Now, you know, Ruth, I can't discuss Miss Bolby with you. Give you an inch and you take a mile. Get a move on, slow coach."

"Becca . . ."

"Yes, what is it now?"

"I should think there must have been a good many arms and legs about, wouldn't you?"

"Where, for goodness' sake?"

"Well, in the sweet queue."

"Oh, get *on*, Ruth," said Becca.

Reenie took a tray of scones from the oven as Otello came into the kitchen.

"Buona sera, signorina."

"How's the old stomach doing, Otty?"

"It complains, signorina. It sighs for pasta and for wine as the bones sigh for the sun."

"Well, you've *had* sun today. Try a scone."

"Grazie, signorina, grazie mille. You should come outside and listen. . . ." His mouth was full of scone now. "To the Signorina Bolby. She sings through the window to the bambini . . . . Ai, Ai, Ai! What a voice! How she sings! But she should let it go. A voice should not be kept in an overcoat, though it should be carefully nurtured. Never before have I heard the English sing. She is English, the Signorina Bolby?"

"Indian."

"?"

Reenie shook some flour on to the pastry-board and, as nearly as she could remember, drew with her forefinger the map of

India. Otello's torrent of astonishment was checked only by Mrs. Williams's entry. He bowed himself out of the kitchen.

"You didn't put no butter on those scones, did you, Reenie?"

"Might as well let the poor —— have it while they can," said Reenie.

"How many more times must I tell you, I will *not* have that word in my kitchen, Reenie. And I won't have you putting butter on the prisoners' scones. And there's one extra for supper in the Schoolroom."

"Not another sec., Mrs. Williams?"

"As if there weren't enough mouths to feed in this house. Another in the kitchen would be more to the point, if you ask me."

"Me too," said Reenie.

"And what beats me, is the way you make yourself understood by them Italians."

"Beats me how they understand me," said Reenie.

As Elizabeth drove the car out from the stables into the back drive she saw Otello come from the kitchen; she put her foot on the brake instead of the accelerator.

"Otello! Buona sera." She pronounced the 'o' in the broad staccato manner of the Italians so that the word fell abruptly from the cramped space of the car into the summer air.

"I must not linger. I go to meet the Signorina Pickford, the new secretary. For me the war is a continual meetings of trains which never ceases. I trust they have treated you liberally in the kitchen? Scones do not seem sufficient food for the sustenance of manual workers. I go! Arriver*der*ci!" The car bounded forward.

"You look very hot and flushed, Ruth. Did you look for my bracelets?"

"Yes, Miss Bolby."

"And you didn't find them?"

Ruth delayed her answer for as long as possible. A picture flashed before her of Miss Bolby searching her bedroom. Miss Bolby made such a fuss about her bracelets, and she, Ruth, hated them; they were gold circular bands, carved, where they clasped the wrist, into cobra's heads.

"No, Miss Bolby."

"But if they are not in my bedroom, they must be there. Are you sure they are not there, Ruth?"

"Yes, Miss Bolby."

"And where is Louisa?"

"Dizzy," said Ruth, beginning to feel it was her fault again, both that the bracelets had been lost and that Louisa was dizzy.

"And where is Lisbeth?" said Jessy.

"Gone to Huggley in the car to meet Miss Pickford, the new secretary." Ruth liked to give news in detail.

"Oh, *gosh*!" said Barby. "Why have we got to have another *secretary*?"

"*Barbara*!" said Miss Bolby.

"She can't have gone to Huggley, there isn't enough petrol," said Jessy.

"I tell you she has," said Ruth.

"She, she, she? Who is *she*?" said Miss Bolby.

"The cat's mother," said Ruth.

"Kindly remember that you are no longer in the nursery, Ruth," said Miss Bolby. Why was Miss Pickford, at the height of summer, and when there was no petrol, being met at Huggley, when she, in the depth of winter, by a succession of dreary halts had had to come to Colsall?

"I wonder what it's like to be a prisoner if you don't hate," said Jessy, hating Miss Bolby.

"Why?" said Barby.

"The Italians don't hate us."

"But they hate the way we keep our churchyards. They

90

say we only put flowers on the graves when they're animals' graves," said Barby.

"But they helped us bury the rabbit, Ravensworth," said Ruth.

"I think it's probably better to hate," said Jessy.

Miss Pickford paced up and down before the station. The stream of passengers from the London train had evaporated; car doors had slammed, kit-bags had been flung on to lorries and she had been alone in a sudden silence.

From the station behind her came a soothing shunting of trains; a distant whistle, the mumbling of a barrow: she did not mind waiting. '*Someone* will meet you at the station,' Lady Rushford had said, and the train had been unusually on time. It was nice to get into fresh country air again. It *was* fresh air, although she could see factory chimneys and a squat gasometer, but green fields lay beyond and soon she would be driving past them, inhaling scent from the hedges, driving deep into the country's heart, further and further from the rattle and tick of buzz bombs and the siren's wail. Though it was not the evil contraption's *sound* she feared, she was used to evil sounds: bumping and thumpings which boomed in her own head; ringings and whistlings which startled. She was deaf. Not very deaf, but deaf enough to lose the cuckoo's song, to be plagued by noises in her own head; too deaf to hear the buzz bomb's first rattled warning, so that she saw it from the faces of others—it was good to get away from those tense faces. . . . She breathed deeply. She did not see that infinitesimal smuts were falling, nor did she hear the car draw into the kerb until its dark shape had overtaken her.

Elizabeth, as she turned the final corner of a tortuous short cut from the High Street to the station, felt uneasy: the lonely figure she saw could be none other than Miss Pickford's. A black cloak floated from its shoulders, a black hat was on its head, a broad-brimmed low-crowned hat, in the distance not unlike a witch's hat with the crown squashed in. No good could come of cloaks and witch's hats—they foreboded an eccentric. She had no memory of a cloak or witch's hat at their hasty interview—hasty because at its beginning they had heard the All Clear and both had wanted to get away in the lull.

The room had been dark, the dark bedroom of Elizabeth's hotel. She had stayed the night at a small obscure hotel; it had made her feel safer somehow, as if a bomb would be less likely to find her out there, though she had wished she had stayed at the Ritz as she heard her first buzz bomb's approach. Just at the beginning of the interview, before the All Clear, one had come uncomfortably close and both had worn an air of unconcern until it had fallen with a bang like that of a giant cracker. 'Oh, thank *goodness*, Lady Rushforth, thank goodness! Though we oughtn't to say "thank goodness" just because *we're* not the ones to get killed. It was an evil day when Man got into the Air; he defiled it.' This unexpected comment came back now. Elizabeth had forgotten it; from then on Miss Pickford had seemed so businesslike, but in the vicinity of a buzz bomb the most normal showed signs of hysteria.

'I took up secretarial work when my fiancé was killed in the *last* war, and it turned out a good thing because I had to earn my living when my father died. Things do turn out for the best, don't they, Lady Rushforth? My father was vicar of Stonechurch, but a very delicate man, and he retired young and we went to live in Wimbledon and there wasn't much money. Dear me! I musn't talk so. But I'm quite proficient, Lady Rushforth. Would you care to give me a test? Shall I take a letter?'

'Oh no, Miss Pickford; I'm sure you're quite fast enough for me.'

'Not fast, Lady Rushforth, oh dear me, no! Just a plodder, that's me.'

Funny that the train was on time; perhaps London had had a quiet day.

Elizabeth braced herself as she opened the door of the car, then she saw with relief that the black cape was a mackintosh.

The London trains poured forth their occupants in a tense, strained state which was apt to break, loosening into a torrent of hair-breadth escapes as they met the country air, but Miss Pickford, contrary to her expectations, talked little, in little nervous spurts; she reminded Elizabeth of a bird.

"I hope you haven't had too bad a day, Miss Pickford."

"Not bad at all; quite a lull, Lady Rushforth."

"Rush*ford.*"

"Oh, I beg your pardon! All this time I've been saying Rush*forth.* I'm such a fool with names!"

"You must be glad to get to the country."

"Oh, I am. Away from all those horrible, evil things."

"I'm afraid we're rather near to an aerodrome. I mean we get a good deal of noise. I like to warn people."

"It isn't the noise I mind. I'm used to noise. I don't mind noise, but they pollute the air. I don't mind anything as long as I can breathe fresh country air."

"Nanny, this is Miss Pickford, who has come to help us out in the Office.

"How do you do, Miss Pickford?" said Becca. They were in the passage.

"You will have to arrange it between you about the bathroom. You can either use the nursery one, Miss Pickford, or share one with Reenie and Vi. Vi is one of our land girls, Reenie is helping us out in the ktchen." Quite early on Elizabeth had hit upon the phrase 'helping us out', it offended no one.

"I'm afraid you have a very small room, Miss Pickford. It's one we generally keep for the land girls, but most of them are billeted out at present and we have to keep a number of rooms free because so many friends and relations use this place as a refuge. I expect you will want to unpack, and you won't mind having supper in the Schoolroom." At this stage the phrase had ceased to be a query.

"May I give you some haddock, Miss Pickford?"

"Thank you, Miss Bolby."

"I hate haddock," said Jessy.

"I'm afraid you must have been having rather a strenuous time in London, Miss Pickford. We try not to discuss bombs before the younger ones, Ruth and Louisa and Bella."

"You don't want to talk about bombs any more than you need, do you, Miss Bolby? I wouldn't mind the bombs so much if I had a nice airy room, but I'm living in 'digs' and I do hate 'digs' don't you, Miss Bolby?"

"What are 'digs'?" said Barby.

"Rooms, dear. Oh, dear me, what dreadful words we get hold of, working in offices, don't we, Miss Bolby?"

"I have never worked in an office, I'm afraid, Miss Pickford. I could never have mastered the shorthand. Mine is not a mechanical mind. And I'm a little older than you, and in my day working in an office was not quite—well, not quite the thing. I wanted a musical career. I wanted to be a singer, but even that was frowned upon."

"Lucky you, never to have lived in 'digs', Miss Bolby!"

"I have a room in Birmingham, just a pied-à-terre, you know. I hope you won't find the noise here too trying, Miss Pickford. We are very near to the aerodrome; I expect Lady Rushford has told you."

"I don't mind noise, Miss Bolby. It helps us deaf ones. I'm a little deaf, you know, but it doesn't impede my work much really. My friends say I'm very clever with it, really. It's funny the way those horrible things make us deaf ones hear. It's lucky *some* good came of Man getting into the Air, but still, that doesn't balance the evil of it, does it?"

"I've always said that the evils of modern times began with Internal Combustion, Miss Pickford."

"With eternal *what*?" said Jessy.

"The invention of the motor car, or was it the steam engine, Miss Pickford?"

"Dear me! Don't ask me, Miss Bolby, I'm no good at science at all, and science doesn't seem to have done us much good; it just makes war more horrible."

"I suppose lorries are pretty horrible when you come to think of it," said Barby.

"And tractors and tanks, like slugs. Particularly when they crawl about the park. I suppose you can't stop machinery, though. Aren't there machines for being deaf, Miss Pickford?" said Jessy.

"Pardon, dear?"

"I mean, aren't there machines to make you hear? Old Mr. Stiles had one, a sort of box you shouted into."

"Very unsightly, even the less old-fashioned ones. And I'm not as deaf as all that, dear."

"What are the new sort like, Miss Pickford? They're not boxes, are they?" said Barby.

"Just the teeniest battery, dear, but they don't improve a woman's appearance and they're expensive and very hard to get, with a war on. You have to write your name down, and I do hate writing my name down, and I don't think I'm deaf enough for that. My friends say I'm very clever, so that you'd hardly notice it really."

"I was thinking of Lord Corwen. He's as deaf as a post, but I suppose he can't afford it." said Jessy.

"I don't know; he's got a Daimler, and he's giving away the prizes at the Gymkhana," said Barby.

"I don't suppose he pays for them, though, does he?" said Jessy.

"Lord Corwen is our neighbour, Miss Pickford," said Miss Bolby. "He lives at Bowborough, with his brother, Lord Archie Meredith, and his sister-in-law, Lady Archie. Lady Archie was a Burraby, a sister of Lord Vallance. She is a close friend of my brother-in-law, Arthur Atherton-Broadleigh, General *Sir* Arthur Artherton-Broadleigh, a son of the Dean of Waterbury; he married my sister, Sita. Lady Archie asked me to go over to Bowborough when I first came here, to see the pictures; they are very fine and you really ought to see them, Miss Pickford. Not as fine as Lord Rushford's, though."

"Lucky you, Miss Bolby!" said Miss Pickford.

"By the way, girls, I am worried about my Indian bracelets," said Miss Bolby. "My Indian bracelets, Miss Pickford, have somehow been mislaid, though we *know*, of course, that they are in the house somewhere and we know that *one* of us will find them. They have great sentimental value; they were given to my mother by an Indian rajah. My people were army people and they spent a great many years in India. Lord Rowfont, I remember, admired them very much—the bracelets, I mean. Rowfont Park was one of my former posts; I was there, in fact, for a great many years, and the Rowfont girls and I still correspond. Lord Rowfont was a great connoisseur of Indian things. Have you been to India, Miss Pickford?"

"Not me, Miss Bolby. I've never had such luck. I've never been further than France. I went to France in the last war, for my fiancé's leave. It wasn't so easy, you know, but my fiancé's father pulled strings. I went to stay with an aunt. My father's sister married a Frenchman, named Laroque, and she lived in Paris. She used to take in girls of good family to learn the language—before the war, I mean. My fiancé was killed, but I couldn't nurse afterwards like all the other girls whose fiancés were killed. I just couldn't do it. Did you ever nurse, Miss Bolby?"

"No, Miss Pickford, I always felt that others were better cut out for it than I. But Rowfont was a hospital during the first world war, a hospital for Officers, and I used to help Lady Rowfont with the running of it.

"This war I've been doing a job with the Red Cross," said Miss Pickford, "paid, you know. Not as paying as some, but I do like to feel I'm doing my bit. There's something to be said for being over call-up age; you do your bit without being told, and there isn't so much heart-break, is there?"

"Get the sugar, Jessica, will you? May I give you some more raspberries, Miss Pickford?" said Miss Bolby.

"I can't get them poor mites out of my head," said Becca.

"Which poor mites, Miss Stroud?" said Reenie.

"All those poor mites in the sweet queue; some of them, no doubt, no bigger than Bella. Something like that doesn't half bring the war back to you. We forget how lucky we are down here."

"That's right, Miss Stroud," said Reenie.

"Ruth wasn't half going on about it, but all she was worried about was how many arms and legs there was," said Becca.

"Queer things, kids," said Reenie.

"Excuse my coming into the nursery without being asked, Nanny. Good evening, Reenie," said Miss Bolby. "I couldn't help overhearing what you said just now, and I really think we ought not to discuss these things. To put about such rumours only causes alarm and despondency. Things are quite serious enough as it is, it seems to me. Whenever we hear good news we always hear something to counteract it. By the way, I missed the nine-o'clock news, I was too busy looking for my bracelets. Was there anything new, Nanny?"

"Not much, Miss Bolby, as far as I could see. To tell you the truth I wasn't rightly listening. I get pretty fed-up with the news; no news is good news, is what I say. Funny the way you get used to things, isn't it?"

"That's just it, Nanny, one gets accustomed to horror. May I have a look in the bathroom for my bracelets?"

"Yes, do. Miss Pickford was in there last, Miss Bolby."

Miss Pickford felt she would suffocate. The low ceiling above made the room seem smaller than it was; it seemed to press down upon her, and the night was hot. It was a shabby room, filled with shabby furniture : an unsteady mahogany wardrobe which rocked when you opened its door, and an old-fashioned washstand with a marble top. Furniture crowded the little room. By taking so much space it seemed to crowd out the air. She turned out the lamp and got out of bed and drew back the curtains. She looked out upon a formal garden; fountains, and flower-beds, and little box hedges, then a balustrade, and beyond that the park. It rolled away into shadow, into dark clusters of trees, into long, wavy humps; she saw that the nearest hump began to move, to break into a number of humps moving slowly out into the open, and that other humps were moving slowly in to fill the spaces, forming a whole again. They were lorries, moving in towards the trees, moving out towards the road. Jessy was right, they were like slugs, caterpillars, creeping : cogs in the machinery of war. There was something horrible and sinister about this silent creeping. They made no sound, or she did not hear it; they were moving stealthily in a shadowy distance over grass.

She wished she had not said to Miss Bolby : 'My fiancé's father pulled strings'; it had sounded as if she had wanted to outdo Miss Bolby, who had been to India. She wished she had not said : 'My fiancé was killed.' It had slipped out somehow; things she did not mean to say had a way of slipping out. Talking about the last war in this one was like reading the headlines in yesterday's newspapers, or talking of some old dead love, yet somehow she found she did so; it made her feel less lost in this one. It was a point in time upon which to focus, a straw to which to cling in the oncoming flood. There was no place in

war for the unattached. There was no one who was saying at
this moment, now: 'I'm glad Rose has gone to the country.'
'At least Rose is safe, out of the buzz bombs' way!' There was
no one who would have said if she had been bombed: 'My
life is bleak now Rose has gone.' Did others in the house feel
as she did? The children had their lives before them, they
belonged here, they were fortunate, they had been protected
so far, and Miss Bolby had seemed so self-assured, as if she, too,
belonged. Yes, she wished she had not talked of her fiancé to
Miss Bolby; had not, all in a moment and before the children
at the Schoolroom table, and for no other reason than that she
had wanted a little to outdo Miss Bolby, bared her soul. . . .
Just because she had wanted to say: 'You may have been to
India, but I, too, might have made a good marriage, just as
good as your sister, Sita. . . .'

'This is my last night, Rose.'

'I know, John. I wish you could have married me this leave,
now.'

'Mug that I was not to think of it—so do I. If we'd thought
of it we could have fixed it up somehow. I mean to on my next
leave, though; by then I'll be twenty-one. No one will try to
stop us then.'

No one would have. Hasty marriages were a daily
occurrence; there had been no less than three in the
road.

'Rose!'

'John?'

'You do love me?'

'Yes, John.'

'With your hair bobbed like that you look like a boy, younger
than you are.'

Upon the mantelpiece, loudly taking toll of the minutes,
there had been a Louis-Quinze clock.

'You're not afraid, Rose?'

'No, John,' though her body had trembled and her heart had bumped.

And then in the morning : 'Well, so long, Rose. Don't forget the days in Gay Paree.' And the sitting-room in her aunt's apartment had looked just as formal as before, just the same. Could that night have been real? Could that which had passed, have passed, in this musty, airless room with its pink frilled lamp-shades and its hard-backed settee? She wanted to get away from the room because it was indifferent to its secret, yet she did not want to leave it because it held an essence of John.

Her aunt had said : 'Well, don't sit up talking too long; John has an early start.' Just as if John had been going back to Cambridge. It had all been so simple and matter-of-fact, and their love had been fulfilled with an economy of words because her aunt was reading in bed in her room at the end of the passage. All other sensation had been eclipsed by terror that she would be found in John's embrace by her aunt.

'Now, Rose, I want to hear all about Aunt Ella, and how you found John.'

'We want to be married on his next leave, Mother.'

She had not known whether her mother had given her a sharp look or whether she had imagined it.

'Well, I don't see why you shouldn't be, dear; he's not likely to have any more before he's twenty-one. We'll make the cake and the dress and then we shall be all prepared.'

'It won't be that sort of wedding, Mother.'

'There's no reason why you shouldn't have a white wedding, is there, dear, even in war-time?' The comment had sounded like a query.

'It's just that we don't want any fuss, Mother.'

The cake and the dress had been ready and a sense of tense expectancy had pervaded Redroof; impossible to tell why, or what it was exactly, but the sourness sent off by the apples in the dining-room had been more sour and the staleness left by last night's supper more stale and the coffee's pungency more pungent. Each Michaelmas-daisy in the border had seemed to stand out separately against a harsh brick wall, each blade of grass to become more separate, thrusting separately through the lawn.

Her mother and father were sitting over coffee and the morning paper : as she could no longer bear to look at the garden, she went out into the hall and out into the road to post the letters; as they fell into the box with a light flat thud, she saw the telegraph boy, and her father open the door and open the telegram, and she saw her father's face. When the boy got back to the gate he began to whistle and this in some way enabled her to cross the road; for the first time she saw that there were finely traced rose leaves in the coloured panes of glass on either side of the door.

'Rose, it is from John's father.'

'I know, Father.'

The days which had followed had been as confused as that day had been clear. Once her fear of the consequences of the night in her aunt's salon had vanished the night itself had dimmed. No one had ever known about it and there was very little to remember now. John's death had made of it an unreality, superseded by pictures of her aunt, propped against pillows in her pince-nez, of the empty salon's formality : that was why she had to talk about John sometimes, but she should not have done so to Miss Bolby. Living in 'digs' made one indiscriminate; when there was someone to talk to, one *talked*.

John had died in the air; he had been one of its first victims. She would surely die for lack of it; she would also be one of

its victims, suffocating slowly for lack of it. These great unwieldy craft bearing down upon the roof—so different from
John's—took the air; they used it, disturbed it and filled it with
their fumes. And the lorries, too, crawling out there in the
darkness, polluted it. As she leaned through the window a
bomber sent a singing through its frame. She did not hear the
lilac and the almond trees bordering the formal garden rustling in the bomber's wake, but in the summer darkness she
saw them move, agitated by the disturbance; and a bat
floundered past, as if it, too, were agitated.

No one had ever heard Miss Bolby swear, but she swore now,
without noticing that she did so; she said : 'Damnation !' For
the last half-hour, ever since she had come down from the
Nursery, she had been pulling out drawers in the Green Dressing Room, not only those containing her own belongings, but
those which held the remnants of Old Lord Rushford's. She
had gone through them systematically; she had peered, crawling upon her hands and knees, into dusty recesses beneath
the furniture, but she had not found the bracelets.

When she had asked Ruth at tea-time if, when she, Ruth,
had looked for them in the Nursery bathroom, they had been
there, there had been an uncannily long pause. Had Ruth
been lying? Was Ruth responsible in some way for their disappearance? Was this some plot between the children? Some
form of revenge because she had threatened that Barby and
Jessy should not ride in the Gymkhana? No, Ruth was a plod-
ding, truthful child; Jessy was the practical joker; but Jessy,
though frequently stubborn and sullen, was not revengeful. No,
it did not seem as though this had anything to do with Jessy, and
Barby, except where the Gymkhana was concerned, was lazy,
and Louisa was a dreamer. How loss made one suspicious.
Already she had begun to suspect the children, and there had
been a moment—a moment only—when Nanny had said, 'Yes,
do; Miss Pickford was in there last, Miss Bolby,' when she had

suspected Miss Pickford. After all, if the bracelets *had* been lying in the bathroom? Miss Pickford was a newcomer and everyone else in the house, even that common girl Reenie, was trustworthy. . . . But Miss Pickford was a gentlewoman; even if a little déclassée through working in offices—her father was in the Church. . . .

Miss Bolby rang for Bob Woodman, the nightwatchman.

Ever since the fire in Old Lord Rushford's day Rushford had had its night watchman, but Bob Woodman had not had to contend with fire. Secretly he was a little disappointed; his secret wish was to ring the great bell which hung by the back door and to break the glass box which held the fire alarm. Earlier on in the war, when enemy aircraft had strayed towards Rushford during the blitzes upon Birmingham, he had had to keep a look-out for incendiaries; now there was little chance of fire from this source, and where fire was concerned he was fearless, though he had a secret fear of lurkers and burglars.

Bob Woodman had been gassed in the first world war. 'Pretty much of an old crock ever since,' he was fond of saying. He wheezed and creaked when he walked, giving a kind of whistle which came from somewhere deep within him : it rasped out through his teeth; sometimes it seemed to come up from his legs, sometimes from his lungs. He suffered from rheumatism in his knees, and as if endeavouring to dispel the creaking in them, he sat warming them before the pantry fire between his rounds. He had just dozed off when he heard Miss Bolby's bell. She was a bad sleeper and she sometimes rang for a cup of tea. He had no objection to taking her one; he was not averse to a gossip, it broke the night's monotony. He had nothing against Miss Bolby, he would say the next day, 'But the night,' he would add, 'doesn't half drawer people together.'

"I feel very disturbed, Bob. My bracelets have gone."

"Gone, miss?"

"I mislaid them earlier in the evening and I can't find them anywhere. It really looks as if they have gone."

"Seems a bit funny, don't it?"

"That's just it. I felt I couldn't go to bed until I'd had a thorough search. I've turned everything inside out and upside down."

Bob looked about the room; he saw no sign of disorder.

"You haven't had them in the Schoolroom or downstairs?"

"I haven't had them since luncheon. I took them off to wash my hands. I thought I had left them in the Nursery bathroom, but when Miss Ruth went to look for them she couldn't see them anywhere. You know what children are, always in a hurry, but they are not there now. I didn't look myself till later. After tea I was busy showing Miss Pickford round."

"Miss Pickford settling in all right, miss?"

"I hope so, Bob. I always feel sorry for anyone on the night of arrival. A first night in a place is never very pleasant and I have no doubt Miss Pickford feels strange she is used to offices. I should be very glad, Bob, if I could have a cup of tea?"

"Yes, miss. I'll get it right away, miss. I'm just racking me brains to think what could become of the bracelets. Indian, aren't they?"

"They were given to my mother by an Indian Rajah."

Bob whistled. A deliberate, not an accidental whistle this time. 'My word, miss! Can't have walked though, can they?"

"No, indeed. No doubt they'll turn up, they must be in the house somewhere, but it's very worrying. It's a great relief to know everyone here is honest."

"Let me see," said Bob. "Who comes into the house? Who's been in the house today? Otello was in this evening talking to Reenie, but Otello wouldn't take nothing, and everyone else is all right, far as I know. Looks like a bit of a mystery." Bob was warming to the mystery. "It's a good ten year since I've been watchman now, and nothing has ever been stolen. Yes, a good ten year before me legs gave out. Before that I was in the

104

gardens. I managed to get back to the gardens after the last war even though I *was* wheezy. Doctors said the open air was good for me lungs, but as soon as me lungs got better me legs began to give out. Well, it's an ill wind, miss. It's me knees that've saved me from this one."

"Indeed, Bob? We don't realise how lucky we are down here."

"No, indeed, miss. Planes are busy tonight, miss."

"Sometimes I find them very trying, Bob. They seem to get on one's nerves in hot weather. I dare say they prevent you sleeping in the daytime?"

"They do that, miss. Hard enough to sleep in the daytime anyhow, specially with me rheumatics. And Fred Finch don't get a wink of sleep at night-times, he's forever thinking a spark'll set a light to the stables. Fred Finch has come into his own again with the war on and horses again in the stables. Hope the fine weather holds for the Gymkhana."

"Will you be going, Bob?"

"I expect me and Mrs. Woodman and Ken'll be going if me knees hold out. I hear Lord Corwen is giving away the prizes."

"I suppose you remember Rushford and Bowborough in their heyday, if you worked for so long in the gardens, Bob?"

"Yes, indeed, miss. Everything out of season in Old Lord Rushford's day. Strawberries the size of plums, we had, but Lord Corwen, he never entertained, not even after Lady Archie come here."

"I remember well at Rowfont how everything was out of season, even in the Schoolroom when there were parties. On special occasions Lord Rowfont was very considerate to the Schoolroom. Those were the days, Bob! I believe Lord Rowfont used to come here visiting, but I suppose you don't remember visitors if you were in the gardens?"

"Memory like a sieve, miss. Went with me legs and me

lungs, after the last war. But you should ast Fred Finch, he remembers them all. Saw plenty of them, driving them back and forth from the station, and to balls and all."

"I suppose you don't remember Lady Archie when she was a young woman, Bob? She was a friend of my brother-in-law the General, General Sir Arthur Atherton-Broadleigh, and of his father, the Dean of Waterbury, but I never knew her in those days. It was through the Dean of Waterbury that I went to Rowfont."

"Is that so, miss? Now Lady Archie, funnily enough, is one of the ones I do remember. She used to come visiting here, with a Colonel Somers, before she married Lord Archie. A very elegant lady, and there was always plenty of talk about Lady Archie."

"Talk, Bob?"

"Well, she and Lord Archie run away. She'd been on the point of it before, only no one knowed which gentleman it would be. They was surprised it was Lord Archie. But you should ast Fred Finch about it; it was he that drove them to the station. He was away with Old Lord Rushford, visiting Lady Archie's brother, Lord Vallance, and she and Lord Archie didn't want to evolve none of Lord Vallance's servants."

"This is news to me, Bob. I have never heard a breath of scandal about Lady Archie from the General or the Dean, no, never a word." But she had. "Well, I mustn't keep you; you'll want to be getting on with your rounds, Bob."

"Thank you, miss, and I'll be getting you your cup of tea."

She had not thought, on the night of her arrival at Rushford, that she had ever heard of Lady Archie, but she had, it was coming back now; a scene she had forgotten came vividly back.

Rowfont, and Lady Rowfont saying: 'As we're such a large

party, Miss Bolby, you won't mind sitting with the children at the little table?"

And Ned Blatchington saying: 'Well, if *you're* sitting at the little table, I shall, too, Bolby.' And from the Big Table: 'They say Blanche is off again.' 'Not really off? And who with *this* time?' Then one of the children said something, and from the Big Table: 'I don't suppose it will come to anything though, I dare say it'll fizzle out like that Indian business. Poor Blanche! Freddie Vallance is trying hard to get her married again; she's a constant thorn in Freddie's side. He can't quite *pin* anything on Blanche, she's just not quite . . . Well, no one but Blanche would keep a drunken thug of a butler like Barrington. . . .'

Then Ned Blatchington said: 'Don't eavesdrop. Listen to me, Bolby.'

Barrington. On the night of her arrival at Rushford Lady Archie had mentioned a butler called Barrington. . . . And *that Indian business.* . . . Had Lady Archie not said that she, too, had memories of India, not of India itself, but of incidents *connected* with India? And had not Lady Rushford said: 'She was a Burraby, Lady Blanche Burraby, a sister of Lord Vallance'?

It seemed as if 'Blanche' had been none other than Lady Archie.

From Rowfont to Rushford had been a long road, but still, in spite of the interlude at Hillstone House, she thought, I know more than most of the 'ins and outs' and scandals of well-known families.

At Hillstone House Rowfont had seemed distant; viewed from Rushford, incidents which had become dim became vivid.

'The bookworm. Still at it, Bolby?'

She had been correcting exercise books by the light of a candle in the Schoolroom.

'How you startled me! You shouldn't come in without knocking, Ned.' The children called him Ned, and she had fallen into the way of it, too. He was Lady Rowfont's younger brother.

'Surely *you* know, Bolby, that it's awfully middle-class to knock on doors.' She flushed.

'But the Schoolroom door is rather different, Ned.'

'The equivalent of a bedroom, you mean?'

'Well, hardly.'

'You don't know the fun I get out of pulling your leg, Bolby.'

'Well, I wish you wouldn't come up here and do so, especially when I'm working. It was bad enough in the dining-room at luncheon, before the children. You're impossible, Ned.'

'Dear Bolby.'

'Must you call me Bolby?'

'Not if you tell me your Christian name.'

'Roona.'

'Roona, my little dusky one, why?'

'Just that. I *was* the little dusky one. I was the youngest of three, and my sisters used to croon it over me. I was born in India, and to them, I suppose, it sounded Indian, Eastern; they chose it for me."

'They chose well. And where are *they*, in India?'

'Sita is; she married an Atherton-Broadleigh.'

'Good heavens! Not Arthur?'

'Yes, Arthur. A son of the Dean.'

'Good Lord! I was at Harrow with Arthur. I was much younger, though. Harry Meredith was his fag, Blanche's son. It was Blanche Meredith they were talking about when you were eavesdropping instead of listening to me at luncheon. She's a wonderful woman, Blanche; all Harry's friends fall in love with her.'

'It was through Dean Atherton-Broadleigh that I came here.

I was to have been a singer, but my father died and left no money.'

'I noticed in church how well you sang. You sing like an angel. Why the devil doesn't my sister get you to sing after dinner?'

'You forget I'm not a guest, I'm only——'

'The Governess. You're too pretty for a governess. My dear Bolby. Surely you're not ashamed of it?'

'Why have you come up here to taunt me?'

'I was bored with the billiard-room. Tonight shaded lights and the click of balls failed to soothe me. I didn't come to taunt you. What would it take to make you a singer?'

She hesitated. 'Training, money, and hard work and the right introductions, and luck, of course.'

'Which is helped by beauty, and you're beautiful. Have you ever thought of marriage?'

Again she hesitated. She remembered a vaguely similar though totally different conversation with Ralph Barnsley.

'Not as a means to an end.'

'That seems very honest of you. What about a rich protector?'

'How dare you say such things to me in the Schoolroom, Ned?'

'Are they worse in the Schoolroom?'

'You have no business to come up here, and I have work to do.'

'You know, the high horse doesn't become you; sometimes you *do* look like a governess.'

'I may be the Governess, but I'm a Bolby. I come from a long line of soldiers and I won't be insulted.'

'My poor Roona, I wanted to help you, not insult you, and now you've spoiled it all!'

'Ned, what do you mean?'

'I'd imagined myself in love with you. In fact I came up-stairs with the idea of telling you so. But I'm a Blatchington, and a bounder, you've just told me. I don't suppose I could ever live up to the Bolbys, but I think you're beautiful. Yes, extraordinarily beautiful, and a bore, and rather bourgeoise. Good night, my dear Bolby.'

Miss Bolby put out the light; it was only then that she remembered she had forgotten to ask Bob Woodman to have a look for the missing bracelets.

2

When Elizabeth came into the dining-room the next morning she saw that Miss Pickford was the first down; she stood by one of the large windows which looked on to the formal garden: she turned as though startled when Elizabeth addressed her; she seemed uneasy.

"You shouldn't have waited; none of us ever wait for breakfast, Miss Pickford. Since everything has become so difficult we all have it together, but we never wait; we just help ourselves as we come down."

"I didn't quite know what to do, Lady Rushforth—I mean ford. It's just like me to do the wrong thing, so I didn't know what to do."

"It seems odd that the children aren't down. I suppose Barby and Jessy sat up talking half the night. Miss Bolby is always a little unpunctual; she is such a bad sleeper, poor thing! I hope you slept well, Miss Pickford?"

"Not too well, Lady Rushforth, that's why I'm such an early bird. Out to blow the cobwebs away. What a lot of vehicles there are in the Park."

"And what a mess they make of it, too."

'It's uncanny the way they creep in and out, isn't it? I was watching them from my window last night. Ever so uncanny."

As Miss Pickford came over to the sideboard Elizabeth

110

saw she wore flat-heeled leather sandals and that her stocking-less feet were damp, as though she had been walking in long grass. Elizabeth reminded herself that the black cape had been no more than a mackintosh and that everyone now wore sandals, yet somehow sandals upon Miss Pickford looked eccentric.

Ruth and Louisa came in together. They took mugs of milk from the sideboard and sat down together.

"Miss Bolby is late," said Elizabeth.

Jessy came in with Barby.

Miss Bolby came in. "You must have thought I had over-slept, Lady Rushford, but it is not the case, I can assure you. Far from it; I was up with the lark, looking high and low for my bracelets. I feel most concerned about my bracelets; it really does look as if they have gone."

"They're bound to turn up if they're in the house, Miss Bolby. Can you remember where you had them last?"

"In the Nursery bathroom. I'm sure it was the Nursery bathroom, yet when Ruth went to look for them she said they weren't there, and they certainly weren't when I went to look later, and they're certainly not in my bedroom. It seems very odd that they weren't in the bathroom when Ruth went to look. Are you *sure* they weren't there, Ruth?"

All eyes were upon Ruth. For an instant she hesitated. She had known yesterday that they were *not* there. Now, upon being asked point-blank, she began to wonder whether, after all, they *had* been. She had not *wanted* them to be there. She had wanted Miss Bolby to have to look for them. Now, because they were *not* there, she knew that Miss Bolby was about to say that they must look for them instead of practising for the Gymkhana, and that Barby and Jessy would think it her fault, because she had not found them. "I was in a hurry, Miss Bolby," she said; "I was late for tea."

"But you must *know*, Ruth."

"If they are in the house, they must be safe, Miss Bolby. I'll tell the servants to look. We'll all look. Who was last in the Nursery bathroom last night?" said Elizabeth.

"Me, I mean I, Lady Rushforth," said Miss Pickford.

"Perhaps, girls, you will look for them for me, after our work this morning?" said Miss Bolby.

"Today is Tuesday and the Gymkhana is next Monday; we have to practise for the Gymkhana," said Barby.

"It is doubtful, remember, that you will ride in the Gymkhana," said Miss Bolby.

"The smoke from Bob Woodman's cottage is floating up straight and the clouds are high; it will be fine for the Gymkhana," said Barby.

"And all the cows are standing up," said Louisa.

"And the glass is going up," said Ruth. Each looked at Jessy. Whether or not they rode in the Gymkhana seemed to depend less now upon the weather than upon Jessy.

"I don't see what difference it makes if it's fine now; there are six days to go," said Jessy.

"What is the matter? You've eaten nothing, Jessy," said Elizabeth.

"I'm not hungry," said Jessy. She had not been able to eat because her impending apology to Miss Bolby, with the bracelets' disappearance, seemed to grow more difficult and distant.

When Elizabeth went into the Office after breakfast she found the poodles heaped in the dog-basket and Eleanor and Doushka, the cats, peeping from the outgoing letter basket like kittens from a Christmas card. Miss Pickford sat before the typewriter with Chang-Kai-Shek, the Pekinese, upon her knee.

"I had hoped, when I had a secretary, that the animals wouldn't feel quite so at home here, Miss Pickford. They come because it's cool, and they move out as it gets hotter, later in the day. Poor Mr. Stiles must be turning in his grave. Mr.

Stiles was the secretary in Old Lord Rushford's day, Miss Pickford, a most orderly person."

"Oh, *don't* disturb them, the dear things! I'm an animal lover, Lady Rushforth."

"Rush*ford*. Wouldn't you find it easier *without* Chang-Kai-Shek on your knee, Miss Pickford?"

Miss Pickford ran a hand down Chang-Kai-Shek's curling tail, picked him up and kissed him and put him into the letter basket with the cats. "Just a ball of fluff with a ragged chrysanthemum for a tail! There I go chattering again, and I wanted to ask you a favour, Lady Rushforth. I want to ask you if before tonight you'll lend me a novel. If I could bury myself in a novel I might be able to forget the lack of air. Don't think I'm complaining, Lady Rushforth, but there *isn't* much air up under the roof there, is there? And there's nothing to take you out of yourself like a good novel. The trouble is, the good authors don't seem to do much good these days. Books have got so psychological."

"I'll try to look something out for you. What sort of novels do you like, Miss Pickford? Historical?"

"Oh, anything, Lady Rushforth, anything but psychological. Thank you *ever* so much! Ready when you are, Lady Rushforth."

Because, since the beginning of the war, lessons for both had been spasmodic and Miss Bolby had not gone away, Barby and Jessy worked for an hour in the mornings with her during the holidays. Today they were late because they had been looking for her bracelets.

Barby looked at the clock: its hands seemed to falter as if attempting to delay the passing of an hour.

"A watched pot never boils, Barby. Unless you can concentrate better than this you will never pass your School Certificate."

"I shall never pass it, anyway," said Barby.

113

"But you must, Barbara. These days you'll get nowhere without it."

"Couldn't I be an Actress without it?" said Jessy.

"Somehow I don't think your father would want you to be an Actress, Jessy."

"Did you pass yours, Miss Bolby?" said Barby.

"In my day it wasn't considered necessary for a gentlewoman to pass examinations, Barbara."

"Is Miss Pickford a gentlewoman, Miss Bolby?"

"I most certainly think so. Her father was in the Church, and were she not a gentlewoman in the strict sense she would most certainly be one of nature's gentlewomen."

In the silence which followed Barby again looked at the clock.

"Very well, you may go now, Barbara." Whenever possible Miss Bolby had ignored Jessy.

"You'll send Ruth and Louisa out to us when you've finished with them, won't you, Miss Bolby?" said Barby. "We want them to work the gramophone."

"I shall see," said Miss Bolby. "At present"— she shut one of the books before her, knocked it gently against the table as if it were a pack of cards—"it is not at all—probable— that you will ride in the Gymkhana. Ruth and Louisa, yes— perhaps, they have done nothing to warrant such punishment, but if you and Jessy are unable to ride it seems hardly worth while getting Ruth and Louisa to work the gramophone." Miss Bolby's whole attention was concentrated upon the books before her. As soon as her voice had ceased, Barby got up and gathered hers together as if she had not heard Miss Bolby, or the words had had nothing to do with the Gymkhana; Jessy, as if they were incomprehensible, looked straight before her. Barby was half-way between the table and the school-room cupboard when there was a knock on the door: it was Ruth and Louisa, who followed Barby's and Jessy's hour of work with a half-hour's reading.

"Come in!" Miss Bolby sang the words no less melodiously than usual. "I thought I had told you *not* to knock on doors, Ruth."

"But yesterday you said I was to knock before coming in, Miss Bolby."

"Ah, a bedroom door, yes. A bedroom door is very different from a sitting-room door, and there is no need to knock when you come into the Schoolroom. Nothing underhand goes on in here, everything is always above-board in the Schoolroom, and it is very *deuxième*, I have always been told, to knock on sitting-room doors. At Rowfont, in fact, I never had to tell my pupils that kind of thing, they *knew*. Come in, come in, Ruth. Come in, Louisa." They had been standing in the doorway.

"Now that you are all here together—wait a moment before you go, Barby and Jessy—I want to ask you once again if any of you remember seeing my bracelets *anywhere* at all yesterday?"

Barby and Jessy and Louisa looked at Ruth.

"No, Miss Bolby, Ruth said they weren't in the bathroom," said Jessy.

"Are they so valuable, Miss Bolby?" said Barby.

"They are Indian; I have told their history before, Barby, and bracelets, as Bob Woodman says, don't walk. It will be very unpleasant, both for the questioner and the questioned, if everyone in the house has to be questioned, therefore I want you all to try to find them, to help me as much as you can. You may go now, Barby and Jessy."

"I hate her," said Jessy.

"But you said yesterday you felt sorry for her."

"I hate her, I hate her. She's going to stop us riding in the Gymkhana just because she's lost her bracelets."

"Not if you say you're sorry for yesterday, Jess."

"I can't. I hate her."

115

"But you must, Jess."

"I could have yesterday, but today I can't because I hate her. She only minds about the bracelets because the Dean gave them to her."

"It wasn't the Dean, it was the Rajah. She's told us fifty times, and she told Miss Pickford last night at supper."

"Well, the Dean admired them then."

"The General, wasn't it?"

"Or Lord Rowfont or somebody. Where are you going, Barb?"

"To the kitchen to see if I can get Reenie to work the gramophone."

"But Miss Bolby'll hear it in the Schoolroom."

"I want her to," said Barby.

"Well, where *are* the bloody bracelets?" said Reenie.

"They're somewhere in the house, they *must* be," said Barby.

"You get along and say you're sorry, Jess, and maybe she'll forget about the bracelets," said Reenie.

"Oh, no she won't," said Jessy; "they're all muddled up with Lord Rowfont and the General and the Dean."

"Oh Lord!" said Reenie. "Drat the ruddy Dean."

In the Schoolroom Ruth and Louisa were about to read 'The Lady of Shalott'.

"You begin, Louisa."

" 'The Lady of Shalott', by Lord Alfred Tennyson," began Louisa.

> "On either side the river lie
>   Long fields of barley and of rye,
>   That clothe the wold and meet the sky;
>   And thro'——"

"One moment, Louisa, please; it should be Alfred, *Lord* Tennyson."

"Why?" said Louisa.

"Well, look what it says, dear. Alfred was his Christian name and his surname was Tennyson."

"But why not Lord Alfred Tennyson?"

"Is his brother a marquess?" said Ruth.

"Was, you mean; Lord Tennyson is no longer alive, Ruth."

"Was, then. When somebody's brother is a marquess it's quite simple."

"I wish you wouldn't be so snobbish, Ruth."

"I'm not being snobbish, Miss Bolby. Really I'm not; I'm trying to help Louisa."

"Well, it's very snobbish to talk in that way about marquesses."

"I know; Jessy says you shouldn't, but I'm not snobbish. I'm not at all snobbish, it's very unfair. I'm trying to help Louisa."

"Begin again, please, Louisa."

" 'The Lady of Shalott', by *Lord* Tennyson.

> "On-either-side-the-river-lie
> Long-fields-of-barley-and-of-rye,
> That-clothe-the——"

"Louisa, take it slowly, *please*! Imagine you are in the field; imagine the wind in the barley and the rye."

"When I take it at a run I can imagine it better," said Louisa. "How do you get made a marquess?"

Ruth said, "Isn't there anything higher than a marquess, Miss Bolby?"

"Ruth, please, I entreat you—such bald bandying about of titles is intolerable, most unladylike, most snobbish. I won't have it. Stop, Ruth! Stop, Louisa! Lord Tennyson was the

117

Poet Laureate, but in future we will refer to him simply as
'Tennyson'. "

"Or Alfred," said Louisa.

"That would hardly be respectful to the Poet Laureate,
Louisa."

"I've forgotten now what Laureate means," said Louisa.

"Couldn't we have that another day?" said Ruth. "We
promised Barby and Jessy we'd work the gramophone."

"I don't think there is very much object in your working
the gramophone, Ruth."

"Oh, why, Miss Bolby?"

"It doesn't look as if Barby and Jessy will be riding in the
Gymkhana, therefore there isn't much object in their practising for it, is there? Before there is any riding in the
Gymkhana Jessy will have to apologise for her behaviour
yesterday."

"I'm sure she will, Miss Bolby."

"She hasn't made any attempt to do so."

"Do you mean none of us will ride? None of us will go
to the Gymkhana?"

"You and Louisa may, but you won't get on very well
without Barby to direct you."

"We couldn't, without Barby. Barby ought to be a Riding
Mistress."

"With Jessy an Actress and Barby a Riding Mistress, your
father *will* be pleased, I must say."

"Is Jessy going to be an Actress?" said Louisa.

"She said so this morning."

"Then she *must* have been in a bate, it's supposed to be a
secret," said Ruth.

"How many times have I told you not to say 'bate',
Ruth?"

"Ken Woodman says it."

"And is there any need for you to copy-cat Ken Woodman?"

Louisa stopped biting her pencil. Ruth sat up. Miss Bolby

118

put down her spectacles. Jerkily, as if the gramophone had been propped up unevenly, 'Run, rabbit, run, rabbit, run-run-run' floated up from the park and in through the windows; the tension eased, the needle had stuck.

Miss Pickford opened the iron gate into the Long Walk. She would come, through the Long Walk, Miss Bolby had said, to the kitchen garden, and she had not yet explored the kitchen garden. The gate, though a light one and delicately wrought, grated against the ground as she pushed it open, though she did not hear the sound.

It was this lack of little sounds that made life seem unreal, she thought, like walking through fog in which sound gave no warning; it cast no shadow as shape did. The gate jarred against her hand and she felt a shock as it shut—she had not expected it to clang.

Broad borders, choked now with weeds, were backed by an overgrown shrubbery; laurels and hollies fiercely crowded out currants and lilacs. Unclipped yew, in a series of arches, threw shadows upon the path which patches of moss had made slippery. Miss Pickford walked on the grass.

Miss Bolby had said : 'The border was a sight in Old Lord Rushford's day. He kept more than twenty gardeners. Bob Woodman, whose acquaintance you will make, Miss Pickford, worked in the gardens.' Just as if she, Miss Bolby, had been the owner of Rushford. It must be nice to feel you belonged, to be so settled in a place, though you could hardly feel settled exactly, on your first day.

'I should be grateful if you would get the Office tidied up, Miss Pickford, just in case Lord Rushford comes home. We don't expect him home, but he has been ill and we half hope he may be sent home,' Lady Rushford had said, but there was something about the Office which had forced her outside. First the animals had left it; one by one the cats had crawled from the letter basket, Chang-Kai-Shek had yapped to be

119

lifted down, and the poodles had whined. The Office had become more and more like a box, filled with the unseen presence of Old Mr. Stiles: somewhere behind the bookshelves, was Old Mr. Stiles. She had taken down a bulky Peerage and then a *Whitaker's Almanack* and had hastily put them back, watched by Old Mr. Stiles. Then a bomber had skimmed the roof and its roar had vibrated through the bookshelves and files, heightening a number of little sounds: birds in the trees outside, rooks crying, and footfalls in the drive, making her conscious, as spasmodic patches of acute hearing inevitably did, of her growing disability. It *was* growing, although on good days she only missed the little sounds, such as the gate's creaking. Worry was bad, they said, for deafness, and who could be free from worry in war, even if you had no one to worry about particularly. It was funny, this, having no one left to worry *about*. Had Miss Bolby some private and personal worry, private and personal because it concerned not only herself, but another? Was it because she was of some importance *somewhere*, that she felt she belonged to Rushford?

When she, Rose Pickford, had left the Office, in much the same disordered state in which it had been before, she had gone up to her room with a borrowed novel. She had been disturbed, less by the bombers above than by the little sounds they magnified, and because she felt she was suffocating, drowning. As a means of distraction she had begun to think about Miss Bolby's bracelets. Poor Miss Bolby. It was too bad to lose something which was of sentimental value. Supposing she, Rose, had lost the locket John Todd had given her with 'Rose' written inside it.

'I can only say I'm thankful, Lady Rushford, that it wasn't the brooch Lord Rowfont gave me. The amethyst brooch I wear in the evenings. He gave it me as a parting gift, and having been so many years at Rowfont, I consequently treasure it.'

120

'I shouldn't worry too much, Miss Bolby. You're sure you didn't leave them *outside* anywhere?'

'No, Lady Rushford, the only time I was outside yesterday was when I was showing Miss Pickford round.'

She, Rose, had felt then that it was her fault in some way. Poor Miss Bolby, how she had gone on about it—all through lunch. But it was horrid to lose anything, and Miss Bolby had seemed such a nice person, eager to explain things and show a newcomer round. All through the conversation the children had sat silent, sullen, as if they thought Miss Bolby had blamed *them* for the loss of the bracelets somehow, until Lady Rushford had said : 'It looks as if the weather is going to change, the blight is coming down. You haven't yet experienced our Midland Blight, Miss Pickford. It gives us no peace, like a fog—it merely dirties everything.' No one had spoken as yet but Lady Rushford and Miss Bolby, and both enunciated clearly—a little as though from a platform, so that she, Rose, had heard—being deaf was sometimes like being at a play—then Ruth said :

'Will they put the Gymkhana off if it pours with rain?'

'You can't put off an event of that sort, unless there's a deluge or a thunderstorm.'

Jessy said : 'I don't see what difference it makes what the weather does *now*; there are six days to go.'

Barby said : 'Crowhurst hates heavy going.'

Louisa said : 'It *is* going to rain : the cows are lying down.'

And Lady Rushford said : 'Well, rain or no rain, you had better mind your "p's and q's" all of you. By the way, Miss Bolby, I want to ask Lord Corwen and Lord and Lady Archie to luncheon on Thursday. Lord Corwen, Miss Pickford, is being very kind and is giving away the prizes at the Gymkhana; he dosen't do much of that sort of thing any more, he is very *deaf* now. He writes letters to *The Times*. We shall be rather crowded if they come, but I don't suppose you or

121

Miss Pickford will mind sitting at the little table, Miss Bolby.'

'Talking of *The Times*, Lady Rushford,' said Miss Bolby, 'today's leader is very well worth reading. If you would care for me to, I will read it aloud later.'

It had been rather like coming in during the second act of a play; both Lady Rushford and Miss Bolby explained so much and told so little. It had seemed as if all in the room had been taking part and she had been watching.

At this point of reminiscence Miss Pickford had got up from her bed and had gone to the window; she had looked out into the park through a yellow film. Last night's dark and slowly moving humps were sluggish now; some, she saw, were hidden under mud-coloured, spinach-splashed sheets. They looked more evil now than in the dark. The zinnias in the flower-beds in the formal garden had dulled. She hurried from her room because she felt she could not breathe. . . .

Now the blight was lifting, wind was blowing it off the gardens and the park towards the moor. . . . It was light again; sunlight fell upon the path and the yew trees threw shadows. With the lifting of the blight her spirit lifted. Perhaps I can stay here after all, she thought. The sunlight, the springiness of the grass beneath her feet and vividness of the moss in the path gave her new courage.

She passed the orangery and went through the rose-garden and through the door which Miss Bolby had said led into the kitchen garden, past a hedge of dahlias and a long line of green-houses. In the kitchen garden all was orderly. She felt she could breathe here, and it was full of pungent scents : rotting cabbages and early chrysanthemums, and carrot-tops and onions hung to dry, smoke from burning weeds, and peaches, which grew upon its rose-coloured walls. She saw the prisoners—earth-coloured overalled figures—stooping; they had not the air of prisoners : they straightened to talk to Reenie—was it Reenie who stood in the cindered path in a full flowered skirt? They stooped and were silent again. She could not hear what they said, but she caught the sound; it came as if from a long way off. Being deaf is like looking through a telescope, she thought. Here I am as near to happiness as anyone can be in war. I should be foolish to go. I must stick it, she thought.

"Good evening, Miss Pickford," said Reenie.

"Oh, good evening, Reenie. It is Reenie, isn't it, the land girl?"

"Kitchen-maid, Miss Pickford."

"Pardon, dear? I don't always hear very well."

"Kitchen-maid, Miss Pickford; Vi, my friend is the land girl."

"Excuse my saying so, dear, but you don't look a bit like a kitchen-maid."

"That's what they all say," said Reenie. "Funny isn't it? To tell you the truth, Miss Pickford, I haven't ever been one before."

"So it's a new experience for you?"

"You're telling me," said Reenie. "Excuse me, Miss Pickford, this is Otello and Nino. Nino and Otello—meet Miss Pickford."

"Buona sera, signorina," said Otello.

"Buona sera, signorina," said Nino.

"Good evening. How do you do? Bon soir," said Miss Pickford. It seemed a little unorthodox somehow, to be introduced to prisoners. "Vous comprenez Inglese? A beautiful evening, is it not?"

"They understand all right," said Reenie, "but they speak in Italian."

"Dear me, however do you manage to carry on a conversation?"

"It beats me how we do," said Reenie. "Has Miss Bolby found her bracelets yet, Miss Pickford."

"She hadn't at lunch-time."

"Jessy said she's sorry?"

"I don't know. To whom, Reenie?"

"To Miss Bolby, before those kids can ride in the Gymkhana."

"Good heavens, what a lot there is going on here. I haven't got to the bottom of it yet. You see, I'm still very new, Reenie."

"Seemed a bit funny when I was new."

"Have you been here long, Reenie?"

"Getting on for seven months. Funny, isn't it? I never thought I'd stick it for seven months, but the place gets you. Melancholy as a morgue and yet it sort of gets you. Miss Bolby came on the same day, and in the grandfather of a fog, too. I never thought *she'd* stay."

"I think I see what you mean, Reenie. If I could be in the garden all the time I think I should want to stay, too. I'm not sure that I like being in the house though, there doesn't seem to be any air. At least, not right up under the roof where I am. Do you and your friend find the same thing?"

"It gets a bit hot up there, but I dare say it's worse in your room, Miss Pickford, it's the scaffolding. Casts a sort of shadow. It gives me the willies that room. They're going to make the window bigger; that's why the scaffolding's there, only something else turned up and the men had to be taken off, just to remind you there's a war on. Perhaps you could change your room; it isn't as if there's a dearth of rooms."

"I don't like to ask, Reenie, not when I've just arrived."

"I'd offer you ours. I know my friend wouldn't mind, only yours isn't big enough for the two of us."

"I suppose there isn't any harm in asking, only I do hate asking. Thanks ever so much for suggesting it, Reenie."

"Don't mench, Miss Pickford. If I were you, I'd go and try my luck now."

124

"Thanks ever so much. Bye-bye, Reenie."

Reenie turned towards the house. Nino and Otello looked up from the work over which they were bending. Miss Pickford saw that they were listening, then she too caught the sound. It was Miss Bolby singing.

First Nino and then Otello took up the air.

Miss Bolby broke off abruptly. She shut down the lid of the piano. How futile it seemed worrying about the loss of some Indian bracelets in the middle of a world war. The effortlessness with which Nino and Otello had answered her, calling forth nostalgia for the singer she had not been, seemed to make its futility doubly poignant, yet such trivialities were like nagging teeth : they would not leave one alone; she could not get the bracelets out of her mind. Better worry about the bracelets than indulge in fancies and memories just because two Italian prisoners had picked up an air, making it sound as she could never make it sound, and the evening was warm and fine. She had opened a drawer in the chiffonier in which were kept the schoolroom knives and forks, imprinted with a large 'R' and a large 'S' for schoolroom below a large coronet —the late Lord Rushford had liked things large—and a spare supply of exercise books and some Rushford-headed writing paper with a smaller coronet: the coronet, she observed, seemed to grow smaller and smaller with time, the present Lord Rushford's being so small as scarcely to be discernible as a coronet; it seemed at first to be some printer's blot or blob. She took some of the writing paper because she had been meaning, for days now, to write to Mrs. Hurst; when writing letters other than to Hillstone House she adhered strictly to her own—writing-paper since the war had become as valuable a commodity as tissue-paper or cotton wool. A letter to Mrs. Hurst would take her mind off the bracelets a little and ease the painful prickings of longings unfulfilled which the Italians' singing had evoked.

125

She wrote with a Relief nib and with the paper at a distance, holding the pen as if it were a quill:

'DEAR MRS. HURST,

'As it is sometime since I had news of all at Hillstone House, and London's long ordeal from the flying bomb has most vividly recalled our difficult days, or—I should say rather— our long cold nights during the Birmingham Blitz together, I feel I must enquire, how, mercifully far from danger, those at Hillstone House are faring.

'Here we are much as usual. Very cut off but for the wire-less and very tried by the bombers which in this fine, hot weather give us no respite. However, we must not complain, as they are our own!!

'Lady Lydia, Lord Rushford's sister-in-law—she was a Bourne-Hervey (pronounced Harvey) and married Lord Rushford's younger brother—is expected at any moment, but has not turned up yet. We were hoping she might have given us some first-hand news—and Miss Pickford, Lady Rushford's new secretary—a daughter of the late Vicar of Stonechurch, I believe—arrived yesterday. An agreeable though some-what nervous woman from whom it is difficult to gauge what is going on. Lord Rushford is half expected home from Italy. It is sometimes very difficult, by the way, to know exactly how to treat our Prisoners. They work, as I think I told you—for the purposes of agricultural produce—in the gardens—it is only on Saturdays that they tend the borders or mow the lawn. (There were twenty-eight gardeners, I understand from our night-watchman, in Old Lord Rushford's day.) When coming in contact with the prisoners—one meets them in the passages and they frequently come into the kitchen— one, I fear, is not uninterested in Reenie, our kitchen-maid (invalided out of the A.T.S., a very common girl)—it is sometimes difficult to know how to address them, especially in my now rusty Italian!

'The children are busily engaged in preparing to take part in a Gymkhana to be held next Monday at Colsall at which the prizes are to be given by our neighbour, Lord Corwen, to whose visit to luncheon here with Lord and Lady Archie Meredith on Thursday I am immensely looking forward. Did I tell you that, by an extraordinary coincidence, Lady Archie (she was Colonel Tom Meredith's widow before marrying Lord Archie *en seconde Noces* and is a Burraby, Lord Vallance's sister) is an intimate friend of my Atherton-Broadleigh brother-in-law, the General, General Sir Arthur Atherton-Broadleigh and of his father, the Dean? Is this not extraordinary? One of those rare doubles!! So nice to have someone in some way connected so near!!!

'Well, my dear Mrs. Hurst, Time, as they say, has an uncomfortable way of marching on.

'I should be grateful if you would give my kind regards to Mrs. Rowcroft and Miss Hines and Mr. Lind, and please remember me to Mrs. Tollmarsh and Milly.

'Yours very sincerely,
'ROONA BOLBY.'

Then she added, as an insertion, with an arrow, after Mr. Lind: 'Not forgetting, of course, Mr. and Mrs. Billings.' Impossible to send regards only to Mrs. Billings and there had been times, especially during the blitz, when she had liked Mrs. Billings.

She overcome the difficulty with regard to Mr. Lorelli by adding, as a postscript: 'Is Mr. Lorelli still with you?'

"That'll serve the old bag right," said Reenie. "What's the betting Miss Pickford gets Old Lord Rushford's room and old Bolb is tucked away under the eaves?"

"One with the voice of a singing bird," Otello made an all-embracing gesture, "should not be called a bag."

"But a bird," said Nino.

"My God!" said Reenie. "You Italians!"

Lucky, lucky Miss Bolby, Miss Pickford thought as she walked towards the house. She frequently thought aloud. Living in 'digs' you did—there was no one to tell you off, as it were. How different I should be if I had a talent, she thought. Think of being able to sit down at the piano like that and sing your soul out. She felt quite elated by the thought. She walked faster. She took large, light strides. After all she might not have to sleep in that dreadful room again tonight; she would go now to speak to Lady Rushford, and she must remember to say Rush*ford*. Rush*forth* came so much more easily somehow.

Elizabeth went into the office to telephone Lady Archie. She had meant to do so earlier in the day, but the extension in the hall was out of order and it was difficult to get a man to see to it; it was difficult to get a man to see to anything. It had been a difficult day: a long series of little irritations. She wanted, too, to look for a letter from Lord Archie, with whom she sat on a number of committees. Lord Corwen, because of his severe deafness and his great age, took little active part in county matters and was deputised for by Lord Archie. She wanted also to have another look for Miss Pickford's letters of reference, not that they would serve much purpose, but she wanted to see what the letters had said. The Office was just as it had been in the morning; there was a strong suggestion of dog and a hint of cat, and nothing had been filed, letters were strewn everywhere. Even with a secretary—one had *still—to do everything—oneself—in order to get anything—done*. The drawers as she opened and shut them jammed.

What had Miss Pickford been doing all the afternoon? Where *was* Miss Pickford?

128

A Week in Late Summer

Elizabeth picked up the telephone. She dialled 'O' and then the number. She rather resented the dialling system. In the old days there had been pleasant little chats with Mr. Curby at the post office. Through twenty years or so as a telephone operator he had lost none of his enthusiasm for the most local of local calls—the more local the better; it seemed hardly necessary to pursue a local call, in fact, having talked to Mr. Curby who already knew its import and kept up a running conversation while the line was engaged. His enthusiasm for trunk calls knew no bounds. It had been a sad business saying goodbye to Mr. Curby. Something had gone from him with his relinquishing of the exchange, though he had stayed on at the post office; age had come upon hm suddenly and his zest for life had waned. Daily, life at Rushford was changing; it had begun to change with the going of Old Mr. Stiles. . . .

"Hullo. Lady Archie?"

"Elizabeth. Archie and I were just talking about you."

"Favourably, I hope?"

"Most. We were saying how beautifully that old man of yours, Benn, keeps the silver. Hughie has taken on ours. He buried it, you know, with the Peerage, in 1940—he almost destroyed his birds and that would have broken his heart. Now he's dug the silver up again and he takes a great pride in it. It keeps his mind off the leaks in the roof and the profits on the cabbages and it prevents him writing letters to *The Times*. I can't read *The Times* any more, I'm so nervous of seeing a letter from Hughie. Of course Hughie'll never get the same lustre on it as Barrington, but there'll never be another Barrington."

"Barrington, Lady Archie?"

"Barrington was our butler when we lived in St. John's Wood, Harry and I. Barrington directed our lives. My maid, Hinton, was in love with him, so much so that there was a moment when Harry said she ought to go. Harry was

129

such a stickler, the young so often are, but in the end she married one of the Atherton-Broadleigh footmen and had a baby—the baby must be well over thirty by now. Barrington was a drunkard so I suppose she was well out of it, but he never lost his sense of direction—in fact if it hadn't been for Barrington——"

"Hold on a moment, Lady Archie; Ruth wants something. Yes, what is it, Ruth? *Don't* bang the door, darling."

"I didn't: it banged," said Ruth. "Barby and Jessy are going into Huggley with Mr. Finch in the trap. He's got to fetch a parcel from the station. Can Louisa and I go too?"

"I should think so. Have you asked Miss Bolby?"

"We haven't got to, have we, if we ask you?"

"I suppose not; I don't really know."

"She's singing, so I expect she's in a better mood."

"All right then. Run along. I'm talking to Lady Archie."

"Sorry, Lady Archie, where were we?"

"With Barrington and Hinton, though I can't imagine why. What *were* we saying?"

"Well, I meant to say I hoped that you and Lord Archie and Lord Corwen would come to lunch on Thursday. I want to talk to Lord Corwen about the Gymkhana—he does so hate being shouted at at the time."

"Wizard!" said Lady Archie. "But I'll have to consult Hughie about the car."

Elizabeth recoiled. "I spend my time telling the children *not* to say 'Wizard', Lady Archie!"

"But why not, my dear Elizabeth? It's time we got a little new blood into the language, and you have the prisoners and the land girls and the A.T.S., while I, on my lonely hill, only have the R.A.F. to draw on. That nice Squadron Leader Langford was over here again the other day—you ought to have more contact with the aerodrome."

"Well, you'll let me know about lunch, Lady Archie?"

"I'll ring you tonight, and I'll do my best to persuade
Hughie. Will that nice Miss Bolby be there? We found, on
that foggy night, that we were curiously connected, through
memories—Indian memories, though very different ones, I
fancy. A sad woman, living in phantasy, in a world far
grander than you and I have ever known."

Lady Archie is becoming very wandery, and very much
hand in glove with the aerodrome, Elizabeth thought. Poor
Lord Corwen, having to listen to Air Force slang. Poor Lord
Vallance, too, he must have suffered in his day—there were
so many stories of Lady Archie's past. There was her love
affair with Harry's friend. Who *was* Harry's friend, who was
always referred to, when the story was told, as 'Harry's
friend'? What had Lady Archie meant when she said she
was 'curiously connected' with Miss Bolby, through memory?
What had she meant by *'Indian memories'*? Hadn't Lady
Archie said something about the Atherton-Broadleighs' footman, too? Could 'Harry's friend' be—could he possibly be
Miss Bolby's brother-in-law? Surely not. No, of course not.
Such a coincidence was quite absurd, and Lady Archie was so
wandery. . . .

Elizabeth heard the door open behind her.

"Were you looking for something, Miss Pickford?"

"For you, Lady Rushforth, and you, I see, are looking at
the room's disorder and wondering where I was. I've been
in your kitchen garden. It's the most beautiful garden I've
ever seen, so safe. I should like to live there, safely within
its walls. It takes me back to my childhood at Stonechurch,
when my father was vicar there, before we went to Wimbledon. There's nothing like a kitchen garden for transporting
you back to childhood. But I've come to ask you a favour
—to ask if I can change my room. It seems dreadful to worry
you so much over trifles when there's so much sadness and
suffering everywhere, but last night I couldn't sleep. I could
get no air, and I need air. . . ."

"Must you change it tonight, Miss Pickford? If you could give me a day or two. . ."

"Oh, I don't want to trouble you, Lady Rushforth. That nice girl, Reenie, not at all like a kitchen-maid, if I may say so, suggested, *offered*. . . . She says her friend wouldn't mind . . . only the room's too small. . . ."

"If you really can't sleep, you'll have to move, Miss Pickford, but it's rather awkward just now. Let me see. . . . There is Miss Bolby's room. . . . I don't know if I could ask Miss Bolby to move into yours, just for a night or two, until we can get another room ready. I don't quite like to ask Miss Bolby. . . . Or there is the State Room, that's airy enough and it's always kept ready. It was done up by Old Lord Rushforth for King Edward VIII's visit; we've kept it open all through the war."

"Oh, dear me, Lady Rushforth, I *am* putting you to a lot of trouble."

"It's no trouble, Miss Pickford. It's just a question of whether I put you there or move Miss Bolby, and if you can't sleep in your room, I'm quite sure Miss Bolby can't. It's a make-shift room which is being altered and never gets finished. I think, on the whole, you and Miss Bolby had better arrange it between you. Yes, you'd much better arrange it with Miss Bolby."

"You *are* kind, and Miss Bolby is such a nice person, Lady Rushforth."

"Oh, it's good at any rate, because Miss Bolby's in a bate, to get out of the house," sang Ruth.

"Oh, *Ruth,* you can't end up just like that; it doesn't scan," said Jessy.

"Well, you do it," said Ruth.

"You might have said you were sorry, Jess," said Barby. "You could have, when she was singing; she seems to melt when she sings."

132

"And I melt," said Jessy, "and you might have said you were. You were rude, after all. You said she had nowhere to go."

"She hadn't, had she?"

"She could have gone to Bertha Barnsley."

"Or the Dean," said Louisa.

"The Dean is dead," said Ruth.

"Oh, who wants to ride in a silly old Gymkhana," said Jessy. "People are being killed all over the place, and all we think and talk about are Miss Bolby's bracelets and a silly old Gymkhana." She saw Barby's mouth droop, and Ruth and Louisa look bewildered and Finch's shoulders sag. He was old now, and she knew that for weeks his life had centred round the Gymkhana, as Barby's and Ruth's and Louisa's, and indeed, until yesterday, her own had. She saw Finch carrying buckets in the stableyard, bustling in the harness-room, whistling songs which were no longer sung: 'Ta-ra-ra Boom-de-ay' and 'Pop Goes the Weazle'... "In Italy, for instance, people are being killed." There was no going back now.

"And in London," said Ruth, "arms and legs are flying about."

"Oh, stop it, Ruth. You're being horrible."

"You began it," said Ruth.

"Are you going to be an Actress, Jess?" said Louisa.

"The greatest Actress there has ever been," said Jessy.

"Not if you're as cross as two sticks," said Ruth.

They had reached a steep incline. Finch edged forward upon the trap's seat, as if to ease the burden from the mare; he clicked his tongue against his teeth and loosened the reins.

"May I come in, Miss Bolby? I hope I am not disturbing you?"

"Certainly not. Please, come in, Miss Pickford."

"I see you are writing letters—I see I am disturbing you..."

133

"Just one or two rather important letters, Miss Pickford, but I've finished with them now." Miss Bolby checked a desire to say : 'I'm through with them,' which savoured of Mr. Billings, and, regrettable though it was, of Lady Archie. It was impossible not to pick up such phrases from Reenie, the girl was always about the house and gardens somewhere instead of in the kitchen.

"Forgive my remarking on it, Miss Bolby, but what awfully posh note-paper. The crest on it, I see. Such a pretty, graceful thing."

"The *coronet*," said Miss Bolby. "There is always a small quantity in the cupboard, Miss Pickford, if ever you wish for any. For anything rather special, I mean. I keep it there mainly for the children's thanks letters, and for my own— well—*important* letters. I wouldn't dream of using Rushford paper in war-time for all and sundry. It isn't fair, is it?"

"Oh, dear me, no! I wouldn't dream of using it, Miss Bolby. I don't think *I* ever have anything—well—important, really. . . . I expect I can buy some ordinary paper in the village?"

"Mr. Curby has a supply of common rough ruled paper."

"So much is common and rough now, isn't it, Miss Bolby? I often wonder what my poor father would have said. He so often used to say he wondered what would be the end of it all."

Miss Bolby looked at the clock. There was a long time yet till supper. She wondered why Miss Pickford had come into the Schoolroom so early. Was it conceivable that she did not know it was not usual for the secretary to sit in the Schoolroom? She, it seemed, was no more used to such houses as Rushford than Reenie. . . .

"Did you come *about* something, Miss Pickford?"

"As a matter of fact it was about my room. I've just been talking to Lady Rushforth———"

"Rush*ford*."

134

"*Ford,* I mean. Silly me, I'm ever such a fool with names."

"I'm afraid I don't quite follow, Miss Pickford, about the room?"

"Lady Rushforth, *ford,* I mean, said I was to have one of the spare rooms, that is, unless you'd rather have it and I have yours. She said we were to arrange it together, so that I could move tonight. Last night I didn't sleep a wink—there is so little air up there where I am, the areoplanes take it all."

"I am surprised I have heard nothing of it, Miss Pickford. Lady Rushford is generally so considerate, and I have been in my room such a long time. I'm quite established there. It would be rather a tall order to move at a moment's notice, you know. There are my books, all my private papers . . ."

"Then please let me have the spare room, Miss Bolby. I think Lady Rushforth thought *you'd* rather——"

"Which spare room is it, Miss Pickford?"

"I believe she said the State Room. I feel ever so excited, King Edward VII slept there, it's so romantic, isn't it? Much more exciting to sleep in King Edward's bed than in Queen Elizabeth's. Coming to a house like this you'd expect it to be Queen Elizabeth's."

"I suppose if this move is to be made tonight, Miss Pickford, we had better begin. We shall both need help with our things. I will call through the window and round up the children. By the way, Miss Pickford, it *was* you who left the nursery bathroom last, last night?—we *did* decide it was you, I think? You will certainly have *air* in the State Room, Miss Pickford, but I wonder if, on second thoughts, you wouldn't be more comfortable in mine?" Miss Bolby wished she had not sealed and stamped her letter to Mrs. Hurst, already a new letter was forming.

"Yes, Miss Bolby?" Elizabeth found it difficult to keep irritation from her voice. All day, whenever she had gone into the Office, someone had caught her there.

It had been foolish to say to Miss Pickford: 'Arrange it between you.' Irritation outweighed all other feeling when she saw Miss Bolby.

"I understand, Lady Rushford, that Miss Pickford is to have the State Room. We have just discussed it and we think, on the whole, she would be better, if you approve of it, in mine."

"Yes, I said, Miss Bolby, that you must arrange it between you. I didn't want to offer her your room, that's all, but do have the State Room if you prefer it."

"Miss Pickford, I think, is unused to large rooms."

"But she wanted a large room. She said she couldn't breathe in the little room upstairs."

"I am very loath to leave the late Lord Rushford's room, but if Miss Pickford feels happier there . . ."

She delights in martyrising herself. Why must they involve me when I tell them to arrange it between themselves? How sick I am of them all, thought Elizabeth.

"I was looking for the children, Lady Rushford. Miss Pickford needs some help with her things and some of mine are very heavy, for instance, my dressing-case with my Indian brushes."

"The children have gone with Finch into Huggley. Why don't you get Reenie, she is strong and able-bodied—or the prisoners?"

"It may be very foolish of me, but somehow I don't quite like the idea of the prisoners, well . . . touching my personal things."

"I see. Then the prisoners can move Miss Pickford's and Reenie yours, Miss Bolby. I'm going down to the gardens now, so I'll get hold of them for you." For several months I have put up with all I have disliked in Miss Bolby because I have found her helpful and because she is, or was, or so I thought, a gentlewoman. I am beginning not to be able to put up with it any more, Elizabeth thought.

She did not go into the kitchen, she called out to Reenie from the doorway.

"Coo-ee. Oh, pardon, I didn't see it was you, Lady Rushford."

"Miss Bolby and Miss Pickford are changing rooms, Reenie. Be a nice kind creature and help them with their things." She did not wait for Reenie's answer, she walked towards the kitchen garden.

She found Otello and Nino in the toolshed, returning tools to their accustomed places for the night.

"Otello! Nino! Before you go home"—then she realised that she should not have said 'home.' "Help me by helping the Signorina Bolby and the Signorina Pickford. They are about to change their rooms. And take Reenie, she is strong, she also will help. The Signorina Bolby has a number of things."

She did not wait for their answer any more than she had waited for Reenie's; she walked on down the kitchen garden and out through a door in its lower wall. She skirted the tennis court and went through a gate into the park; she walked until she reached the river; it was turgid and defiant because about to be constrained—it raced towards a hump-backed bridge which must narrow and congest it. There was no peace in the river. The yellow-green waters of the canal which ran through the field beyond would soothe, but no impetus carried her on to the canal. All my energy goes into the house, she thought. I no longer see beyond the house. I am going down in a back-wash of pettiness which keeps me too busy to survey it. I no longer look beyond the house. It is time Larry came back. And if Larry comes back . . . ?

Because Elizabeth stood still, and she seldom stood still, she became aware, as Bella on the stair and Miss Bolby on the night of her arrival had become aware, of a bomber's distant burr—a sound by now so customary that it was seldom heard : how often was its dark descent upon the house unnoticed. She turned in the sound's direction as it gathered; already low in the sky, its perpetration rose from the wood behind the house —seemed to hover before it turned above the elms and lurched towards the river; she resisted an impulse to squat down into the grass. There is no peace anywhere, she thought; we are lulled by the countryside into a false peace. There is something in what Miss Pickford said : there will be no peace, even when the war is over, as long as there are black devils in the sky. I am becoming as cracky as Miss Pickford.

"The prima donna, she moves, and Miss Pickford, too, she moves," said Reenie, "what did I tell you?"

"We have already been informed, we have seen the Baronessa. We come to assist the removal of the Signorinas," said Otello.

"Come on then," said Reenie.

"I come, I come," said Nino.

Miss Bolby surveyed the State Room. The bed, beneath its dust sheet, loomed; no one had said who was to make it or remove its covering. She ran a finger over the chest of drawers and saw that it was dusty. She opened a cupboard and shut it because of an overpowering odour of moth-ball. It evoked memories of Hillstone House. Just such an odour had overpowered her on the day of her arrival there.

Milly had shown her to her room, and before beginning to unpack she had opened the cupboard. . . . How vividly now she could see the room . . . and the drawing-room, as she had first seen it, with Mrs. Hurst and Mrs. Billings and Mrs. Rowcroft and Miss Hine in chairs drawn to the fire. There had been a moment's uneasiness when she had not known whether she or they should be the first to say good evening, and then she had thought: It is I, I am a Bolby, and she had said: 'Good evening.'

'Miss Bolby, I take it?' It had been Mrs. Hurst who had effected the introduction: 'Mrs. Billings, Mrs. Rowcroft, and Miss Hines: meet Miss Bolby.'

'And Mrs. *H*urst,' Mrs. Billings had nodded.

Mrs. Hurst continued to knit and all were silent.

'May I ask, Mrs. Hurst, if I am too late for tea?'

'You ring when you want it, Miss Bolby.'

'And Elsie will bring it,' said Mrs. Billings. '*H*ave you come from far, Miss Bolby?'

'From Worthing, Mrs. Billings. I have been visiting an old friend, a Miss Barnsley, Bertha Barnsley. She is a pianist of some repute and we studied together. She has a large house in Worthing, left her by her parents.' There was a silence.

'You musical too, then, I take it, Miss Bolby? My word! Hillstone House isn't half coming on. Mr. Lorelli upstairs and Milly in the Tollmarsh's sitting-room and now you, Miss Bolby!

'Though you could *h*ardly call Milly musical, Mrs. *H*urst,' said Mrs. Billings; 'Mr. Billings and I once went for a *h*oliday to Worthing, Miss Bolby. Rather full of old fogies, isn't it?'

She, Roona, had thought of the shelter where she had sat on the morning after Ralph Barnsley had proposed.

'I think the old fogies, Mrs. Billings, as you so rightly call them, have left the South Coast since the war. There were plenty about when my parents and I lived there—they retired there after India. I was born in India.'

'Then you won't like our Midland fogs, Miss Bolby. Whatever 'as 'appened to Elsie?' Mrs. Hurst touched the bell with a knitting needle. Then Mrs. Rowcroft said: 'You

are lucky to be musical and to have been to India, Miss Bolby.'
And from somewhere upstairs had come a violin's first faint
feeble puling, the forerunner of Mr. Lorelli. . . .

It had been a number of weeks before they had discovered
that the lessons she gave were unconnected with music, and it
had been she herself, who had revealed their nature, by
accident, as it were, one night in the smoking-room after
dinner.

'Pretty hard luck an incendiary falling on Medway Hall,
the whole place has been gutted,' Mr. Howland said, looking
up from his evening paper.

'Too bad, when one of those old places goes up, isn't it?'
Mr. Lind said. Mrs. Hurst said : 'None of the family treasures
saved, Mr. 'Owland?' And for once she, Roona, had thought
aloud and was glad that she had, she had been waiting for an
opportunity to talk about Rowfont : 'Medway is within a
mile of Rowfont, Mr. Howland. I hope nothing has happened
to Rowfont,' and in the silence which followed : 'I taught the
late Lord Rowfont's girls. I spent a number of years at
Rowfont, it was Lord Rowfont who gave me my amethyst
brooch.'

'Well, I never! Fancy you never telling us, Miss Bolby!'
Mrs. Hurst scratched her head with a needle.

'Rowfont, Rowfont. Let me see now, Jacobean, isn't it? I
once went past it with my cousin on a bicycling tour. My
cousin, in fact, had permission to fish in the river. Lady
Rowfont was a fisherwoman, was she not, Miss Bolby?'

'And a Blatchington, Mr. Lind.'

Mr. Lorelli, whom she, Roona, had not seen, sat at the
dark end of the room and had not so far spoken : 'Incendiaries,
Miss Bolby, seldom fall singly . . .'

This was hardly the time to think of Hillstone House, though
she would have liked a picture of the State Room to be
flashed before those who were there. . . .

She opened the drawers in the chest of drawers and then

another cupboard. King Edward had used these very cupboards; she would like to tell this, too, to Mrs. Hurst and Mr. Billings, and particularly to Mr. Lorelli. . . .

She opened the windows and propped open the door so that a current of air might dispel the moth-balls' odour. How easy it was, she thought, to become a prey to memory, to drift off into it with the opening of a cupboard door. . . .

She walked down the passage, resisting a temptation to hurry past dark chests and pictures from which tormented souls looked down.

As she reached her old room, Lord Rushford's room, she heard voices, Reenie's, and then the prisoners': cadences of Italian filled the stair well. She had barely shut the door before there was a knock upon it.

"We've come to move your things, Miss Bolby," Reenie came into the room, followed, a little hesitantly, by Nino and Otello.

"We have been bidden by the Baronessa to move the Signorina's things. From the gardens we have heard the Signorina sing. To hear the voice of the Signorina is a pleasure," said Otello.

"Dear me, how I am forgetting my Italian. *Grazie, Otello, grazie.*"

"You should see them, Miss Bolby, when you sing! You've no idea what you do to them when you sing!"

"I perfectly understand what Otello says, Reenie. Singers, you know, know Italian, though it is a great many years since I sang. And where, may I ask, Reenie, have *you* learned Italian?"

"Me? Oh, I just pick it up as we go along, Miss Bolby. Which of you are we going to move first?"

"Had the children not gone into Huggley without my permission none of this would have been necessary."

"Well, just tell us what it is you want moved and we'll get going."

"Everything will have to be moved, Reenie; Miss Pickford is coming into my room, and sad I am to leave it. I have been very happy in the late Lord Rushford's room. Quite at home here. I have become even more attached to it than I was to my room at Rowfont. If Nino and Otello can manage the heavy luggage you and I can take my more personal things. My papers, for instance, and my sari, and some of my Indian things. I had expected you, Reenie, but not Nino and Otello."

"Just as well I brought them along, though. It looks as if you've got a good deal more than Miss Pickford."

"Working in offices as Miss Pickford has, Reenie, things don't accumulate in the same way. I have my mother's Indian things and so much that Lord Rowfont gave me. I don't like to leave them all in my pied-à-terre."

"Pardon, Miss Bolby?"

"My pied-à-terre, my room at Hillstone House. Since they seem to understand your English better than my Italian, be so good as to ask Nino and Otello to take the suitcases, Reenie."

"It's where you're going to put them all beats me."

"I'm afraid I don't quite follow you, Reenie."

"Seems like it's going to be a tight fit in Miss Pickford's room."

"In *Miss Pickford's room*?"

"Isn't that where you're going, Miss Bolby?"

"Lady Rushford has arranged for me to have the State Room, Reenie."

"Christ!" said Reenie.

"Archie," said Lady Archie, "you know, I quite look forward to going to Rushford on Thursday."

"My dear Blanchie, why?"

"I look forward to seeing that poor Miss Bolby again and now that he is a general, I want to hear more about Arthur, and, I must confess, Sita. . . ."

"Hadn't you better let sleeping dogs lie?"

"For goodness' sake don't go making any mischief, Blanchie," said Lord Corwen.

"If one is spared the horrors of war, one should surely do one's best to mitigate its monotony. You know that tomorrow one of us has to Hoover out the library."

"Bags I," said Lord Corwen.

"My!" said Becca. "Gallivanting into Huggley without permission! Whatever next, I wonder! Not that it's anything to do with me, now that you're in the Schoolroom."

Becca sighed and held a cheek towards the iron. "Sometimes, out here," she said, "you forget there's a war on, even with the bombers' racket going on. Ever such fun and games while you've been gone. . . ." Veins stood out in her right arm as she wielded the iron.

"What fun and games?" said Ruth and Louisa and Jessy together.

Barby sat at the window; she stared out into the park at nothing in particular. Vague, inexplicable disturbances which could not be put down solely to her desire to carry off a prize with Crowhurst in the Gymkhana had made her uneasy lately. She had sensed, though the thought had not formed as such, that the acuteness of this desire was due to her not belonging wholly, as Jessy and Ruth did, to Rushford, and now that Jessy no longer seemed to care about the Gymkhana some of the zest had gone out of it; Jessy, somehow, in the trap on the way to Huggley, had voiced a feeling of futility.

"Miss Pickford has moved into Miss Bolby's room and Miss Bolby into the State Room," said Becca. 'Not that I'm saying nothing *against* Miss Bolby, mind, but in my day governesses were governesses; things have changed since my day. If ever there was a topsy-turvy house in a topsy-turvy world, it's this one. Goodness knows what your father would say. Sometimes I think it is a good thing he *is* at the war. Miss Pickford can't sleep in her room, and Miss Bolby, instead of going into Miss Pickford's, goes into the State Room, and the State Room, between you and me and the gatepost, wasn't meant for governesses. Not that I have anything *against* Miss Bolby, mind you, only it seems funny, just now, opening up the State Room." Becca ran the iron adroitly into the armhole of a sleeve. "And while you were all gallivanting with Mr. Finch in Huggley we've had Reenie and the prisoners all over the house, moving their things."

Jessy and Ruth and Louisa watched Becca's movements as if hypnotised by the iron.

"Not that I don't feel sorry for Miss Pickford, not being able to sleep; she says she can't breathe, poor thing!"

"Do you mean she's balmy?" said Ruth.

"Whoever said such a thing? Goodness gracious me, Ruth!"

"You did; you said they all were."

"All who, Ruth?"

"All the governesses and secretaries."

"Well, if that isn't making mountains out of molehills, I don't know what is, Ruth."

"Perhaps, Jessy," said Barby from the window, "now that she's in the State Room she'll be in a better mood."

"Perhaps, Jess, she'll be in such a good mood——"

"Oh, shut up, Ruth!"

"Can't Ruth and I have supper in the Schoolroom, Becca? She's been singing, and she likes us to sometimes, when she's been singing," said Louisa.

"And it's fried fish," said Ruth; "I haven't had fried fish for years."

"And now that Picksie has supper in the Schoolroom, supper is more fun," said Jessy.

"It is not often I am honoured by the presence of Ruth

144

and Louisa," said Miss Bolby. "We will cast a veil over the fact that no one asked my permission to go to Huggley. In any case it should not have been Ruth and Louisa, but Barby and Jessy, and Barby and Jessy seem to have lost their sense of responsibility lately. Will you have sauce, Miss Pickford?"

"Thanks ever so much, Miss Bolby."

"And while you were gone on some errand of which I know nothing, Miss Pickford and I have been busy, *very* busy. We could have done with your help, in fact. As it was, we were assisted by Reenie, and Nino and Otello, and no one particularly likes to have her intimate belongings handled by Prisoners, well-behaved and polite though Nino and Otello are, and by—well—Reenie——"

"I don't know what we should have done without Reenie," said Miss Pickford.

"If only she would restrain her language a little," said Miss Bolby.

"She worked in a bar once," said Barby.

"She was an usherette once," said Louisa, who, uncertain of its meaning, had taken a fancy to the word.

"Before her boy-friend was killed and she went into the ATS," said Ruth.

"We've had a funny lot of kitchen-maids," said Jessy.

"Do you remember Lil, who had lice in her head?" said Barby.

"We all had them," said Jessy.

"Louisa had them for weeks," said Ruth.

"In fact, Otello thought she still had them when he cut her hair, that's why he cut it like an umbrella," said Jessy.

"Must we discuss such very unpleasant subjects at meals?" said Miss Bolby.

"We are always told that those horrible little creatures are a part of war, but what a very horrible experience for you, oh, you poor dears!" said Miss Pickford.

"Miss Pickford has moved into my room, your grandfather's room, and your mother has put me in the State Room," said Miss Bolby.

"Why?" said Louisa.

"It seems to be the only one available; your mother offered it to Miss Pickford because it has more air, but Miss Pickford felt she would be happier in mine. When you ask a direct question, try to put it a little less bluntly, Louisa."

"But there isn't nearly as much air in Grandfather's room as there is in the State Room, Miss Bolby." Louisa had long ago adopted Old Lord Rushford as her grandfather.

"I am very happy in Miss Bolby's room, dear. It's ever so nice of Miss Bolby to turn out for me."

"But why did she, if you could have had the State Room?"

"We thought I should be a little lonely in the State Room, it's such a *grand* room, dear."

"King Edward slept there," said Barby.

"Which King Edward?" said Louisa.

"King Edward VII, of course," said Jessy.

"There is no 'of course' about it, Jessy," said Miss Bolby. "Rushford is a very historic house. More than one king, no doubt, has visited it, and on one occasion a queen. Queen Adelaide, whose portrait hangs in the dining-room. Your stepfather, I expect, knows the ins and outs of it."

"Or Mr. Finch," said Ruth. "Mr. Finch knows everything."

"Old Mr. Stiles knew more, only he was so deaf he couldn't hear the questions," said Jessy, and on seeing Miss Pickford's face she said: "He couldn't hear nearly as well as you, even with his box, Miss Pickford."

Into the silence which followed Miss Bolby said: "The State Room here is not unlike the State Room at Rowfont, only the State Room at Rowfont is larger. Yes, it brings back many memories. During my early days there quite a number of Royalty visited it. I well remember the shooting parties and a certain day at tea—the ladies of the party wore tea-gowns

146

in those days—when we, the girls and I, were asked down to meet King Boris of Bulgaria. The next day we, the house-party, including the girls and I, were photographed—a group upon the front door steps was taken. I have the photograph somewhere, if you would care to see it sometime, Miss Pickford?"

"Oh, I should indeed! Thanks ever so much, Miss Bolby."

"Did the King of Bulgaria have ladies-in-waiting, Miss Bolby?" said Louisa.

"Kings don't have ladies-in-waiting, you silly fool," said Jessy.

"Oh, but they do! I know they do, I read it somewhere," said Ruth.

"You mean mistresses, don't you?" said Jessy.

"What are mistresses?" said Louisa.

"Favourites, women," said Jessy.

"There you are," said Ruth, "I told you they had women. Can I have a little more fish, please, Miss Bolby?"

"Lady Alice," said Miss Bolby, putting a curled piece of plaice on to Ruth's plate, "Lady Alice was a lady-in-waiting —Lady Alice Atherton-Broadleigh."

"To King Boris?" said Ruth.

"Don't be such a fool, Ruth," said Jessy.

"Your sister's mother-in-law, you mean?" said Miss Pickford. "You *are* lucky to know such interesting people, Miss Bolby."

"Before she married the Dean," continued Miss Bolby. "I remember the first time I stayed at the Deanery, hearing about it. It was just after my sister Sita got engaged to Arthur, the General—in those days he was a young subaltern. They met in India, he and Sita; she was staying with Lord Chipperfield." She did not say: 'My sister chaperoned Lord Chipperfield's girls out or she could not have got to India because we could not have found the fare.' Instead, she said: "Sita became very friendly with Lord and Lady Chipper-

field's girls, Lady Pearl and Lady Lavender Thrufell—
written '*Through*fell', such a difficult name for foreigners.
Lady Pearl had just come through, or rather, Lord and Lady
Chipperfield *hoped* she had come through, an unhappy love
affair. She had been secretly engaged to the younger children's
holiday tutor, Roger Leaming, and Lady Chipperfield, not
unaturally, disapproved. Roger Leaming was working on a
thesis and he did some holiday tutoring to make a little money,
but Lord Chipperfield was obliged to say, very tactfully, I
feel sure—Lord Chipperfield was a very tactful man—that he,
Roger Leaming was wasting his time tutoring. Lord Chipperfield took the whole thing very well, and would, I believe,
have sanctioned it, in spite of the fact that Roger was penniless and that his mother lived in Hove—at the far end, almost
in Portslade—but unfortunately some empty whisky bottles
were found in Roger's room, and Lady Chipperfield was
distressed by the way the affair was conducted. Roger used
to meet Lady Pearl in the shrubbery and Lady Chipperfield
discovered this, so she took a telescope which had once
belonged to Lord Nelson from the hall and propped it up in
her bedroom window, and one morning when Roger was in
the shrubbery with Lady Pearl he saw a suspicious glint
between the leaves—a flash from the telescope with the sun
upon it, so he went straight to Lord Chipperfield and out it
all came. They remained closeted in the library for a long
time and the next day Roger packed his bags and all the
younger children cried. He hid the empty whisky bottles
under the bed, but the housemaid found them. The younger
children were very fond of him, he taught them history and
flew kites with them and they called him 'Mr. Rog'. Roger
was a friend of my sister Sita's." She did not say : 'It was
because of this sad affair that Roger implored my sister Sita
to apply for the post of chaperon so that she could act as a
go-between when the girls went to India." What she said
was : "Fortunately, just after this, Lord Chipperfield went

148

out to take up an appointment in India. Lady Chipperfield
was obliged to remain behind at first to get the younger ones
settled, but she hurriedly sent out the older girls. Sita became
Lady Pearl's confidante upon the voyage, which turned out
to be very fortunate for Sita; it was through Lord Chipperfield
that she met Arthur, the General, as he is now, Arthur
Atherton-Broadleigh. He was Lord Chipperfield's aide-de-
camp. Lady Pearl and Lady Lavender were Sita's brides-
maids."

"I feel ever so sorry for Lady Pearl, Miss Bolby," said
Miss Pickford.

"It was pretty beastly of Lady Chipperfield to look through
the telescope," said Barby.

Ruth said : "But what did she *see* through it?"

"It would have served the old cow right if they'd married
after all," said Jessy.

"I regret to say they did, and that is not the way to refer to
Lady Chipperfield, Jessy. They eloped and married in the
end, in spite of Lady Pearl getting engaged to someone much
more suitable first. My sister has always felt responsible."

"Why?" said Louisa.

"Sita, you see, conveyed messages to and from Roger; she
began, you see, by being Roger's friend. She had no idea,
needless to say, that her own life would be so influenced by
the Chipperfields. It was very awkward for Sita, because once
she met Arthur she felt a debt of gratitude to Lord Chipperfield."

"Where is Lady Pearl now?" said Louisa.

"In Hove. They are getting on in years now, and very
badly off. Roger is teaching mathematics, and when I last
went over from Worthing they seemed very down-at-heel,
living, I regret to say, in—well—almost a council house, not
at all in the way she is used to. She was de-heading dead
roses in the back garden and she looked very worn, and, I

regret to say, there were a great many empty whisky bottles about. It is very sad, she sees none of her former friends."

"I *do* like to hear of true love running smooth, though, Miss Bolby," said Miss Pickford, "just *once* in a while. Except for the ones who get killed, men are so nearly always all the same."

"Isn't it because they get killed that you think they're not?" said Jessy.

"Dear me, Jessy! How *cynical*. But youth *is* cynical, isn't it, Miss Bolby? That's the modern trend."

But Miss Bolby was not listening. She was back at Worthing, she had just come back from her visit to the Deanery, she had paid off the cab.

'Roona, is that you dear? Come in, and tell me all. I want to hear all, child.'

'Can't I go and take my things off first, Mother. I'm tired.'

'If you must, dear, but hurry. I am impatient to hear who Lady Alice was.'

She had dawdled about upstairs, anxious to delay what she had to tell, to think of some way in which to minimise the humiliation, the set back. . . .

'Roona, are you coming, dear?'

'Yes, Mother.'

'You look tired and drawn, as if all had not gone well.'

'It has been a long journey and it's hot, Mother. Can I go and ask Enid for a cup of tea?'

'Ring, dear, that is what servants are for. . . .'

"Lady Meredith, I mean Lady Archie, was a something, wasn't she?" said Barby, bringing Miss Bolby sharply back from the Worthing drawing-room to the Rushford school-room.

"What do you mean, a something?" said Jessy.

"Well, a lady-in-waiting or something."

"She can't have been, she ran away," said Jessy.

"What do you mean, Jessy?" said Miss Bolby. "You may take the plates and pass the sweet, Barby."

"With Lord Archie," said Jessy.

"Lady Archie was Lord Vallance's sister and Colonel Tom Meredith's widow. I think you have made a mistake, this is nothing but servants' gossip, some tale of Bob Woodman's. I have never heard a breath of scandal about Lady Archie, Jessy."

"But Lord Archie had a wife, she was an Actress," said Jessy.

"Mr. Finch knows all about it, he drove them to the station," said Ruth.

"She was a suffragette, though. Perhaps that's what you're thinking of, Barb," said Jessy.

"Who was? The Actress?" said Louisa.

"No, you idiot, Lady Archie."

"Couldn't a suffragette be a lady-in-waiting?" said Ruth.

"Don't you know what a suffragette was? Haven't you ever heard of a suffragette?" said Jessy.

"I think we have had quite enough of this sort of talk, Jessy," said Miss Bolby.

"How odd life is. I always thought it was the Actresses who married secretly and ran away," said Miss Pickford.

"Another day has gone by and nothing has been seen or heard of my bracelets. Is it not very odd, Miss Pickford?" said Miss Bolby.

"I feel ever so worried; it was me—I mean I, who was last in the bathroom. I'm beginning to think it was me—I mean I—who must have taken them, Miss Bolby. When I was secretary-companion to Mrs. Staines-Close she lost a brooch, and, believe it or not, before the day was over I thought I'd taken it. I know it's ever so silly, but that's what nerves do to you, Miss Bolby."

"Oh, come! You mustn't let imagination run away with you to that extent, Miss Pickford. The bombers seem very active tonight, and I know it *is* sometimes very difficult not to let them get on your nerves."

"I suppose we should derive some sort of comfort from knowing they are our own. If only they wouldn't use up the air so! If only they weren't so evil . . ." said Miss Pickford.

"There is a mist rising over the river, it's going to be fine, fine for the Gymkhana," said Barby.

"It is time you went to bed," said Miss Bolby.

"There are five days to go," said Ruth, "and there is always a mist over the river."

"I wonder if Lord Archie's Actress was a *great* Actress," said Jessy.

I am an old fogy; even I, who was a beauty, have become an old fogy, Miss Bolby thought. If I were to see myself in the Worthing shelter now I should see myself as an old fogy.

The self Miss Bolby saw in the State Room mirror, because it was ill-lit, was shadowy: this mirror, a larger and better mirror, did not show, as those in Jessy's room and the room at Hillstone House had shown, new sags and furrows, but her body, as if it floated in some dark distant pool, seemed to have shrunk and her shoulders to have drooped. Was it some trick of light because the mirror was large, reflecting a large room? Those distant figures in the shelter, too, were shrunken; it was dangerous to delve so much in memory. She seemed to see in the mirror a series of rooms. How different her life might have been had she not been confined to two sorts of room, a bedroom and a schoolroom.

Drawing-rooms and dining-rooms were as passages, her presence in them transitory: she had been forced to grope as a moth gropes before flying out into the night. But she had not been a moth, far from it. Guests at Rowfont had proved this, they had not always lowered their voices; many had assumed they were voiceless, it seemed, or that governesses were deaf.

'Why do we see so little of Miss Bolby?'

'She is the children's governess.'

'She won't be for long; she can't be, looking like that.'

'Who was the dark, good-looking one who came in to tea with the children?'

'She is the children's governess. Her sister married the Atherton-Broadleigh boy.'

'Good Lord, she's a scorcher! Never let her leave the Schoolroom.'

'Your new Miss Bolby is a beauty. You might have told me *beforehand* that I was sitting next to the Governess.'

'If the Littlebridges come, we shall be thirteen.'

'We can always ask Miss Bolby.'

'So and so has failed us at the last minute, Miss Bolby. Lord Rowfont and I would be most grateful if you would help us out by coming down?'

On Sunday nights, and on nights when Mr. Grayling, the agent, came, on the children's birthday nights, and if she had been there, on Christmas night she had come down. How different a life from Sita's. . . . Not so different from Mavis's. Mavis had married Lord Chipperfield's agent.

Had I made a marriage such as Sita's, she thought, or had I been a singer—I should have been famous as a singer—I should have stayed in rooms such as this, where King Edward stayed. Not now, when I am middle-aged and sour and shrunken, but when I was young and in beauty, and perhaps —who knows?—I might have stayed, not only in houses *where*, but *when* King Edward stayed. How much fuller a life, though, is mine than Miss Pickford's, whose social peak has been Mrs. Staines-Close.

There had been a moment last night at supper, and again in the afternoon as they discussed the change in rooms, when she had felt that it was Miss Pickford who had taken the

153

bracelets. How trying, how worrying, how disturbing if it had been Miss Pickford who said she was a gentlewoman. These days all and sundry, all at least, who sought posts as companions and governesses said they were gentlewomen. Had she not seen them in Mrs. Barton's Agency, carefully mended, colourless creatures, horribly like the creatures in the shelter?

"Roona," she said aloud, "it is only the Old who become suspicious."

And seeing the old in the Worthing shelter, she dived under the bed and heaved out a suitcase and began another search in its pockets.

How wasteful, Miss Pickford thought, were the Rushford windows; they seemed to screen off more air than they let in : they could not be opened to the full, but must be secured, noisily protesting in the process, by means of a peg and a bar in which there were holes.

She was on the other side of the house now, and she missed the formal garden with its lilac trees; there had been something steadying in its formality, something which had seemed to say : 'Though bombers may thunder and we are at war, here all is in order. Pay no heed to the creeping things beyond,' and although last night she had not been able to sleep, she had become accustomed to the creeping things. On this side of the house no moving humps defaced the park, which undulated of itself, unhindered until it ceased to be park and was gathered into mist; she was tempted, because of the strangeness, to draw the curtains and look out into it to appease her thirst for air—a temptation to which she could not succumb.

Life is full here, she thought, so much is happening; the house is full, and full of life. How different from life with Mrs. Staines-Close, and yet I am outside it. Is it because of my disability or because I am a personless person? Yes, I must be a personless person because I feel the presence of others in empty rooms. Is it because I am always occupying others' rooms? She began to think of all the letters she had written, others' letters, neatly typed and correctly taken down. However disorderly the room, words as they formed upon the typewriter seemed to bring forth order, her fingers as she tapped the keys to hold a purpose, but she was adrift again once the letters were signed and sealed. Before the typewriter I am *there,* she thought, not a wraith, an outsider who watches the scene from the wings.

She looked about the room; it was a pleasant room : long, and narrow and graceful, with inset cupboards and mirrors. She shied away from the mirrors in case she saw Miss Bolby. The room held more of Miss Bolby than the Office held of Old Mr. Stiles, though the table was bare without Miss Bolby's sari, and the dressing-table blank without her brushes. There had been books, too, and photographs in silver frames; a mauve embroidered cushion in the chair and a cover upon the bed and brass trays upon the mantelpiece; even the cupboards seemed bare without Miss Bolby's moth-proof bags.

'This is my room, Miss Pickford; a very pleasant room, as you see, and a very convenient room. All the cupboards and mirrors were put in by the late Lord Rushford, so, you see, you will have plenty of room for your clothes. The far cupboard, I should explain, still holds some of the late Lord Rushford's things.' Just as if she had been on intimate terms with the late Lord Rushford.

'I see you admiring the sari, it was my mother's. And this little photograph here, is of Mr. Ned Blatchington, Lady Rowfont's younger brother—we were talking about the Blatchingtons, you will remember, the night you arrived. Perhaps I shouldn't say so—though it hardly seems an indiscretion after so many years—he wanted to marry me. . . . I won't show you the photograph of us all with King Boris

155

now, Miss Pickford; it is put away somewhere, but remind me. . . .'

Lucky, lucky Miss Bolby, with interesting connections and a talent, and positions in which she had met Royalty, and beauty, the traces of which could still be seen!

Her own things, the photograph of John beside her bed, and John's dog, and the Vicarage at Stonechurch with her father before it and a white patch of light upon his bald head, seemed out of place here. When she opened the far cupboard and found traces of Old Lord Rushford she felt more at ease.

I am as I am because of my dull life, she thought, because of the Vicarage, and Wimbledon, and a brief, bruised love-affair, and posts with respectable elderly solicitors, and years with ageing gentlewomen such as Mrs. Staines-Close, and then the war, and offices again, working with gentlewomen whose work was voluntary when mine was paid and living in 'digs' alone. . . .

She began to wonder what Miss Bolby would think if she knew of her love-affair with John and to feel a little envious of the down-at-heel Lady Pearl's cosy security in a council house in the shelter of a good man's love—Roger Leaming, she thought, must surely be a good man, he had stuck to Lady Pearl through thick and thin.

Miss Pickford shut the door upon the traces of Old Lord Rushford, and avoiding the mirrors, came out from the shadow into the bedside-lamp's glow, determined to make *this* room her own.

On the way to the bathroom Reenie put her head round Jessy's door. Jessy lay at full length, head resting upon clasped hands; she had thrown back the sheet.

"How you doing, Jess?"

"You know, it's a funny thing, Reen, but I don't really care about the Gymkhana any more."

"You mean you're not going to say you're sorry to Miss Bolby?"

Jessy did not answer.

"I suppose you haven't thought of Barby eating her heart out over Crowhurst? And you've forgotten about the sack race and the egg and spoon race, and Ruth and Louisa?"

"Reen, have you ever *been* to a Gymkhana?"

"Not on your life, Jess."

"Then how do you know about it?"

"Haven't you and Barby, to say nothing of Mr. Finch and Ken Woodman and Ruth and Louisa, talked of nothing but the Gymkhana? And what *about* Ken Woodman, and Mr. Finch, and Mrs. Woodman, and the whole bloody village? It's going to fall a bit flat, isn't it, if they all go and none of you take part in it? Jesus Christ! Listen to me talking like an Old Retainer." Reenie had come into the room. She went over to the window and rested her sponge-bag upon the sill.

"What made you go off the Gymkhana, Jess?"

"The war. It's a funny thing, you want a thing desperately and then suddenly you don't want it any more. The war makes it seem silly."

"My godfathers!" said Reenie. *"You'd* feel better if you went along and said you were sorry to Miss Bolby."

"You're all on Miss Bolby's side now and it's not fair."

"I don't like to see all you kids going about looking wretched because you can't ride in the Gymkhana, but it doesn't mean I've changed my mind about Miss Bolby."

Jessy lay for some time in silence.

"Reen, are you in love with Otello?"

Reenie tightened the string of her sponge-bag and took it from the sill. "And what if I am, Jess? It's just too bad. All part and parcel of the bloody war. I should think Miss Bolby would still be up, Jess, settling into her new room."

157

"Writing her letters to India."

"Though it beats me why she's got the State Room."

"Well, it's far enough away, and King Edward slept there."

"Oh, go on! Don't be silly, Jessy," said Reenie.

Jessy heard the water from Reenie's bath gurgle out into the waste. She heard Reenie open and then shut the bathroom door. She heard her pad along the passage and open her bedroom door and say something to Vi. She got up and put on her dressing-gown, but she did not put her feet into Barby's worn cast-off slippers. An errand of apology must be soft-footed and secret, almost a secret from oneself, she thought, it was so indescribably horrid.

She would say in the morning: 'By the way, it's all right about the Gymkhana.' Or she might say nothing at all, she would let it be felt somehow. She began to think how pleased she would feel in the morning, of the eagerness with which Ruth and Louisa would drag out the laundry basket and wind up the gramophone; of Barby's face as she mounted Crowhurst and of Finch's as he held him, and of how the tunes themselves would float out more hopefully over the grass. . . . Then she thought of Miss Bolby in the State Room.

She went over to the window and leaned her elbows upon the sill. Mist reached up from the river, extending long white feelers into the park; it already encircled the elms.

I love Rushford more than anywhere else on earth, she thought; I want never to leave Rushford. I shall never marry. I shall be a great Actress, but I shall have my roots here. I shall be Jessica Rushford. Not the Jessica Rushford who is looking out into the park, but the Jessica Rushford who everyone comes to see.

She heard Bob Woodman's step: long *short*, long *short*, with a creak in it because of his gammy knees. It must be after ten; he has begun his first round, she thought. The uneven rhythm of Bob's step made it easier to face Miss Bolby in the State Room.

She opened her bedroom door. A board creaked as she stepped upon it. A bulb burned feebly at the end of the passage, the stair leading to the passage below was in semi-darkness; it protested feebly against her bare-footed descent. She hurried down the length of the Blue Passage—so-called because of the colour of its carpet—passing dark chests, and doors which hid empty, dust-sheeted rooms, and pictures of tormented souls.

She knocked upon the State Room door.

"Come in!" Miss Bolby sang. If only she would say it, not sing it, Jessy thought.

"What on earth are you doing out of bed at this time of night, Jessy? Come in. Come in, my dear child. Don't stand there with the door open, the room is full of draught. I can't think how King Edward stood it."

Jessy came in, but she did not advance into the dimly lit room. Miss Bolby stood in shadow, beyond the pool of light about the dressing-table lamp; she had been stooping above a half-open drawer: she had not yet undressed; about her shoulders was Sita's shawl.

"Far be it from me to criticise the late Lord Rushford's taste—he did the room up, you know, in honour of King Edward's visit—but it is dark, dark and draughty." She shut the drawer. "The King came for some occasion, I think, a ball."

"A shoot," said Jessy. How could she say she was sorry when Miss Bolby rattled on about the King?

"You know, Jessy, I sometimes wonder if you forget how lucky you are?"

"How, Miss Bolby?"

"You come from a very old historic family."

"Yes, Miss Bolby."

"But you don't always behave as if you did."

159

"No, Miss Bolby."

"You should have been in bed long ago. Why have you come here?"

"I came to say I'm sorry. . . ."

Miss Bolby moved out from the shadow into the pool of light. "Ah! So you *have* come. I thought you would come. I thought you would realise in time, and it has taken a long time, that your will was less strong than mine. Why didn't you come at once like a sensible child? Well, now that you have admitted you are in the wrong, have you lost your tongue?"

"No, Miss Bolby."

"And that is all you have to say, Jessy?"

"Yes, Miss Bolby."

"Well, at least you have said you are sorry, a little reluctantly, so that I have had to drag it out of you, but you have said you are sorry, and that, for you, I must admit, Jessy, is a great deal. But why, may I ask, did you go into Huggley without my permission?"

"Mr. Finch had to go, for a parcel."

"And did you have to go with him? Always with the servants, and you encourage this in the younger children. You seem to prefer the company of your social inferiors. This is a trait in your character which should be discouraged; someday you will find yourself friendless, friendless in your own class, and you will be sorry."

"Do you mean like Lady Pearl?" said Jessy.

"Roger Leaming," said Miss Bolby, "came from quite a good family, he was the grandson of a rector; I'm afraid you rather misunderstood me there, Jessy."

"May I go now, Miss Bolby?"

"Yes, if you are genuinely sorry."

"Yes, Miss Bolby."

"And for this evening, too, I hope. You were nowhere to be found when you were needed; and why did you make

Ruth sneak off to your stepmother to ask permission? You are rather cowardly sometimes, aren't you, Jessy?"

"Ruth isn't a sneak and I'm not a coward. We wanted to go for the run, Miss Bolby."

" 'For the run' sounds very much like Reenie. 'For the drive' would be better. You spend so much time with that girl that soon you will find yourself talking just the way she does, and you are becoming impertinent, just the way she is. To tell you the truth, Jessy, I have a feeling that Reenie won't be with us for very much longer."

"Why, Miss Bolby?"

"She is far too familiar with the prisoners. If and when your father comes home I don't think he will like it."

"But she's not really at all keen on Otello, Miss Bolby. He's not her 'boy-friend'—she just likes him."

"I should hope not indeed, but you only confirm my opinion that the girl ought to go; I have thought for a long time that she was seeing too much of Otello; and 'keen on' and 'boy-friend' are not, by the way, very ladylike phrases. Why is it you are walking about without slippers?"

"I didn't want to make a noise on the stairs."

"You should have come at a sensible hour."

"I thought you'd be busy settling into your new room."

"Ah! My new room. . . . I hope that poor Miss Pickford will be happy in my old room. It makes me very sad to leave Lord Rushford's room, but I thought Miss Pickford would be happier there than here, she is unused to large rooms. Unused to large houses, houses of this sort, and she has had a bad time in London with the flying bombs. I feel very sorry for Miss Pickford."

"Now, may I go, Miss Bolby?"

Becca was asleep when Bob Woodman came into the nursery. He saw that the door was open and that the light was on and one of his duties was to put out lights, though feeble bulbs were left burning in the passages.

Becca sat slumped in a low chair by the fire: the chair in which she had nursed Larry, Jessy and Ruth and Bella. Her large hands lay loosely in her lap: her large feet, fore-shortened, rested upon a stool, so that she seemed all feet and hands and lap. Hair had strayed from a greying bun and had fallen into a figure of eight. In disarray she looked younger than her years, Bob Woodman thought; he remembered her as a painfully-flushing girl from Four Ways Farm.

The creak in his step and his wheezing breath woke her.

"My word, Bob Woodman, you gave me a start!"

"I'm ever so sorry. I didn't see you was asleep, Miss Stroud." Because he had been a boy working in the gardens when she had come to Rushford and until he had become night-watchman had remained an underling, and night-watchman was something at which one arrived by accident and to which one did not rise, he had remained 'Bob Woodman', while she, 'Rebecca', as nursery-maid, had in the course of years become 'Miss Stroud'.

"Not often you catch me sleeping, Bob Woodman. Too many babies through me hands. And how a body *can* sleep with this racket going on, I should like to know." She pointed ceilingwards. When the noise had subsided, Bob said: "With the noise me knees is making tonight, I wonder I didn't wake the dead, Miss Stroud. Things not too good, are they?"

"What things, Bob Woodman?"

"News isn't so good, for one thing, and then all them kids in the sweet queue."

"To tell you the truth, I don't listen to the news no more. 'This is the nine o'clock news, and this is Who-ever-it-is reading it'. . . . I'm fed up with the news. Terrible the way you get used to war. Who told you about those kids in the sweet queue?"

"Reenie."

"Trust Reenie and Ruth for spreading a tale."

"Terrible, though, isn't it?"

"Terrible, Bob Woodman."

"Doesn't look much as if you and me'll last the war out neither."

"Speak for yourself, if you please."

"What with me knees, and the roof falling in."

"Whose roof, Bob Woodman?"

"This roof. It was falling in before the war and it's falling in still, and you and me haven't got no idea what it costs, roofing a place like this, Miss Stroud. Place'll be sold when the war's over."

"Not on your life, Bob Woodman, not while he's in it, not Master Larry—just listen to me!—can't get out of the habit when I'm talking to you or Mr. Finch or some of the old ones. They'll be living in one room before *he'll* sell."

"What, all of them?"

"Well, two rooms, then."

"It's less of an old barn of a place than Bowborough."

"It is that. I wouldn't live at Bowborough, not if you paid me. They say Lord Corwen's in a bad way. Given all his money to the birds. Lord Archie won't never be able to take it on."

"Lot of old crocks like me'll be out of work when these old places go."

"Things is better for some though, the way things are going."

"Better, you mean, than they were?"

"That's what I mean, Bob Woodman."

"Better for some and worse for others."

"Bound to be that, the way human nature is."

"That's what I say, Miss Stroud."

"Mrs. Woodman and Ken all right?"

"Mrs. Woodman's not too good."

"I'm ever so sorry to hear that. Is it her eye again?"

" 'Nother sty. She's afraid she won't be sightly enough to take Ken to the Gymkhana."

"Ken can come with us all right."

"But I thought none of you was going, because of Jessy."

"We'll be going all right. You know what Jessy is. Won't say she's sorry till the last minute. Wilful as a mule, our Jessy, and if it's a battle of wills I'll back Jessy. She'll get round it somehow; she'll beat Miss Bolby, trust Jessy."

"Miss Bolby'll be ringing for a cup of tea in a minute; she generally likes a chat and a cup of tea."

"On with your decorations, then. Out with the red carpet. Tonight, Bob Woodman. Her Ladyship is in the State Room."

3

When the telephone operator told Larry Rushford there would be a two hours delay he felt relieved. Suddenly, and for no explicable reason, he wanted to put more, not less distance between himself and Elizabeth. Not because he did not want to see Elizabeth, but because it was two years since he *had* seen her, and as the meeting drew nearer he became a little afraid of it. How much would she have changed? How much had he? Her letters had told little. Little could be told in an airgraph, and she had seldom answered his questions, or, if she had, he had forgotten them by the time she had answered them. 'Your last letter is upstairs and I'm writing in the Office.' Or : 'I'm writing upstairs and your last letter is somewhere in the Office.' Well, after six years of marriage wives did not carry cold, shiny airgraphs next their hearts, and Rushford had a number of stairs.

And what changes would he find at Rushford? Had they cut the beeches? How often had the beeches made a leafy roof to memory. . . . How often had he looked down upon Rushford with his feet upon last year's leaves through leaves floating and flying towards Rushford, square and squat in

the hollow, flanked by its formal garden and its oval lawn,
with the park spreading out beyond. . . . Each year the
wood-cutters' thuds had come nearer. Had they yet reached
the beeches?

Instead of telephoning he sent a telegram:

'Back arriving 5 10 will make my own way from station
love Larry.'

Then he crossed out 'back'. Homecoming seemed to do
something to the intellect.

He did not want Elizabeth to meet him at the station
because his first sight of Rushford following so closely upon
his meeting with Elizabeth would be more than he could bear.

He almost began to wish he had not come.

He would get out of the taxi—were it possible still to get
a taxi—at the stables, sending it on with his luggage to the
back door. He would come up the back drive because there
was a point in the front drive where something uncomfortable
happened to his heart. . . .

Ruth sat in the swing-seat. By sitting in a curved, almost
supine position she could just reach the ground with her toe;
the seat's motion smoothed out the jarrings of an unsmooth
day. It had begun badly. Breakfast, instead of being a beginning, had been a sort of aftermath of the night.

She had heard Jessy go to Miss Bolby's room last night,
and without waking Louisa she had slipped into Jessy's
bed.

'Is it all right, Jess?'
'Is what all right?'
'Have you said it?'
'Said what?'
'Haven't you been to Miss Bolby?'
'Yes, of course I have.'

165

'Then, did you say it?'

'What do you think I went to Miss Bolby's room for if I didn't say it?'

'There's no need to be so cross, is there?'

'You always spoil everything so.'

Ruth swallowed. When she had control of her voice again she said: 'Was it all right, though?'

'I suppose we're riding in the Gymkhana, if that's what you mean.'

'But didn't she say so?'

Jessy this time, was silent.

'Was she beastly, Jess?'

'Sometimes she *is* beastly. You'd better go now. I want to get into my bed.'

Then, in the morning, when she, Ruth, had told Barby and Louisa that Jessy had said she was sorry, Barby had said in a matter-of-fact way: 'Then it's all right about the Gymkhana. Directly you and Louisa get away from Miss Bolby, you must bring out the gramophone. Today is Wednesday. We've got four more days.'

At breakfast Elizabeth had said: 'I feel worried about Miss Bolby's bracelets. I've been thinking about them all night. I do hope no one has taken them:' and she, Ruth, had said: 'No one could have, no one from outside has been here— except Miss——.' And then Pickford came in and Elizabeth talked of something else and Barby said: 'As it's all right about the Gymkhana, Miss Bolby, couldn't we, just for once, practise all the morning?'

Miss Bolby, about to help herself from the hot-plate, paused. 'I am not at all sure that it *is* all right. I wasn't at *all* pleased with any of your behaviour yesterday, and Jessy was very impertinent last night. It is no good apologising on one hand and being impertinent on the other. I should feel quite differently if I thought Jessy were *truly* sorry. You have all day to practise and it seems to me that an unnecessary fuss is

166

being made about this Gymkhana. However, I am very busy. My mail has arrived from India, so I will let you off this morning.'

'Poor old Finch will be disappointed and the village will be disappointed. We have a great gala always, Miss Bolby, for the Colsall Gymkhana,' Elizabeth said.

Miss Pickford said : 'I have never *been* to a Gymkhana.'

Miss Bolby sat down. 'We will see what the day brings forth, Lady Rushford.'

After breakfast she, Ruth, had gone to fetch the laundry basket and Louisa the gramophone records. The door of the Office had been ajar.

'I'll question the servants, Miss Bolby, and the prisoners. It's hateful, but I quite see I shall have to.'

'It is equally hateful for me, Lady Rushford, to put you in such a position.'

'If we had had strange land girls here, or anything of that sort, but there has been no one strange in the house—except Miss Pickford.'

'And we must naturally count Miss Pickford out.'

'I don't see why. Either all of us or none of us are under suspicion, Miss Bolby.'

'Miss Pickford is a daughter of the late Vicar of Stonechurch, and a gentlewoman, Lady Rushford, and far be it from me to *suggest* that anyone is under suspicion.'

Louisa had come back with the records, and the laundry basket, which she, Ruth, should have dragged out, was still under the stair. She wished she had less facility to overhear. Conversations behind doors became intensified when doors were shut or ajar; they penetrated—took on a new urgency.

There was a tension in the house which seemed to be mounting : Miss Bolby and Jessy were both growing more bad-tempered as Miss Bolby grew more agitated.

The words, 'Run, rabbit, run', had seemed absurd today, harsh and jarring as they had floated out over the grass, rising above the elms, growing more and more absurd, till they seemed to fill the park with harsh sound, letting forth a last shriek of inanity as Louisa bumped against the gramophone so that the needle slipped. Crowhurst and Dove, being ridden in a ceaseless circle by Barby and Jessy, had stopped.

Jessy said: 'It's all so silly, practising for a thing you're probably not going to be able to do. It would serve her jolly well right if we said we didn't *want* to ride in the Gymkhana, said we wouldn't go near the thing.'

Barby said: 'I shall go on practising till the very last minute. I don't care what she says. We shall ride in the Gymkhana.'

Ruth wished again that she had not overheard the conversation in the Office, and that she had not said at breakfast: 'No one from outside has been here except Miss——' because it had sounded as if she, Ruth, had thought that it was Miss Pickford who had taken the bracelets, and, of course, it wasn't, and no one until today had, *in words,* connected Miss Pickford's name with their disappearance, although last night at supper an uncomfortable silence had fallen in the Schoolroom when Miss Pickford had said: 'I am beginning to imagine it is I who must have taken them,' and she and Barby and Jessy and Louisa had looked at their plates, not because they thought she *had,* but because they had known that Miss Bolby thought so.

Words, at this point, snatches of conversation which had flashed before her with the clarity of captions at a foreign film, ceased to be words in Ruth's head; as she rocked in the seat she began to see wordless scenes: King Boris of Bulgaria with Miss Bolby, a different Miss Bolby. And Sita, in a long white gown, reclining upon a deck, on her way to India, and Lady Pearl in the shrubbery with Roger Leaming, and herself and Louisa flying a kite with Roger Leaming who had somehow taken the place of Miss Bolby. . . .

She put out a hand in order to steady herself because she was slipping sideways and her fingers as they grasped the mattress's edge touched something hard and cold. With both hands she lifted a corner of the mattress: Miss Bolby's bracelets leaned like hoops against the seat's side; one, like a coiled snake lay beneath it.

Larry paid off the cab as he had planned. Splashes of cloud were washed into the sky and sunlight bathed the house, turning its bricks to the colour of a pale tea-rose, paling its green copper dome; he could see only the top half of the house as yet, the rest was hidden by a dark hedge of rhododendron. Already this year's leaves were dark, and dark to the touch, coated with Birmingham's smuts. He walked slowly toward a small gate which led through to the front of the house—slowly so that he could better hear and feel the gravel beneath him. He saw Ruth's legs hanging over the swing-seat's edge, but he could not see they were Ruth's—the top half of her body was hidden by the seat's side. The house was silent, partly in shadow: no sound floated out from its open windows. A long shadow fell from the sundial upon the lawn; his retreating taxi had rattled away into the drive.

Where was Elizabeth? Had there been a delay, too, over the telegram so that she had not yet received it? If so, his arrival would be a shock—as if he had wanted to catch her out in some way. . . .

Homecoming was not so joyous after all.

He advanced towards the seat, wishing now that he had telephoned.

Ruth was staring before her, as white-faced as if she had just seen a ghost.

In the excitement of Larry's return Ruth forgot Miss Bolby's bracelets. When she remembered them later she went to the Schoolroom.

Miss Bolby was writing a letter. Sheets, Rushford-headed sheets, Ruth saw, fully covered in her large hand, lay spread upon the table. One of those long letters to India in answer to the morning's mail, Ruth thought.

"Miss Bolby, Larry's back. He's come back, Miss Bolby."

"I know, Ruth. The news has already reached me. I am immensely looking forward to meeting Lord Rushford." She looked down at, and then up from, the letter as if she were reading from it. "You must be glad, Ruth." She said this as if against her will, grudgingly.

"Now that he is back, are you going to let us ride in the Gymkhana, Miss Bolby?"

"There seems no particular reason why I should grant concessions just because your father is back. It will depend upon you, Ruth."

"How, Miss Bolby?"

"On all of you. You have been very insubordinate lately, as if wishing deliberately to antagonise."

I wish she wouldn't use such long words, Ruth thought.

"But Jessy said she was sorry," she said.

"In a very half-hearted, off hand, insolent way."

"But she *was* sorry. I know she was. Truly she was, Miss Bolby. You know how Jessy *hates* saying she's sorry."

"You don't have to tell me that, Ruth. I don't want to disappoint your father, but at the same time I don't want to make any rash promises. We shall have to see about the Gymkhana."

"Yes, Miss Bolby." Ruth smothered a desire to ask if the letter was to India, then she said : "Miss Bolby, would it make any difference if I found your bracelets?"

"What on earth do you mean, Ruth?"

"I mean *then*, would you let us ride in the Gymkhana?"

"The two matters are entirely separate and you know perfectly well that they are. I see no connection whatever.

Are you insinuating that I am forbidding you to go to the Gymkhana now because I have lost them?"

"No, Miss Bolby." Ruth was a little hazy as to the meaning of the word 'insinuating'.

"Then what, exactly, do you mean, Ruth?"

"I thought that perhaps if you found them you'd be in a better mood."

Miss Bolby rose. She held firmly to the table with both hands. They were ugly hands with many rings upon them and the veins stood out, notched and swollen, as if all her anger had gone to her hands.

"You are very insolent, Ruth, as insolent as Jessy. You think because you are a Rushford, because you belong to an old historic family, you can be insolent to those who are forced through circumstances to earn their living. You will have to learn to behave differently. You won't get very far in life if that is your attitude. Never in all my born days have I known such insolence. None of my other pupils, even in houses I have been forced to frequent in Birmingham, have ever behaved with such insolence. How *dare* you be so insolent? How *dare* you?" She let go the table and sat down. Ruth saw that she was an old woman.

Miss Bolby was different when her hands were hidden. Ruth felt hollow, as if she had been hit, lashed for something she had not done with a hidden whip, yet somehow it did not hurt because Miss Bolby was an old woman whose anger had drained from her face, leaving a waxy pallor and traces of beauty which Ruth saw but did not recognise as such. Not knowing what else to say, she said: "I'm sorry, Miss Bolby."

Miss Bolby brought her hands back on to the table, gathering together the closely covered sheets.

I hate her, Ruth thought, looking at the hands, because she hates Jessy. When she says she'll let us ride in the Gymkhana I'll let her have her bracelets.

"It's so *exciting*!" said Miss Pickford. "So awfully, extremely *exciting*! Just fancy! Lady Rushford thought he wouldn't turn up and he's back. Not like a lord at all, so young and sunburned. You must be ever so excited!" She seemed to radiate excitement.

Barby and Jessy, and Ruth and Louisa—in the Schoolroom for supper as a treat because Larry was back—were silent.

Miss Bolby said: "The sun is hotter in Italy, Miss Pickford. I have had the good fortune to have met Lord Rushford already. Lady Rushford introduced us when we met in the hall. Have none of you children anything to say upon your father coming back? No one could more assiduously advocate restraint than myself, but too little show of feeling will never make you a great Actress, Jessy."

"I don't see how we're all going to get round the Big Table when Lord and Lady Archie and Lord Corwen come to lunch tomorrow," said Ruth.

"Someone will have to sit at the little one," said Louisa.

"Who did you say was coming, dear?" said Miss Pickford.

"Lord and Lady Archie and Lord Corwen, our neighbours, about whom I have already told you, Miss Pickford," said Miss Bolby.

"It's lucky for me Lady Rushford does so much of her correspondence by telephone. I shouldn't know how to address the envelopes to all these people," said Miss Pickford.

"You don't exactly correspond by telephone, do you?" said Barby.

"Miss Pickford meant communicate, Barby," said Miss Bolby.

"Well, you know what I mean, Miss Bolby. I never do know what I mean unless I've got it all down in shorthand before me."

"That's where you're so clever, Miss Pickford. Very few of us can say *that*," said Miss Bolby.

172

"Will it be Barby and Jessy and you, Miss Bolby, or will it be Miss Pickford and Louisa and me who will sit at the Little Table?" said Ruth.

"Miss Pickford is very shy, she might prefer to sit at the Little Table. Am I not right, Miss Pickford?" said Miss Bolby.

"Well, it's just that I don't always hear very well, Miss Bolby, but I'd awfully *like* to meet Lord and Lady Archie and Lord Corwen."

"You're not nearly as deaf as Lord Corwen, really you're not, Miss Pickford," said Jessy.

Miss Bolby opened the State Room window. Mist advanced across the park; it forced its feelers through the balustrade. She felt its cold damp breath upon her hair; it stirred the magnolia so that the great leaves lifted. Her thoughts strayed towards the dark protuberance which held light, and warmth, and love, because it held Larry and Elizabeth.

As her eyes, growing accustomed to the darkness, traced the jutting mass which threw shadow into it at the house's further end, balancing the State Room, a thin strip of light pierced it—the accidental movement of a curtain. She waited, watching for it to be righted, but it remained, a vivid horizontal ray, piercing a total darkness.

Did they not know? Had they forgotten that light must not be shown? Were they too occupied with love?

Miss Bolby withdrew her head and drew the curtain, then she switched on her own light. She had not yet undressed. Somehow in the State Room it was not easy to undress; the truth of the matter was that she was not easy in the State Room. She wished now that she had let matters rest, had let Miss Pickford have the State Room.

Ruth had hit upon the truth, she was taking it out on the children because she had lost her bracelets and because she had begun to suspect Miss Pickford.

Suspicion is taking hold of me, she thought. I must control it, take hold of it. Keep my head.

She switched out the light and wrapped herself more firmly in Sita's shawl, and as though drawn by some force she could not resist, drew back the curtain so that she could look through the window again. The light from Larry's and Elizabeth's room pierced the darkness steadily, its narrowness seemed to give it fiercer intensity. So strong was the desire to go down the Blue Passage and through the swing doors which led to the far wing where the light burned, and knock on the door, saying : 'Forgive me for disturbing you, but a light is showing,' so that the falling words would instantly disrupt the harmony within, that she had already reached her own door when a cold voice inside seemed to say : 'It would not be ladylike to do such a thing; it is the kind of thing Miss Pickford would do.' She rang instead for Bob Woodman and switched the light on again and got into a dressing-gown so as to set further temptation aside. She re-wrapped Sita's shawl about the dressing-gown and put the eiderdown over her knees. Advance waves of mist had brought a chill into the room. She waited in the armchair for Bob. The fringe of bobbles which fell beneath its chintz cover brushed against her bare heels—a remnant of a past era.

King Edward must have sat just as she was sitting now, in this chair.

And others had sat, before removing their finery, while a maid or valet hovered, and floating up from the ballroom below came the last strains of a waltz—dying notes, bewailing the dying night, and a grinding of wheels and a rustle of skirts and a shutting of doors; then the first call of a thrush and the last lament of an owl. . . .

Had she been a great singer or married as well as Sita, she too might have heard these sounds : not from the Schoolroom, woken from a cold uncomfortable sleep, cramped in a chair because she could not bring herself to go to bed while others

174

were festive, while servants watched, hidden behind pillars, from the gallery or the top of the stair—she, the Governess, could not very well watch with the servants—but from a room such as this. . . .

She looked up and caught sight of herself in the mirror, a little shrunken figure in a flannel dressing-gown, sitting as the figure she feared to see so often sat, in a dark pool of distance, its face a pale blur, insignificant in a spacious room, a little shrunken figure, half its normal size.

A failure, who had not lived fully in any sphere—who had always lived upon the fringe.

So intent was she upon the figure that she had not been warned by his wheezing breath or his creaking knees of Bob's approach. She was startled by his knock.

"Come in!" With the sound of her own voice the figure in the mirror seemed to swing back into normality; as it enlarged, the room's spaciousness seemed to diminish. 'You have no need to feel inferior,' it seemed to say; 'you are a Bolby.'

"Good evening, Miss. You rang, Miss?"

For an instant she had forgotten why she had rung for Bob. "Ah, yes, Bob. Good evening, Bob. I rang because I saw a light showing. It is difficult to tell in such total darkness from which window it comes, but it looks like Lady Rushford's room, and I felt it my duty to report it."

"Trust me to find a light. I'm just setting off on a round now, Miss. Not that it's doing much 'arm, if you ask me. Jerry's a bit too busy in other directions to go bothering about the Murky Midlands. Mighty thankful we ought to be we've had our turn and them infernal buzz bombs can't reach us."

"Certainly, Bob, but I feel, all the same, that you should go into the matter of the light."

"Maybe it's Miss Pickford's room. She's forever opening windows so as the curtains gets pulled back. Always after air. She'd 've been better in this room, if you ask me."

"I think she would have felt uneasy in it, Bob. When one is used to small rooms, furnished rooms which are vulgarly known as 'digs', I mean, such a large room with so much history attached to it is, to say the least of it, a little overwhelming. I suppose you hardly remember the momentous occasion of King Edward's visit, Bob?"

"I was only a lad at the time, Miss. I remember watching 'im drive away, though. And me father was in the Gardens then, and I remember 'im telling about the ivy on the photograph frames, trailing from one to another like. Plenty of frames there was about too, and palms right up to the ceiling. None of your modern stuff in the late Lord Rushford's day. All the fal-da-lals were burned in the Fire. But Fred Finch is the one you ought to ast, Miss. It was Fred Finch who met the King at the station with all 'is retinoo."

"I shall make a special journey to the stables tomorrow in order to do so, Bob."

"Planes not so busy tonight, Miss."

"The mist, I suppose, is keeping them off, and we need a little respite. Their continual approach seems to set up a nervous tension. Sometimes I find it more trying than the blitz itself."

"Miss Pickford must find it a bit trying, coming as she does from London, I should think." Bob shook his head; unlike the rest of his body it did not protest.

"It's splendid news, Lord Rushford being back, Bob. A house is always better with a man in it, I think."

"You could have knocked me down with a feather when Mrs. Woodman come in and says, 'Good news for once, and you'll never guess what, Bob.' Never thought I'd see Master Larry, as Miss Stroud and me privately calls 'im, alive again. Makes you wonder these days when you see someone alive, don't it? Now, I suppose, the young ladies will be riding in the Gymkhana?"

"That, Bob, depends solely upon the young ladies. I think

you should go and enquire into the matter of the light in case it distracts one of our own incoming bombers. We don't want one crashing into the house, do we?"

"I should think not, indeed. Tonight, of all nights!" Bob gave a little chuckle which seemed to come huskily up from deep in his chest as if strangulated by the wheeze there.

"I think you should go at once, Bob."

"O.K., Miss."

Even the manners of old servants were deteriorating. No servant in Lord Rowfont's house—had such an expression been in use—would have said O.K. Whenever addressing her, Roona, whatever advantage had been taken, whatever insolence intended, servants—who had been servants and not sluts, as Elsie, or war-time make-shifts as Reenie, had kept up a semblance of respectfulness. It was disappointing of Bob. She had liked Bob, but Bob had been singularly disappointing tonight; there were odd gaps in his memory, and all he had been able to talk about tonight was ivy, and he should not have said 'Tonight, of all nights' so suggestively. Her thoughts strayed back to the room where the light was.

The late Lord Rushford's room was below Elizabeth's, so that Miss Pickford could not see the horizontal ribbon of light, but her thoughts, too, strayed to the room above.

They are together, they are lost together in love, she thought.

She looked at the photograph of John, and it meant nothing.

I am nothing, she thought, because I have lived without love. My brief love with John was too brief and bewildering to be love.

She looked out into the park, it rolled away into darkness; it gave no such reassurance as the formal garden had, and she did not hear Bob Woodman's step. She felt she was alone in a dark world. But upstairs, there is love, she thought, and love brings forth goodness. I would rather have had my love with John than no love.

"I can't think, Larry, why you didn't telephone."

"I thought a telegram might be less disturbing."

"It might have, if I had received it." Elizabeth brushed her hair before the dressing-table mirror. It fell to her shoulders. As burnished as the copper which hung in the kitchen, Larry thought. It sent off a light sizzling into the pool of space between them. He would have liked to brush it himself, but he made no move to do so. He sat deep in an armchair.

"I'm awfully sorry, darling, but the fault wasn't mine, I particularly didn't want to come without giving you some sort of warning."

Though Elizabeth thought, she did not say: 'Anyhow, I'm glad you're back, Larry.' She said instead: "I'm afraid you'll find the most ghastly muddle in the Office."

"What about the new secretary, Miss What's-her-name?"

"She has only been here a few days and she doesn't seem to have got into her stride. You've no idea how difficult it is to get a secretary these days."

"Well, for goodness' sake don't let's worry about the Office. What about the beeches, I haven't been up there yet. Have they cut the beeches?" He did not say, 'I couldn't look, I hadn't the courage.'

"No, the ones near the house are still there. We may be able to save them yet. By the way, Larry, Lord Corwen and Lord and Lady Archie are coming to lunch tomorrow. I don't suppose you'll want to see them the moment you've got back. I'll put them off, if you'd rather."

"No, I'd like to. I always like seeing Lady Archie."

"All men do."

"Is something wrong . . .?"

"Nothing, only Lady Archie has become rather absurd lately."

How little she has changed, Larry thought.

"And she's as thick as thieves with Squadron Leader Langford."

"What's the matter with Squadron Leader Langford?"

"Nothing, only he's frightfully common."

"You musn't run away with the idea that everyone in the Forces is common."

"Well, it's all very different from Father's day, and I get irritated by Lady Archie and her attempts at democracy and modernity, she goes to the other extreme. By the way, can you, by any chance, remember the name of Lady Archie's lover?"

"Which one?"

"The one there was all the scandal about, 'Harry's friend'."

"No, it's gone from me, that shows how long I've been away. Why do you ask, darling?"

"No particular reason. I was just wondering. . . . Poor Lady Archie, she must have been a great trial to Lord Vallance in her young days."

"She was. Father always said he forgave her for all the scandals, but he never got over her being a suffragette—but why in heaven's name are we sitting here discussing Lady Archie?"

Bob Woodman advanced into the mist, reluctant to leave the warmth of the house behind him. It closed in about him, swathing the dark mass. It drifted about his head and forced its way into his lungs so that his breath came faster, in little short gasps, fighting at odds against floating vaporous wreaths. His uneven tread was muffled by grass as he walked into a filmy wall in order to be better able to survey the house. Miss Bolby was right about the light; it hung, vertically suspended, a bright ribbon in a dark wall. No doubt she knew, too, where it came from—that was why she had sent him out to look for it; clear as day, it was now. Wanted to spoil the fun she hadn't had, that was what that was. Damned if I'm going to say nothing about *that* light, he thought. The little rasping chuckle forced its way up again. Interfering old bitch, spoiling others' fun, he said.

4

"There is no marmalade; which of you has eaten all the marmalade?" said Larry.

No one answered. Only Larry and the children were in the room. Larry got up to ring the bell.

"It's rationed," said Ruth.

"I know perfectly well it's rationed, Ruth. I haven't been to the North Pole, but that doesn't explain why there's none left. You can't have eaten a whole week's ration between you this morning. It's not very good manners to clear the board before everyone else is down. Which of you finished the marmalade?" Larry went over to the hot-plate where the coffee stood. "And there is no coffee. Why is there no coffee? The one thing I've been looking forward to for weeks is my morning coffee; for weeks I've pictured brown jugs steaming and all I see are dregs of tepid mud. What on earth is the matter with you all this morning? And why isn't Miss Bolby down, and does Miss Pickford usually have breakfast first and drink all the coffee?"

"She goes out early to get air," said Ruth.

"But where is Miss Bolby? The object of a governess is to keep order, surely?"

"She is late because of her insomnia," said Ruth.

"And can none of you speak this morning, except Ruth?"

Barby said: "Today is Thursday. There are three more days before the Gymkhana."

"You say it, Barby, as if it were a sort of death knell."

"It is," said Ruth. "Miss Bolby won't let us ride in it, and it isn't Jessy's fault, she said she was sorry."

Then the bracelets, coiled, curved gold rings came between her and the breakfast table. "But she'll change her mind I'm sure she will." She felt Barby's and Jessy's and Louisa's eyes simultaneously turn upon her, as if they knew that everything hung upon her now, in place of Jessy.

Intermittently, since she had found them, a number of questions concerning the bracelets had tormented her. If, when Miss Bolby came down, she said: 'I have made up my mind now, you may ride in the Gymkhana," she, Ruth, would go to the swing-seat when no one was looking and collect the bracelets and take them to Miss Bolby as if she had just found them. Then she thought: But this is deceitful, and though Miss Bolby says I am, I have never been deceitful. It would be a little difficult to go cold-bloodedly to the swing-seat and get them now; she would feel it was her fault in some way that they were there. Then she thought of the savage look she had seen on Miss Bolby's face when she had said to Jessy: 'Too little show of feeling will never make you a great Actress, Jessy.' The words 'assiduously advocate', whatever that meant, had been mixed up in the sentence and Miss Bolby had said them with a sort of relish, as if she had been sticking a pin into a ripe plum and the plum had been Jessy.

"I'm glad Miss Bolby keeps some sort of discipline," said Larry, "but it seems a shame if you can't ride in the Gymkhana. Old Finch will be so disappointed, perhaps I can persuade her by playing hard on the returning father. I do wish, though that you'd leave me a little marmalade. Is Miss Pickford a great coffee-drinker?"

"Early risers often are. I hope you'll forgive me for being a little late, the mornings are a great trial. Good morning, Lord Rushford. Just as one gets off to sleep one is disturbed by an incoming bomber."

181

"One of our own, which is something, though. Good morning, Miss Bolby. I'm afraid there's no coffee, and Benn doesn't seem to answer the bell. Ring again, will you, Jessy?"

"Why are you ringing the bell, Jessy," said Elizabeth as she came in.

"I'm afraid I told her to," said Larry.

"It's no good ringing bells, Larry. Benn only stays on condition that he doesn't have to answer bells, it's too much of a strain on his lumbago. One of the children must go to the kitchen. What is it you want, Larry?"

"I can't see the point of having servants if you do all the work yourself. There's no coffee."

"But it's the only way you can keep servants. You don't seem to realise things have got worse since you've been away. Why is there no coffee? Miss Pickford must have taken it all, she comes down early. Go and get some more coffee, Barby."

"*And* marmalade," said Larry. "Why does Miss Pickford take the air so early?"

"She is a little eccentric, poor thing, and a little deaf. I think she finds meals difficult, she doesn't hear half of what we say."

"May not the root of the matter be that Miss Pickford is perhaps, not quite, in the strict sense, a gentlewoman, Lady Rushford?" said Miss Bolby.

"She says she is," said Larry. "When I was tidying out the Office this morning I found her letter."

"How irritating of you, Larry, I've been looking for it for days. What were you doing in the Office? I told you it was in a muddle and I didn't mean you to see it until it was in some sort of order."

"It's remarkable for its disorder at present, darling."

"One must remember that Miss Pickford has had a very bad time," said Miss Bolby.

Barby came in with the coffee on a small round tray.

"You've forgotten the marmalade," said Larry.

"Oh — !" said Barby.

A calm seemed suddenly to have fallen upon a choppy sea; into it Larry said: "On the whole, Barby, less unsuitable words might be found for use at the breakfast table. It isn't so much the words you use, it's when and where you use them."

"Sorry, it just came out. Reenie says it. Is it a very bad word, Larry."

"Mr. Finch said it when he couldn't get Crowhurst into the horse-box," said Ruth; "it means——"

"We don't wish to hear what it means, Ruth," said Miss Bolby.

"When I'm old enough I shall live with a man, I shall never marry," said Jessy.

"Jessica——" began Miss Bolby.

"Why, Jessy? It seems rather irrelevant," said Larry.

"Oh, well, I don't know, you keep your own name and it's more jolly, and there wouldn't be any of these hateful breakfasts. I hate breakfast. I think breakfast's horrible, and I want to keep my own name. I want always to be Jessica Rushford."

"The *great* Jessica Rushford," said Barby.

"Oh, shut up, Barby," said Jessy.

"Actresses don't marry," said Ruth.

"Yes, they do, you silly fool, only they keep their own name," said Jessy.

"Girls! Girls!" said Miss Bolby. "I feel greatly distressed, Lord Rushford. Clearly some obnoxious influence is at work."

"If you mean Reenie," said Barby, "she's not obnoxious."

"Who is Reenie?" said Larry.

"The kitchen-maid, only she's not really a kitchen-maid."

183

"She was in the A.T.S. and then in a bar and then an usherette and she loves Otello only he's not her boy-friend," said Ruth.

"Ruth, please! I'm sure Lord Rushford doesn't wish to hear all this, and it's time we left the table," said Miss Bolby.

"What about the Gymkhana?" said Barby.

"You said you'd persuade Miss Bolby you were our father, Larry," said Louisa.

"We will discuss the Gymkhana later. Try to think before you speak in future, Louisa," said Miss Bolby. "I am sorry, Lord Rushford, for this exhibition, but one must endeavour to be lenient, as General Sir Arthur Atherton-Broadleigh used to say."

"Good God! Miss Bolby's got it, got it in one and it's been worrying me all night," said Larry.

"Got what?" said Elizabeth.

"Arthur, Arthur Atherton-Broadleigh, 'Harry's friend', Lady Archie's lover."

"Did *Lady Archie* have a lover?" said Jessy.

"She is supposed to have had many. She was a great fascinator, Lady Archie."

"Was she beautiful?" said Barby.

"A deadly wielder of a sunshade, I should think. But she was already getting on a bit when she went off with Lord Archie—that was after Arthur. Father used to tell the story so well. They were all staying with Lord Vallance, and Fred Finch drove them to the station. Before that she had a Colonel Somers in tow, who was after her money. He followed her for years and they used to come here together. When he had gone through it all she found Arthur—Arthur was Harry's friend, a son of the Dean of Waterbury. It all comes back to me vividly now. It was one of the scandals of the time, and poor Arthur was sent to India where he married a——"

"Larry!" said Ruth, who watched anger contort Miss

Bolby's face and tranfer itself to her hands. "Larry! Stop! Arthur is Miss Bolby's General. . . ."

Miss Bolby rose; with both hands she held on to the table. Ruth felt the tremor of the cloth as anger pulsated in them and the veins swelled. Miss Bolby's voice, when she spoke, was singularly melodious, as if anger, smothered so that her words might be sweet and cool, revenged itself upon her hands. Six pairs of eyes watched her as the sentences rose and fell.

"Lord Rushford, I wish to inform you that the woman who married Arthur, Arthur Atherton-Broadleigh, General *Sir* Arthur Atherton-Broadleigh, is my sister Sita, and that they met in the house of Lord Chipperfield, under the auspices of Lady Pearl Throughfell, with whom my sister Sita became friends on the voyage out to India. I myself knew the Atherton-Broadleigh family. I visited the Dean and Lady Alice at Waterbury before my sister Sita's marriage and I have never, never, then, or since, on any occasion, heard any breath of scandal connected with Arthur. The fact that there was none, I think, can be corroborated by the present Lord Rowfont, whose family also knew the Dean. Therefore, Lord Rushford, I regret to say that I cannot sit here listening to scandal, nothing more than vile malicious gossip—if I may say so—and allow insults to be directed at my sister Sita. You must excuse me, Lord Rushford, this has been a great shock to me. I feel extremely unwell."

"Larry," said Elizabeth, "what on earth made you embark upon *that* saga?"

"You asked me last night, you know, who Lady Archie's lover was."

"I know, but I didn't expect you to pour the story out like that, and before the children, too."

"It won't hurt the children. Children can't be kept in cotton wool these days and I thought they'd enjoy the story. It's pretty rotten for them not being able to ride in the Gymkhana. It all came back to me when she said the name Atherton-Broadleigh. Lady Archie's past has always fascinated me and I let it all out somehow."

"It was foolish of me not to have remembered. Ever since Miss Bolby has been here the name has worried me, and I couldn't think why. If I'd only known last night I could have warned you. Now she'll leave, of course, and I don't see how we can ask her to sit at the same table as Lady Archie at lunch. I was going to put her at the big table and Miss Pickford at the little table with Ruth and Louisa; I thought she and Lady Archie could have hobnobbed together about India, and now this upsets everything. It's really very tiresome of you, Larry. I thought everything would be easier once you came back."

"In fact you don't seem very pleased I'm back."

"Oh, nonsense, darling."

They sat for some time in silence. Bacon-fat had congealed upon the children's plates.

"I suppose we had better move," Elizabeth said, "so that Benn can clear."

"Benn must wait today."

"But we are three extra for lunch."

"Then the three extra must wait for lunch."

"You're in a very bellicose mood, Larry."

"No, darling, but it's my first day home and I mean to enjoy it, that's all."

"You're not going to let the question of the Gymkhana rest with Miss Bolby, are you?"

"To tell you the truth, I don't feel much like interfering with Miss Bolby. Who generally makes the final decisions about the children?"

"Miss Bolby. I have so much else to contend with."

"You'll have less now that I'm back."

"I hope so, but not if you sit all day over breakfast and

upset the servants. I think Miss Bolby is being a little unfair about the Gymkhana."

"Let's see what happens later in the day. She may have gone by this evening. Poor Miss Bolby! She must have been a beauty at some time or other. I think I see why Arthur fell for Sita. But something pretty awful must have happened to make her so sweetly sour."

"Or an accumulation of little things. She was to have been a singer, but when her father died there was no money. She sings remarkably well. When she sings the prisoners pick up the air and Italian opera floats between the gardens and the house."

"Then let's make her sing."

"You'd far better leave well alone, Larry."

"You know, you've been shut up with all these women for far too long, darling."

"I know, Larry. And these bombers perpetually bearing down upon the house sometimes get on one's nerves."

"I can believe it. They've got on mine already. Elizabeth, you *are* glad I'm back?"

"Of course, darling."

"Am I allowed to ring the bell as a signal to Benn that the meal is over?"

Larry felt adrift when he left the breakfast table. Purposeless: although there was plenty to be done, to do it, somehow, would be to take something from Elizabeth; in spite of the muddle in the Office, she seemed so adequately to have filled the gap made by his absence.

He pushed open the Office door. Miss Pickford sat at the typewriter with her back to him. Chang-Kai-Shek was on her knee; Eleanor and Doushka lay curled in the letter basket and she tapped away merrily—or so it seemed. She did not hear him come in, and he felt he was intruding and shut the door.

187

He went to the morning-room, *his* room. It was as dust-sheeted as it had been yesterday, only yesterday it had seemed to say: 'I am the only room which has mourned you.' He had half-hoped to find it freed from its shrouds, awakening, as it were: now its silent emptiness seemed to resent him, as if he had been neglectful.

Caught as if by a searchlight in the sun's slant, dust undulated towards him from the window. There was an essence in the room so strong that it made him sneeze: a concentration of carpet and furniture long confined together. Stifled by its presence, yet reluctant to let it go, he opened a window: through it, rasping feebly, their first impact already dissipated, came the words, '*Run*, rabbit, *run*, rabbit, run, run, run. . . .' He saw Barby and Jessy circling upon Dove and Crowhurst, and Ruth and Louisa crouched upon the grass beside a laundry basket upon which was drunkenly perched a gramophone; they were intent with a fearful urgency.

He heard the door open behind him.

"Excuse me, Lord Rushford, I've come to take the covers off. Winnie's kids are ill again and she can't get up from the village. Seems a shame you should be all covered up when you get home. Nicest room in the house, too, sort of cosy. Just give me a hand, Lord Rushford, and we'll have them off in two shakes of a lamb's tail."

"Thanks awfully, I——"

"Just in case you don't know, I'm Reenie."

"How do you do, Reenie?" said Larry.

"Pleased to meet you, Lord Rushford. I'm ever so glad you're back."

"Thanks awfully," said Larry.

"Listen to those kids," said Reenie; "seems a shame they can't ride in the Gymkhana."

"They may yet," said Larry.

"That's the stuff; you put your foot down, now that you're back."

"You're right, I will, Reenie."

Reenie gathered together the folded covers.

"Time I was off, or Mrs. Williams'll be screaming her head off in the kitchen, what with Lord and Lady Meredith and Lord Corwen coming. Bye-bye, Lord Rushford."

"Thanks awfully, Reenie," said Larry. "Bye-bye."

After Miss Bolby she is like a sea breeze, he thought. Thank God there is still someone sane and whole in the house. Thank God for Reenie.

"All set, Hughie?" said Lady Archie.

"All *what,* my dear?" said Lord Corwen.

"In other words, my dear Hughie, Archie is waiting and the car is at the door."

"I wish you'd talk in good plain English instead of jargon. What have you got in your hat, my dear? It looks like the corner of a conservatory."

"What you see, my dear Hughie, is a garden rose and a frond of fern. I'm tired of transferring the trimmings of my winter felt to my summer straw. I do wish you'd sometimes spend a little money on something besides the birds. The roof and I have to suffer so. Elizabeth, by the way, says they're having trouble with the Rushford roof and they're having to sell some of the beeches."

"It will break Larry's heart to cut the beeches," said Lord Corwen.

"All our hearts are breaking. Cracking, crumbling, slowly disintegrating, like our houses—the Crumbling Aristocracy. I feel singularly crumbly today. Hurry up, Hughie, I'm hungry."

"May I come in, Miss Bolby?"

"Please don't feel you must knock upon the Schoolroom door, Miss Pickford. No one ever knocks upon the Schoolroom door except the servants."

189

"I thought I'd come along so that I could go down to the dining-room with you. I feel a little—well—you know, Miss Bolby—shy."

"When one meets few people one becomes shy. I well understand what you mean, Miss Pickford. Let me look at you, children; are you tidy?"

"Who is going to sit at the Little Table?" said Ruth.

"We are agreed it shall be Miss Pickford, are we not, Miss Pickford? The Big Table, as I well know, is something of an ordeal when one is shy. Unless, of course, Miss Pickford particularly wishes to meet Lord Corwen and Lord and Lady Archie, in which case she had better sit at the Big Table. Conversation with the Big Table is not very easy if one is at the Little Table, and I have no particular wish to renew *my* acquaintance with Lady Archie, and I feel Miss Pickford will be happier at the Little Table. Are you all ready now to go down?"

"You know Miss Bolby, Lady Archie. And this is Miss Pickford, who is helping us in the Office," said Elizabeth. *"This is Miss Pickford, Lord Corwen."*

"A little sherry, Miss Bolby?" said Larry.

"Thank you, Lord Rushford."

"A little sherry for you, Miss Pickford?"

"Thanks *ever* so much, Lord Rushforth."

"Can't I persuade you to change your mind, Lady Archie?"

"Drink before luncheon goes to my head," said Lady Archie.

"Which is the object of drink, my dear," said Lord Archie.

"In fact, if it hadn't been for drink, or rather Barrington, Archie and I would never have got together, would we, Archie? But I like to keep my head, don't you, Miss Bolby?"

" 'If you can keep your head . . .' Lady Archie," said Miss Bolby.

"Very fine sherry, Larry," said Lord Corwen.

"Does drink make you feel more cheerful?" said Barby.

"More *what*?" said Lord Corwen, and then, under cover of an incoming aircraft: "Cheerful? Yes, of course it does, my dear child. Tearful and cheerful, eh, Larry?"

"Bring your drinks in with you," said Elizabeth.

They filed into the dining-room.

"Now, how shall we sit?" said Elizabeth. "Let me see. Perhaps Miss Pickford will sit with us, and we'll put Miss Bolby at the Little Table with Ruth and Louisa. I'm sure Miss Bolby won't mind, and Miss Pickford hasn't met Lord and Lady Archie and Lord Corwen before. Will you sit on Lord Corwen's other side, Miss Pickford? And then you, Jessy. And Barby, you had better sit on the other side of Lord Archie."

"Hughie," said Lady Archie, "just look at the silver!" In an aside to Larry she said: "A little competition is a good thing. Hughie has taken the silver on, it keeps his mind off his worries and makes a change from the birds."

Aloud she said: "We ought to be drinking Larry's health. Pour a little of your sherry into my glass, Larry. Here's how!"

Ruth, at the Little Table, said: "What does it mean, Miss Bolby, 'Here's how'?"

Jessy, at the Big Table, said to Miss Pickford: "She's got it wrong, hasn't she?"

Louisa, at the Little Table, said: "Poor Picksie, I'll bet she's shy. Lord Corwen won't hear a word she says."

Elizabeth thought: I have made a foolish mistake. I shouldn't have put Miss Pickford next to Lord Corwen.

"So you're a new arrival, eh, Miss Pickford?" boomed Lord Corwen.

"Pardon, Lord Corwen?"

"Deaf, too? Well, own up to it, Madam. Why mind? Don't be shy about it. Be bold. It makes so much easier for the other fellow. There'll be some more aircraft over in a minute, and they're a help, ain't they? Give me a nice noise and I'll defy you to find me at fault with a syllable."

"But we oughtn't to be *thankful* for them, ought we, Lord Corwen, when they're so evil?"

"Evil? Why evil? They're defending the country and aiding the deaf. What's evil about them?"

"But they must be evil when they cause tumult and terror and death."

"All machines are evil, if it comes to that, my dear woman. Look at the motor car. Plenty of deaths caused by that."

"Not so many though, surely, Lord Corwen."

"Not much difference in peace-time, if you ask me. I'm not talking about war. What the machine has done to war is another kettle of fish."

"That's what I mean, Lord Corwen. They're evil."

"It isn't *they* that are evil, my dear woman, it's war."

"Oh, I'm *so* glad you think so, Lord Corwen. I've always been against war."

"All the same," said Lord Corwen, "if I had my way I wouldn't have a motor car."

"As machines are a part of progress, I suppose they are with us for ever," said Elizabeth.

"Hughie doesn't believe in progress; if he did he'd tile the roof. Mushrooms are beginning to grow in the hall. How is your roof, Larry? I hear you are selling the beeches," said Lady Archie.

"They're gradually being taken, whether I want to sell or not, but I shall fight for the ones above the house. I'd almost rather sacrifice the roof than the beeches. I went up this morning to have a look at the damage. Truncated trees do something terrible to me."

"I know, it's horrible. To see them is to wound the soul," said Lady Archie.

At the Little Table Ruth said: "Birds steal things, don't they, Miss Bolby?"

"What birds, Ruth? Don't sprawl in your chair."

"Rooks, for instance?"

"Lord Corwen is the ornithologist. When there is a silence at the Big Table I will ask Lord Corwen," said Miss Bolby.

"Eh? What are you young ones talking about?" said Lord Corwen. Miss Bolby's clear enunciation and the high key of Ruth's voice had come across to him with clarity.

"With your great knowledge of birds, Lord Corwen, perhaps you can tell us whether rooks are thieves? Or whether it is solely the magpie?"

"Rooks? Thieves? Nonsense, Madam. What are children taught these days? Professor Middlewitch's book on birds is a good one. That'll tell you all about rooks and magpies."

"I bet that was Ruth's question," said Jessy.

Ruth wished she had been silent. Lord Corwen looked like a rook, she thought. He was like a rook the way he craned his neck forward. His voice was like a rook's. It fell the way the rooks' voices fell when they dived into the elms. *'War!'* he had cried, just like the rooks, and in the next sentence his voice had fallen, just like the rooks. Rooks flew above the swing-seat on their way to the elms. Bella sat in the swing-seat imitating them. Could it be not the rooks but *Bella who had taken the bracelets?* "Will you excuse me, Miss Bolby?" she said. "It's frightfully important. It's something I've got to ask Bella."

"Certainly not, Ruth. There is a luncheon party. You must wait until after luncheon. You can't behave just anyhow, you know, because you are sitting at the Little Table. Supposing there was someone very important at the Big Table? Royalty, for instance, as there frequently was at Rowfont?"

"King Boris?" said Louisa.

"When King Boris came the girls and I *were asked to the Big Table.* Anything you have to say to Bella, Ruth, can perfectly well wait until after luncheon."

"We've heard none of your adventures yet, Larry, and nothing about Italy," said Lady Archie, "and there are so many questions I want to ask. Is there anything left, for instance, of the Scala, in Milan?"

"I can't tell you that, Lady Archie, but in the meantime we can stage a little opera for you here. Miss Bolby, you know, is a singer, and I'm sure she'll sing for us, won't you, Miss Bolby? And we'll get hold of the prisoners."

"Well said, Larry. By getting the prisoners to entertain us, we shall entertain the prisoners. So few seem to think that prisoners, poor things, need entertaining. By all means let us entertain the prisoners."

"When you were a suffragette, Lady Archie," said Jessy, "how did you tie yourself to the railings? Did you tie each other, or did you get someone to tie you?"

"I was never militant, my dear Jessy. Had I put my brolly through a masterpiece it would have killed my brother, poor old Freddy Vallance. Poor Freddie was very rigid. Some of my activities, I'm afraid, must have caused him suffering. It was the Dean of Waterbury, *Miss Bolby's friend,* who enlisted me in the fight for women's suffrage. We used to have long talks about it in the Conservatory. He was a great man, the Dean, and—ah, dear me, what a superabundance of vitality! He thought nothing of delivering a sermon and opening a boys' club and visiting the East End and playing five sets of tennis, to say nothing of making love to Lady Alice, I feel sure, all in the same day. Poor Lady Alice, I think she found him a great trial. Some day, Miss Bolby, you and I must get together and compare notes about our Atherton-Broadleigh days. And I want to hear more about Arthur. My son Harry was Arthur's fag, and after Arthur had left Harrow Harry asked him one night to dine with us and go to the play —something at the Haymarket, I think it was. After that Arthur often visited us; he was very handsome in those days, a younger edition of the Dean. . . . You must tell me all about your sister Sita, too, Miss Bolby. . . . "

With a simultaneous movement knives and forks were downed, all but Miss Pickford's and Lord Corwen's; then, as though sensing some disturbance, they too arrested theirs in the journey from plate to mouth. Ruffling the taut silence came the disentangling of Miss Bolby's skirt from the table-cloth and the movement of her chair. She stood up.

"You will realise, Lord Rushford, that, in view of this morning's episode, it would be impossible for me, totally impossible"—she tidied her chair in under the table and laid her napkin down upon the cloth—"for me to sing before Lady Archie, and equally impossible for me to sing with the prisoners. In fact, I wonder, Lord Rushford, how you have the effrontery to ask me such a thing. It is a double insult. Once again, Lord Rushford, I must ask you to excuse me." Her journey from the table to the door seemed to leave a wake, dispersed only by the door's thud.

"Oh, Lord!" said Ruth. "We shall *never* get to the Gymkhana."

"And who were the ladies, Larry?" said Lord Corwen as he climbed into his car.

"Miss Pickford is the secretary, Lord Corwen."

"The little deaf one, sitting next to me? Quite a young-looking woman, too. Ah, it's sad, sad for the deaf! They should have aids when they're as deaf as that. So like a woman not to make use of an aid. And the dusky, sultry one with a musical voice? I could hear *her* now, clear as a bell, except for that last speech. She must have been a smasher."

"She is Miss Bolby, the governess, Lord Corwen."

"No governesses about like that in my day, m'boy. All the governesses in my day were as plain as they make 'em. You must come over to Bowborough, Larry. Blanchie wants to ask those nice fellows from the aerodrome again. Must be lonely for 'em, shut up there with their great blundering craft. Bring Miss Bolby."

"Nice woman, that Miss Bolby. Nice-*looking* woman, too. Couple of eyes like saucers in her head," said Lord Corwen.

"A little myopic," said Lady Archie.

"Must have been a smasher," said Lord Corwen.

"A smashing bore, you mean," said Lord Archie.

"You must have heard the music in her voice and not what she said. You're not following in Arthur's footsteps, are you, Hughie? When Miss Bolby becomes Lady Corwen, Archie and I will live in the Bothy. There's one thing I really couldn't do. I couldn't live under the same roof as Miss Bolby."

"Eh? Speak up, can't you, Blanchie?"

"Nothing I say is ever of any importance, Hughie."

"But there's plenty of sense talked in nonsense, Blanchie," said Lord Archie. "God preserve us from Miss Bolby."

"What was all that rigmarole about at luncheon?" said Lord Corwen. "I hadn't noticed what a good-looker she was until she stood up like that, and then I couldn't hear a word she said. Bad acoustics in the Rushford dining-room. Always were bad. Never could hear a word in old Bertie Rushford's day. Larry's girls must be old enough for tennis now, ain't they? Get them to come over the next time you ask those fellows from the aerodrome, Blanchie."

"Elizabeth doesn't mix with the aerodrome, and Miss Bolby, when she rose so majestically, seemed very angry with us all. She seemed to think Larry had insulted her in some way."

"Some of your mischief-making, no doubt, Blanchie."

"You'll see Miss Bolby at the Gymkhana on Monday, Hughie," said Lady Archie.

Ruth sat in the swing-seat. It gave a series of little jerks as she climbed into it, bumping against its poles. She touched the ground with her right toe, then she withdrew her legs into it; its motion now was gentle—even. She shut her eyes because the slant of the sun-dial and the rise and fall of the balustrade made her feel sea-sick: out there beyond stood the laundry basket and the gramophone. Would they or would they not ride in the Gymkhana? What was she to do about the bracelets? How could she take them to Miss Bolby in her present mood? No one had seen Miss Bolby since she had left the dining-room. No sound came from the State Room. No help had been gained from Bella. All Bella had said was 'War! War!' like the rooks and Lord Corwen. War! War! the rooks cried, as if resenting the black monsters from above bearing down upon them. Ruth's eyelids were heavy, infected by the afternoon. Blight had engulfed the park in its yellow film—like the drop curtain in last year's pantomime, she thought—the elms loomed, cumbrous and shadowy through its gauzy transparency: it seemed to muffle the bombers' roar and the rooks' cry. . . .

Lawn sloped steeply upward from the house towards dark growths of rhododendron fringed by shrubs of lilac and laburnum; paths forming little lanes ran between dark hedges of rhododendron. Beyond, spreading forth branches in a vaulted ceiling, stood what was was left of the beeches.

Larry looked down upon the house from a clearing.

From here it looked as it looked in old prints—as it had looked before the fire. Park stretched to north and to south of it. There was serenity in its formal garden: army huts and humped rows of vehicles, all the ugliness of war, from the angle from which he looked, was hidden; the sole signs of life were the laundry basket and the drunkenly perched gramophone.

Jessy's eyes encompassed the same view as Larry's, with Larry superimposed upon it. Each footfall made a crackling and crumbling of dead leaves as she came up behind him, but he did not turn until she had almost reached him.

Leaves lay upon leaves, dried leaves upon sodden leaves. Year upon year's leaves lay beneath her. It was like ploughing through loose sand : dry sand upon wet sand, and as sand was washed and sifted by the sea, wind sifted the leaves, leaving a firm bed of leaves as there must be a firm bed of sand below the sifting sand. Leaves, unlike sand, were springy. Jessy seemed to bound upon a springy mattress; she felt as light as a leaf.

"You look a bit lonely, Pa." It was a long time since she had called Larry 'Pa'.

"I am. I have a sort of nostalgia for Italy."

"Aren't you glad to be back?"

"Glad to be back, but just wondering how long I shall remain here. How much longer we shall be able to live here."

"If you've got a house you might as well live in it."

"With it falling to pieces?"

"I'd rather live at Rushford in ruins than anywhere else on earth."

"Me, too. But it's not very practicable."

"Who would want it, if we didn't live in it?"

"I suppose it would make an institution of some sort; a school, or an asylum, or an old persons' home."

"And where would we live?"

"In some gimcrack villa, probably, like millions of others, all on top of each other."

"It sounds horrible. *Must* we? And you belong here. You belong to Rushford."

"I know, Jess, but those days are over. It's no good growing up with that sort of idea."

"But couldn't we stay here if you sold all the beeches?"

198

"We might be able to scrape along for a few more years, that's all."

"Couldn't you give it to the National Trust, so that we could go on living here?"

"Having had its interior burned, I'm afraid it's not of much interest to anyone but us."

"And Miss Bolby."

"Why Miss Bolby?"

"King Edward stayed here. If it was burned down again, the whole of it, I mean, and the land taken, I think something in me would die."

"Me, too. But possibly we only think that because we're lucky, we don't know what it is to be rootless. Here in England it's difficult to imagine it. I began to see a little of what it must mean when I was overseas. Here everything is just the same as when I left. A few more lorries in the park and a little more mud, and a few more huts, and certainly more noise, because of the aerodrome, but otherwise nothing has changed. Finch still polishes the harness and Elizabeth fusses about the servants and Bob Woodman creaks through his night rounds. It's wonderful, Jessy, a sort of balm, but for all that, we're heading for a new way of life and we might as well face it."

"Don't say that to Elizabeth."

"No, I shan't. Not at present, anyhow."

"She can't bear to think Rushford will ever change, yet she doesn't love it the way you and Ruth and I do; none of them do. How can they, they're not Rushfords."

"She loves it through us, I think. You sound a little like Miss Bolby."

"Oh, Larry, don't be beastly. I'm not being snobby, am I?"

"I don't think so, only over some things it doesn't do to express feeling."

"Miss Bolby says I shall never be a great Actress unless I do."

"Well, there's something in that, too. You're a bit ungainly for an Actress, you sprawl like a drinking giraffe. Ruth, on the other hand, has the grace of a doe."

"Ruth wants to be a teacher."

"A teacher of what?" said Larry.

"Riding and poetry. She wants to keep a riding school with Barby, and teach poetry in her spare time. She doesn't like the way Miss Bolby does it."

"And Louisa?"

"Louisa always feels dizzy. All the money I make can go towards it."

"Towards what?"

"Rushford. It's not as tumbledown as Bowborough. Is Lord Corwen poor, or just mean?"

"Mainly cranky, and a little of both, I think. He spends such a lot on the aviary and he gives large sums of money which he can't afford to the Society for the Protection of Birds."

"Did you see the way he looked at Miss Bolby? I think old men are horrible."

"Perhaps he admired her. There's no reason why he shouldn't look at her if he admires her, is there?"

"But he's so old."

"Age hasn't got much to do with it, and you can see she's been good-looking."

"She's got a beautiful voice; you ought to hear her sing."

"I asked her to, but it didn't go down very well."

"Was it true about Lady Archie and Arthur?"

"Absolutely, I believe. Arthur fell madly in love with her."

"But *she* must have been so old."

"Not then."

"Much older than he was, if he was Harry's friend."

"Love, as you will learn, knows no rules, my dear Jessy."

"Then I suppose Reenie loves Otello. It must be horrible to love the enemy."

200

"I see strong signs of Miss Bolby's influence. He won't be the enemy after the war."

"But it must be pretty horrid, almost as horrid as being a prisoner."

"Horrid, but then war and everything to do with war is horrid."

"I wish Miss Bolby would marry Lord Corwen and leave before the Gymkhana."

"That seems to be leaping ahead a bit too far. Don't worry too much about the Gymkhana. If she doesn't relent I'll try and fix it somehow."

"Larry . . ."

"Yes, Jess?"

"You'll hang on to Rushford as long as you can?"

"Until my dying day, if I can," said Larry.

Ruth did not know how long she had been asleep. It might have been moments or it might have been hours; no sound or movement agitated the elms—as if the rooks slept. The blight had dispersed, had been melted by the evening sun, whose warmth she felt, and whose glow bathed the west side of the house and fell short of the sundial; beyond it all was in shadow. She reached forward and lifted a corner of the seat's mattress; there lay Miss Bolby's bracelets, cold and coiled. She took one and dropped it over her left hand, and as it slid to her elbow she felt the elasticity of its spring : she was held between two finely finished cobra's heads.

"Dear me ! I knocked on the Schoolroom door, Miss Bolby. Habit. I quite forgot you didn't like us knocking on the Schoolroom door. I came to see if you were all right. I didn't like to come before in case I disturbed you. When you went out of the dining-room I thought you must be unwell. Nothing wrong, I hope, Miss Bolby?"

"Nothing at all, I assure you, thank you, Miss Pickford."

"It was ever so nice of you to let me sit at the Big Table, most unselfish. I quite enjoyed sitting next to Lord Corwen. So easy, isn't he? Even if his manner *is* a little gruff. So understanding. No airs at all. You'd never think he was a marquess."

"When you have lived amongst the Aristocracy as long as I, Miss Pickford, I think you will find that about most families, at least the *old* families."

"You couldn't have anything much older than the Rushfords, could you? I looked them up, and they take about three pages."

"But these, Miss Pickford, are not the *true* branch. And they have made a number of *mesalliances*, which always comes out sooner or later. Lord Rushford, I must say, is not at all what I expected."

"But very charming, Miss Bolby, and so young-looking."

"I understand he has had a very unorthodox upbringing, and Men do not keep their Integrity in Marriage in the same way as women."

"Women have to put up with so much more, don't they? They're better able to withstand things. Forgive me asking, Miss Bolby, but who *was* Lady Rushford?"

"Before her previous marriage she was a Wishart, daughter of a Colonel Wishart. She was a widow, you know—a Mrs. Michael Crone when she married Lord Rushford. Her husband was killed in a motor accident in the South of France, the car fell over a cliff—Nannie knows about it. I got Mr. Lind at Hillstone House to look it up for me. Mr. Lind is most interested in heraldry and he looked it up for me in the Birmingham Public Library, where they have a more up-to-date Peerage. I am thinking of returning to Hillstone House for a time, Miss Pickford."

"Not leaving? Oh, Miss Bolby. Something *is* wrong. I sensed it. Oh, I am sorry. Not bad news, I hope, from India?"

"No, Miss Pickford, but I have private matters to see to, and I like to return from time to time to my pied-à-terre. I have said nothing to Lady Rushford yet, and before I go it is essential that I find my bracelets."

"Oh, you *must* find them, Miss Bolby, but it's difficult to know just where to look now."

"I have been thinking, Miss Pickford, that should someone have taken them and then changed her mind about taking them, a kleptomaniac, for instance, or some one who was not ordinarily a thief, there are a number of places where they might be hidden."

"But who *could* have taken them, Miss Bolby?"

"Well, there is Reenie; her background, from all I hear, has not been too savoury. She must have mixed in some very rough company."

"Oh *no*, Miss Bolby. I'll swear it's not Reenie."

Miss Pickford had been getting nearer and nearer to the door. She opened it now and almost collided with Barby.

"Miss Bolby, Lord Corwen on the telephone. He wants Jessy and you and me to go to Bowborough on Sunday, to play tennis with Squadron Leader Langford. He's hanging on."

"You and Jessy are not good enough to play with Squadron Leader Langford and you know I don't play tennis. Have you consulted your mother?"

"I can't find her. Squadron Leader Langford doesn't mind us being bad. He likes just knocking the ball about, and Lord Corwen wants to speak to you, he's hanging on."

"To me? My dear Barbara!"

"Well, what shall I say, Miss Bolby? Shall I go back and say you can't speak to him? We might as well go. There's all Friday and Saturday and Sunday to get through, and we can't ride on Sunday and they have jolly good teas at Bowborough and Squadron Leader Langford is rather fun. He says 'Wizard!' when you hit a ball and 'Duffer!' when he misses."

"Just one moment, I must think this out, Barbara."

"But Lord Corwen is hanging on, Miss Bolby."

"He didn't say whether Lady Archie would be there?"

"I expect she will be, she always *is* there."

"I have always been very anxious to see the pictures at Bowborough, particularly the Reynolds Lady Archie talked of. Yes, I think you may accept the invitation, Barby."

"But he said he wanted to speak to you, Miss Bolby."

"It is extremely nice of him. I have always noticed that Lord Corwen is an extremely polite man. I will go down and speak to him, Barby."

"Isn't it funny," said Barby to Miss Pickford, "he's not a bit deaf on the telephone. He heard every word I said."

Ruth put the bracelets back under the mattress. It would not be wise to take them to Miss Bolby in her present mood.

"Barby and Jessy and I are very much looking forward to our visit to Bowborough on Sunday. I expect Barby has told you about it, Lady Rushford," said Miss Bolby.

"No, Miss Bolby, I had no idea you were going," said Elizabeth. "Lady Archie said nothing about it at lunch, and I don't quite know how you're going to get there. We're very short of petrol and we must keep what we've got for the Gymkhana. Even if the children don't go, the whole household will. And Finch will have a hard day on Monday, so I don't see how he can take the trap out on Sunday."

"They *must* go," said Ruth. If Miss Bolby goes to Bowborough, she may change her mind, she thought.

Already a change had come upon Miss Bolby. When she had come into the room at teatime Elizabeth had said: 'I hope you have had a good rest, Miss Bolby?' and her rest, as if by a miracle, seemed to have erased her anger. She seemed to have become, in fact, a new Miss Bolby.

"When did Lady Archie ring up?" said Elizabeth.

"She didn't, Lord Corwen did," said Barby, "and he specially asked to speak to Miss Bolby."

"How odd of Lord Corwen. I mean, he hates the telephone, and he's so unsociable," said Elizabeth. "What did he ask you *for*, Miss Bolby?"

"For tea, Lady Rushford. He wants the girls to play tennis."

"Squadron Leader Langford is going," said Barby.

"What an awful bore! I don't want to go in the least," said Jessy.

"We might as well go, Jess. There's nothing to do here on Sunday," said Barby.

"I can't think why Lady Archie sees so much of Squadron Leader Langford," said Elizabeth. "It's all very well to ask some of them up from the aerodrome sometimes, but not every five minutes as Lady Archie does."

"He can't play tennis for toffee," said Jessy.

"Nor can we, and the lawn's like a hay field," said Barby.

"Every time anything goes into the net he says 'Prang.' He's an awful bore, really," said Jessy.

"You must go," said Ruth. "Barby can drive the trap. She drives as well as Mr. Finch, and you can go by the lanes."

"What does Miss Bolby think?" said Elizabeth.

"I should be very interested to see the pictures, Lady Rushford. The day we called, on the way to your meeting, you remember, our stay was very brief. Lady Archie didn't have time to show me round."

"You'll have to go into the aviary," said Jessy, "in amongst all those awful squawking birds who look exactly like Lord Corwen."

"Aren't you being rather disagreeable and ungracious, Jessy? It is extremely kind of Lord Corwen to ask us."

"I can't think why he has," said Jessy.

"You must go," said Ruth. "If you like I'll run down to the stables and say you want the trap."

"And it must be Bess. All the other ponies must rest," said Barby.

'All the ponies must rest.' Just as if the children *were* going to the Gymkhana. How irritating the child was, blatantly ignoring her decision. How irritating they all were, Miss Bolby thought. It had been a disturbing and distressing day.

First of all the dreadful scene before the children at breakfast, the revelation concerning Lady Archie, at which Lady Archie herself had had the bad taste to hint on that first evening: at which the Dean had hinted during that long-ago visit to the Deanery, and of which Sita knew nothing. Life played strange and shabby tricks indeed. Who would have thought that that 'other woman', that 'older woman' of whom the Dean had spoken, would turn out to be none other than Lady Archie? And Lady Archie boldly talked about Arthur as if there had been nothing between them, and yet in such a way that anyone who knew the story must know what Lady Archie was thinking.

So the anecdotes disjointedly told by Bob Woodman were not merely servants' gossip, they were true. There was reason for 'plenty of talk' about Lady Archie, and the 'plenty of talk' concerned Arthur. But Arthur had become impregnable, and with him, Sita. No old scandal could harm Sita now, though it was unfortunate that she, Roona, had mentioned Lady Archie so often in her letters to Sita.

Until the moment when she and Miss Pickford, sherry glasses in hand, had walked into the dining room she had decided to ignore Lady Archie, to reply to whatever Lady Archie said in monosyllables, should it be necessary. To put up a cold front towards Lady Archie and to refer—making plain the respect that was felt for Sita—to Sita: to take her revenge upon Lady Archie somehow. To hint, perhaps, that there was *something* that Sita knew which she considered Arthur's youthful folly: she had meant very gently and very subtly to mock at Lady Archie, but this would only have been possible from the Big Table, and with the force of a sledge-hammer's blow had come the words: 'Miss Pickford will sit with us, and we'll put Miss Bolby at the Little Table.' And Miss Pickford had talked to Lord Corwen without a trace of shyness and he had devoted his whole attention to Miss Pickford, and Lady Archie had embarked upon a long discourse upon her friendship with the Atherton-Broadleigh family and upon intimate details of the Dean's way of life and had thrown out the suggestion that they should reminisce to her, Roona, as a condescending crumb. Then, to crown it all, Lord Rushford had asked her to sing before Lady Archie *with the prisoners,* just as one might ask something of the servants.

How often had she wished in the past that Lady Rowfont would say: 'We will ask Miss Bolby to sing.' When King Boris came, and the night Ned Blatchington had come to the Schoolroom. How different *that* night might have been. But Lady Rowfont had only said: 'We will ask Miss Bolby to sing,' when Mr. Grayling, the agent came, as if to remind her that Mavis had married an agent; as if to remind her, in fact, that she was on the same level as Mr. Grayling, since both were in Lord Rowfont's employ. . . .

After she had left the dining room Miss Bolby had gone to her room to lie down. I must be calm, she had thought. I have never lost my head, I must not lose it now. I am a Bolby. Then she had gone into the bathroom—the State Room had its own bathroom. No sharing the nursery bathroom now. No waiting for Reenie and Vi. . . . She put a cold compress upon her brow and fell into a sleep.

She had been writing to Mrs. Tollmarsh to make sure

that the room at Hillstone House was free, when first Miss
Pickford had come into the Schoolroom, and then Barby
with the message that Lord Corwen was on the telephone.
Lord Corwen, with whom she had hardly exchanged a word,
had wished to speak to *her,* Roona!

'Miss Bolby?'

'Yes, it is I, Lord Corwen.'

'Speak up then, my dear woman, can't you? Ah! That's
better. Clear as a bell now. Nothing like the telephone for
the deaf, Miss Bolby. But *your* voice, my dear woman, would
penetrate the tomb. Handsome voice. Fine voice. Musical.
Ought to have been a singer, that's what you ought to have
been. Barby says you're comin' over on Sunday for a game of
tennis?'

'It's extremely kind of you to ask us, Lord Corwen, and
I'm sure it will give us great pleasure. The girls will enjoy
the tennis, but they are not very good, I'm afraid, and I fear
I'm hardly young enough for tennis any more.'

'Not young enough? Nonsense. Young enough to watch,
ain't we? Those young Air Force fellows are comin'.'

'I should very much like to see the pictures, Lord Corwen.'

'Interested in pictures, eh? If that Canaletto in the hall
at Rushford is a Canaletto, I'll eat my hat. Plenty of pictures
here, but you'd better see the aviary, Miss Bolby.'

'I should be most interested, Lord Corwen.'

'Three-thirty sharp, then.' He had slammed down the
receiver.

Had Lord Corwen, with the deaf's sixth sense, realised
she had been insulted? Was he trying, under cover of his
bluffness, with some old-world chivalry, to atone for it?

She looked into the glass: it was not the Roona Bolby of
the Worthing days, but a figure from the shelter she saw
there.

It had indeed been a disconcerting day.

5

"Archie, have you seen *Mrs. Jackson's Gentle Art of Cookery?* Mrs. Meadows is coming from the village and it is very important to have a good tea. A chocolate cake I think, and plenty of scones. And how is the lawn?"

"I don't see why you have to make quite such a fuss about Hughie's party, Blanchie. Silly old fool!"

"There's no fool like an old fool. Consequently we must encourage it, Archie, like mad. *Throw* them together, see that they are closeted together in the aviary, that should finish it. Poor Hughie. A man is as ardent at eighty as he is at eighteen."

'DEAR MRS. HURST,' Miss Bolby wrote.

'I hasten to reply to your letter received yesterday, in answer to mine. I was more than glad, delighted in fact I may say, to hear from Hillstone House.

'I am sorry indeed to hear of Mrs. Tollmarsh's trouble and of the unfortunate incident concerning Elsie. I certainly do not approve of "followers" being admitted to the kitchen, after all, anything might happen. Milly should take the reins into her own hands and get rid of her. She is not at all the right type of girl for that type of house. *Mais qui voulez-vous? C'est la guerre!*

'Now for my news, Mrs. Hurst. You will be interested to hear, I know, that the elder girls and I are going over to Bowborough today for a little tennis (the girls, of course, not I!!) Lord Corwen rang me up after he had been here for lunch on Thursday and suggested that we should go and meet some of the officers from the aerodrome. Some of them are, rather—well—to put it mildly, out of a very *middle* drawer. Lord Corwen is an extremely kind man and I think he feels that they are lonely. We are very isolated here, isolated in fact *but* for Bowborough and the aerodrome, and *he* (Lord Corwen, I do not think that Lord and Lady Archie feel that way) feels that the old should *Do Their Bit,* and Lord Corwen, I must say, certainly does it.

'I am looking forward to another glimpse of the pictures, particularly the Reynolds, which is infinitely superior to the Canaletto here about which there is some doubt. Lord Corwen, in fact, says that it is not a Canaletto at all.

'Well, Mrs. Hurst, as it is now five minutes to one and the Schoolroom is such a long way from the dining-room I must make my way down to lunch. (We have no gong here.)

'My kind regards to all and please tell Mr. Lind that I am writing under separate cover to thank him for so kindly attending to that little matter at the public library for me.

'Yours very sincerely,

'ROONA BOLBY.'

"All the arrangements must be made today. Today is Sunday and we shall have to start early tomorrow," said Barby.

"It's a pity Nino and Otello can't go. There is going to be no one left behind at all except Nino and Otello," said Jessy.

"That's if *we* go," said Ruth.

"We shall go," said Barby.

"My word! Nothing like being certain of yourselves, is there?" said Becca.

"You *will* be nice to her, Jess?" said Ruth.

"Nice to whom?" said Jessy.

"Well, Miss Bolby, of course. Everything depends on what happens at Bowborough."

"It doesn't depend on me, it depends on Lord Corwen," said Jessy.

"You *are* lucky, Miss Bolby," said Miss Pickford; "you have been to so many interesting places and met so many interesting people. I hadn't ever met anybody much until I came here. I met a few titled people when I was in the Red Cross, of course. Otherwise I haven't met anybody much except Mrs. Staines-Close."

"My Atherton-Broadleigh connections enlarged my circle of acquaintances enormously, and there was so much *va et vient* at Rowfont," said Miss Bolby.

"I wish you were coming, too, Picksie," said Jessy.

"It is quite unnecessary and rather familiar to call Miss Pickford 'Picksie'," said Miss Bolby.

"Are we ready? Mr. Finch is at the door with the trap," said Barby.

"Bye-bye! Have a nice time," said Miss Pickford.

"Bye-bye!" said Barby.

"*Goodbye, please, Barbara,*" said Miss Bolby.

Miss Pickford opened the schoolroom window. The war she waged daily for air was growing more intense : Miss Bolby felt the cold. Already there was a sharpness in the early morning air which gave her a tingle of exhilaration when she, Rose, kicked off her sandals and wriggled her toes in the dewy grass. Mists rose in the evenings from the river, having nothing to do with the yellow film which lifted as suddenly as it fell during the day upon the park.

Movement played upon the stillness of a Sunday afternoon. War paid no heed to Sunday. Relentlessly its evil machinations continued. Shapes crept in, replacing those which crept out from beneath the trees where all should have been still. Sly, sinuous—from the Schoolroom barely perceptible : the slow stretching of the tenacles of evil testing its strength against evil : war.

211

It was just as busy in the sky. A shadow, as a bomber flew homeward, dipped into the formal garden. Because the house itself was so silent and still, Miss Pickford tautened, a conscious reinforcement against its roar. How many times a day do we subconsciously tauten? she thought. How much evil do they do us, these evil things of the sky? Then she began to wonder what sort of a man Squadron Leader Langford was, and whether he looked like John. She felt glad she had not been asked to Bowborough, in case he looked like John. Not that the pictures of the moustached pilots she had seen in the papers had resembled John. But the air, as well as the sea, seemed to bend those it embraced to the pattern of its will, and she did not want any more to be reminded of John. Memories concerning John were best thrust aside, and because this was so the poor dead creatures began to revive, to press forward. Shadowy scenes in a motion picture, which took on the vividness of 'stills', as if seen, not through the telescope of time, but with the naked eye.

Tennis with John. . . .
'Sorry.'
'Fault.'
'Out.'
And the thud of a ball.
And from the house : 'Tea-ee !'
'Coming, Mother.'
'Bend, Rose, as if you were looking for a ball, as if there was one in the border. Let the others go on.'
The garden at Redroof was just large enough to hold the tennis court and the border, so that all the summer the border was full of balls. John thrust his racquet into a clump of bushes which made a soft swishing sound as they recoiled from it.
'Will you marry me, Rose.'
'Yes, John.'

'Cooee-tea-ee.'

And during tea a band playing. Troops marching:

> 'It's a long way to Tipperary,
>   It's a long way to go,
>   It's a long way to Tippera-rr——'

and the band turned the corner. Voices rounded it with less suddenness, voices behind those voices followed, flagging—and the tea-table was surrounded with silence, because John was going tomorrow.

Ordinary memories, memories like a million others' memories, as though memory and Suburbia had gone hand-in-hand. Not exciting ones like Miss Bolby's, of large Country Houses and Parties, and Princes, and India. . . .

Miss Pickford sat down at the Schoolroom piano. In the Vicarage at Stonechurch, before the move to Wimbledon she had learned the piano. There was only one tune she could remember now, not a First World War tune, not a signature tune of her generation, one that came later. One she had been taught by Mrs. Staines-Close's nephew. He had not recurred with the consistency of John. He had been less, less and yet more, but he had not been her 'affianced'—her 'intended'.

> 'What'll I doo-do-do-do-doo—do-do-doo-do.'

She had played it upon the upright piano in 'digs'.

"I didn't know *you* played the piano, too, Miss Pickford," said Louisa.

"Oh! I don't, dear, I don't. Just strumming, that's all. I don't play like Miss Bolby. I wish I could. People with a talent must be happy."

"Play it again," said Louisa.

"But it's such a silly sort of tune, dear."

213

"That's why I like it."

"You've made me shy now."

"Is it easy to learn shorthand?" said Louisa.

"Easy when you know it. Don't shout, dear; I can hear you quite well, Louisa."

"I'm sorry, Miss Pickford; I didn't think you could."

"Sometimes I can and sometimes I can't, dear."

"But how can I know when you can?"

"That's just it, dear."

"Well, is it?"

"Is it what, dear?"

"Easy to learn shorthand?"

"I have just said it is easy when you know it, like everything you do."

"But is it easy to *learn?* How long would it take me to learn it? I want to learn it so that I can write things to Ruth without Miss Bolby knowing it. When Miss Bolby spells things out sometimes, you know, in a horrible sort of way, making words sound different," said Louisa.

"Whatever shall I write, dear?" said Miss Pickford, drawing lines upon a piece of Rushford-headed paper which had been lying upon Miss Bolby's sealed letter.

"Write: 'If Lord Corwen asks Miss Bolby to marry him we shall be able to go to the Gymkhana'. "

"Oh, Louisa! I can't write such a thing. What a dreadful thing to say! How wicked of you!"

"But it's true. Jessy says she knows Lord Corwen wants to marry her because of the way he looked at her, and that's why they've gone to Bowborough. Barby says if he asks her to marry him she knows we will ride in the Gymkhana."

Then Miss Pickford said: "Well I'm blest! If Miss Bolby doesn't get all the plums, and at her age, too! Well, I'm blowed!"

She wrote on a piece of paper:

214

"Let me see," said Louisa. "Write underneath it so that I can see which is which." And Miss Pickford wrote:

Miss Roona Bolby to marry the Marquess of Corwen.

"Just think of it, Louisa; it will be in all the papers."

"And she will leave," said Louisa. "Now write something easier. Write 'The Cow has a Silver Tail'."

"Surely, dear, you mean 'The Cloud has a silver lining'."

"No, 'The Cow has a Silver Tail'."

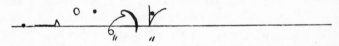

"Now write underneath it, so that I can see which is which," said Louisa.

" 'The Cow has a Silver Tail'," wrote Miss Pickford underneath it.

"Oh! I do not want to learn shorthand!" said Louisa.

"How are we going to know if he has asked her?" said Miss Pickford.

"She's going to say we can ride in the Gymkhana."

"But she might change her mind, even if he asked her. Dear me! I shouldn't be gossiping to you like this, Louisa, but I do like a wedding, and I should like *someone* to be happy."

"You're coming to the Gymkhana, aren't you?" said Louisa.

"No, dear; I shall take the day off. I shall have it all to myself and I shan't go near the Office, so that Old Mr. Stiles won't know where I am."

"But Old Mr. Stiles is dead. He's been dead a long time."

"Not entirely dead; his spirit lives on. It peers out at me from the shelves, it gets in between the leaves of the reference books. It's because I'm so disorderly. I can't seem to get any sort of order into the Office, not with Old Mr. Stiles watching me all the time, though Lord Rushford *has* tidied it up a bit."

"*He* likes the office. He goes there when he's lonely. Perhaps he goes there to be with Old Mr. Stiles. Where will you go tomorrow, Miss Pickford?"

"To the woods. I shall lie on the ground and listen for the birds as I used to in the Vicarage garden at Stonechurch. I knew all the bird calls then. The blackbird's flute and the throstle's full-throated trill—the willow-warbler's water-fall and the swallow's sweet twittering, the chaffinch's strident chatter, the wren's piercing perseverance and the skylark's joy. I knew them all because my father knew them all. He knew about birds, like Lord Corwen. I shall listen for other sounds, too, little sounds : the bee's jazzing as he plunges into a flower's heart, the landing of a leaf upon leaves, the broken fall through undergrowth of some ripe berry : little scurryings and burrowings. Oh, Louisa! I do wish sometimes that my head wasn't full of cotton wool."

"Is it?" said Louisa. "My head is a bit woolly, too."

"It muffles some sounds and magnifies others. It seems to know no discrimination."

"It is a pity, Picksie, that *you* can't marry Lord Corwen," said Louisa.

Birds flying off with sound, almost before sound went forth, and the deaf who waited for it, were alike, there was some affinity between them. This is what Louisa, in her own way, thought.

"But, Louisa, things like that don't come my way," Miss Pickford said.

"Punctual to the minute. Capital! Capital!" said Lord Corwen. "Meadows will put up the pony, Barby. Off with your bonnets and shawls. Nice of you to come, Miss Bolby.

Those Air Force fellows are late again. No sense of punctuality. Always waiting on their craft, I suppose. Blanchie is fussing in the kitchen."

When they had removed their coats Lady Archie came into the hall. "How do you do, Miss Bolby? Hughie has been on the look-out for the last half-hour. I was afraid Elizabeth might have sent Miss Pickford instead of you, and Hughie must show you the pictures and the aviary while the children are on the tennis court. I left a message at the Lodge for Squadron Leader Langford and Flight-Lieutenant Mead to go straight there, so as not to waste any time. Archie has been working like a Trojan on the lawn."

"Many prangs?" said Lady Archie. She sat behind a silver teapot which stood upon a silver tray. "We clean it all ourselves, Miss Bolby." She had been watching Miss Bolby survey it. "It's Hughie's job mainly. He polishes from nine to one— quite an undertaking. Dear me! I had meant to give you China tea and it seems to be Indian. Our Indian tea is so plebeian. Yours, I expect, comes from your sister Sita, Miss Bolby. I don't remember Arthur being much of a connoisseur about tea. I suppose you have nothing but Indian tea in your mess, Squadron Leader Langford? It's a curious thing, one has no picture of an Indian drinking tea, yet I vividly see a Chinaman holding a handleless cup and burning his fingers upon its bowl. Do you like the milk in first or last, Miss Bolby? Tastes differ and one has to keep up with the times."

"How about coffee? Any rule about that, Lady Meredith?" said Squadron Leader Langford.

"Speak up, can't you. I can't hear a word you say," said Lord Corwen.

"My mother always used to say there were a number of ways by which you could tell a lady," said Miss Bolby.

"What were they, Miss Bolby?" said Lord Archie.

"The milk, the way the milk was put in, Lord Archie, and the wearing of gloves, for instance, and well-mended shoes."

On a June afternoon, uneasy and tired from a long cross-country journey, she, Roona, had watched Lady Alice Atherton-Broadleigh put the milk in last.

'Tell me more details, Roona, more of Lady Alice's little ways. You did nothing, I hope, to make it seem that you were not used to such houses.'

'No, Mother. Nothing, Mother.'

And later, before Mrs. Butler-Clitheroe came to tea, she, Roona, had said : 'Mother, when *Lady Alice* pours the tea she puts the milk in last.'

'There is no need for you to tell me things of that sort, Roona'; and her Mother had said to Mrs. Butler-Clitheroe : 'Milk, Mrs. Butler-Clitheroe? I expect you like it in *last*.'

"Nobody wears gloves any more," said Jessy, "and Becca says putting the milk in last makes it taste horrid."

"If you like it in first, I can't see that it much matters," said Lord Archie.

"In matters of etiquette taste must be thrown to the winds, Lord Archie," said Miss Bolby.

As clearly as if she had seen it upon a printed page, Jessy could detect in Miss Bolby's voice an exclamation mark.

"Drink much tea in Ceylon?" said Lord Corwen to Squadron Leader Langford.

"As a matter of fact, we didn't, er—actually drink much tea, sir—actually."

"Ha ha!" said Flight-Lieutenant Mead.

"Boozing, I suppose," said Lady Archie.

"You're wizard, absolutely wizard, Lady Meredith," said Flight-Lieutenant Mead.

"I see I shall have to call you by your Christian names. Squadron Leader becomes a little unwieldy when repeated a number of times, and Flight-Lieutenant singularly cumbersome—like a great bat floundering. What *is* your Christian name, Flight-Lieutenant Mead?"

"Graham," said Flight-Lieutenant Mead.

"Then I shall call you Graham; and you Hugo, Squadron Leader Langford," said Lady Archie.

"Suits me all right," said Squadron Leader Langford.

"Down to the ground," said Flight-Lieutenant Mead.

"This fashion for Christian names makes everything so much easier than it was in my day. Friendship instantly flowers. It's so much easier to be intimate. Don't you agree, Miss Bolby?" said Lady Archie.

"More tea, Miss Bolby?" boomed Lord Corwen.

"Thank you, Lord Corwen, one cup is sufficient," said Miss Bolby.

"Eh——" said Lord Corwen.

"One is enough, thank you, Lord Corwen."

"Then why don't you say enough? Enough is a good old English word. Nothing wrong with enough," said Lord Corwen.

"I hope you got on well with Hughie in the aviary, Miss Bolby?" said Lady Archie.

"Lord Corwen and I have got on very well indeed, extremely well. We found we had a great deal in common, but we have not yet visited the aviary. Lord Corwen is reserving it for his *pièce de résistance,* his *bonne bouche,* Lady Archie," said Miss Bolby.

"We find it very damp here in the winter, you know, Miss Bolby," said Lady Archie.

"Give Miss Bolby some sugar, Langford. She hasn't seen the Reynolds yet. She must do that after tea. She has got to go round the house yet," said Lord Corwen.

"When I was in Florence with Lord Rowfont's girls, we visited the Uffizi Galleries every day," said Miss Bolby.

"My dear woman, what on earth for? You can't see

pictures in a gallery. Pictures should always be seen in a house, where they were meant to be seen."

"But if all the pictures in the world were in houses they wouldn't be seen," said Jessy.

"Well said, Jessy. Pictures should be for the People," said Lady Archie. "We must open our houses—at a small charge, of course, so that Hughie may have more birds and Archie can buy me a new hat."

"If the Populace is allowed in our Great Houses we shall be left with little privacy," said Miss Bolby.

"Privacy, my dear Miss Bolby? Privacy died with the hansom cab. You can't even elope any more in a good straightforward fashion."

"I should love to elope. I think it must be *wonderful* to elope," said Barby.

"Well said. Top-hole, Barby," said Lady Archie.

Lord Corwen rose. "Finish your dish of tea and let me take you to the aviary, Miss Bolby. Allow me to assist you, Madam."

Miss Bolby's foot had become wedged between the table leg and her chair.

'Sufficient, Sufficient.' The word shuffled about in Miss Bolby's head as they drove home. Day had ceased to be day and dusk was not yet dusk, and light had become a deception.

'More tea, Miss Bolby?' Lady Alice Atherton-Broadleigh had said on that June evening which had seemed so long ago until this evening when it had once again become vivid. 'Thank you, Lady Alice; one is sufficient.' She, Roona, had intercepted the look which was barely a look because Lady Alice looked at the tea-tray, but which would have been a look had Lady Alice allowed it to traverse the tea table and reach the Dean : it had shied off, instead, into the raising, which was barely so much as the raising, of an eyebrow. And she had not known then what the look had signified. Later she had noticed that neither Lady Alice nor the Dean used the word 'sufficient'. She had made a mental note of this and she had not used it again, it had sunk back into some recess of the subconscious, until she had gone to Hillstone House. It had been hard at Hillstone House not to fall into boarding-house ways—they were insidious, though, generally speaking, she and Mr. Lind had managed to keep upon a higher level somehow.

Lord Corwen's bluffness had not wounded the way Lady Alice's sly insinuation had. Lord Corwen was both bluff and courtly. One could not take offence at what he said.

"It must be nice to be old in some ways," said Jessy, as though her thoughts had verged on to Miss Bolby's track. "You can do what you like and say what you feel."

"But Lord Corwen is careful to say what he feels without hurting others' feelings," said Miss Bolby.

"Why is it he says 'ain't'?" said Barby. "It doesn't sound right for someone like Lord Corwen."

"It was the fashion when Lord Corwen was young. Both Lord Rowfont and Lord Chipperfield used to say it," said Miss Bolby.

"Lord and Lady Archie don't."

"Lord and Lady Archie have lived less sheltered lives. They are not isolated by deafness as Lord Corwen is."

"And they're a bit younger," said Jessy.

"I have never heard anyone say 'top-hole' before, either. Is that a bit younger?" said Barby.

"It was much used when Lady Rowfont's girls had their first season. It had already come into vogue, I believe, when Roger Leaming married Lady Pearl Throughfell. I remember Roger Leaming saying it."

"After the war I suppose there will be no seasons," said Jessy.

"Well, not for you. You are going to be an Actress," said

221

Barby. "How many seasons did Lady Pearl do, Miss Bolby, before she married Roger Leaming?"

"Only one, then Lord Chipperfield went to India."

"Did your sister Sita do a season before she married Arthur?"

"When my father died we were left extremely badly off, Barby. Otherwise I should have been a singer. But Sita had the opportunity of going out at once to India. Had she not done so, and had my father not died, I feel quite sure that my mother would have arranged for us girls somehow to have had a season."

"How did she find the money to get to India?" said Jessy.

"There are always ways of arranging things, Jessy, and it was a long time ago. I have almost forgotten such mundane matters as money."

"Did Lady Archie have a season?" said Barby.

"Certainly, Barby; she was Lord Vallance's sister."

"You wouldn't think so sometimes, would you? She says such extraordinary things."

"Lady Archie is not a serious woman," said Miss Bolby, "one must not judge her too harshly."

"About her lovers, you mean?" said Jessy.

"How many lovers do you think she had? It must be wonderful to have lovers," said Barby.

"Barbara!" said Miss Bolby.

They drove on for a time in silence, then Miss Bolby said: "I have been thinking about it, girls, and as your behaviour today was exemplary I have decided to reverse my decision about the Gymkhana." Silence closed in upon the words for a moment; they seemed to be suspended. A newspaper, curved into a ghostly shape, came to life in the middle of the road. It hissed upon the tarmac as the wind shifted it, and the pony shied: the trap swerved and then righted itself. . . . Barby stood up, and then sat down. "I say, Jess, here, take the reins for a minute, will you?"

"You're not going to faint, are you, Barby? Put your head between your knees while I look for my smelling salts. When you see something in the middle of the road at which you think the mare may shy you should try to avoid it," said Miss Bolby.

"Mr. Finch says that you should always drive straight into it," said Jessy.

THE GYMKHANA

1

NIGHT died. Light moved painfully in from the horizons; in its birth pangs it pierced the pantry window and woke Bob Woodman. The clock in the corner hiccuped as if to herald it. Bob stretched, he was stiff and chilled; ash coated the charred remains of the fire.

Time for his last round. He eased his arms into his coat and put the torch, which stood upon the table, into his pocket. The torch gave him confidence; it was during this last round, when the growing light turned transparency into reality, when forms grew out of shadows and trees became trees and stone became solid, that he half expected to find some figure lurking beneath its solidity. Dew lay upon the oval lawn before the house with the sharpness of frost, though its touch was softer, it did not kill; it brought to its full the scent of fresh-cut grass. As the light hardened, mist, which lay shifting above the park, changed its tactics. Instead of moving forward it withdrew slowly, wavered, and drifted forward again, reaching beyond where it had withdrawn with the fitful certainty of an outgoing tide.

As Barby woke she heard Bob Woodman's step. She stretched out a hand for her watch, which she had put as near as she could to the pillow. She had left a message last night for Bob Woodman to call her early. Becca had insisted that they had gone early to bed; she had also washed their hair.

Not content with leaving a message for Bob Woodman, Barby had listened for his step. She had called out of the window: 'I say, Bob, you will call us early, won't you?'

'Early as you like, Miss. What sort of time, Miss?'

'Sixish, I should think.'

'Six is a bit early, isn't it, Miss?'

'But we want to see Mr. Finch and the new lad start off early with the ponies, they're taking them over early, and you will wake Reenie, too, won't you, so that she's not late with the breakfast?'

' I shan't forget Reenie, Miss.'

'Nino and Otello are going to help her pack the lunch in. The lunch will have to go in the station van. It must be awful to be a prisoner, mustn't it? To have to watch everyone else go off, when you can only pack the lunch in.'

'Seeing as they are prisoners, they might do worse, Miss.'

'Bob, was the last war as bad as this? Was it awful?'

'You bet it was, Miss.'

'Gas and trenches, and all that?'

'That's right, Miss. That's how I got me dicky lungs.'

'Miss Pickford's fiancé was killed in it.'

'Is that so, Miss?'

'Bob, do you suppose Miss Bolby had a fiancé?'

'I don't rightly know, Miss.'

'You know she is going to marry Lord Corwen?'

'Good Lord, Miss! You *have* taken my breath away.'

'She must be going to, or she wouldn't have changed her mind about the Gymkhana.'

'Lord Corwen has been looking for a wife these thirty years, they say, but I didn't know he had his eye on Miss Bolby. Well, I never, Miss!'

'It was very sudden, it happened at lunch on Thursday. Louisa says Miss Pickford isn't coming tomorrow. I wish Miss Bolby wouldn't, but I expect she will if she's going to marry Lord Corwen.'

It seemed hardly possible, as she heard Bob Woodman's step now, that the day, the great day for which she had waited so long, had dawned—that its sickly feebleness was strengthening into day, and today of all days, her watch had stopped. She did not wait to thrust her feet into an old pair of slippers of Elizabeth's, but pad-padded across the linoleum to the window on bare feet: "I say Bob, is it early—is it sixish?"

"Just about, Miss."

"And you haven't called us yet."

"I was just going to, Miss."

"Well, there is no need to now. I'll wake the others. What is the weather going to do?"

"Looks all right to me, Miss, from the way the mist is lying."

"And the cows aren't lying down?"

"Can't see any from here, Miss."

"And you can't feel any rain in your knees?"

"N'more than usual, Miss."

"And you won't forget Reenie?"

"No, Miss."

"O.K., Bob. Thanks awfully for calling us."

Ruth heard Barby call out of the window, so that she was awake and already out of bed when Barby came in.

"Wake up, Louisa, it's the Day. The Great Day. Get up, Lazy Bones!"

Louisa reluctantly struggled into wakefulness; then, as if the meaning of Barby's words had at last penetrated the sluggish remnants of sleep, she said: "Hurray! Hurray! It's the Day."

"Well, hurry up then," said Barby, "or we shan't be in time to see Mr. Finch start off."

Ruth was silent. She was thinking of Miss Bolby's bracelets.

During breakfast Elizabeth said: "You are coming with us, of course, Miss Bolby?"

"I think, Lady Rushford, that with your permission I shall take the day off. I have had a very heavy mail this week, and I have not yet written my weekly letter to India. And I have a number of other matters to see to—such little trivialities as mending. At Hillstone House I was always able to get Elsie to mend for me in her spare time. I am rather inexpert with my needle, not good at practical things."

Again Jessy felt she could hear an exclamation mark.

"One was not brought up to be practical, more's the pity! My mother, I know, little thought I should have to fend for myself in the way that I have. My poor mother thought, no doubt, that I should be as lucky as my sisters, Sita and Mavis. I often think how lucky it was for my mother not to have lived to see what so many of us have come to. I know you will excuse me if I do not come with you, Lady Rushford. There is a little matter which I feel it is my duty to try to clear up once and for all, this mystery of my missing bracelets. I should be distressed, indeed, were suspicion to fall upon anyone."

"You look as if you're going to burst. Is anything the matter, Ruth?" said Larry.

"No," said Ruth. "I was just thinking about the Gym-khana."

"We had better arrange who is going with who," said Barby. "Jess and I had better go in the brake as we have to get there early."

"And you had better take the Woodman family and Winnie from the village," said Elizabeth, "and Becca and Bella, and Benn and Mrs. Williams and the lunch and I will go in the van."

"And Reenie and Vi are going to cycle," said Barby.

"Oh, please let Louisa and me go early too," said Ruth.

With the day, and the Gymkhana, and the honours they would win there behind her, she would be able, in the evening, to get the bracelets and to take them to Miss Bolby, Ruth thought, and to say: 'Look Miss Bolby, I've *found* them.' And Miss Bolby, exultantly, would say, 'Well done, Ruth, splendid child! I, too, have news for you and I shall tell you first so that you may tell the others. I am to marry Lord Corwen.' It seemed odd, somehow, that Miss Bolby had not told them already. No one in the house had said as yet: 'Miss Bolby is

to marry Lord Corwen.' Was it possible that after all Lord
Corwen had not asked her to marry him?' Barby and
Jessy and herself and Louisa had taken it for granted that
Lord Corwen had asked her to Bowborough in order to ask
her to marry him, just because Jessy had said: 'Did you see
the way Lord Corwen looked at old Bolb? Wouldn't it be
wonderful if he married her, then she'd go,' and they had all
seen how Lord Corwen had looked at her. Nothing must be
said, though Barby had told Bob Woodman through the window. Nothing must spoil it. Nothing. Nothing. Then Miss
Bolby would go. Just in the same way nothing must be said
about the bracelets now, so that they would not spoil the
Gymkhana—although they had to a certain extent already
done so. They had come between her and the Gymkhana
ever since she had found them.

'What about Miss Bolby's and Miss Pickford's lunch, if
they are not going?" said Barby. Since the news of Miss
Bolby's reversed decision she had played the part of a general
nearing the zero hour before a long-planned battle.

"They must have a cold lunch here in the dining-room,"
said Elizabeth, as if they were not there, and then as if remembering their presence: "And one of you, I am sure, Miss
Bolby, won't mind clearing away. I want the servants to
have as much of a holiday as possible. We shall be back late,
I expect—probably about seven. The Gymkhana is such a
festival, and it is always so difficult to collect everyone together
and to get the children away. Just as we are about to leave
one of them disappears into the crowd. There are sports and
side-shows and a flower show, and there is generally a raffle
and a jam-making competition. It's a pity you're not coming,
Miss Bolby."

Jessy thought she could detect a certain satisfaction in the
way Elizabeth said this, as though, knowing that she was on
safe ground, she said it with a sort of relish.

Ruth thought she had heard an onimous note in Miss Bolby's

voice as she had said: 'I should be distressed indeed *were suspicion to fall upon anyone.*'

Barby and Jessy, and Ruth and Louisa, and the Woodman family, and Winnie from the village, climbed into the brake as it ground to a standstill before the front door.

Nino and Otello hung about the van. Picnic baskets had been packed into it. "We shall make a slower start, but I expect we shall overtake you," said Elizabeth to the brake's occupants.

"But we have got to be there first, to arrive early," said Barby, "otherwise the point of it all goes."

"It would be like an Actress not arriving at the theatre before the audience," said Jessy.

The brake lurched forward, its wheels bore down upon the gravel heavily as it circled the oval lawn. It blundered through the gate and down the drive. Reenie's and Vi's bicycles skimmed the ground lightly behind it. Louisa's thin flat voice rose above the wheel's mumbling, Jessy's and Barby's and Ruth's joined it and Nino and Otello took up the song. Nino took an earth-stained handkerchief from his pocket and waved it. Miss Bolby and Miss Pickford stood upon the steps within the porch's shade and Miss Pickford took out *her* handkerchief. "Oh, Miss Bolby, they're happy! It does you good to see people happy. I'm ever such a fool when I hear singing." She buried her nose noisily in it. "You ought to have joined in the singing, with a beautiful voice like yours it seems a pity to keep silent."

"Children have a habit of singing, and the prisoners have little reason to be happy, and a *good* voice should be carefully tended, not wasted. It is never a good thing to let emotion get the upper hand, Miss Pickford," said Miss Bolby.

In the brake Barby said: "Today everything seems to have gone right, and yesterday I thought nothing would. Isn't it funny?"

"Laugh in the morning and you'll cry before night. I don't like the looks of it when things goes too right," said Bob Woodman.

"Haven't had your sleep, that's what's the matter with you, Bob Woodman. Always look on the black side of things when you haven't had your sleep, you do," said Mrs. Woodman.

The house was silent. A collection of empty rooms in which clocks ticked more than usually loudly, as if to emphasise the room's emptiness; so strident, in fact, was the clock in the hall that Miss Pickford heard it on her way to the dining-room. Essences, too, were more sharp; that of lavender which lay about in bowls, and of bees-wax, with which Winnie from the village had polished the furniture; they seemed to penetrate the room's furthest recesses.

Miss Bolby was already in the dining-room.

"Well, Miss Pickford, so you and I are alone."

"It does seem strange, Miss Bolby, doesn't it? After so much movement in the house it seems a little uncanny."

Miss Bolby removed the cover from the dish on the sideboard, exposing the cold remains of a joint. Beside it stood a salad, and behind it some stewed fruit and a hardened piece of cheese. "The kitchen doesn't seem to have troubled greatly with our lunch, Miss Pickford. I suppose it was left to Reenie, and that young lady, I think, would hardly exert herself to any great lengths over lunch for *us*, with a Gymkhana in view."

"But they were very busy in the kitchen, especially Reenie. I have never seen a girl work like Reenie. She works as if for love of it, and you should have seen the lunch they took, Miss Bolby."

"In any case a little more might have been done for those who were left behind. I call this a very meagre and carelessly served meal. Hillstone House would have done better. Indeed, considering the difficulties of rationing, Milly Tollmarsh did us very well, but Mr. Howland and Mr. Lind were very particular about their food."

"Men are," said Miss Pickford.

Both sat down, Miss Bolby at the head of the table.

Little sounds which Miss Pickford did not usually hear seemed to loom out at her today. Fate is being kind, she thought, I shall hear the birds. But she wished for once that fate were not so kind. Not just at the present moment, with Miss Bolby sitting so close to her in silence, with all the little sounds crying out against it. She felt glad of it when a bomber came in, not this time to accentuate, but to belittle them. When its torrent of sound had subsided they got out of hand again.

Miss Bolby did not seem so friendly today. Had she been wrong about Miss Bolby? Wrong in thinking her friendly?

"I do hope the children will enjoy themselves," she said, wishing she had not said it. "I am glad you relented. They were looking forward to it so."

Well, it was out now. The whole of what she had wanted to say and had not meant to say, and realised that she should not have said. Why not, after all, *be* glad, and let Miss Bolby know she was glad? "Yes, I am *glad*, Miss Bolby," she said.

Miss Bolby swallowed, drank from her glass, and put it down and said : "I think I shall enjoy myself, too, Miss Pickford. Everything is thought of for the children, little for those in whose charge they are." She poured more water into the glass and it fell from the jug with a splash which Miss Pickford heard. "Especially in this house, this chaotic slapdash house in which there seems to be no rules or routine, little, in fact, that one expects in an aristocratic house, or even a gentleman's house, but this afternoon I shall enjoy myself, I feel."

"Sitting at the piano, I suppose, singing. You don't know how lucky you are, and it *does* seem a waste with no one to hear you but me, and with me up in the woods there will be no one but the prisoners. Why don't you get the prisoners to sing with you, Miss Bolby?"

"I don't approve of this familiarity with the prisoners. I totally disapprove of the way they are allowed to come in and out of the house, treated as if they were members of the household, almost. Cosseted, one might say, and fed by Reenie. To suggest that they sing with me, Miss Pickford, is insulting, though Lord Rushford, who would, one would think, know better, made the same suggestion."

"I'm dreadfully sorry, Miss Bolby. I wouldn't for the world insult you. Everything I say seems to be going wrong today, and yet my hearing is perfect and I'm so looking forward to hearing the birds. When I first arrived, Miss Bolby, you seemed so happy here, as if you loved Rushford, almost as if you belonged to it. Now you—well, you don't seem to like it any more. It isn't anything *I* have done, is it? I haven't offended you in any way?"

"No, you haven't offended me, Miss Pickford."

"Then if you'll excuse me, Miss Bolby, I'll go. I want to get up into the woods as soon as I can, so that I can have a long afternoon with the birds."

"Lady Rushford wished one of us to clear away the lunch, Miss Pickford, but in that case I will do it."

"Oh no, Miss Bolby! Please don't trouble. I'll do it before I go. It won't take me a jiffy."

"But I haven't quite finished, Miss Pickford. I was just about to take a biscuit and cheese. They fill up the cracks, as the children say, in a—well, a very *plain*—scarcely a chef-cooked meal! Don't wait, Miss Pickford, please. I expect I can manage, bad as I am at domestic duties. It doesn't require a great deal of skill to clear away a meal."

"Must it be done right away, Miss Bolby? Why don't you leave it? There isn't a soul to see it and I'll do it when I come in. You don't want to hang about either; I expect you want to get

232

off to your singing. Artistic folk like you shouldn't waste time hanging about clearing away meals."

"Before I can get to the pleasure of my singing with a peaceful mind, I have a great deal to do, Miss Pickford. I have to find my bracelets."

"You mean you have a suspicion where they are, Miss Bolby?"

"I have, Miss Pickford. A very shrewd suspicion."

"Oh, Miss Bolby!" And instead of asking Miss Bolby where she thought they were, Miss Pickford thought of Mrs. Staines-Close's brooch. She saw the brooch rise and fall upon Mrs. Staines-Close's bosom. It was a bee-brooch, with diamond wings and a mother-of-pearl body and little shifty ruby eyes. When the brooch had been lost, she had felt all day that it must have been she, in some moment of aberration, who had taken it; she had felt this until it had been found. In the same way she had felt one evening in the Schoolroom that she had taken Miss Bolby's bracelets, and she felt it now. Miss Bolby would not look at her so searchingly unless *she* thought so. She looked just as Mrs. Staines-Close had looked when she had thought that she, Rose, had taken the bee. There was the same strained note in Miss Bolby's voice as there had been in Mrs. Staines-Close's. In the Schoolroom that evening there had been a kind of query, a suggestion of the jocular, as if it were *absurd* to be suspicious, and yet because she, Rose Pickford, was under the same roof, in the same employ, Miss Bolby must clear her mind of such suspicion. Her voice held none of these pryings now, it was an accusing voice. Miss Bolby, who had seemed to be her friend, who had taken her round the house and down the garden, was accusing her, Rose, of stealing the bracelets! Miss Bolby, who had explained the pictures, who had initiated her into the ways of the house; who had told her so much about India, and her mother's friends, and Bertha Barnsley, and Rowfont, and King Boris, and Ned Blatchington's proposal, and her sister Sita, and her

233

Atherton-Broadleigh connections, and the Dean of Waterbury!
Miss Bolby, who knew so many famous people! Who had
given up her room so that she, Rose, might have it instead of
King Edward's room—instead of King Edward's room. . . .
Had Miss Bolby been false? Had *she*, all the time, wanted
King Edward's room for herself? Had all Miss Bolby *said*
been false. . . ?

Miss Bolby's eyes were no longer upon her. She liberally
buttered a biscuit and she looked at the biscuit, spreading the
butter carefully so that none overlapped its edge—as if she
were wholly absorbed in the task, unconscious of another's
presence. No, Miss Bolby could not have meant it. Naturally
she was worried about her bracelets. Who wouldn't be?
Had they not been given to her mother by an Indian
Rajah?

"Well, bye-bye. I'm off to the birds, Miss Bolby," she said.
But the words, *her* words, sounded false, as if *she* no longer
trusted Miss Bolby.

Having haphazardly cleared the table, Miss Bolby left the
dishes upon the sideboard, then she went to the Schoolroom.

She put her feet up upon the chintz-covered chaise-longue
beneath the window. She put her hands beneath her head,
resting it in them, leaning back against faded cushions. From
this position she surveyed the room.

As schoolrooms went, it was not a bad room. Not too
frugally furnished; many had been worse and some had been
better: an upright piano across a corner, a round table in
the room's centre, covered with a faded cloth upon which were
faded inkstains; delf vases stood upon the mantelpiece and
the chiffonier. Today they were filled with dahlias—top-
heavy heads, drunkenly falling forward, slipped from the
position in which she had arranged them. Today *she* had
arranged them. She had gone down the garden when the
house had emptied, free to pick what she willed, because

Gibson, the head gardener, had gone to the Gymkhana; he had taken fruit and vegetable exhibits to the Flower Show, and no underling would dare to say: 'Those are not for picking, if you don't mind, Miss Bolby.' She had not so much as looked for the prisoners, but they had been singing, and against her will she had had the urge to sing: to break down the barriers, to let principles go, to sing in their own tongue—lines were coming back from Verdi and Puccini, and with them the dark room in Mr. Middlethorpe's house in Worthing, and the Barnsleys' house, and Ralph, and Bertha. . . . So she hurriedly picked the dahlias, the largest and the best she could find because it was Miss Pickford who had first filled the delf vases and she wanted to outdo Miss Pickford.

'I hope it's not impertinent of me, Miss Bolby, but I've brought in a bouquet; flowers brighten a room so. They make it *live*, my father always used to say. Mrs. Staines-Close used to like me to do the flowers for her, she said I had a delicate touch. Perhaps you'd like me to arrange them for you, Miss Bolby?'

'It's very thoughtful of you, Miss Pickford. Flowers, as you say, are so important. Lady Rowfont used to leave many of the vases to me when there were parties at Rowfont. She asked me to do the centre-piece for the dinner-table one night when King Boris came, and the King was gracious enough to draw me aside after dinner to tell me how much he admired it. After that it was always I who did the flowers. By the way, Miss Pickford, the head gardener here, Gibson, is most emphatic about the *best* flowers *not* being picked, at least not for the Schoolroom. Now, with so little of the flower garden tended, he likes to save them for the front of the house. In some of my other posts, in pre-war days, it was different—the Schoolroom was a veritable bower.'

'Oh, I *am* sorry, Miss Bolby. I don't want to offend Mr. Gibson.'

' "Gibson" I think he prefers *us* to call him, Miss Pickford.

His bark is worse than his bite, you know. I don't think you need have any fear of Gibson.'

'I almost feel I oughtn't to arrange them now,' and Miss Pickford, hesitantly fingering them at first, had arranged them —delicately, so that the lighter flowers cascaded, against a background of fern. They had been an irritant to her, Roona, every time she, Roona, had come into the room, because it was irritating that anyone who was such a fool as Miss Pickford could do anything with taste and delicacy. It had not been possible to throw the flowers away until today, because Miss Pickford had filled the vases daily, rearranging a leaf here and a fern there and snipping off dead heads like a pecking bird. But this morning, when the house had emptied, she had thrown them away and taken a basket down the garden, singing. Before she knew where she was her voice was out and letting itself go—only when she heard the prisoners from the kitchen garden did she restrain it.

She hastily gathered some fern, because she knew Miss Pickford was in her room and she wanted to do the vases while Miss Pickford was out of the way; then she hurried back and tried her hand at them, but the fern wilted and fell sideways, so she took it to the waste-paper basket in her room so that Miss Pickford should not see she had been unsuccessful, then she wrestled with the heavy-headed dahlias.

Now that they had fallen forward they made islands of colour in the room, more showy by far than anything Miss Pickford had done. Miss Pickford was not artistic, she knew nothing about pictures. When she, Roona, had taken her round the house, she had said : 'Oh, what a pretty piece of china ! I *do* like Dresden, it's so dainty, Miss Bolby !' hardly noticing the pictures. How could such a person be artistic? And why should she be? She had no background, she was not a gentlewoman.

No, most decidedly not a gentlewoman. How could such a fool as Miss Pickford have taken the bracelets? The notion was absurd, one of those dreadful suspicions that came upon one when something was missing. How fortunate that she had said no more to Miss Pickford, that she had not openly accused her in a moment of insane jealousy and hatred, because the suspicion had been growing. The uneasy atmosphere in the house, the restlessness of it; the noise from above, and the children who had created an atmosphere about the Gymkhana, had all helped to make her, Roona, lose her balance about the bracelets—her balance, not her *head*. No, it was not poor foolish Miss Pickford who had taken them, but they must be found to prove that it was not—or that it was. . . .

Miss Bolby withdrew her hands from beneath her head and rested them at her sides and shut her eyes. The whole afternoon lay before her in which to find the bracelets. The less she thought about them the more likely she was to come upon them.

She would write a letter or two in order to forget them. Letters always calmed her, and she had not yet written her weekly letter to Sita, and *this* letter to Sita was a little difficult, knowing what she now knew about Lady Archie. But she would describe the visit to Bowborough and Lord Corwen's little courtesies—so unexpected and so sudden, because, with the intuition of the deaf, he had sensed that she was not treated as one of her station should be treated—and because of the light, insulting way in which Lady Archie had talked to her on Thursday at lunch—she was in no doubt now that Lord Corwen had sensed this.

She would write to Mrs. Hurst, too, to describe the visit, and this she wanted to do while the memory was fresh.

She got up—it was not so easy to get up now middle-age was beginning to make itself felt through the bones. She went over to the piano; she lifted the lid and struck a chord, and then another chord—then she shut down the lid and took her blotter and her inkpot and pen from a drawer in the chiffonier.

She put them on the table and drew up a chair and arranged herself in the position in which she liked to write: an upright position a little away from the table. She opened the blotter and smoothed its pages and shifted it a little to one side before dipping her pen into the ink. 'Dearest Sita', she wrote, and while thinking out the next phrase she turned over one of the blotter's porous pages: beneath it lay a slip of paper upon which were written hieroglyphics, and below the hieroglyphics phrases: this was so surprising that the phrases at first were as senseless as the hieroglyphics.

Miss Roona Bolby to marry the Marquess of Corwen.

The Cow has a Silver Tail.

So senseless were the words that she had to re-read them before their meaning sang out at her: then they seemed to fill the room and to thunder in her ears with the force of a waterfall before subsiding, before rearranging themselves as phrases upon a slip of paper in Miss Pickford's hand. It was a clear hand, and there was grace in the hieroglyphics, and yet the meaning was mad. *Un peut detraqué*—the poor woman had taken leave of her senses. Miss Bolby said this aloud, tapping her brow. 'Miss Roona Bolby to marry the Marquess of Corwen.' Yes there *was* meaning here. Not only meaning but malice. The woman was not only a thief, but a malicious maniac, a *klepto*maniac, leaving nasty little notes about which might be found by the children, because she had not been asked to Bowborough. She was jealous, and this was her revenge. Just because she *had* been asked to sit at the Big

Table on Thursday she thought that she could make fun of her, Roona, suggesting that Lord Corwen had wanted to marry her, Roona, and that *she,* Roona, had wanted to marry Lord Corwen, when it had not entered her head any more than it had entered Lord Corwen's. How *dared* the woman suggest such a thing? and '*The Cow has a Silver Tail*', what did that mean? Was the whole thing madness? This sounded a little like the children. Had Miss Pickford been making fun of her with the children?

Her first impulse was to tear the paper up, and her hand trembled in her eagerness to do so; but no, Miss Pickford must suffer for this : explain it, when she explained why she had stolen the bracelets. A woman who would stoop to this sort of indignity would not draw the line at theft, and were she a kleptomaniac she probably *could* not.

Miss Bolby folded the paper and put it in a black handbag which she carried about the house with her.

"I must be calm," she said aloud. "At this, of all times, I must be calm, I must not lose my head." She took a bottle of eau-de-Cologne from the drawer in the chiffonier and shook some on to her handkerchief. Then she lay down again upon the chaise-longue.

I will rest a while until I am calm, she thought. Then I will go to her room and search it thoroughly. There is plenty of time. She will be in the woods all the afternoon.

Miss Pickford lay upon a spongy, springy bed. She thrust her hands deep into it, churning the top layer of leaves, grasping clods which lay beneath them; those loose upon the surface hissed, they made the sound of a distant sea retreating upon shingle, but she did not hear it. All the lesser sounds had faded out; those which lived in her own head had replaced them. She was being duped. How was she to know now, that the thrush was the thrush, when these false sounds intervened, startling and misleading? It was Miss Bolby's fault, she had

worried and agitated her just when her hearing was clear.
When there was only one wave-length, tricks could not be
played with the machine, and soon she would be reduced to
relying upon a machine, and even were it small and not
unsightly employers would not care to employ one who had
to rely upon a machine. And yet Old Mr. Stiles had had a
machine which had sat upon the desk in the Office while Old
Lord Rushford dictated. Bob Woodman had told her this.
He had knocked at her door one night.

'I'm ever so sorry to disturb you, Miss, but you're showing
a light.'

'Oh, Bob, I *am* sorry. When I'm trying to let in more air
I forget about the light.' She had wondered whether she
should have called him 'Woodman', or 'Mr. Woodman', or
'Bob Woodman', instead of just Bob. Etiquette at Rushford
was so confusing.

'Care for a cup of tea, Miss? I've got me kettle on and I'm
just taking one to Miss Bolby.'

'Oh, thanks ever so much, Bob,' and again she had felt that
it was not quite right somehow to call him 'Bob', and they
began to talk, and he had told her more about Old Lord
Rushford and Old Mr. Stiles, and he had said : 'But you ought
to ast Fred Finch, Miss, his memory's a deal better than mine,
Miss,' and she had said : 'I find it so hard to hear what Fred
Finch says, Bob,' and Bob had said : 'It's inconsiderate of 'im,
never puts 'is teeth in, that's the reason of it, Miss. One lame
dog ought to help another over a stile.' And the next day Miss
Bolby had looked at her as if she had known about the cup
of tea, and as if she, Rose Pickford, had been trespassing upon
Miss Bolby's rights and should not have had it.

This growing hatred, yes, hatred, of Miss Bolby must be
curbed. It was wrong. Her respect, yes, respect—she had
never *liked* Miss Bolby—had turned in the last day or two
to dislike, and now, because Miss Bolby had upset her hearing
just as she was about to listen to the birds, it had grown to

hatred, and to hate was wrong. Miss Bolby was not evil, she
had not deliberately upset her, Rose's, hearing. She had only,
after all, been trying to *find* her bracelets; had been searching
for help, perhaps, but she had looked like Mrs. Staines-
Close. . . .

It was wrong to think evil. 'Look for evil and you'll find it,'
her father had said. 'Look for good and you'll find good.'

It must be getting on for tea-time, and Miss Bolby would
want a cup of tea and she would not know her way about
the kitchen because she was not on friendly terms with Reenie,
and she, Rose, could do with a cup of tea herself because the
afternoon had been so disappointing.

Miss Pickford scrambled to her feet. There were leaves on
her clothes and in her hair, and a fragment of leaf had
attatched itself to her spectacles and she blew it away and
watched it bob before her nose and float and fall, and lose
itself in a milliard leaves. She kicked her way through them,
so that leaves sprayed about her in showers, in flakes more
gentle than snow—languorous and elusive.

Although there was no hurry and it was early, Miss Bolby
could not rest for long upon the chaise-longue.

She would go out for a little, she thought, before she
searched Miss Pickford's room—*her* room which Miss Pickford
had taken.

She was calm now; she would feel better outside in the sun-
shine. She would sit out in front of the house for a while. It
would be pleasant to sit alone before it when it was deserted—
almost as if it were her own. Or as if she were a visitor and
the other guests had gone to the races—in Old Lord Rushford's day.

She took her bag. It was not safe to leave anything un-
guarded now.

As she went through the silent corridors she began to think
of how life must have been here at Rushford, when maids who

were maids—cap-and-aproned maids—must have hurried in fresh print frocks, carrying cans, brass cans which they filled from cupboards at the end of the passages—this was where taps had lived at Rowfont in pre-bathroom days—cans which would be taken to bedrooms and left in basins, enveloped in small, finely embroidered towels. There had been basins and towels and cans in *her* Rowfont days, three times a day. There were no such luxuries at Rushford.

When she reached the stair, the front stair—at the foot of which, carved upon each pillar, danced a dolphin—she paused. With what grandeur and exhilaration, with what an air of satisfaction could one sweep down such a stair towards a dinner party or a ball. She swept down it now.

White light, daylight, sunlight, driving the dust before it, fell through the open door into the hall and the illusion vanished. The dolphins stared blearily at her.

Miss Pickford was right, there was something about this silence and emptiness which was uncanny.

Miss Pickford again! She did not want, just now, to think about Miss Pickford—for the last few moments her thoughts had ranged over subjects which had been pleasanter.

She took *The Times* from a table in the hall. *The Times* would soothe and steady her, distract her a little from the unpleasant task which lay before her.

She went out into the light; three-quarters of the house lay in light, a quarter in shadow. She sat in the corner of the swing-seat which would soon be in shadow; shadow brought quietude and sun made her dizzy. She spread *The Times* upon her knees. She was not as calm as she thought. Not calm enough to read *The Times*. She began to swing gently, and because the swinging motion eased, she began to sing, and as always when she sang, almost inaudibly at first, from somewhere in the kitchen garden the prisoners' voices joined her. When a distance lay between them there was no harm in it, it was as if it were an accident—as if she were taking a walk

in Italy. Because the afternoon was still and no one moved
in the house and gardens, it was as if the three voices were
enclosed within an opera house and they sang to a silent
audience—but not for long. Purring in towards the sound to
disrupt its pattern and break its continuity came a bomber,
and with it reality. Miss Bolby remembered Miss Pickford.

In order to stop the seat's swinging she ground her right
toe into the gravel, and the sudden jerk which made it bounce
upset her balance so that she fell sideways and grasped the
mattress. As she did so she felt something hard and cold.

Miss Pickford had gathered a bouquet for the schoolroom :
fern, and the seed-heads of wild campanula, and a spray of
blackberry which fruited and flowered at the same time.
She carried it gently so that its flushed petals should not
fall.

She was at the wood's edge now, and the beeches' smooth
boles were thinning; in the tracery above there were gaps of
sky, as if a fine shawl had been torn. Presently she came out
into the clearing from which Larry and Jessy had looked at
the house : a path ran horizontally before her, marking the
wood's end, and from its furthest edge lawn ran steeply and
unevenly, seeming to run abruptly up against the house itself,
hiding the gravel strip which decorously divided them. She
knew, as she saw it from here, that she was beginning to love
Rushford, to love its squat serenity—it looked squat from
where she stood—pushed down into the hollow, with the lawn,
rough and unruly, tumbling towards it. She understood how
Miss Bolby had felt now, when she had shown her round—
the pride with which she had said 'we', as if she belonged to
Rushford. She, Rose, was beginning to love the mist which
strayed up from the river, seemingly casual and fragmentary
yet implacable in its melancholy. She would not be driven
away by Miss Bolby; it was one of Miss Bolby's bad days, that
was all. One must make allowances for Miss Bolby. One who

was so talented must surely possess an artistic temperament.

As Miss Pickford thought this, a single note and then the first phrase of a melody floated through to her. Had the haze of cotton wool in her head cleared? She leaned forward, straining, eager: this was no sound of her own fabrication, tricking her, it was Miss Bolby—and the prisoners! Oh, joy! Miss Bolby would be nice again, and she would be wanting her cup of tea.

Forgetting the tender care she had lavished on the blackberry blossom, Miss Pickford ran down the slope before her; to resist the temptation to run down a slope when there was a slope to be run down was beyond her powers.

So Miss Pickford *had* taken them! She had taken them, and then when enquiries had been set afoot and the servants questioned she had been afraid and she had hidden them where no one would think of looking for them, and by the merest chance they had fallen into her, Roona's, lap as it were. It was simple now. She, Roona, would not have the unpleasant task of searching Miss Pickford's room. She would *take* the bracelets there instead and put them in a drawer, then she would go to Miss Pickford and say: 'If I am not disturbing you, Miss Pickford, I would like a word with you. Far be it from me to spoil your afternoon, but if you could spare a moment, I should like you to come to the Schoolroom.' Then she would produce the slip of paper from her bag and say: 'I think there must be some misunderstanding, Miss Pickford; this piece of paper was in my blotter. The writing is yours, *and* the hieroglyphics, I take it, as you are the only member of the household who is a shorthand writer. As I am unable to read shorthand, perhaps you will transcribe it for me? Perhaps you will also be good enough to explain the *longhand* phrases to me?' Then she would say: 'And there is another little matter. I have just been to my room, or rather *your* room which I relinquished in order that you should not feel out of place in the King's room,

244

and in *this* room, *your* room, I have found *my Indian brace-lets*, in a drawer. . . .'

Miss Bolby took the bracelets and put them in her bag. There was no time to be lost now, she must make certain of getting them into the drawer before Miss Pickford came in.

It seemed a shame to break into Miss Bolby's song with a cup of tea, she would relish it more later on, Miss Pickford thought, so she went first to the Schoolroom to arrange the bouquet.

She felt so light-hearted that she sang as she went down the corridor. The evil moment at lunch which had been so preg-nant with suspicion had been born of her own imagination, had come forth from her own head; thoughts as well as sounds were beginning to trick her. But what did it matter now, Miss Bolby was in a good mood or she would not be singing.

When Miss Pickford opened the Schoolroom door and saw the dahlias she felt she had been hit.

Harsh, red splashes, hurting the eye because they were with-out pattern, leaning their great heads together as if they had been thrown into the vases and left to support each other, mocked at the slender sprays she held in her hand. Then she thought: Oh! if only I could arrange the poor things—take the weight from them and make them sit up and blaze at me. Used in the right way, scarlets and crimsons are just the thing. How clever Miss Bolby is. She has seen what I should never have dared to see, but she has not yet arranged them.

She put down her poor pale bouquet and began to take the dahlias from the vases. . . . 'By the way, Miss Pickford, the head-gardener, Gibson, is most emphatic about the *best* flowers not being picked. . . .' And the flowers she, Rose herself had arranged had not been dead. Had Miss Bolby deliberately thrown them away so that she might fill the vases with dahlias which she, Rose, was not allowed to pick?

As if its red petals scalded her, Miss Pickford put down the head she held. She listened, but she heard no sound. From this side of the house she would hear no sound; the Schoolroom faced the formal garden, and the sound she had heard from the wood's edge had not seemed to come from there.

The silence, and this new uneasiness concerning Miss Bolby so disturbed her that instead of going down to the kitchen she went to her own room. The shock which met her there was greater than that which she had received in the School-room.

Miss Bolby stood before the chest of drawers, leaning over an open drawer; her hand seemed to be inside the drawer. She was just a figure at first, as Miss Pickford opened the door and faced the light, then, as her eyes became adjusted to it, Miss Bolby became Miss Bolby, and as she did so she straightened and faced Miss Pickford. It was not possible to see her mood upon her face, the strong light at her back protected it, and it threw back light from the room's green walls which gave her an unusual pallor.

"Ah, Miss Pickford! I thought you were in the woods, or I should have asked your permission before coming to your room, in spite of the fact that it is *my* room!"

"Oh, don't mention it, Miss Bolby. Can I help you at all? Were you looking for something?" Then Miss Pickford remembered the bracelets, and she added, because she felt uneasy, with a new uneasiness now, which seemed to attack the pit of her stomach: "I was just coming to look for you, Miss Bolby, to see if you'd like a cup of tea."

"Your character, if I may say so, Miss Pickford, is curiously complex, extremely interesting psychologically. You insult me, you leave little notes about concerning me so that they may be seen by the servants and the children—for all I know you collaborate with the children in order to make fun of me—and, not content with that, you *thieve* from me, and then you have the impertinence to offer me cups of tea! Will you be so kind as to shut the door, Miss Pickford? We are in a draught, and it looks as if we shall be here for some time. I must ask you for an explanation."

"But I don't understand, Miss Bolby; I . . ."

"Be so good as to shut the door, Miss Pickford, and please come over here into the light; there are one or two little things I want to show you."

Miss Pickford shut the door. She felt she had become an automaton, there was no feeling in her legs any more. She could not have heard Miss Bolby aright. Just when she needed it most, her head was beginning to play tricks again.

Miss Bolby opened her bag and took a slip of paper from it and put both down upon the writing table in the window. She unfolded the slip of paper and smoothed it.

Miss Pickford edged away from the bag. It was a low squat bag with a snap-fastener; it seemed to bulge with evil.

"Perhaps now, first of all, Miss Pickford, you will explain *this* to me?"

Miss Roona Bolby to marry the Marquess of Corwen.

The Cow has a Silver Tail.

"Oh, *Miss Bolby,* I must have left it in the blotter! It was just a little bit of fun Louisa and I had together in the School-room when you were at Bowborough and she asked me to teach her shorthand so that she could—well, she wanted to see what shorthand looked like, and I couldn't think of anything to write and that was what she said: 'Write, "Miss Bolby is to marry the Marquess of Corwen" '; and before I knew where I was I'd written it, and she said it was true, and ever since I've wanted to congratulate you, Miss Bolby, but I didn't quite like to, in case—well, just *in case* it *was* some nonsense of Louisa's."

"And what reason have either you or Louisa for supposing Miss Pickford, that Lord Corwen wishes to marry me?"

"That was what Louisa said, Miss Bolby, and he did—well, he did ask you over to Bowborough, and knowing how nice he was, having sat next to him, I felt glad. I began to think of the wedding——"

"And 'The Cow has a Silver Tail'—how do you explain that, Miss Pickford? That, I suppose, is also some nonsense of Louisa's?"

"That was what she said, Miss Bolby. She said: 'Now write something else,' and I couldn't for the life of me think of anything else. I'm such a fool when asked to write something suddenly, and she said: ' "The Cow has a Silver Tail." ' She is such an imaginative child, Louisa."

"A very backward, dreamy child. Sometimes, I think, not quite all there. Has it ever occurred to you, Miss Pickford, that there is something a little odd about your mind? But a kleptomaniac can hardly have a very well-balanced mind. Your explanation is not a very satisfactory one. Louisa is not a *malicious* child, and it is a little difficult to believe such things from the mind of a child in view of what I know about *you,* Miss Pickford. For a week I have been suspicious and have thrust away my suspicions, but now I *know* that it is you who took my bracelets, and here is the evidence. Kindly look, Miss Pickford—in the drawer. You took them, and then when Lady Rushford began to make enquiries you hid them away because you knew I suspected you, and then, when nothing came to light, you grew bold again and you brought them back to the drawer. Look, Miss Pickford! You can hardly explain this away!" Miss Bolby took the bracelets from

248

the drawer. She held them up and slid them over her wrist
so that they made a light jingling. "But I shall not put them
on. Oh no! They will remain in the drawer until Lord and
Lady Rushford come in."

The colour had gone from Miss Pickford's face, and she
sat down because the strength had gone from her knees. Then,
suddenly, something seemed to click in her head, and the room,
and the cold coils lying in the drawer, and all that had happened in the past week fell into a pattern so sharply defined
that she lost her fear: anger took its place, surging upward
through her and bringing her whole body back to life. She
stood up, she had no need now to hold on to the table; words
rushed into her head with the force of a torrent, so that those
at the back shot the first ones forward.

"How dare you call me a thief, Miss Bolby? How dare
you? I see through you now. I see the kind of person you
are. You hid the bracelets away yourself somewhere, so that
you could accuse someone, and you picked on me because you
want to drive me away from here, and you brought them up
and put them in my drawer. Of course you did. You must
have, or how could they have got there? You were putting
the bracelets into the drawer when I came in, of course you
were. Oh, you're wicked, Miss Bolby! Yes, wicked! I looked
for good and I found evil, and you're not even a lady—Reenie
is more of a lady. You're a snob, Miss Bolby. I see now why
you took King Edward's room—so that you could write to all
your friends at Hillstone House and tell them you'd slept in
King Edward's room. You're false, Miss Bolby. You're a
fraud, and you're horrible and I hate you. Why you're not
even artistic—you've just got a voice, and anybody can have
a voice, it's an accident! And you're not driving me away,
but I'm going. Oh yes, I'm going this instant. I won't be
alone in the house with you another minute. Here, take your
horrible bracelets and leave my room and let me pack my bag,
and everyone will know why I've gone and what you've done

to me and the sort of person you are, even Lord Corwen, and I hope for his sake he doesn't marry you!"

Miss Pickford took a suitcase out of a cupboard and began feverishly to throw things into it.

"Wait a moment, Miss Pickford!" said Miss Bolby. "Calm yourself. Let us try to arrive at some sort of understanding about this thing before you go. Let me tell you, you are wrong if you think Lord and Lady Rushford will take your word against mine. With references and connections such as mine this is hardly likely!"

"Oh, they will, they will! They're nice people—and anyway, I don't care!" said Miss Pickford, continuing to throw things into the suitcase. "I must get out of this house as quickly as I can; I can't stay in it another minute with you."

"You may find you will have to, Miss Pickford. There is no one left, you must remember; they are all at the Gymkhana. Who do you think will drive you to the station?"

Miss Pickford had forgotten the Gymkhana. She felt suddenly cold and powerless, and anger seemed to drain from her. She leaned forward over the bed, upon which she had thrown the suitcase, clasping her left side. "Oh, Miss Bolby," she said, "you're cruel." Miss Bolby seemed as hard and cold and cruel as the gold cobras which were her bracelets. "I can't breathe," Miss Pickford said, "I must have air," and she ran from the room.

She would feel better, she knew, when she had been able to breathe in fresh air, and because the higher you go the more air there seems to be, she ran to the top of the house and into the room which had first been hers—the little room with the scaffolding round the window, because it was high; she leaned as far as she could through it, holding on to the scaffolding— had the window been less small she would have climbed out on to it—it enabled her to lean further out, it supported her, made her feel she was *in* the air and so could breathe it in more easily. Below she saw Nino and Otello in the formal garden.

"Nino! Otello! Help me!"

"Take care, Signorina! If you lean so far through the window you will fall!"

"Non parlo Italiano. Je ne comprend pas, non comprendo!"

"Stay still! Don't move! Take care!" said Otello.

It was only then that she realised how far out she was leaning; something in his voice gave her warning.

"Help me! Help me! I'm coming down," she said, and she wished that she *had* fallen—that she had *thrown* herself down.

I must get away, she thought; somehow I must get away. A bomber roared in as she withdrew. It sent its vibrations singing through the scaffolding and the window's frame; it seemed to suck the fresh clean air which had been coming in towards her away from her, augmenting her desire to get away which was now so strong that her whole being was fixed upon it. She ran down through the empty house and into the formal garden. "Nino, Nino! Otello! Help me! Get me away from here. One of you must take me to the station; they're all at the Gymkhana. *Stazzione! Automobile! Vite, vite! Comprenez?* The Signorina Bolby"—she pointed to the house—"she accuses me, me, of taking her bracelets! She wants me to be sent to *prison! Prisoniero, comme-vous.* She is wicked, evil, *mechant!* Get me away!"

Her distress was so great that it communicated itself through the barrier of language, and Otello, by intuition more than understanding, grasped the gist of her words. He said in English: "The old bag!"

"I take you, Signorina," said Nino; "I drive the Fiat. In Italy I drive a Fiat."

"Yes! The Fiat, Nino! Lord Rushford's Fiat is in the stables, they didn't take the Fiat. Get the Fiat, Nino!"

"It is forbidden that a prisoner of war should drive a car," said Otello. "It would result in grave consequences."

"Oh, but you must let him take me, Otello, you must! Oh, don't stand there arguing! *Vite! Vite! Presto! Presto!*"

"In the Fiat of the Signore Barone, no one will see," said Nino, demonstrating the Fiat's nearness to the ground.

"Take me to Colsal Halt and I'll wait till a train comes. Oh, take me! Take me, Nino!"

"If the Signorina will get her valise," said Nino, and as she ran back into the house Nino and Otello began to run towards the stables.

She ran up to her room and seized a hat and a coat and her bag and the suitcase, just as it was, without waiting to put more into it. The door of her room was open and the drawer was open, but there was no sign of Miss Bolby.

She hurried down the dark stair which ran down from outside her door, and through the hall and down to the stables, lugging and bumping the suitcase. Though her breath came in little short gasps, the problem of breathing no longer worried her, she had forgotten it.

When she reached the stables Nino had got the Fiat started. She did not hear the engine's purr, but as she dragged the suitcase towards it it slid out of the coach-house which served as a garage, with Otello running beside it.

When Miss Bolby left Miss Pickford's room she went to the Schoolroom and lay down upon the chaise-longue.

Though outwardly calm she was inwardly shaken. Her plan had miscarried.

Fortunately it was Miss Pickford and not she who had lost her head.

She had not expected denial and abuse, such an ugly scene. It was difficult to know now what exactly she had expected . . . a confession? So that she might say: 'As we are alone in the house together, Miss Pickford, no one need know about this very unfortunate incident. I know you will not wish to remain here under such circumstances. It will be assumed that I have found my bracelets, and you, you will just give your notice in, as if you didn't care for the place. And let us hope that in new surroundings you will find some way of curing this miserable malady.' It was a kindness to call it a malady. One must be humane. Or, perhaps . . . but it was difficult to see the way things would have gone if she, Roona, had been able to secrete the bracelets in the drawer before Miss Pickford had come in. . . . And the flow of abuse, the outrageous things Miss Pickford had said had altered everything.

Careful thinking was needed now. Miss Pickford would soon find she could not get away, and it would not do to have her saying—well, all *that* to Lord and Lady Rushford. At all events it was good to have the bracelets back. They jingled as they slid back and forth upon her forearm.

Here, upon the chaise-longue, in the fading light, with a cashmere shawl at her feet and the cedar to the right of the formal garden gently swishing, she felt she might have been back in the White House at Worthing—that it might have been her mother and not herself who lay upon the chaise-longue. . . .

It would not do, at this point, to begin dreaming.

It would be as well now to go and see if she could find Miss Pickford; it could not be very long now before they were back from the Gymkhana.

Miss Bolby tidied her hair, without looking in the mirror— she did not want just now to look in the mirror.

She went downstairs—not by the little dark stairway which ran down from the Schoolroom passage and Miss Pickford's room and which would have been quicker—but by the front stair into the hall.

The house's silence seemed to press in upon her now; in the last half-hour it seemed to have grown more silent.

Miss Pickford was somewhere outside probably, thinking she would find some stray underling who would take her to the station.

Miss Bolby went to the piano at the far end of the hall. Oh, joy, after the Schoolroom one, to strike a chord upon a grand piano.

She raised its lid and sat down upon the stool.

She paused for a moment, made uneasy by the overbearing silence, almost wishing now for an incoming aircraft to disturb it. The sounds which did so were gentler, fainter and more feeble : the distant spasms of a car starting; little feeble, futile paroxysms, spitting at each other before gaining in power, before smoothening and running together so that the sound became one.

From where she sat she saw the Fiat crawl out like a small beetle from the dark copse which hid the stables and swing into the main drive . . . and diminish in size and vanish into space where the drive and the park humped into a hillock.

Well, that was that. Miss Pickford *had* gone, and who could have taken her but one of the prisoners? Trouble would certainly come of *that*, which would teach the prisoners that they were prisoners. Miss Pickford using the Fiat, and the prisoners—the audacity of it! Who would have thought it! Foolish, feeble woman!

Once again the pattern for the future shifted. All the afternoon it had been shifting, falling into new and unforeseeable shapes with the suddenness of the particles in a kaleidoscope.

The Schoolroom would be wholly hers again; she would return to Old Lord Rushford's room : new vistas would open up before her, not the vistas of discontent into which she had looked in King Edward's room.

And might it not be possible, conceivable, that there had been some truth in what Miss Pickford had said, that Lord Corwen *had* asked her over to Bowborough because he had

wanted to marry her? That she would leave Rushford, when
the time came, not for Hillstone House, but for Bowborough,
as the Marchioness of Corwen?

Oh, glorious snub for Lady Archie!

Oh, glorious, after all the disappointments, to outdo Sita,
to be a Marchioness, the Marchioness of Corwen!

Elated, exultant at the thought, Miss Bolby crashed out the
opening chords of Liszt's Liebestraum.

Bella slept in Becca's arms, Ruth and Louisa sleepily sang,
Barby and Jessy were silent as Fred Finch drove the brake
home. Winnie from the village and the Woodman family had
gone home early; Harry Williams and 'the new lad' had
taken the ponies.

When Larry and Elizabeth, who had left before the brake,
in the van, broke down and were overtaken by it, silence had
overtaken the brake; though the mare's pace quickened as she
headed for home, all heads began to nod.

As they slowed to a walking pace in the last lap of drive,
Bella stirred, and first Barby and then Jessy, and then Ruth
and Louisa, sat up: sound came towards them from the house,
made more resonant by its emptiness—the sound of a piano,
of great crashing chords.

While Becca lifted Bella out they climbed down and filed
into the hall.

As they did so they heard the telephone, drowned until now
by the piano: angry, feeble, futile; impatient to be answered.
Barby lifted the receiver, and Miss Bolby, sensing rather than
hearing a disturbance—she had been playing for so long she
had forgotten where she was—lifted her hands from the keys.

Into the silence Barby said: "Hullo? Yes. . . . Who? . .,
No, she hasn't come back yet from the Gymkhana. I'll get her
to ring you. She and my stepfather had a breakdown. . . .
Yes? *Who?* The Infirmary? . . . Yes. . . . *Who?* . . . Oh,
how? . . . Not *killed*? . . ."

She put the receiver down. "Miss Pickford," she said, "has been killed. The Fiat ran into a lorry, and Nino is in the infirmary.

"Killed," she repeated, "Miss Pickford has been killed."

2

"If the funeral is at Rushford," said Lady Archie, "you or Hughie will have to go to it."

"I don't see that it is really necessary, Blanchie," said Lord Archie.

"We must show our sorrow somehow, and Hughie sat next to the poor woman at lunch. Poor woman! A sad struggling woman. Not only is death a tragedy, but it's so inconyenient. It seems that she had no relations. Elizabeth has wired to a Mrs. Staines-Close, to whom she was a sort of secretary-companion, to see if any can be traced, so as to find out what is to be done about the funeral. Think of it! That poor woman was driving to her death just as we were enjoying ourselves at the Gymkhana."

"All the same, I don't really see why we should go to her funeral, my dear Blanchie."

"Hughie will probably want to, to see Miss Bolby, though I have a feeling that we have been mercifully delivered from Miss Bolby. Hughie seems quite off her. Something must have gone wrong in the aviary, and she is leaving."

"I told you we should encourage it," said Lord Archie.

"*I* told you, my dear Archie."

"It seems to be asking for trouble to encourage him to see her again, though. We can't have her vamping him. When is she going?"

"If the funeral is at Rushford, after the funeral. And no one says vamp any more, Archie."

3

"Miss Bolby isn't coming down to breakfast," said Barby, as she came into the dining-room. "She is having some tea in bed. She has got one of her headaches. She doesn't feel well."

"What happened?" said Jessy. "How did she find the bracelets?"

When Elizabeth and Larry had come back last night, almost immediately after the news had come through about Miss Pickford, Elizabeth had sent them to bed. They had had milk and biscuits in the nursery instead of the usual Schoolroom supper, so that they had hardly seen Miss Bolby.

"In the swing-seat," said Larry. "She seems to think that Miss Pickford took them, was a sort of kleptomaniac and hid them in the swing-seat."

"Oh, but she didn't," said Ruth. "I found them. Bella must have put them there. I *know* it was Bella. I saw her rolling something down the crack yesterday. She is like a jackdaw, or magpie, or a rook, is it?"

"But, Ruth," said Larry, "*when* did you find them?"

"Oh, two days ago, I should think."

"Then why on earth didn't you tell somebody, or give them back to Miss Bolby? Do you mean you left them there?"

"I was going to give them back if she said we could ride in the Gymkhana. She was beastly to Jessy."

"But she did say you could ride in the Gymkhana."

"I know. I thought—I thought, somebody might have hidden them there if it wasn't Bella. Not Picksie, but Jessy, for fun or something. I thought—I thought that there might have been a row, or something. . . ."

"When you find something which has been lost, it is always better to say so at once," said Larry.

"I know Picksie wouldn't have taken them, she loved birds. *She* should have married Lord Corwen," said Louisa.

"Is that why Picksie left, I mean because Miss Bolby thought she had taken them?" said Jessy.

"Oh, it's my fault! It's all my fault! It's my fault that Picksie was killed!" said Ruth. There were tears in her voice, and her face, Louisa thought, was almost the colour of the red-leather seats of the dining-room chairs.

"It's Miss Bolby's fault," said Jessy. "I'll bet she was beastly to her."

"It's nobody's fault," said Larry. "Such things happen. You might as well say it was Nino's fault for driving her to the station."

"There'll be an awful row about that, won't there?" said Barby.

"I have spoken to the Camp Commandant," said Elizabeth, "and he has decided to treat Nino leniently, but he is moving him, and Otello, from here. Otello thinks it was *his* fault for letting Nino go."

"Poor Reenie!" said Jessy.

"I'll bet you Reenie will go," said Barby.

"Everybody seems to be going except Miss Bolby. I wish Miss Bolby would go," said Ruth.

"She *is* going," said Larry; "she feels she can't stay here now. I expect she may feel it was her fault and it is only natural she would want to go, and very much better that she should. The whole thing has been very sad and unfortunate. It is a great pity Miss Pickford lost her head—if she did lose her head—and didn't wait to rush off until we got back."

"When is Miss Bolby going?" said Jessy.

"It depends," said Elizabeth, "on the funeral. If it is here she feels she must stay for it. If there is no will and if Miss Pickford has no relations who wish it elsewhere it will be very much simpler to have it here. I hope to get some sort of answer from Mrs. Staines-Close this morning."

"Perhaps we ought never to have gone to the Gymkhana,"

said Ruth, staring at the white expanse of cloth which should have held Miss Pickford's empty cup and marmaladed plate.

"Isn't Miss Bolby going to marry Lord Corwen?" said Louisa.

"Why should she?" said Elizabeth. "What an extraordinary idea!"

"It's rather jumping to conclusions to suppose Lord Corwen wanted to marry her just because he asked her to Bowborough," said Larry.

After finishing her fourth cup of tea, Miss Bolby felt stronger.

I must face the world, she thought. This tragic happening is not, in any way, my fault. I must not behave as though it were my fault. I must be brave. I am a Bolby.

She put on a dark dress. To have worn a bright colour at such a moment would have been unseemly; not that she was addicted to bright colours, though many had said she should wear them. Mauves and dusty pinks and crushed strawberries were less *outreé* and more becoming and occasionally she wore purple. But although purple was a mourning colour, it was not a summer colour and it did not seem right for today. She would wear a touch of purple for the funeral in case Lord Corwen came.

Early in life she had begun to wear violets and purples. It had been Ralph Barnsley who had said: 'Good Lord, Roona! your eyes look absolutely violet when you wear that mauve thing, like those whopping great ones you see in greenhouses, not the little wild, hedgerow fellows. You ought to wear purple.' And at about the same time Bertha had said: 'Heavens alive, Roona! All the boys will be like bees about the honey pot around you if you go on wearing that sort of colour. Come over into the light, dear. Yes, they *are* violet. What wouldn't I give for those eyes of yours. You're a ripper, Roona!'

Bertha had been full of warm good-heartedness, without a trace of jealousy or malice, but then Bertha had been successful, though from a social point of view she had not made a good marriage—she had married a little wisp of a man, a then penniless composer—but she had become a successful pianist. It seemed surprising that anyone so large and good-hearted and—well, vulgar—should have become a good pianist. Poor Bertha! As she had become larger she had become louder. Yet she would keep a whole hall hushed, enraptured, as if she had thrown an invisible mantle about herself, so that no one saw the large figure who played. And in the Worthing days she had not lacked admirers. It was surprising on looking back that she, Roona, with those great violet eyes, had not had more. Never before had she voiced this thought: whenever it had been in the offing she had rejected it. Many men had 'followed' her, many when she had been teaching, and later chaperoning, the Rowfont girls, had sought methods of getting into conversation with her. Many of the guests at Rowfont, besides Ned Blatchington, had found some excuse to come to the Schoolroom. Few, considering this great number, had proposed. This was not the moment to analyse the reason why.

There was no doubt about it, on going over Sunday carefully, that she had made an impression on Lord Corwen. And if Lord Corwen came to the funeral . . .

She looked—because in order to do one's hair one must look—at least briefly into the mirror, and in order to look at one's hair one could not avoid one's eyes—they were undoubtedly large and beautiful eyes. Eyes did not shrink as the body shrunk, but they faded. Yes, they were faded, but large and indescribably beautiful as they had always been.

She hurried downstairs. There might, by now, have been some reply from Mrs. Staines-Close. It was not impossible that some decision had been reached about the funeral. She hankered, as she hurried, for Old Lord Rushford's room from where she had been so well able to see who came up the drive.

"Ah, Miss Bolby, are you better?"

"Thank you, Lady Rushford, I am quite restored, though distressed, not unnaturally."

"As we all are, Miss Bolby."

"I came to see if I could help you in any way, with telephoning, or the writing of letters."

"Thank you, Miss Bolby, I *should* be very grateful if you could go through some of the drawers for me. As you know, Lord Rushford could find nothing in Miss Pickford's room to show any trace of relations, and really this Office is in such a muddle, in spite of Lord Rushford's attempt to tidy it, it is impossible to find anything."

"Poor Miss Pickford had no sense of order," said Miss Bolby.

Barby came in with a telegram.

"This must be from Mrs. Staines-Close," said Elizabeth.

"What does she say?" said Barby.

'Only relative known of George Pickford Willow Trees Windsmoor Road Wimbledon   telephone number probably obtainable Telephone Directory   if can be of any assistance please wire   Mildred Staines-Close.'

"Well now, I suppose, we must try to telephone George Pickford. Find me the London Telephone book, Barby."

It relinquished no such address as Willow Trees, though it revealed the fact that there were other George Pickfords.

"Perhaps they have just moved. In any case it's an old book," said Barby.

Elizabeth rang the Directory, which seemed in no hurry to reply.

"Poor Mr. Curby, he doesn't know what he's missing," said Barby. "How he'll wish we weren't on the dial."

Elizabeth said: "This is just the moment when I should have been thankful for Mr. Curby; within no time he would have had all the ins and outs of Miss Pickford's family at his finger tips."

Receiving no reply from the Directory, Elizabeth sent a 'Reply Paid' telegram to George Pickford.

'Deeply regret have to inform you of Rose Pickford's sudden death in car accident yesterday please wire or telephone Colshall 233 wishes concerning funeral Elizabeth Rushford Lady Rushford Rushford Colshall.'

Then she said: "Now, Miss Bolby, I will leave you to see if there is anything helpful in the drawers. I haven't yet been to the kitchen."

"Isn't it awful that you have to eat when somebody dies?" said Barby.

When Elizabeth and Barby had gone, Miss Bolby began systematically to go through the Office desk. It had not been possible to make much headway while Elizabeth was telephoning.

As she began to read and arrange in neat piles the letters which she had taken from the drawers, she felt an unexpected quiver of excitement. Nothing had been sorted for years, it seemed, goodness knew what she would find: letters of Old Lord Rushford's, perhaps. She had long ago begun to feel that she had intimately known the late Lord Rushford; now, at any moment now, she might literally do so. But old bills and receipts, letters concerning Red Cross matters, letters from the Forestry Commission and forms from the Ministry of Food were all she could find until she came upon Miss Pickford's letter to Elizabeth. She felt the quiver of excitement again.

'To Lady Rushford,

'DEAR MADAM,' it ran,

'I do not know if this letter will find you as I have been staying with a friend where I saw your advertisement in *The Times*, and I foolishly lost the piece of paper on which your address was written down.

'I think I had better say at once that I am a middle-aged woman and a gentlewoman, and Church of England, and that my father was in the Church—he was for some time Vicar of Stonechurch—and that I am a little deaf, though I do not think my slight disability affects my work, and I have shorthand (Pitman's) and typing, and am fond of the country and of nature, except of cows, of which I am a little afraid.

'I was for some years secretary-companion to Mrs. Staines-Close—a sister-in-law of Admiral Sir Martin Staines-Close—of Witherly Wood, Camberly. Latterly I have been doing secretarial work for the Red Cross and St. John Joint War Organisation (paid) not being young enough or strong enough to nurse, but being anxious to do some sort of war work.

'If this application is of no use to you, please do not trouble to reply, but should you be glad of the help of a woman like myself I will send my written references.

'Yours truly,
'ROSE PICKFORD.'

Miss Bolby put the letter down. Its note of diffidence disturbed her, as did also the reference to Admiral Sir Martin Staines-Close. On no occasion had Miss Pickford mentioned him. It was almost as if she had borrowed or invented him, although there was little similarity between 'Staines-Close' and 'Atherton-Broadleigh', and 'Admiral' was very different from 'General', and she, Miss Pickford, was not personally connected with him, and at the time she had written the letter she had never heard of her, Roona Bolby.

Although she would have preferred it not to do so, her own letter to Lady Rushford rose before her; sentence by sentence it jumped up upon the photographic plate of memory, with a difference and a similarity:

'To *The* Lady Rushford'—the underlining was upon the plate only.

'DEAR MADAM,

'I have today been given your name and address by Mrs. Barton's Agency, and I understand that you require a permanent resident Governess.

'I must tell you that I am a Gentlewoman (connected by marriage with the late Dean of Waterbury and Lady Alice Atherton-Broadleigh, my elder sister having married General Sir Arthur Atherton-Broadleigh—and through my other sister with Lord Chipperfield's family). I was for ten years with the Dowager Lady Rowfont, at Rowfont Park, Marlbury, and have lately been with a Mrs. Kenneth Bonder, here in B'm.

'I think I may say I am well grounded in general subjects and I am able fluently to speak and to teach French, and have a slight knowledge of Italian. I also taught Lady Rowfont's girls—with whom I still correspond—the piano.

'I must add that I am most anxious to find a permanent post in the country, my last post not having been entirely "simpatica", and that I am free to come if you wish.

'Yours truly,

'ROONA BOLBY.'

Miss Bolby put Miss Pickford's letter at the bottom of a drawer, it would not be needed again. She put a large wodge of business letters and bills on the top of it, anxious to have done with Miss Pickford, and to get on with the search of another drawer. Then her eye was caught by a hand which seemed familiar: there was something familiar about the paper, too; one did not often see *good* paper these days. It was half concealed by a bill from the local chemist and a letter from the Food Office. Was it? Could it be? Yes, it *was*, it was! The letter she had always wanted to see! What memories that smooth, fine-textured paper with its small blue coronet revived!

She withdrew it from under the letters which partly covered it:

'The dowager Lady Rowfont thanks Lady Rushford for her letter, and is able to say that she found Miss R. Bolby honest, trustworthy, and of good moral character when in her employ.'

Beneath this lay a form upon which was printed:

'Mrs. Barton's Governesses' & Domestic Servants' Agency
Warrior's Row,
Birmingham.
Established 1859

In respect of Lady Rushford's kind application we beg to introduce a Governess who has applied to us for a situation and given particulars as under:

Register	
as	*Governess*
Name	*Miss Roona Bolby*
Address	*Hillstone House, Hillthorne Road, B'm.*
Age	*58 active*
Denomin.	*Church of England*
Height	*5 ft. 6 ins.*
Character	*6 months*
with	*Mrs. Kenneth Bonder*
Previously	*10 years*
with	*Dowager Lady Rowfont*

'Mrs. Bonder states that Miss Bolby has had a good deal of experience as a governess and was satisfactory and is a gentlewoman, connected by marriage with the late Dean of Waterbury.

'Formerly with the Dowager Lady Rowfont with whom she served as governess and finishing governess for a period of ten years.

'The Dowager Lady Rowfont writes: "Miss Bolby was in my employ for 10 years. I believe her to be a fit and proper person for you to recommend." '

4

"Nino's leg didn't come off, did it?" said Ruth.

"No, of course not, it was broken, you silly fool," said Jessy.

"I expect there was a lot of blood though," said Louisa.

"Oh, I know it was my fault," said Ruth.

"Oh, shut up, Ruth, it was all our faults in a way," said Jessy.

"What do you think they're like?" said Louisa.

"Who, for goodness' sake?" said Becca.

"Mr. and Mrs. George Pickford."

"Little people, I should think. I'm sure they're little people," said Jessy.

"They'll have an awful journey, with the buzz bombs and everything," said Barby.

Ruth said: "They're staying the night at the Rectory. Poor Picksie! What is a funeral *like*, Becca?"

"You needn't think you and Louisa are going to any funerals; you'll have plenty of funerals before you've finished, and I don't hold with it at your age."

"We can watch from the window, though, can't we?"

"If Barby and Jessy can go, I don't see why we can't," said Louisa.

"Barb and I had supper with her in the Schoolroom every

night, which sort of makes it different, and, anyway, it makes more people—there won't be enough people if we don't go." said Jessy.

"It's odd the way you're alive one day and dead the next, when you come to think of it," said Barby.

"Here today and gone tomorrow, that's life," said Becca.

"Poor Picksie, she always hated Eternal Combustion," said Jessy.

All day they had shunned the Schoolroom, and as if seeking protection, and wanting to be together, had spent most of it in the Nursery with Becca.

"I'm glad Hughie is going to the funeral," said Lady Archie, "even if it's only to settle his mind once and for all about Miss Bolby. I feel sorry for them all. Sorry for Miss Bolby, too. We shall never know what happened exactly, but I expect she *drove* that poor woman away—and even if it wasn't, she'll always feel it was her fault. I expect she bragged about her aristocratic connections, and she probably told Miss Pickford she wasn't a lady. She seems to suffer from a sort of *folie de grandeur* which has its roots in India. Poor Miss Bolby! I feel sorry for those little people coming all the way from Wimbledon to a strange house for the funeral of a cousin, and sorry for Nino for having driven that poor little Miss Pickford to the station, and sorry for Otello for letting Nino go, and sorry for Reenie for losing Otello. But one can't go on being sorry for everyone; one would die of exhaustion, in an excess of compassion. Ah dear me! How difficult it is to find a happy medium about anything. I feel sorry for Elizabeth, too, having to cope with it all."

"Elizabeth is an excellent manager, my dear," said Lord Archie.

"Perhaps not always tactful, though. One must remember that Elizabeth isn't quite . . ."

"Isn't quite what, my dear?"

267

"Well, not *absolutely* out of the *topmost* drawer."

"Surely that isn't a modern phrase, Blanchie?"

"Not modern, just vulgar, but one has to try to keep up with the times, my dear Archie."

After this they were silent for a time; they sat together upon a sofa. Then she put her hand in his. "Odd though it may seem and old as we are, you know, I still love you, Archie."

"And I you, my dear Blanchie."

"And all because Barrington was drunk, and Cyril was new and didn't know the ropes and let you in."

"All because of *what,* my dear?"

"Nothing. Reminiscence is the first sign of senility, take no notice, Archie."

5

In the morning the blight came down. Mr. and Mrs. George Pickford drove through it from the station to the Rectory. It had been arranged that the funeral should be in the afternoon so that they might have time enough for their long journey.

Becca and Bella and Ruth and Louisa watched them arrive at the church from the nursery window. They were a little early as they had come up in the Rector's car. They awkardly carried wreaths.

Miss Bolby heard the car in the drive and looked through the State Room window. She was obliged to lean out, to crane her neck forward: in Old Lord Rushford's room she would have been able to see without craning. There was something undignified about having to crane, yet the temptation to do so was too great to resist.

Had she known the pictures of the Douanier Rousseau, she might have seen Mr. and Mrs. George Pickford as squat, dark figures, overshadowed by tall trees, but she would have tossed both them and him on to the dump heap of 'modern art' had she done so.

'I don't understand modern art,' she had said to Mr. Lind
one night at Hillstone House in the smoking-room.

To which he had replied : 'Is it possible, that you don't *know*
it? And by "modern" meaning what, exactly, Miss Bolby?'

'I have seen a great many of the world's pictures, Mr. Lind,
and at least a number of the world's *famous* pictures. I
travelled a good deal, you know, with Lord and Lady Rowfont's girls. I think I may say I have an *average* knowledge
of the *great* masters.'

'Yes, but up to what *date*, Miss Bolby? And don't you
ever say to yourself, "This man, this *new* man, will be a *great*
master"?'

'I don't count upon my judgment the way you do, Mr.
Lind.'

That night she had hated Mr. Lind as much as she hated
Mr. Howland and Mr. Billings and Mr. Lorelli.

But she did not think of Mr. Lind and Mr. Howland and
Mr. Billings and Mr. Lorelli as she looked through the window
now. She did not see Mr. and Mrs. George Pickford as
awkward, struggling figures, tired from a long journey, come
to perform an awkward duty; instead she thought : They are
mediocre, ordinary little people, singularly out of place in
the family church here. They are types one would see in the
underground; they are just what I expected of Miss Pickford's
relations.

Then she began to think that the whole idea of burying Miss
Pickford in the Rushford family church was absurd, absurd
and incongruous. Miss Pickford, who not only had no aristocratic relatives, but no aristocratic *connections*. What would
the late Lord Rushford think of this intrusion? That Miss
Pickford, so insignificant in life, should be treated so after
death was excessively galling.

The bell began its toll. 'I will get you, too,' it seemed to
say. 'You ... ! You ... ! You ... !' Out of the context of
its chime the note was sombre.

The Gentlewomen

As Miss Bolby pinned on her black straw hat trimmed with a purple band, the spacing between each toll lost its evenness —as if the ringer had taken his eye from his watch, or his hand from the rope in order to blow his nose—so that the note lost its solemnity. In Miss Bolby's ears it almost changed its tune to a wedding chime.

About her neck she tied a violet scarf. Would Lord Corwen come?

The congregation was small. Mr. and Mrs. George Pickford sat with the Rector's wife in the front pew; behind them Elizabeth and Larry and Lord Corwen, and behind again Miss Bolby and Jessy and Barby, and behind them Reenie and Vi, and in a side pew, because they habitually sat in a side pew, Bob Woodman and Gibson, the gardener, who had made a number of wreaths so that the coffin should not want for flowers, as if he sensed Miss Pickford's love of flowers.

Barby and Jessy, having scrutinised the backs of Mr. and Mrs. George Pickford through the space between Lord Corwen and Larry, now shifted their attention to large black prayer books which rested in the pew, awed by the service's solemnity, eager to savour its newness. Reenie cried quietly for Otello. Miss Bolby found it difficult to keep her eyes upon her book and to concentrate upon the service; because her thoughts were solely with Lord Corwen, it became a meaningless droning.

He had come into the hall beforehand as she had hoped he would, but he had brushed her aside as it were, with a 'Howdy do, Miss Bolby?', and he had not so far looked round during the service. He seemed very old today, but the blight had temporarily thinned, and a broad band of sunlight, deepened almost to ochre by the layers of blight between the earth and the sun's rays, slanted across the aisle and the front pews, making Lord Corwen, too, seem yellow—yellow and shrunken, with his neck thrust forward—accentuating his age as it caught Barby and Jessy immediately behind him, throwing upon them the pinkish yellow bloom of ripe apricots.

He is like an old bird, she thought, and she did not like birds—except at a distance and in song. She had been uneasy when they had fluttered and squawked about her head in the aviary, so uneasy that Lord Corwen must have seen her flush and withdraw when he said : 'Don't move, don't be frightened, my dear woman. Nothing to be frightened of, stay still and let them get to know you.' But was it not natural that an entry into an aviary full of birds fluttering about one's head should be disconcerting? Lord Corwen's brushing her aside just now had been nothing more than his brusque manner. . . .

They were moving out towards the graveside now.

Again Barby's and Jessy's youth accentuated Lord Corwen's age. A light wind lifted wisps of hair so that it floated out from under their hats, they stood tense and awed, as though fascinated by the scene's barbarity : the wind filled the Rector's surplice, ballooning and distorting it; it agitated the prayer book's leaves and blew the blight down again upon the church-yard so that the sky seemed to come down suddenly, to settle above the heads of the group about the grave in a yellow pall. The Rector's droning ceased, and Mr. and Mrs. George Pickford moved forward to scatter earth into the grave; Mrs. George Pickford unpinned a bunch of violets from her lapel and it fell with a little light thud upon the coffin as she tossed it forward, then the droning began again, but before the mumbled words had dispersed into the blight they were drowned : an incoming bomber cut through the pall above and swooped low over the churchyard, oblivious of all beneath it.

Suddenly the ceremony was over. Although it had reached its end, it seemed to have been interrupted—broken. The little procession moved raggedly towards the gate, aimless, dis-integrated now, fragmentary, no longer a procession.

Elizabeth, as if anxious to draw it together, moved forward to speak to Mr. and Mrs. George Pickford; Larry moved protectively, as if anxious to hasten them away from contact with death, towards Barby and Jessy; Lord Corwen and Miss Bolby walked through the gate together, then Lord Corwen said: "Well, goodbye, Larry," and climbed into his car.

Barby and Jessy reached the hall first. Larry had told them to run on ahead and they had hurried, feeling it indecorous at first and then breakng into a run, glad to be free of the churchyard.

Ruth and Louisa were waiting in the hall.

Ruth said: "It's all my fault that she's dead. I saw how dead she was from the window."

"But if you're dead, you're dead," said Barby; "it doesn't make any difference how dead."

"But it's my fault, I tell you," said Ruth; "if I'd given the bracelets to Miss Bolby she wouldn't be dead—not shut up in the earth so that she can't get out like that. It's my fault, I tell you."

"No, it isn't," said Jessy, "and she's only shut up in the earth because she's dead. You don't want to get out if you're dead."

"But she might," said Louisa.

"And it's my fault if she can't," said Ruth.

"Why are you all standing here in the hall?" said Miss Bolby.

"I am trying to tell Ruth it's not her fault Miss Pickford is dead, Miss Bolby," said Jessy. "If it's anyone's fault it's yours, yes, yours, yours!"

"Don't speak to Miss Bolby like that, Jessy," said Larry. They were all in the hall now. "What are you all standing about here for?"

"Ruth thinks it's her fault Miss Pickford is dead," said Jessy, "and it's not, of course, of course it's not. If it's anyone's fault it's Miss Bolby's."

272

"You are not to speak like that, Jessy. I've told you before, it's nobody's fault, and this is not the time to discuss it. You are being rude and unkind and unjust to Miss Bolby. Go upstairs at once," said Larry.

"Then it's the war," said Jessy. "It won't even let you have a funeral in peace. It makes everybody horrible, yes, horrible. It's this awful, evil, filthy, stinking, beastly war! It's made Miss Bolby horrible. You killed Miss Pickford, Miss Bolby, you *killed* her! I *hate* you, Miss Bolby, you're *horrible*!"

Something rushed past Miss Bolby's head and she felt her straw hat lift—caught by a rush of air—and settle itself again: Jessy's prayer book lay spreadeagled upon the floor, wrenched from its secrets: a pressed violet, a white-heather spray, a snapshot of Larry and a ribbon marker. No one moved or spoke until Barby said: "Perhaps, Jess, you will be a great Actress after all."

HILLSTONE HOUSE

1

NOW THAT Miss Bolby was coming back—'buck', Elise pronounced it—she would have to take a bit more trouble with the bath.

'Elsie! El-see!' Miss Bolby's voice would rise and fall in the stair well, fill the corridor where the bathroom was. 'Elsie, I see a dark rim. This is no way to clean a bath.'

'I 'aven't got me Vim, Miss. I ast Miss Milly, and she 'aven't given me no more yet.'

'A bad workman blames his tools, Elsie. Kindly reclean the bath.'

Elsie vigorously polished the brass.

Bit of a shock it was, Miss Bolby coming buck so sudden. After breakfast Mrs. Tollmarsh had called her into the Tollmarsh's sitting-room. 'Miss Bolby is returning to us today, Elsie. Turn out her room, will you? And you had better get her trunk down from the attic. Well, don't stand there looking daft, Elsie.'

Fancy Miss Bolby coming buck.

Elsie hummed as she polished. She didn't mind polishing. Bright brass brought a gleam of light into the dark house. It made her think of merry-go-rounds, and gypsies, and jingling harness, and the bright brass on the barges as they slid down greenish-yellow waters; the plod-plod of the barge-horse, and voices, though one seldom heard voices—barge people were singularly silent people, static: carved figure-heads, dark shapes against a greenish sky, enveloped in the water's calm. This, in her own way, was what Elsie thought. She had been born and bred by the waters of the Grand Union Canal.

Humming still, because she was no longer at Hillstone House but sitting in a pink pinafore upon the towpath, she took her Brasso and the stained and tattered rag and went up to Mr. Lorelli's room.

"Beg pardon, sir; I thought you was out, sir."

"Don't mind me, Elsie. I'm just going out, as a matter of fact. Bit early this morning, aren't you?"

"I've to turn out Miss Bolby's room, sir."

"Good Lord, Elsie! That old bag coming back?"

"Yes, sir."

"You'll have to get her trunk down from the attic then, won't you? You'd better let me help you. What the devil is she coming back for? Since she so much prefers them to us, why doesn't she stay amongst the upper classes? Why? I'll tell you why, because, between you and me and the gatepost, Elsie, they don't like her any better than we do, and if you want my opinion, she's no better off there than she is here."

"This is only her pi*a*deter, sir."

"Her what, Elsie?"

"Her pi*a*deter, sir."

"Oh, her pied-à-terre? Good Lord, I didn't know you spoke French, Elsie. Let's get her blooming trunk down, shall we?"

Now the fun and games in the dining-room would start again, and Mr. Lorelli's accent was more Frenchified than Miss Bolby's, Elsie thought.

" 'Eard the news, Mrs. Billings?" said Mrs. Hurst.

"I can't say that I *h*ave, Mrs. *H*urst. *H*as something *h*appened?"

"New arrival expected tonight."

"Well! You *always* know the news, Mrs. *H*urst. Will *h*e or she not *h*ave to *h*ave Miss Bolby's room?"

"That's right, *she* will, Mrs. Billings."

Mr. Billings blew in. He literally blew in, there is no other means of expressing it, he brought a current of air in with him.

"Nice little bit of news for you ladies. Miss Bolby is returning to the fold. Vive the Taj Mahal!"

"If you 'aven't gone and spoiled my little surprise, Mr. Billings!"

"I wonder if that accident had anything to do with it," said Mr. Lind, who sheltered behind a book in a corner.

"What accident, Mr. Lind?" said Mrs. Hurst.

"Didn't you see? I meant to tell you. There was a paragraph in Tuesday's evening paper. A Miss Rose Pickford, secretary to Lady Rushford, was killed in a car accident last Monday, it ran into a lorry and was being driven by an Italian prisoner."

"How very unorthodox," said Mr. Howlard who had at that moment come in.

"Sounds like a bit of a drama," said Mrs. Hurst.

"Doubtless we'll hear," said Mr. Lind.

2

A strong south-westerly wind blew rain into Miss Bolby's face as she got out of the train at New Street Station. It hurled leaves prematurely from trees, it waltzed them along the gutters and landed them in outlandish places and blew them through the glassless roof and left them on the platform where they skidded round passengers' feet until they were trodden on. Rain spat in Miss Bolby's face and fell upon her suitcase —a sort of colourless confetti.

Confetti indeed! There seemed little hope of confetti *now*. She was so angry with Lord Corwen that she scowled at a porter: "Take these through to the Queen's Hotel, my man." He did not immediately answer, he was too astonished, it was so many years since he had been called 'My man'.

"You'll have to wait, 'm, till I've finished the job I'm on." And she had to wait, with the wind tugging and the rain spitting. Then she followed him up the steps, holding on to her hat with one hand and her zip-bag with the other until she reached the shelter of the Queen's Hotel, where the porter, under her direction, transferred her luggage into the hands of the hotel porter.

"Afternoon, Miss. Not with Lady Rushford today?"

"Not today, Digby. I have had to return to Birmingham upon private business. I had an urgent letter from India which necessitated my seeing to some affairs here. I'm just going into the lounge to have a cup of tea before returning to my pied-à-terre."

"All well at Rushford, I hope, Miss?"

"All is *very* well at Rushford, thank you, Digby. Lord and Lady Rushford were most concerned that I had to leave them in the lurch in such a hurry. Lord Rushford is back, you know."

"Well I'm blowed! Right glad I am to hear it, Miss. Nasty accident, I saw there was the other day."

"*Very* nasty, Digby. Send a waiter in to me, will you? So that I can order some tea."

Trains shrieked in the station: they shunted into it: they wailed a warning to the world that they were about to leave it. They stood, static in it, hissing forth steam. Trolleys rumbled and porters whistled a noisy accompaniment to the clatter of tea-cups.

I am pausing here between trains, Miss Bolby thought, Tonight I am taking a sleeper northwards, upon my wedding journey. Hughie and I have been lent some great house in Scotland, and the shooting. Then she thought: No, an ornithologist would not shoot. Far from it. Hughie was going northward to give a lecture upon birds, and the protection of birds, in Edinburgh, for which purpose they were to stay in some big house locally, and there was to be a big party of his friends to meet the new Marchioness—it was the latter half of the wedding journey. They would have separate sleepers, first-class sleepers, surely, and new suitcases upon which there would be coronets and in which there would be teagowns. . . .

The thin hum of an aircraft travelling at great height pierced the station's symphony—she had forgotten the war.

Time was getting on now. Tea would be over at Hillstone House. Between tea and dinner seemed a suitable time to arrive; she would have time to unpack a little, to shake out the sari and get out a few nicknacks before the gong sounded. . . .

Elsie would be washing up the tea-things in the dark kitchen, Mr. Lorelli getting out his violin upstairs, Milly Tollmarsh banging out the first bars of Beethoven's Minuet in G, while Mrs. Tollmarsh's cough rumbled up from deep in her chair.

Mrs. Hurst and Mrs. Billings and Mrs. Rowcroft and Miss Hines would be sitting round the drawing-room fire—autumn came early in the Midlands, and on a day such as this there would surely be a fire.

Mr. Lind and Mr. Billings and Mr. Howland would be coming home from offices. Leaves would be skidding on the sills of tall, cold windows, falling through the hollies and floating above the laurels clumped darkly on either side of the gate. . . .

I am a Bolby, I must be brave, Miss Bolby thought. Then she finished her tea and called the waiter so that she might pay her bill.

Dinner was over. When Mr. Lind and Mr. Howland and Mr. Billings and Mr. Lorelli followed Mrs. Hurst and Mrs. Billings and Miss Bolby into the smoking-room from the draughty linoleumed dining-room—Mrs. Rowcroft and Miss Hines were already knitting in the drawing-room—they took up their accustomed places. Mrs. Hurst and Mrs. Billings made room for Miss Bolby upon the sofa.

"I *hope*," said Mrs. Billings, "that you will tell us about your post, Miss Bolby. Mr. Lind tells us Rushford is a very beautiful *h*ouse."

"A very fine house, Mrs. Billings, a very *historic* house, though not so fine and less historic than Rowfont, Lord and Lady Rowfont's place, my former post, you remember—though hardly a post, if I may say so, we were all such friends. Rushford, though, has a very fine Canaletto and some interesting bedrooms, the State Room in particular. King Edward slept there." Miss Bolby paused.

" *H*ow very interesting," said Mrs. Billings; " *h*e must have slept in so many places, and yet after *H*enry VIII and Queen Elizabeth we never *h*ear where any of them slept."

"Charles II, you mean, don't you?" said Mr. Lind.

"Dear me, dear me!" said Mr. Howland, *"les dames!"*

"King Edward's room was *my* room," said Miss Bolby. "It will be a sad day indeed. Ah, yes, a *sad* day when these old houses go, and from the way things are going I doubt if Rushford will last much longer."

"Go they certainly will, I'm afraid," from behind his book said Mr. Lorelli.

"And that is what *you* want, what *you* hope, is it not, Mr. Lorelli?"

"Well, no. You misunderstand me. I never said *that,* exactly, Miss Bolby."

"Seeing as it's Miss Bolby's first night back and we're cosy, let's cut out the politics, shall we, Mr. Lorelli?" said Mrs. Hurst.

" Here, here!" said Mrs. Billings.

"Well said, Mrs. Hurst," said Mr. Howland.

"And how!" said Mr. Billings

Mr. Lind said : "You'll never stop progress."

3

For the next few days Miss Bolby watched the post. Whenever she saw the postman from her bedroom window she ran down into the hall. She watched and waited with such feverishness she might almost have been her mother, she thought, waiting for the cable from Sita. Then, one afternoon, when she had seen the postman come and had run down to the hall and found nothing for herself upon the marble slab, she went back to her room and got out her paper and pen—she had been down to the centre of the town to get the best paper in case of this necessity—and wrote to Lord Corwen.

'MY DEAR LORD CORWEN,

'Ever since your kindness in asking me to Bowborough, I have felt that I must write to tell you how much, how *very* much I enjoyed every moment of my visit. It is with a very real and great pleasure that I look forward to a future visit when I have settled some tiresome private affairs which necessitated my return—for a short time—to my pied-à-terre here in B'm.

'I send my kind regards to Lord and Lady Archie, and, of course, to the birds!!

'Yours very sincerely,

'ROONA BOLBY.'

After this Miss Bolby watched the post with increasing eagerness, but she received no reply.

THE END